# SNEAK ATTACKS!

Elimax raised his blaster. The ugly snarl of the weapon filled the cramped space as he sent two high power beams on tight focus into the heads of the sleepers.

In the silence that followed, another sound erupted—the buzz of a single-shot needler, fired at close range. Elimax crumpled forward; his blaster fell to the deck.

Beka stepped out of the shadowed corner where she'd stood watching. . . .

**Also by Debra Doyle and James D. Macdonald, from Tor Books**

# STARPILOT'S GRAVE

## DEBRA DOYLE AND JAMES D. MACDONALD

A TOM DOHERTY ASSOCIATES BOOK
NEW YORK

STARPILOT'S GRAVE

Cover art by Romas

A Tor Book
Published by Tom Doherty Associates, Inc.
175 Fifth Avenue
New York, NY 10010

Tor Books on the World Wide Web:
http://www.tor.com

Tor® is a registered trademark of Tom Doherty Associates, Inc.

ISBN: 0-812-51705-9

First edition: June 1993

Printed in the United States of America

0  9  8  7  6  5  4  3

*For Peregrynne*

# ACKNOWLEDGMENTS

Special thanks this time are owed to Cliff Laufer, without whose (former) hard drive the manuscript for this book would have occupied far too many floppy disks; and to Kate Daniel, for checking this volume to see if it would make sense to someone who hadn't yet read *The Price of the Stars*.

# Prologue
## Pleyver: Flatlands

DARKNESS HAD fallen over the city. Light from the streetlamps lay in stark white circles against the warehouse walls, with pools of blackness falling in between. Overhead, the fixed star of High Station—Pleyver's giant orbiting spaceport—burned down through the skyglow. No one saw Owen Rosselin-Metadi pass by like an unheeded thought, skirting the edges of the lamplight and pausing to catch his breath in the safety of the dark.

He wasn't sure how long he'd been running. Hours, it felt like—ever since leaving his sister back at Florrie's Palace, in an upper room where the acrid stink of blaster fire mingled with the heavier smell of blood. He didn't think anybody had followed him out of there; he'd put most of his remaining energy into staying unseen, and Beka had taken care of the rest.

Owen didn't like the favor he'd asked from her, that she take on the risk of drawing away the armed pursuit, and he didn't particularly like himself for asking it. But Bee was a survivor, the kind who could fight her way from Florrie's to the port quarter and blast off leaving a legend behind her. He'd seen that much clearly; far more clearly, in fact, than the outcome of is own business on Pleyver.

Nevertheless, he had lied to her.

Well, not exactly lied. But he *had* let her think that the datachip he'd given her, packed with information from the locked comp-files of Flatlands Investment, Ltd., was unique. He'd never mentioned the other datachip, the one that he'd come to Pleyver to obtain. The information on the second chip belonged to Errec Ransome, Master of the Adepts' Guild—or it would if Owen lived long enough to deliver it.

*Maybe I* should *have given it to Bee.*

Owen shook his head. He'd briefly considered asking her, but the presence of her copilot had killed that idea. The slight, grey-haired man she called the Professor gave Beka an unquestioning loyalty—that much Owen had perceived without any difficulty—but it was a loyalty that would put Beka first and the Adepts' Guild a far-distant second.

No, it was better to let the two of them go their own way. From the look of things, Beka had kept her promise to distract the ordinary hired help, the ones who did their fighting with blasters and energy lances. Dodging the others should have been easy, if only he hadn't been so stupid as to get caught once already tonight. . . .

Owen had shown up outside the portside branch office of Flatlands Investment, Ltd., just before dusk. He'd hoped to get there earlier, but intercepting Beka at the spaceport and convincing her to abandon her own designs on the company's data banks had taken longer than he'd anticipated.

Beka wanted revenge, plain and simple: revenge on

whoever had planned their mother's assassination and revenge on whoever had paid for it. She'd get it, too; Bee in
pursuit of a goal had a straightforward single-mindedness
that made a starship's jump-run to hyperspace look like a
sightseeing trip. But that same trait could make her dangerous to be around if your purposes and hers happened to
diverge. Owen didn't think that the Guild's interest in FIL
was going to put him in Beka's way, but he didn't want to
chance it.

Besides, he reflected as he approached the grey, slab-
sided FIL Building, it was easier for one person to work
unnoticed than for two. He could slip in, get enough from
the files to satisfy Master Ransome and his sister both, and
slip out again before Bee was through eating dinner.

The front door of the building was secured by an electronic ID-scan. Owen palmed the lockplate like any authorized visitor. Inside the mechanism, the electric current
flowed through its appointed paths and channels as the
door made ready to reject the identification. Then, without
changing his expression or his physical posture, Owen
reached out, using the skills that for more than ten years
had made him Errec Ransome's most valued—and most
valuable—apprentice.

The flow of electrons altered its course. The lock
clicked quietly and the door slid open.

A stranger waited in the unlit lobby, a thin, hunched
man in the plain garb of a low-level office worker. Owen
tensed, but the man didn't make any threatening moves.

"I've got the password," the worker said.

Owen paused. He hadn't expected anyone to be here at
all. But he hadn't sensed any wrongness as he approached
the office building, and the man himself didn't project any
great amount of menace either.

*He must be one of Bee's contacts,* Owen decided. *He's
certainly the type—his coverall might as well have a tag
on it saying "Disaffected Employee."*

"Well?" he said aloud.

The man licked his lips. "We need to talk about the money first."

Money . . . Owen knew he shouldn't feel surprised. His sister was a merchant-captain, and dealt in the purchase and sale of whatever goods might find a market. But when Owen worked, as now, in the persona of a down-at-the-heels drifter, he carried as little cash as possible. A spaceport bum with money was a contradiction in terms.

"I'm just the messenger boy," Owen said. "You can pick up your fee at the General Delivery office." In addition to handling electronic and hardcopy messages, local branches of the giant communications firm made convenient, no-questions-asked cash drops for all sorts of legal and semilegal business exchanges. "I'm not authorized to carry cash."

He braced himself for an objection, and made ready to counter it in much the same way as he had dealt with the door. He was mildly surprised when the man only nodded, said, "Right," and began fishing in the pockets of his coat.

After a few seconds, the man came up with a thin slice of plastic. "The password's on here."

He held out the keycard. Owen reached out a hand to take the card, and felt the first undefined stirrings of premonition as their fingers touched.

*Something's wrong. He ought to have made a fuss about the money.*

Owen looked at the man again, this time using the physical contact to enhance his perceptions. Under that deeper scrutiny, the patterns of the office worker's consciousness showed up like a dark and knotted skein, with fear and duplicity and greed tangled into an unlovely network.

*Now I see it. He doesn't mind that he might not get Bee's money. Somebody else has already paid him more.*

Owen smiled inwardly, though the face he presented to the office worker never changed. *Sister mine, it's a good thing I came to this party instead of you. You were about to walk into a trap.*

He tucked the keycard into the breast pocket of his coverall. Then, in a continuation of the same movement, his right arm snapped forward, and he smashed the edge of his hand against the bridge of the other man's nose. Cartilage and bone crushed inward, and a fine spray of blood misted out.

Owen caught the man as he fell and eased him silently to the floor. On his knees beside the unconscious man, he searched quickly and methodically through the other's pockets, but found nothing of interest except a second keycard, a twin to the first, equally unmarked. He pocketed it and stood up again.

He looked down for a moment at the sprawled form of the office worker. Perhaps the man would drown in the blood draining from his crushed sinuses, or perhaps not. Owen left the worker there for those who had hired him, and went about his own business.

He took the emergency stairs, not the lift, to the top floor, and paused briefly before the lockplate of the office at the end of the hall. The security system here presented no more challenge than the lock on the outside door. In a moment he was in, with the door closed and secured behind him. He'd probably taken care of any problems by silencing the man below; if he hadn't, whoever had set this trap for his sister would find more in it than they'd expected.

The desk comp had a slot for the keycard. Owen paused for a moment, considering.

Without a physical card in place to complete the circuits, not even an Adept's tricks could shunt the electron flow to perform the task he needed. But which card to use? Owen weighed them in his hand, assessing them as he had the office worker below. One of the cards, the one that he'd been given, felt limited, probably crippled on purpose. He discarded it without any more thought and switched to the card he'd taken from the office worker's pocket.

The password worked. He had Bee's datachip full within minutes; her need for information was narrow and specific, and easily supplied. Errec Ransome's chip took longer. The Master of the Guild cast his nets wide, and in strange waters, for the welfare of the galaxy's Adepts.

Errec Ransome had been a junior Adept in the Guildhouse on Ilarna when the Magewar broke out. Those days had seen slaughter done all across the galaxy, but few places had suffered worse than Ransome's home planet. Only Sapne and Entibor had experienced more destruction than Ilarna. Sapne, depopulated by plagues and reduced to barbarism, had no inhabitants left alive who could remember its ruined cities in their prime; and Entibor was an orbiting slag heap with nothing living on its surface at all.

Seeing all his friends dead and the Ilarna Guildhouse smashed into rubble, Errec Ransome had left the Adepts for a time. He had joined the privateers of Innish-Kyl in their hit-and-run war against the Magelords, fighting other men's battles for his own purposes. The Mageworlders had been crushed now for twenty years and more, and Master Ransome had long since returned to the Guild; but his vigilance never ceased.

Owen completed his second download and withdrew the keycard. And then—

*Danger!*

The premonition slammed into him full force. His senses clamored with the awareness of enemies nearby, and he clutched the edge of the desk with both hands.

*Danger! Too close—*

He lifted his head to looked around the office, and cursed under his breath at his own arrogance and stupidity.

What had seemed to be alternate exits—windows and an inner door—he saw now were only illusions, holographic projections with their reality enhanced by his own willingness to believe. The trap had closed on him in a room with no escape except by the door through which he had entered. He would have to fight his way out.

He crossed over to the door and put his hand against it, still expecting little more than blaster bravos and hired thugs, the sort of vermin who were his sister's enemies. Instead . . .

Worse and worse. His enemies waited for him on the other side. *His* enemies, and not Beka's at all.

Owen paused again in the deeper shadows beside a trash bin and looked around. Still no visible pursuit. Closing his eyes and drawing a deep breath, he centered himself and cleared his senses as best he could.

*Nobody near. I've lost them. I hope.*

He couldn't be certain; he didn't have enough energy left to make certain and still keep himself hidden. The fight at the Flatlands Investment Building had taken too much out of him—single-handed and unarmed against too many opponents, while most of his inner resources were diverted into hiding the datachips in his coverall pocket.

He'd lost the hand-to-hand fight, but he'd won the other struggle: he still had both datachips concealed when his enemies dragged him off to Florrie's Palace. There was somebody at Florrie's, they gave him to understand, who was slated for the honor of finishing him off.

He'd never expected to find his sister Beka waiting for him at the other end of a blaster. Once he saw her face, he thought for a few seconds that she was going to kill him after all. But she shot the guard instead, and cut another man's throat, and then surprised Owen even further by agreeing to draw away the inevitable pursuit.

If Master Ransome's datachip ever made it back home to Galcen, Owen reflected, it would be mostly Beka's work. For his own part, he'd been half-blind from the moment he came here.

The blindness wasn't entirely his fault, he supposed. The enemy must have been clouding his vision ever since he showed up on Pleyver—the old enemy, the ones who had laid siege to the planet of Entibor for three years, and not abandoned it until Entibor was dead; who had broken every fleet the civilized worlds had sent against them except the last; who had massacred the Adepts of Ilarna and half a hundred other planets besides.

There were Mages on Pleyver, and not mere apprentices or self-taught dabblers in the ways of power. The great Magelords had returned.

# PART ONE

# I. Nammerin: Namport;
## Space Force Medical Station
## Galcen: The Retreat

W HEN THE courier ship from Galcen Prime arrived on Nammerin, a light but steady rain covered the entire Namport landing field like a fine mist. Lieutenant Ari Rosselin-Metadi ducked out through the hatch of the courier, cast a resigned glance upward at the low grey sky, and climbed down the steep ramp to the ground.

The metal creaked under his boots as he descended. Along with his father's dark hair and his late mother's elegantly chiseled features, Ari had inherited the size and strength of some unknown ancestor on the Metadi, or spaceport-mongrel, side of the family. As a result, he was considerably taller and heavier than the average Space Force trooper the ramp was designed to support.

With both feet planted on the tarmac, he reached up a hand to steady the courier's other passenger as she emerged. It wasn't a long stretch; his head brushed the side of the courier vessel in spite of the landing legs that raised the ship a good seven feet off the ground. His traveling companion—a short, brown-skinned woman with long black hair twisted into a knot at the nape of her neck—took the offered hand and paused for a moment in the open hatch.

"Rain," she said. "Why am I not surprised?"

"Because it always rains in Namport," said Ari. "The Space Force 'Welcome to Nammerin' booklet says that this part of the planet has a wet season and a dry season, but that's a lie. The only two seasons I've ever noticed are rainy and rainier."

The young woman laughed and jumped down to the tarmac, ignoring the ramp completely. Ari didn't feel her weight as she came down, even though her small, trim body carried more muscle than the appreciative eye might suspect. She'd taken his hand as a courtesy only, and he knew it.

Like Ari, the woman wore the uniform of a member of the Space Force Medical Service, but where he wore a lieutenant's bars, she wore no marks of rank at all. Mistress Llannat Hyfid was an Adept, and while the rules of her Guild allowed her to serve in the Republic's Space Force, they barred her from holding formal rank.

As far as anyone could ever tell, Llannat Hyfid accepted her in-between status with cheerful equanimity. Most of the time, Ari himself almost forgot that she was anything more than a fellow-medic and a good friend. Almost, but never quite.

He let go her hand as soon as she straightened from the slight crouch in which she had landed. "Time to collect our baggage before it gets mixed in with the mail sacks," he said. "Then we can see about an aircar rental."

They rescued their carrybags just as the Nammerin Mail hoversled pulled away from the side of the courier. The aircar rental, though, turned out to be unnecessary. When they got to the spaceport's vehicle lot, they found Bors

Keotkyra from the medical station waiting for them beside the Med Station scoutcar. The stocky, fair-haired young officer was flanked by two of the hospital's senior enlisted personnel, wearing Ground Patrol brassards.

"I'm impressed," said Llannat as she and Ari tossed their carrybags into the scoutcar's cargo compartment. "Are you people that eager to see us back?"

"The CO wants to talk to both of you," was Keotkyra's oblique answer. "Nobody's sure whether he wants to kiss you or write you up for Punitive Articles 66 through 134, inclusive."

"How are the bets going?" asked Ari.

"Even money either way." Keotkyra peered into the cargo compartment. "Is that all you brought with you?"

"We left without stopping to pack," Ari said. "I've got ten credits that says we'll be in official disgrace before dinnertime."

"I'm not going to take your money," said Llannat as they climbed aboard and strapped in. "Gambling depends on luck—and I quit believing in things like that after I joined the Guild."

The Medical Station, when they got there, looked almost deserted. At the same time, Ari felt as if he and Llannat were the focus of a multitude of curious eyes. By the time Keotkyra and the Ground Patrol escort had finished marching them across the compound to the CO's office, he'd prepared himself to face the worst.

As far as anybody at the station knew, Ari and Llannat had last been heard of as a pair of kidnap victims, seized during an emergency medical call to the far side of the Divider Range and spirited off-planet by a heavily armed ship with an unprecedented turn of speed. Nobody here knew the truth: the pilot of the ship had been Ari's sister Beka—who had already died, officially and messily, in a spaceship crash on Artat.

Beka hadn't bothered to ask her older brother if he'd

like to join her in tracking down the men who had planned
and hired out their mother's murder. She'd snatched him
away from the Space Force without asking anybody's permission, least of all his own; and now that she was done
with him she'd left him on his own to straighten out the
mess.

Ari paused outside the door of the office and looked
over at Llannat. The Adept had a nervous, intent expression on her face, as if she were listening for something too
faint for others to hear.

"Well?" he asked. Llannat had "heard" things before,
apparently pulling knowledge straight out of the air; she'd
saved his life that way at least once.

But this time she gave a helpless shrug. "Your guess is
as good as mine."

Behind them, Bors Keotkyra cleared his throat.

Ari glanced over his shoulder at their escort. "All right,"
he said. "We can take a hint."

Ari palmed the doorplate and the panels slid apart. The
office looked just as it had the last time he'd stepped
across the threshold, several months before. Printout flimsies covered the desk like fallen leaves, the CO's pet sand
snake drowsed atop the office safe, and the CO himself
wore his habitual expression of gentle regret.

He also wore his dress uniform—something that happened at the Nammerin Medical Station about as often as
a month without earthquakes. Ari snapped to attention.
*That settles it. They're going to throw the book at us.*

Out of the corner of his eye, he saw Llannat standing at
attention beside him. Her left hand brushed the short
silver-and-ebony staff clipped to her belt, and Ari felt a
moment's flash of envy. *She doesn't have to worry; even
if she gets reduced in grade all the way down to a spacer
recruit, she's still Mistress Hyfid, and the Guild takes care
of its own.*

That wasn't fair, of course. Llannat hadn't chosen to get

caught up in his sister Beka's half-mad quest for vengeance. The Adept had been in the wrong place at the wrong time, that was all; and if Master Ransome could spare her any of the consequences, Ari promised himself he wouldn't begrudge her the good luck.

Caught up in his thoughts, he barely noticed when the CO rose and said, "Follow me." It took a cough from Bors to get the whole procession moving again. They left the office by the side door, and marched back across the compound to the Main Supply Dome.

If protocol hadn't required that Ari keep his face expressionless, he would have frowned in puzzlement. *Busting a couple of junior officers for Unauthorized Absence doesn't need a building big enough to park a spaceship.*

Then the doors of the supply dome opened.

The crates and boxes normally held in Main Supply had been shoved aside. Where they had been, in the center of the dome, all Ari could see was dress uniforms lined up in formation.

*I don't believe it,* he thought. *They've turned out everybody but Intensive Care and the gate guards.*

The CO stepped up to a lectern facing the assembled ranks and nodded to the chief master-at-arms.

"Lieutenant Rosselin-Metadi and Mistress Hyfid," the master-at-arms called out, "front and center!"

*This is it,* Ari thought, as he and Llannat took their places in front of the lectern and came to attention. *They're going to make a public example of us "for the good of the service." Maybe I should have asked Father to take care of things after all.*

But he'd never in his career asked for favors because he was General Jos Metadi's oldest son, and his father had never insulted him by making such an offer. Jos Metadi had begun his climb to rank and respectability as a privateer—some of his enemies said as an out-and-out pirate—and his ethics remained, to say the least, flexible; but on that subject father and son were in agreement. Ari squared his shoulders and prepared to take what was coming to him.

*If they throw us out,* he thought, *I can always see if the Quincunx needs a couple of representatives back on Maraghai.*

Ari's honorary membership in the civilized galaxy's largest criminal guild—an unintended byproduct of the Med Station's need to obtain a supply of tholovine faster than normal Supply channels could operate—was a secret he devoutly hoped his superiors in the Space Force didn't share. When a simple business deal involving the exchange of cash for a perfectly legal but hard-to-obtain drug had degenerated into arson and armed pursuit, Ari had expended considerable creative thought on keeping the Brotherhood's role out of the official reports. He'd never expected that the Quincunx would be grateful, or that their gratitude might come in handy later.

The CO glanced down at a sheet of heavy paper resting on the lectern, then looked back at Ari and Llannat.

"Lieutenant Rosselin-Metadi, Mistress Hyfid, it is my extremely pleasant duty to inform you that you have both been awarded the Space Force Achievement Medal."

Ari heard Llannat's breath catch and become irregular as she fought the urge to laugh. The Achievement Medal was the smallest award the Space Force had the power to bestow, ranking even below the Good Conduct Badge. It meant only that the recipient had completed four satisfactory years of active duty. It also implied, to the initiated, that the officer giving the award was mildly surprised that this should be so.

For his own part, Ari felt a perverse indignation. *If they're not going to break us,* he wondered, *why are they going out of their way to insult us?*

The CO looked down at the lectern again for a moment, and then went on. "The citation for this award," he said, "cannot be read aloud at this time, because it is classified. It is, in fact, classified at such a high level that I myself am not cleared to read it. The name of the classification level is also classified."

He paused, and looked out over the assembly before going on. "I am allowed, however, to say that the award was signed by none other than the Head of the Grand Council."

*I should have known Father would do something whether I asked him to or not,* thought Ari, as the CO stepped in front of the lectern to shake first his hand and then Llannat's. *He must have called in some debts from a long way back to get this—there's no way he could have told anyone the truth.*

A bellowed command from the master-at-arms signaled the end of the official part of the festivities. The dress-uniformed ranks broke up, revealing a loaded buffet table behind them. The half-melted ice sculpture in the center of the table could have been either a spaceship or a shooting star, but the trays and plates spread out around it were unmistakably food.

"Broiled groundgrubs," Ari heard Llannat murmuring in the dreamy tones of one who has been too long on space rations. "Tusker-ox riblets. Pickled gubbstucker."

"Go ahead," said the CO. "Help yourselves. After all, you're the guests of honor."

Several minutes later, Ari had a heaping plate of Nammerinish delicacies in one hand and a glass of the locally distilled purple aqua vitae in the other. He made his way through groups of well-wishers to the stacks of boxes at the edge of the cleared area. Llannat was already there, working on a dish of the broiled groundgrubs. A bottle of Tree Frog beer rested on a packing crate near her hand, and most of the station's junior officers clustered around her.

Bors Keotkyra lifted his bottle in a toast as Ari approached. "Here's to the returning heroes," he said. "Whatever you did, it must have been exciting."

Ari exchanged glances with Llannat. He was no Adept like his brother Owen, who could see another's ideas almost before they took shape, but it didn't take any particular gift to know that the thoughts behind the young woman's dark eyes were echoes of his own—memories of blood and death and treachery, of his sister Beka reborn as the one-eyed starpilot Tarnekep Portree, of black smoke rising from the Citadel on Darvell.

He blinked hard to clear the images away, and took a long swallow of the aqua vitae.

"Yes," he said to Bors, as the astringent fumes of the liquor chased the last of the pictures back where they belonged. "It was more exciting than it strictly needed to be."

The Adepts' Retreat on Galcen stood on an outcrop of grey rock in the mountains of the planet's northern hemisphere. Over the centuries the massive, high-walled structure had been fortress and storehouse and hermitage by turns, and even among the Adepts, not many knew its true age. Other planets had their Guildhouses, where Adepts could live and study and go about their tasks—but the Retreat on Galcen was the heart of it all.

To study at the Retreat was a privilege granted to very few, to teach there, an honor granted to even fewer. For Owen Rosselin-Metadi, who had done both, the Retreat was home. The longer he had been away, the more its high grey walls seemed to beckon to him on his return, promising shelter and the company of friends and a chance to let go of the everlasting watchfulness that his work demanded.

This time, as always, he left his rented aircar in the valley below and went the rest of the way on foot. He could have stayed in town and called for someone to come get him—the Retreat had excellent aircar and comm link connections, and the hike up from Treslin was an all-day proposition—but he preferred not to advertise his comings and goings.

The apprentice Adept who stopped him at the gate was new since Owen had left for Pleyver, and painfully young-looking. *The boy can't be a day over sixteen,* Owen thought, forgetting for the moment that he had come to the Retreat himself when he was even younger. *Master Ransome is really robbing the cradle these days.*

The apprentice couldn't have been long on gate duty, either. He stumbled over the traditional greeting. "Welcome, friend. What is your name, and have you—have you—"

" '—have you come to seek instruction?' " Owen finished for him. "My name's Owen, and I'm an apprentice in the Guild already. Could you tell Master Ransome that I've come back?"

The youth stared at him for a moment. Owen wasn't particularly surprised by the reaction. It wasn't often that an apprentice showed up at the Retreat looking like an out-of-work day laborer and asking for the Master of the Guild by name.

"Uh—right," said the boy after a pause. "You wait here and—I mean, let me call somebody to take you to him."

Owen waited patiently while the apprentice spoke over a comm link to an unfamiliar voice farther inside the Retreat. In time another, somewhat older apprentice showed up. Owen didn't remember her, either.

He let her lead the way through the stone-walled passages to the room that served Master Ransome as an office. Like everything else about the Retreat, the room was immeasurably old—so old that its tall, narrow windows had no panes, not even glass ones. In the wintertime, a force field kept out the driving wind and snow, and a ceramic heat bar glowed on the granite hearth. But this was summer; the hearth was bare, and a cool breeze blew through the chamber unimpeded.

A slight, dark-haired man dressed in tunic and trousers of dull black stood at one of the windows, looking out. The apprentice cleared her throat.

"Master Ransome. An apprentice calling himself Owen is here to—"

She got no further than the name before the man turned. At the sight of Owen, Ransome's face broke into a smile of delight that made him look twenty years younger. He strode forward and clasped Owen tightly by the shoulders.

"It's good to see you home," he said.

Owen returned the hug. "Believe me, sir, it's good to be here."

The apprentice spoke up again, somewhat diffidently. "Will you need anything else?"

"Not at the moment," Ransome told her.

As soon as she had left, the Master of the Guild drew Owen over to a pair of chairs beside the empty hearth. The momentary happiness that had passed across Ransome's features was already fading, leaving his face as somber and weary as before.

Owen saw the change come and go, and felt a chill, like the feather of some dark bird drawn across the back of his neck. Errec Ransome was a good ten years younger than Owen's father, but there was something about him these days that made him look all of General Metadi's years and more.

"I'd almost given you up for dead this time," Ransome said as soon as they both were seated. "And Jos was starting to ask some awkward questions."

All trace of welcome was gone now. If Owen hadn't seen the Guild Master's momentary change of expression and felt the strength of his embrace, he would have stiffened himself to endure a spectacular tongue-lashing, as befitted an apprentice who'd fallen below his expected standard.

"I'm sorry," he said. "I almost got caught."

He looked away for a moment at the bare stone of the hearth—some of the memories from Pleyver were still vivid enough to be painful—then turned his head back to meet Ransome's dark, inquiring gaze. "I did get caught, in fact. My own stupid fault, and if Beka hadn't been in town I'd never have gotten away. I couldn't make it off-planet, though; I had to hide out dirtside until everybody forgot about me. It took a while."

Ransome smiled, a quirk of the mouth that scarcely touched his eyes. "That's an understatement," he said. "We have apprentices at the Retreat who've never seen your face—two seasons' worth of them at least."

"I know; I met a couple of them just now. A bit young, aren't they?"

"No more than the usual," Ransome told him. "You, of course, are about to grow a long grey beard."

Owen gave a short laugh. "After the last few months, I feel like it."

He paused, hating to destroy the Guild Master's good humor, however faint—but it had to be done. He drew a breath and went on. "They were Magelords, you know, on Pleyver."

Master Ransome's features grew very still, and his dark eyes seemed to focus on something long ago and far away. "So," he said. "It begins again."

"I'm afraid so," Owen said. "We're not dealing with half-trained agents smuggled through the Net to do a bit of spying, or with a few talented locals who've put together a Mage-Circle out of what they've seen in the holovids. At least one of them on Pleyver was a Great Magelord in the old style—as strong by himself as any Adept I've ever known, even without the power of the others to back him."

"The First of their Circle, he would have been," said

Ransome. "If they're working as they did in the old days." His voice sounded as though he had tasted something bitter. "How did you slip past?"

Owen shook his head. "I didn't. I spent the past two seasons on Pleyver working as a cargo handler down at the spacedocks. Eventually the First gave up looking for me, and the rest of them weren't strong enough to give me any trouble."

"The First gave up looking for you," Ransome said. "Do you have any idea what happened to make him stop?"

"No," Owen said. "But the whole time he was looking for me I could feel it, even in my sleep. Once or twice he backed off a bit, trying to fool me into making a run for the port, but he was too strong to be very good at hiding. Then one day he just wasn't around anymore."

"Off-planet?"

Owen sighed. "I don't know. Maybe. But Pleyver wasn't a total loss, anyway. I still have this."

He pulled the datachip out of the breast pocket of his coverall and handed it to Master Ransome.

"I thought about smuggling it out to you," he said, "but I couldn't think of any way safer than carrying it myself."

Ransome's hand closed over the coin-sized slice of plastic. Another time, Owen thought, he would have looked pleased; but now he barely seemed to notice that he held it. "Is the information still good?"

"Most of it, I think." Owen leaned back in his chair and gave a tired sigh. The datachip had weighed on him more than he'd known. This was the first time in months that he didn't have it somewhere on his person, and its absence left him feeling almost light-headed. "There's a lot of trade and economic data—it looks like we've got stuff crossing the border zone into the Mageworlds that would give the Grand Council fits if they knew about it—plus a bunch of encrypted files I didn't have time to break."

He paused. "There were some other files that had to do with what happened to Mother. I gave those to Beka."

"Was that wise?" Ransome asked. "Your sister is headstrong, to say the least. The rumors I've been hearing say a good deal more than that."

"She's also Domina of Entibor now that Mother is dead—whether she wants the title or not. If anybody has a right to those files, it's Bee."

Owen studied Ransome's dubious expression for a minute and then added, "If she hadn't drawn off the armed pursuit, you probably wouldn't have your data right now. And the fact that all those files were taken while she was on-planet may have sown some useful doubts about exactly who was looking for what in FIL's data banks."

Ransome nodded slowly and tucked the datachip into an inside pocket of his black tunic. "A persuasive argument," he said. "And I am grateful, both to her and to you. But I need you to go out again as soon as possible . . . we have another situation that needs attention."

Owen's heart sank. He could feel his longed-for time of quiet safety receding before him like a wave drawing back from the beach. But he was Master Ransome's apprentice, and had promised long ago that he would serve.

"How soon?" he asked.

"Tomorrow."

"I was hoping to stay here through the fall and winter at least," Owen protested. "Teaching a bit, maybe, and meditating. After all those months hiding out on Pleyver, I'm so jumpy I twitch whenever the wind changes."

"We don't have that kind of time left, I'm afraid," said Ransome. His voice was firm, in spite of the regret and weariness in his dark eyes. "The wind has changed already, and the storm is coming sooner than anyone thinks."

Ari had been back at the Med Station for over a week before he remembered to drop by the station post office and pick up his accumulated mail. Being himself a dutiful, rather than an enthusiastic, correspondent, he didn't expect to find anything of particular interest waiting there for him.

The crew member on duty had been at the awards ceremony with everyone else. He handed Ari a mixed bundle of printout flimsies and sealed envelopes with nothing more than a half-apologetic "You've been gone awhile, so the junk messages had a chance to pile up."

Ari glanced at the top item in the stack—a four-color 3-D flyer announcing a special bargain rate on the purchase of ten or more cases of Tree Frog beer.

"They certainly have," he said, tossing the flyer into the trash-disposal unit. He hadn't felt the same about Tree Frog beer since the affair with the Quincunx, when somebody had tried to poison him by slipping mescalomide into a bottle of Export Dark. The gaudy little advertisement made an unpleasant reminder of a night that had begun with fire and attempted murder, and had ended with Llannat Hyfid fighting a black-masked Mage assassin for Ari's life.

That particular enemy was long dead, but Llannat herself had said once that the Mages preferred to work in groups. . . . Ari growled an oath deep in his throat, and distracted himself by sorting through the rest of his mail at the counter instead of taking it to his quarters.

He recycled five more advertising flyers and the catalog of a firm dealing in exotic herbs; scanned the printout flimsies notifying him of private messages in the electronic files (three from his father and one from Beka's old school chum Jilly Oldigaard, all six months out of date); and set aside for later reading an equally outdated but probably still amusing letter from his friend Nyls Jessan, formerly of the Nammerin Medical Station and last officially heard from at the Space Force Clinic and Recruitment Center on Pleyver.

That left the newest item in the stack, a plain envelope with a local postmark and no return address—just his own name and Space Force directing codes, written in a light, even hand.

Ari worked at the sealed envelope with his thumbnail. Namport's moist equatorial climate had already weakened the adhesive; after only a little urging the flap peeled back and he was able to extract the square of cheap paper inside.

The letter had no salutation and no signature, and only three neatly lettered sentences:

> If you think you see me, you're mistaken. It's somebody else; I'm not here. Stick with Mistress Hyfid and stay out of trouble.

Even if the handwriting hadn't been familiar, Ari thought, the elliptical style would have been a dead giveaway. Out of the entire population of the civilized galaxy, only his brother Owen habitually addressed him with that kind of half-condescending obscurity.

Frowning, Ari tore the envelope and the note into confetti-sized pieces, then dropped the scraps into the trash disposal unit. *"Stick with Mistress Hyfid and stay out of trouble,"* he quoted glumly to himself. *Good advice . . . but I don't think it's going to help me very much.*

"C APTAIN."

"Mmh?" Beka didn't look up from the comp console. *Damned Space Force paper pushers; this checklist is longer than all of Councilor Tarveet's speeches pasted together.*

"Captain, it's late."

She nodded absently and flipped to the next screen. "Mm-hm."

"Captain—"

The change in tone caught her attention. She blinked, wiped a hand across eyes gone bleary from too long at the console, and leaned back in her chair to look at the speaker for the first time.

*Warhammer*'s gunner/copilot looked back at her in mild concern. Nyls Jessan—lean and fair-haired, with light grey eyes and pleasant if unremarkable features—had the appearance of a small-time free spacer in a dangerous part of the galaxy, all the way down to the war-surplus blaster.

But appearances could be deceiving, especially where Jessan was concerned. Her partner spoke Standard Galcenian with an upper-class Khesatan accent; he played cards and handled weapons like a professional; and he'd abandoned a perfectly good career in the Space Force Medical Service to join Beka on *Warhammer* after her old copilot had died in the fighting on Darvell.

*A man of many talents, is our Jessan,* she thought, and smiled in spite of herself. "Now I'm listening. What's the problem?"

"You," he said. "You've been working over that checklist since 0400, and *Warhammer*'s not going to get any cleaner than she already is. It's time you got some sleep."

"Is that what you had in mind . . . sleep?"

"Absolutely," Jessan assured her, straight-faced.

She hesitated a moment, watching him, and then shook her head with a faint sigh. "We can't afford to fail our blockade inspection just because some busybody in a Space Force uniform decides that I haven't done my paperwork right."

"Let me handle it," he offered. "I'm used to the style."

"No. If I'm going to sign for something, I want to make all the mistakes myself."

He shrugged and stretched out on the padded acceleration couch on the other side of the common room. "Fine, then. I'll stay up and keep you company."

"Your choice," she said.

She turned back to the screen and worked diligently for a few minutes until a faint snore broke the silence behind her. She glanced over at the couch. Jessan's head had fallen back against the cushions and his eyes were closed.

"Damned idiot Khesatan," she muttered, and hit the button to close the comp session.

The console folded itself back into its bulkhead niche,

and Beka stood up. She went over to the couch and touched Jessan lightly on the shoulder.

"All right, Nyls," she said. "You win. Let's go to bed."

The chronometer in the captain's quarters aboard *Warhammer* sounded its usual wake-up signal at 0500 Standard. Beka slid out from beneath Jessan's arm and swung her feet down onto the deckplates. The alarm button for the chrono had been set into the bulkhead on the far side of the cabin, and she couldn't turn it off without getting out of her bunk—which had probably been the designer's intention in the first place.

Once the alarm had been silenced Beka started getting dressed, but not in the plain shirt and trousers that she'd worn yesterday. Today she wore the lace and ruffles of a well-groomed but somewhat androgynous young man of fashion from Mandeyn's Embrigan district, with long brown hair braided into a queue and finished off with a black velvet ribbon. This particular Mandeynan, however, carried a double-edged dagger hidden up his sleeve, and had a Gyfferan Ogre Mark VI blaster in a worn leather holster tied down against his thigh.

She finished arranging the folds of her white spidersilk cravat, tucked a lacy handkerchief into one ruffled cuff, and contemplated the result with satisfaction. Beka Rosselin-Metadi, master of *Warhammer* and Domina of lost Entibor, had all but vanished, replaced by Captain Tarnekep Portree: starpilot, gunfighter, and killer-for-hire.

*Now for the final touch.*

Beka reached into the storage compartment that held her dirtside gear, took out a red optical-plastic eye patch, and fitted it into place. The patch covered her left eye socket from cheekbone to brow ridge, giving Tarnekep Portree an oddly piebald gaze. Most people found the glittering red plastic disturbing, with its hints of extensive prosthetic work lying hidden underneath; they would flinch and turn

away without looking closely at the rest of Tarnekep's pale
and angular face.

*All part of the disguise,* she reflected. *The Prof knew
what he was doing when he thought up this identity. Nobody wants to get close to Tarnekep Portree.*

Well, almost nobody. When she turned back toward the
bunk, Nyls Jessan was awake and watching her.

"How's the effect?" she asked.

He smiled. "Excellent as always, Captain. Elegant, but
with a distinct aura of indefinable menace."

"Good. Let's hope it fools the inspectors."

Inspection came at 0911.54 Standard, when *Warhammer*
dropped out of hyper at the edge of the Net—the artificial
barrier to hyperspace transit that the Republic had imposed
upon the Mageworlds at the end of the war. Making a new
jump would be impossible until the inspecting officer sent
word to the generating station to open a hole and let the
*'Hammer* pass.

Like a vast spiderweb spun out in magnetic fields from
thousands of generating stations, the Net hung between the
Mageworlds and the rest of the civilized galaxy. Any starship coming or going had to to drop out of hyper and run
in realspace, where the Republic's Net Patrol Fleet pa-
trolled in force, sensors always alert for vessels trying to
sneak undetected across the border.

One could, Beka supposed, go the long way around,
skirting the edges of the Net. Space was too big for any artificial construct to enshroud the Mageworlds completely.
Even in hyperspace, though, such a journey might take
years.

*But Ebenra D'Caer believed he could make it to the
Mageworlds in a single jump from Ovredis,* she thought as
she waited with Jessan for the inspection party to arrive.
*And* somebody *sure fished him out of his cell back at the
asteroid base.* Llannat said it was Magework, all the way
down the line. "The Mages make long plans," she said.

*And the Professor, too ... he talked about five hundred years as if it was nothing.*

She bit her lip. Thinking about her old teacher and co-pilot wasn't going to do her any good, not with a shuttle coming across right now from Net Station C-346—one of the checkpoints where all ships seeking passage had to register and submit to inspection. She concentrated instead on the details of *Warhammer*'s cover ID as the armed merchantman *Pride of Mandeyn* (Suivi registry, Tarnekep Portree commanding).

Soon a muffled clunk and a faint tremor in the deckplates told her that the shuttle had docked. She toggled open the *'Hammer*'s dorsal airlock and let the inspection party come in: two Space Force enlisted personnel, one short, redheaded and female, the other dark-skinned, gangly, and male, under the command of a wide-eyed young ensign who had clearly never seen anything like Tarnekep Portree before in his life.

Beka suppressed an urge to laugh. *So this product of a sheltered upbringing gets to sit across the table from me while we go over the paperwork with a magnifying glass. If I'm lucky, he'll be twitching so hard he forgets half his questions.*

The wide-eyed young ensign, however, wasn't one to let his personal opinions get in the way of efficient customs procedure. He consulted the clipboard he carried in one hand, then asked for—and got—the sheaf of printout flimsies that contained the *'Hammer*'s pre-inspection paperwork; the official forms that confirmed the vessel's registry as *Pride of Mandeyn*, and Tarnekep Portree's legal ownership of same; and the imitation-leather folders that held all the relevant licenses, ID flatpix, and passports (Mandeynan and Khesatan, one each) for the captain and copilot of the *Pride*.

He passed the IDs through the clipboard scanner, which beeped quietly as it communicated with the link aboard the shuttle. The shuttle would relay the IDs to the Net Station's main data banks and pass any relevant information back to the inspecting officer.

"Tarnekep Portree," the ensign said after the beeping had stopped. "The data net has you down as Wanted For Questioning back on Mandeyn."

Beka didn't blink. "This isn't Mandeyn," she pointed out. "And a WFQ isn't a warrant."

"Granted," said the ensign. "Nevertheless, the Space Force is legally obligated to pass any word on your whereabouts back to the Petty Council of Embrig Spaceport."

"Fine. Tell the council I said hello. I love them too."

The ensign pressed his lips together as if suppressing a hasty reply, and glanced back at his clipboard. When he looked up again at Jessan, his expression had changed from dubious suspicion to active distaste.

"Nyls Jessan," he said. "Formerly of the Space Force Medical Service. Lieutenant commander, no less. Cashiered."

Jessan bowed. "The same."

The ensign's lip curled. He turned his back on Jessan completely and spoke to Beka. "Captain Portree, I'll be going over the *Pride*'s paperwork with you. Please direct your . . . associate . . . to assist my people in a physical inspection of the vessel."

"Sure." Beka waved a hand at Jessan. "You heard the nice man, Doc. Show our friends around."

"My pleasure, Captain."

Jessan headed off into the depths of the ship with the two enlisted personnel trailing after him, and Beka sat down at the common-room table with the ensign. The young officer ran through the paperwork line by line, consulting frequently with his clipboard.

"Energy guns dorsal and ventral, shields bow and stern—you carry a lot of firepower for a merch, Captain."

Beka raised an eyebrow. "We're an armed freighter, like

the registry says. When you work in the outplanets, you can't always depend on the Space Force to show up in time."

The ensign looked offended. "This isn't a war zone, Captain Portree. I'm afraid we'll have to seal your guns for the duration of your stay in the Mageworlds."

Beka had been expecting to hear something of the sort; the *'Hammer'*s guns were latest-generation technology, newly upgraded at the shipyards on Gyffer. Nevertheless, she scowled. "What am I supposed to do if somebody over there across the border starts taking potshots at me? Yell for help and hope the fleet comes running?"

"You're not in the outplanets any longer, Captain. The Mageworlds aren't in any shape to give you trouble." He glanced at his clipboard again. "You don't have a cargo listed."

"I'm going in empty and looking to pick up a cargo once I get there," Beka said. "Like it says on the form, I'm interested in rare earths and botanicals for the medical-research trade."

"Any Republic currency you've got has to stay on this side of the border," said the ensign. "Sorry if it complicates your business dealings, but that's the law."

*You're not the least bit sorry, you little bastard,* thought Beka. *Well, I'll fix you. Just watch me do it.*

She emptied the money from her trouser pockets onto the table: five or six decimal-credit pieces, a rumpled ten-credit chit, and a silver Mandeynan mark with a pinpoint blaster hole through the middle.

"Here you go," she said. "Maybe Doc has a couple of ten-chits on him, but otherwise that's the lot."

"How do you plan to pay for your cargo, Captain?"

"I don't," she said. "I'm a pilot. Other people pay me."

The ensign looked like he'd bitten down on something sour. He went on with the paperwork, going back and forth between the *Pride*'s forms and the data appearing on his clipboard.

*Hunting for something else he can call me on,* thought Beka. *Aha—now he thinks he's got it.*

"About your crew, Captain. You have only yourself and the copilot listed, but you have berthing space for at least six."

Beka shrugged. "The *Pride*'s a *Libra*-class freighter; she was built to run with a full crew. She's been upgraded a lot since the old days, but nobody ever bothered to take out the extra berthing. We use it for slopover storage mostly, when we've got a lot of cargo on board."

The ensign made a note on his clipboard. "Understood. But Mageworlds nationals can't pass through the Net in civilian vessels, so don't plan on picking up any passengers."

"Don't worry. The damned Mages can rot on their side of the Net for all I care. I'm looking for a cargo that doesn't talk back."

"Wise of you, Captain Portree. We don't tolerate the other sort."

*I'll bet you don't,* Beka thought, as the ensign continued his way through the stack of printout flimsies. *It's a good thing I've got work to do, or I'd smuggle an entire Mage-Circle out through the Net just to prove that I could.*

Eventually the paperwork came to an end. Beka signed the several forms, in triplicate, in Portree's angular, slashing hand, and the ensign stamped and dated all the signatures. He was down to the last one when Jessan came back with the two enlisted personnel.

The redhead approached the table. "Everything's clean, sir," she told the ensign. "And the guns are sealed."

"Very good." The ensign gathered up the signed and dated forms, and returned the registration papers and both of the personal-information folders to Beka—pointedly ignoring Jessan, who was regarding the proceedings in general, and the ensign in particular, with an air of bland amusement.

When the inspection party had departed and the shuttle had pulled away for Net Station C-346, Beka put the papers and the folders into the ship's safe. Then, from a snug and very well concealed locker, she removed a compact but effective scanner. Only after she had located and deactivated both of the listen-and-record devices the inspectors had left behind—one in the *'Hammer'*s cockpit and the other, somewhat more imaginatively, underneath the bunk in the captain's quarters—did she allow herself to relax.

"Trusting souls, those Space Force types," she observed to Jessan. "Do they plant a snoop or two on every freighter that goes through the Net?"

"Probably," said Jessan. "And most of them probably get scanned and deactivated. But if you leave a couple on every ship you inspect, and collect the ones that are still there when the ships come back, eventually you get lucky."

"You have a natural bent for this sort of thing . . . are you sure you were a medic before they threw you out?"

"It's all on the record."

Beka snorted. "We know how much that's worth, don't we?"

"Not everything in there is fiction," Jessan protested. "Most of it's the plain truth, in fact. Easier to keep things consistent that way."

She looked at the Khesatan curiously. "Nyls, just what does the record say about the end of your Space Force career? The way that ensign looked at you . . ."

"Beautiful, wasn't it?"

"I'm serious."

"Black-market trafficking in underage sapients," Jessan said. "Quite a nice little racket."

"If you call twenty-to-fifty at hard labor 'nice.' How did you get off?"

"The prosecution was thrown out as void on a technicality, so I was merely discharged with prejudice." He shook his head mournfully. "It was terrible, really. Pull up a copy of the court transcript, and you'll see that my quarters were illegally searched, so all the evidence seized was inadmissible."

"Very artistic all around," Beka said. "So that's what you and Dadda's aide were cooking up over the secure comm link, our last night on Innish-Kyl. I'd been wondering."

"Captain, I'm shocked. Falsifying official records is a criminal offense. Would I accuse a Space Force officer of Jervas Gil's reputation of suborning a felony?"

"In a heartbeat," she said. She juggled the pair of small, button-shaped listening devices in the palm of her cupped hand. "Right now, we have some waiting around to do until the 'Hammer gets jump clearance, and I've still got these little knickknacks to dispose of. I think I'll head down to the forward hold for a bit of target practice."

"Mind if I come along?"

"Not at all. I rather enjoy your company."

They made their way along the plain steel decks of the ship and through the hatch into Forward. Beka toggled a switch to bring up the work lights. She glanced about, finding the hold a shadowy and oddly echoing space without the crates and pallets that normally filled it. It was a good thing, she reflected, that the inspection party hadn't bothered to take measurements and compare them with the real stats for a *Libra*-class freighter. They might have noticed that the forward cargo bay was considerably smaller than it ought to be—and after that, it wouldn't take them long to figure out about the engines.

*Warhammer* held a number of secrets, but the oldest and best kept went back to the time when General Jos Metadi had commanded her. Early in his privateering days, then-Captain Metadi had put his ship into the yards on Gyffer for an expensive and unrecorded stay. The Gyfferan ship-wrights had removed the original engines; then they had filled all the empty space plus a portion of the cargo compartments with the realspace and hyperspace engines of a vessel half again the 'Hammer's size. Those engines, coupled with newer and heavier energy guns, had turned an armed freighter into a ship of war, strong enough to outfight a dozen Magebuilt fighters and fast enough to outrun the mothership that carried them.

Not even Metadi's copilot of those days, Errec Ransome, had known exactly how fast Warhammer could travel when the need was on her. Beka had pushed the 'Hammer close to that limit more than once—but not since the ship's most recent visit to the Gyfferan yards, where those outsized engines had been yet another of the items on the upgrade list.

*With no cargo on board,* Beka thought, *we could probably outrun a dreadnought if we had to.*

The idea pleased her, and she smiled a little as she affixed the pair of snoop-buttons to the bulkhead near the hatch. The two buttons showed up as dark, coin-sized circles against the steel.

With Jessan following, she crossed to the far side of the hold and pulled out her blaster. She checked the charge—ninety-seven percent—and scaled the setting down to a fine beam at lowest power.

"No use drilling clear though the hull to vacuum," she observed. Then she settled the Mark VI into its holster and turned her back on the target.

Without warning she whirled, drawing the weapon at the same time, and fired twice down the length of the bay. The bolts left glowing trails of ionized air behind them, and the snoop-buttons sparkled briefly. She took a two-handed stance and sent five more bolts into each of the buttons, then switched to a one-handed grip and stood sideways to the target as she fired. Finally, she lowered her arm, thumbing the blaster back up to full power as she did so, and put the weapon away.

"Whoever that was," said Jessan, "I think he's dead."

"We'll see."

They walked over to the bulkhead where Beka had placed the snoop-buttons. Both of the recorders were lumps of slag and charred plastic, and tiny pits had been etched into the steel behind them. Beka tapped at the pattern of blaster-points with one close-trimmed fingernail.

"A decent group," she said, "but I'm not getting any better. Dammit, I wish the Prof could be with us for this one."

"You still miss him, don't you?"

"Yeah," Beka said. "I miss him."

She pried the carbonized snoop-buttons off the bulkhead and dropped them to the deck, then ground the bits of glass and plastic into the metal with the heel of her boot. "But he's dead, so there's no point in talking about it. Let's get moving."

Jervas Gil—full captain, Republic Space Force—leaned back in the command chair in RSF *Karipavo*'s Combat Information Center. The comp screens around him showed no activity beyond the usual status reports, and the battle tank, the big holovid setup that displayed any current action, was blank and dim. The cruiser was in peacetime watch sections and the CIC was empty except for Gil.

General Jos Metadi's former aide, promoted to captain and commodore of the Mageworlds Fleet, had soon discovered that his new rank presented him with more care and responsibility that it did privacy. He found the deserted CIC an excellent place to think and to be alone, or as alone as anybody ever got on shipboard. Footsteps sounded on the deckplates of the CIC as Gil's aide—these days, he rated an aide of his own—approached with a clipboard full of flimsies.

The aide, a young lieutenant named Bretyn Jhunnei, saluted and said, "Daily reports for you, sir."

"Anything interesting?"

Jhunnei had black hair and a long, sallow face. She tilted her empty hand back and forth like a scale coming to a balance. "Same same."

"Thanks."

Commodore Gil took the clipboard and flipped quickly through the sheets. Most of the reports were generally unsurprising, the same as the day before and the day before that: lists of food endurances on the other ships in the fleet blockading the Mageworlds; fuel-consumption reports; a daily situation estimate from Space Force Intelligence (based, as far as Gil could tell, on his own reports from the week before); and the record of all civilian ships passing through the Net, with the results of any boarding searches.

Gil scanned the last set of papers without much interest. Anything portentous or disturbing uncovered as a result of those searches would already have been forwarded to him in a separate message. This would be the leftovers, the little ships doing the sort of decimal-credit trade that made up the Mageworlds' limited contact with the rest of the civilized galaxy—ships with names like *Redstar*, *Lucky Vi*, and *Pride of Mandeyn*.

He suppressed a start. Somehow he hadn't expected anything so normal from the likes of the General's daughter, just a one-line report two-thirds of the way down the list of ships, an ordinary boarding and search for contraband, with the results listed simply as "routine."

Gil forced himself to keep on flipping through the stack of flimsies as if nothing had happened. At last he handed the printouts back to Jhunnei for recycling.

"Well," he said under his breath, "it's begun."

"What's begun, sir?" Jhunnei asked.

Gil looked at the fresh young lieutenant—first in her

class, the pride of the Service Academy, no combat experience.

*A whole generation,* he thought. *Has it really been so long?*

"The Second Magewar," he said. After a pause, he added, "Not a word of that to anyone, eh?"

Jhunnei's expression didn't change. "Word of what, sir?"

Gil regarded the lieutenant with approval. Discretion was one of the chief marks of a good aide, and Jhunnei was shaping up nicely. For a fleeting moment he thought back to his own recent tour as aide to General Metadi, and wondered if the General had ever thought the same thing about him.

"Nothing, Jhunnei," he said. "Nothing. But I'd like to make this month's training schedule concentrate on combat readiness. Write a message to the fleet instructing all captains to exercise their crews at General Quarters."

"Yes, sir."

"And work up a fleet training plan."

She nodded. "Will that be all, sir?"

"For the moment. And forget what I just said about the war. The action really started over two years ago. It's just that no one noticed at the time. That's all."

Jhunnei saluted and left. Gil sat alone for a while, thinking, then leaned over and punched the call button for the commanding officer's quarters on the *'Pavo.*

"Captain," Gil said as soon as the red "listening" light came on. "Please put your vessel in Condition Three."

"Aye aye, Commodore," the captain's voice replied. "Anything I should know about?"

"No," Gil replied. "There's nothing to know."

He relaxed back into his seat and waited while the clean-cut young men and women of the *'Pavo,* those whose Wartime Cruising watch stations were in Combat, filed into the CIC and brought the display screens and status boards to life. Commander Erne Wallanish, the *'Pavo*'s executive officer, walked up to the command chair.

"XO reporting," Wallanish said. He was a stocky, sandy-haired man with a strong outplanets accent—Pleyver, Gil thought, or maybe Innish-Kyl. "What's the situation?"

"Apparently peaceful," Gil replied. "Carry on."

"Yes, sir."

Gil stood and stretched. One good thing about shipboard routine was that it had enabled him to recommence his exercise regimen and to watch his diet. He'd gotten rid of most of the flab that five years of dirtside duty had put on him.

"I'll be in my quarters," he said. "Any messages can reach me there."

The vacuum-tight door sighed shut behind him as he walked quickly from the space. Once in his cabin, he opened the fold-out desk beside the bunk. He pulled over a sheet of flimsy and began to write a report—in longhand, using the service-issue stylus he carried in his uniform pocket to initial reports and sign messages.

The General had insisted that anything of the supremest importance needed to be encrypted before transmission, without entering it into anything electronic. "Too many ears, Gil," he'd said. "Electrons have no friends; they'll work for anyone as easily as they'll work for you."

Gil constructed the code grid from memory and encrypted his message. With luck, even broken down into plaintext the brief sentence would have meaning for only one person. "Vessel of interest entered Magezone" was all it said. And remembering the Mages and what rumor claimed they had been able to do, Gil wished that he hadn't needed to think about those words as he wrote them down.

What were the odds, Gil wondered, that the Magelords had a spy somewhere in the fleet? Nearly a hundred percent, he decided. The Adept who had gone with *Warham-*

*mer* to Darvell and back—Mistress Hyfid, that was her name—claimed that Ebenra D'Caer had been working for the Mageworlders all along, and that the Mages had extracted him without a trace from his prison cell on Beka Rosselin-Metadi's asteroid base.

*Right,* thought Gil. *And what Mistress Hyfid knows, the Master of the Adepts' Guild also knows. He'll have his own agent somewhere in the fleet, I'm sure. The Guild isn't supposed to run intelligence operations, but "not supposed to" never stopped anybody yet.*

Gil shrugged, and put both the Magelords and the Adepts' Guild out of his mind. Let the Mages and the Adepts play their metaphysical game of hide-and-seek. With any luck, they would neutralize each other. He had another mission: to keep the Mageworlds from rearming; and if that effort failed, to keep the war from touching the Republic.

That was enough of a job for one man, and if he did it, he would have done enough.

# III. Nammerin: Space Force Medical Station Downtown Namport

THE SUN had not yet risen. In the Bachelor Officers' Quarters of the Med Station, most of the rooms were still dark and their occupants asleep. Except for the fading starlight coming in through one unshaded window, Room 231A was as dark as the rest; its occupant, however, was awake and had been for some time. Llannat was alone—the room had bunks and closet space for two, but Housing hadn't seen fit to assign her a roommate—and she stood in the middle of the bare floor with a short ebony staff in her right hand, fighting against shadows.

*Here,* she thought, blocking where her imagined opponent struck. *And here. And the counterstrike—now!*

Faster and faster she went through the sequences, until the ebony staff became only a dark blur, almost invisible against the night. Llannat was sweating, and the dark coverall she wore clung to her back and shoulders, but her breathing was steady. She practiced every day, if not always for so long or at such an early hour. This morning, though, she'd awakened in the silent time before dawn and hadn't been able to sleep.

She'd been dreaming again—not of Darvell, with its blood and fire, but of Beka Rosselin-Metadi's hidden base in an uncharted belt of asteroids, and of the soft-spoken, grey-haired Entiboran who had bequeathed it to her. Llannat had never known the man's true name. Beka had called him "Professor," which suited his demeanor; he had called Ari's sister "Captain" and "my lady" in return, and had given her loyalty until death.

Nor had Llannat ever learned the Professor's true age. He was older than he looked, impossibly old; she'd heard him speak of centuries as though they were nothing. He had been Armsmaster and confidential agent to House Rosselin for a long time when the Magewars began. And before that he had been something else.

"... *I foreswore sorcery long ago, when I gave my oath to House Rosselin.*"

"*Adepts don't practice sorcery.*"

"*No. Adepts don't.*"

But the Mages did, and the silver and ebony rod the Professor had carried with him to Darvell was a Mage-lord's weapon and badge of office. The Professor hadn't returned from that journey, but his staff had. Beka had picked it up, either not knowing or not caring about its true nature, and had given it to Llannat without understanding what she did.

Llannat's own staff, the long one of plain wood that marked her as an Adept, had vanished somewhere in the grey nothingness that those who worked with power called the Void. Some people—Ari's sister, for one—might think it was chance that had brought Llannat the Professor's staff in exchange.

*But I know better*, Llannat thought. *If this staff came to me, it's because the Professor wanted it to.*

She hadn't told Master Ransome about the staff. She'd spoken with the Guild Master more than once in the aftermath of the Darvell affair, but she'd left the staff at Prime Base with her luggage every time. Nor had she told Master Ransome anything about the Professor, except in his role as Beka's copilot. The omissions worried her. She ought to have told the Master of the Guild everything that had to do with the Magelords and the use of power.

*It looks like I inherited the Professor's secrets along with his staff. He never told anyone what he was, except me—and what am I, now? What would the Guild Master call an Adept who carries a Magelord's staff, and who acknowledges a Magelord as her teacher?*

She didn't need any special wisdom to answer that one. Errec Ransome had never forgotten what the Mages had done to the Guildhouse on his homeworld of Ilarna; nor, so far as Llannat could tell, had he ever forgiven it. He dealt ruthlessly with those remnants of the old Mage-Circles that still surfaced from time to time, and he would not be gentle toward an Adept who had betrayed the Guild by choosing to learn from the enemy.

*But you can't always pick your teachers,* Llannat thought. *Sometimes the universe picks them for you.*

The learning didn't always stop just because the teacher was dead, either. In her dream, she and the Professor had been practicing staffwork in one of the corridors deep beneath the surface of the asteroid base. Sometimes in these dreams she won the practice bouts, and sometimes she lost them, but almost always the Professor talked with her as they fought.

Tonight he had spoken of Ari Rosselin-Metadi. *"My lady's brother is not a man who works to avoid trouble."*

*"Ari couldn't be inconspicuous if he tried,"* she had answered, countering the Professor's blow as she spoke and striking out in turn. *"But the hand of the Guild is over him."*

The Professor turned the stroke aside with ease. *"The Guild's hand? Or your own?"*

*"I'm an Adept,"* she said. *"My hand and the Guild's are the same."*

She missed her block then, and the Professor's next blow came in against her side. He struck again without waiting for her to recover.

*"Mistress, are you sure?"*

*"When I came to the Guild,"* she said, blocking again, *"I told Master Ransome I would obey—"*

*"—in order that you might learn,"* the Professor finished for her. The third blow in his sequence came crashing down past her guard and ended the match. *"Apprentice vows. But no one remains an apprentice forever."*

After that she had awakened, to lie staring up at the darkness with her ribs aching from blows that she had taken in a dream. Now she moved through the sequences as she had dreamed them, taking the blows and blocks and counterstrikes and working with them until they flowed together without need for thought.

She didn't want to think, particularly. It didn't take dreams and prophecies to know that trouble was coming, and that when it arrived, the vows of a single medic-turned-Adept would dwindle to matters of no importance at all.

The old section of downtown Namport dated from the first few decades of the planet's settlement. In those days, the buildings had been thrown together using local materials whenever possible, to cut down on the cost of importing fixtures and fittings. Later, in the good times after the end of the Magewar, Namport had grown too fast for the old section to keep up. The wooden-frame buildings with their shuttered balconies weren't fashionable anymore. Prosperous citizens moved out to newer parts of town, leaving the run-down older houses for the workers who provided casual labor around the port and the industrial districts.

Namport's traffic, like its architecture, was a mix of galactic technology and local materials. Most of the city dwellers drove nullgrav-assisted hovercars that didn't need roads in order to operate; and the small-time farmers who harnessed the native tusker-oxen for draft animals had no use for pavement at all. Pedestrians like Owen Rosselin-Metadi had to pick their way through the mud from puddle to puddle.

Owen lived in one of the old quarter's oldest buildings—a slowly decaying clapboard structure painted a faded and peeling green—and his current job, in the laundry room of a bathhouse at the edge of the spaceport, had him working nights and walking home along the unpaved streets as the sky grew light. Today the street outside his apartment building was deserted except for the neighborhood drunk sleeping propped up against a trash bin. Even the one or two streetwalkers who worked this part of town had gone home.

The main door of the building was open, as usual; whoever owned the place and collected the rent wasn't going to waste good money on scan-locks or security guards. Owen climbed up the four flights of stairs—ignoring the lift, which had been broken for so long most of the tenants didn't realize that it existed—and unlocked the door to his room.

His apartment was "furnished," which in this section of Namport meant that it contained a table with one leg shorter than the other three, a folding metal chair with dents in the seat and back, and a narrow cot with a lumpy mattress. The sheets on the mattress were Owen's, purchased out of his first week's pay. Master Ransome had supplied him with enough funds to cover his expenses, but he preferred to work his own way as usual, leaving the roll of credit chits tucked inside the mattress cover for an emergency backup.

Nobody had come into his room since he'd left it the evening before. He would have known if anybody had. After Pleyver, he'd taken precaution upon precaution, but if there were any Mages left on Nammerin they were keeping their distance. Owen had counted on setting something in motion with his arrival, anything from a disturbance in the currents of Power to a physical attempt on his life, and he found the lack of interest disturbing.

*The Mages ought to be here,* he thought, as he stripped out of his working clothes. *They've had a functioning Circle on Nammerin for a long time, and it shows. All the patterns have knots and kinks in them; they've been twisted out of shape by sorcery. I should have startled the Circle into action just by showing up.*

He folded his discarded garments and laid them on the chair, with his shoes side by side on the floor beneath, then stretched himself out on the lumpy cot. Sleep tugged at him like an undertow, trying to pull him away from the shore, but he forced himself to stay awake and keep thinking for a few minutes longer. He had work to do, and—if Master Ransome was right—little enough time to do it in. If the Mages on Nammerin weren't going to reveal themselves of their own accord, then he would have to stir them into action.

*Tomorrow,* he told himself. *Tomorrow's a better time for it. I can wait. Time isn't just on the Mages' side. It works for me as well.*

In the quarters he shared with another of the Medical Station's lieutenants, Ari Rosselin-Metadi squeezed a dollop of shaving gel out of the tube and rubbed it onto his cheeks and chin. While the depilatory was doing its work, he laid out his uniform on the neatly made bottom bunk.

He'd gotten dressed as far as socks and trousers when he was interrupted by a pounding at the door.

Bare to the waist, with the greenish shaving gel stiffening on his face, Ari padded across the room. The old scars of an encounter with a *sigrikka*—one of the great predators on the planet Maraghai—stood out against the massive, heavy muscles of his bare back and arms. He palmed the lockplate and the door panel slid aside.

Out in the hallway, the greyish pink light of early morning filtered down through the skylight onto the tousled hair and short, stocky form of Bors Keotkyra. The younger officer was carrying a thick bundle of printout flimsies in one hand.

Ari scowled at him. "What's the racket about? Thomir just got in from being night officer, and you're pounding loud enough to wake the dead."

"Promotion lists are in," said Bors. "Three people from the station made lieutenant commander, and you're one of them." He rattled the sheaf of flimsies. "And new orders came in along with the promotion lists—you've got some of those, too. Orders, I mean. You're getting out of this mud-pit. Some people have all the luck."

"I'll trade my luck for yours any day," Ari said. "You don't happen to know where they're sending me, do you?"

Bors shook his head. "You're getting a ship tour; that's all I know. See you at breakfast—I have to go finish spreading the good word. Later!"

"Later," said Ari. He hit the lockplate again, and the panel slid shut.

Over in the top bunk, Thomir lifted his head off his pillow far enough to ask blearily, "What was that all about?"

"Orders and promotions."

"Oh," Thomir said, and yawned. "And here I thought it was something important." Ari's current roommate was both a recent arrival on Nammerin and a newly minted lieutenant; promotion and reassignment wouldn't be coming his way again any time soon.

"Well, it isn't. Go back to sleep."

Ari wiped off the shaving gel with a damp facecloth—actually, a square of the standard-issue reclaimable synthetic that the Space Force used for everything from bandages to blankets—then stuffed the cloth into the recycler and began putting on the rest of his uniform. He slid his arms into the sleeves of his tunic and shrugged it into place, then sealed the tabs and went back over to the closet. A leather gun belt hung from a hook inside the closet door.

The gun belt supported a heavy, war-surplus blaster. Ari belted on the weapon and straightened it so that that holster lay along the outside seam of his trousers. He gave his uniform a final check in the mirror, then headed out of the room and down the corridor to the officers' mess.

The doors of the dining hall slid open, and Ari caught the Nammerin station's distinctive early-morning smells of water-grain porridge and fresh-brewed cha'a. A babble of voices mingled with the clink of glasses and tableware. Even the people who usually didn't speak to anybody until after the third cup of cha'a were talking, passing the print-out flimsies of the promotion and reassignment lists back and forth and checking for news of friends and acquaintances.

Ari got himself a bowl of porridge, a mug of cha'a, and a mug of the sludgy local drink called *ghil*. He carried his tray over to the nearest table. Esuatec from Outpatient waved a handful of flimsies at him as soon as he sat down.

"Hey, Ari!" she said. "You made lieutenant commander."

"I know," Ari said. "Bors told me. Who's got the list of billet assignments?"

"I do. I'm going to the supply depot on Agameto."

"Not bad."

Esuatec nodded. "Could be worse. You know what they

say: 'Why die? Go Supply! Stay in the rear and count the gear.' "

Ari drained his mug of *ghil* in one long swallow, and followed it up with a mouthful of cha'a to rinse the grit out of his teeth. As far as he was concerned, *ghil* ranked as one of Nammerin's better contributions to the problem of breakfast—it combined the high protein of a nourishing soup with the added bite of a mild stimulant—but even native-born Nammeriners admitted that the texture required some getting used to.

"I suppose supply clerks on Agameto get sick once in a while," he said. "And I hear the weather's nice there. What about me?"

"You've got—" Esuatec flipped through the pages. "—oh, this is a good one—you've got a berth as head of the medical department on board RSF *Fezrisond*."

"The *Fezzy* hasn't gone anywhere outside the Infabede sector in years," Ari said. "And she's Admiral Vallant's flagship, to boot. Formalities. Spit and polish. Inspections and visiting diplomats and dress uniforms at breakfast."

The complaint was mostly for ritual's sake. Ari was not at all displeased with the assignment: nothing flashy, but a good, solid promotion into a responsible position. He turned to his bowl of water-grain porridge with a sense of satisfaction and a general feeling that the day had begun on a propitious note.

A shadow fell across his tray as somebody else sat down across the table from him. He looked up. It was Llannat Hyfid in her customary unmarked uniform, with the ebony staff clipped as usual to her belt. She looked thoughtful. He watched her as she put milk and sugar into her cha'a and drank half of it before setting the mug down again on her tray.

"The orders are in," he said finally. He didn't suppose she would care much about the promotion list, since Adepts didn't carry rank.

"I heard," she said.

"Bors?"

"Who else?" Llannat sighed. "He means well. But all that boundless enthusiasm makes me feel old sometimes."

"Wait until he's been in the service a couple more years," said Esuatec. "He'll be as ancient as the rest of us."

Ari shook his head. "No such luck. Bors will still be young and enthusiastic when he's a hundred and two." He turned back to Llannat. "So what did you get, anyway?"

"Didn't Bors tell you? They love me so much here on Nammerin they're keeping me around indefinitely."

"Oh." Ari took up a spoonful of porridge, looked at it for a moment, and let it fall back into the bowl. He turned the empty spoon over in his hand, then turned it bowl-up again and laid it down on the tray. "It'll save you packing and unpacking, I suppose."

"Yes." She drank more cha'a. Her dark eyes seemed focused on something halfway between the far side of the table and the rim of her mug. "You have a ship tour?"

He nodded. "On *Fezrisond*."

"That's good."

"I suppose it is. Or maybe not. I don't know."

Llannat put the empty mug down without looking at it. "You were probably right the first time."

Esuatec looked from Llannat to Ari and back again, then stood up. "I've got to go," she said. "They need me early over in Outpatient this morning."

Ari pulled his thoughts together enough to say something polite, but Esuatec was already gone. Llannat was still gazing out into the empty space over the tabletop.

"I thought you'd be glad to stay on Nammerin," said Ari finally. "You told me one time that it reminded you of home."

"Parts of it do," Llannat said. "But I didn't join the Space Force because I wanted to stay on Maraghai."

"I guess not." Ari thought for a moment. "You could always ask the Guild—"

"No," she said. "It doesn't work that way. I decided to stick with the Space Force, and that means I go where the Space Force sends me. Or doesn't send me."

"We're—you're stuck, then," Ari said. "Nammerin until further notice."

She sighed. "I know. Think of us dirtsiders once in while when you're out there zipping through hyperspace and touring the galaxy."

"If the *Fezzy* makes it outside the Infabede sector while I'm on her," Ari said, "I'll pay you fifteen credits and buy you a drink the next time we're on liberty in the same port."

Llannat smiled for the first time that morning. "Make it twenty credits and dinner," she said, "and I'll take your bet."

The afternoon sunlight falling across his pillow roused Owen from sleep. He lay for a moment with his eyes closed, testing his surroundings for danger. Nothing. The currents of Power flowed as they always had, their patterns undisturbed except for the constant underlying distortion that marked the presence of a working Mage-Circle.

*I learned to recognize* that *on Pleyver,* he thought, *even if I didn't accomplish much else in all the time I spent there.*

He got out of bed, yawned, and stretched. From the stretch, he moved smoothly into the ShadowDance routines that the Adepts at the Retreat taught to all their students. He could have performed the ShadowDance for much longer than it took him to finish the basic sets; he enjoyed losing himself in the slow, graceful movements that needed only a small change in emphasis to become quick and deadly.

But he had things to do, and a limited time to in which to do them. When he'd finished the last set, he sponged the sweat off his body with cold water from the sink in the kitchen nook—the shower in the apartment's tiny bath-room didn't work any more than the lift did—then dressed in his second set of work clothes, the clean ones, and set-tled himself cross-legged on the bare floor to meditate.

This time his meditations took a more active form. Much as he had tested the apartment and the neighborhood for trouble when he first awoke, he extended his awareness out further, taking in more and more of Namport. He was look-ing for Mages, which was nothing new—he'd done that ev-ery day since he first arrived on-planet—but this time he wasn't bothering to hide his tracks.

*Let the Circle notice me,* he thought. *If they get nervous, they'll do something rash. And then I'll have them.*

Nothing happened, however. He was almost ready to end the session and get on with his normal workday when he felt the patterns alter. Someone was coming—someone was looking for him, with more than physical senses. The approaching presence brought with it something of the pat-tern he had learned to recognize as Magework.

*I've found them,* he thought. And then corrected him-self. *No. I've found* somebody—*but I don't think it's the Circle.*

For there was no malice in the presence, and no fear. Whoever came seeking him wasn't an enemy, as any of the Nammerin Mages certainly would be, and might even be a friend.

He waited. Before long, he heard the stairs creak, and a knock sounded on his door.

"The lock's an easy one," he called. "Come on in."

He heard a click, and the door opened. The young woman who stepped across the threshold wore a Space Force uniform without insignia, but her rather plain, dark features were familiar enough. He'd known Llannat Hyfid when she was an apprentice at the Retreat on Galcen—a confused and uncertain medical-service ensign with a late-blooming sensitivity to the currents of Power.

"Mistress Hyfid," he said, giving her the courtesy due to the title while he continued to assess the changes time and experience had brought.

She'd made progress, no question about it, steadying and strengthening more than he'd expected in the time since he'd last met her. There were other changes, too, chief among them the short, silver-trimmed ebony staff she wore clipped to her belt. The distinctive aura of Magework clung to the staff like purple fire, its patterns clearly visible to Owen's already-sensitive perceptions.

*Where did she get that thing?* he wondered. *And how can she touch it without knowing what it is?*

"Owen," she said. If she noticed his reaction to the staff, she didn't show it. Ignoring the cot and the rickety chair, she sat down on the floor across from him. "It's been a while—and this isn't where I expected to see you again."

For a moment Owen was uncertain how he should deal with his unexpected visitor. He watched her, not speaking, while he sorted through the possibilities in his head.

*Does Master Ransome know what she's carrying? Should I tell him . . . no. She's Adept, not apprentice; she has the right to make her own decisions, and she doesn't feel like a traitor.*

But the staff made him uncomfortable just the same. If the local Mages could sense it, they might do—who knew what they might do? Unless the power it represented in the hands of an Adept made even them nervous.

*It ought to. It makes* me *nervous.*

"You shouldn't be here," he said finally.

"Maybe you're right," Llannat said. "But you might as well be broadcasting yourself over all the holovid networks in Namport. You were certainly giving me headaches as far out as the Medical Station."

"You should have taken the hint and stayed away." He leaned forward a little, catching her gaze and holding it.

"Listen to me. You being here is dangerous. For me, for you. Don't ask why. Just go."

She didn't look surprised. "Not yet," she said. "I have a question for you first. Guild business."

"I doubt if I can answer it for you," he said. "I'm just an apprentice, remember?"

Llannat shook her head. "You're more than that, and every Adept in the Guild knows it. I want you to tell me what's going on with Ari. Master Ransome sent me here to play bodyguard for him—so why is he being shipped out when I'm not?"

"I don't know," said Owen truthfully. Master Ransome hadn't mentioned Ari in their discussions back at the Retreat. Even the cautionary note Owen had sent to the Medical Station had been his own idea. He and Ari had never been close—quite the opposite, in fact—but there was always the chance his brother might spot him by accident in the Namport crowd. "The orders probably have something to do with Space Force policy, whatever that is."

"That's what I mean," she said. "The last time I got any orders, Master Ransome pulled strings or pushed buttons or did whatever it is he does. Next thing I knew, instead of going to Galcen South Polar and treating recruits for snow blindness, I was wading through the water-grain paddies on Nammerin with your brother. This time, though, nobody did any such thing—and I want to know how I'm supposed to be protecting Ari if he's off on a ship somewhere and I'm stuck down here on the mud flats until further notice."

"It could be that Master Ransome has assigned someone else to look after my brother. Or he may not need looking after any more. Who knows?"

"I think you do. Are you here to guard him?"

Owen hesitated. The question was coming too close to matters that shouldn't be spoken of aloud—not to someone who carried a Magelord's staff on a planet where a Mage-Circle still worked as Circles had in the old days.

"I think you ought to go now," he said.

He saw her drawing herself together, as if gathering her resolve. Then she spoke, quietly and with a touch of reluctance. "I don't want to do it like this," she said. "But it's Ari's life we're talking about. I'm an Adept, Owen Rosselin-Metadi, and you're still an apprentice in the Guild. You owe me an answer. I'm waiting."

"As you will, Mistress," he said formally. *She really has changed. The Llannat Hyfid who left the Retreat for Nammerin would never have had the nerve to ask me like that.* "No, I didn't come here to guard my brother."

"Then why are you here?"

"I'm here because I was sent here, like you. But unless Master Ransome told you to make contact with me, please leave. You're putting us both in danger as long as you stay."

He didn't wait for her reaction this time, but closed his eyes and let himself sink back into deep meditation. It was flight, pure and simple: questions he didn't hear, nothing would oblige him to answer. Eventually, she would grow tired of waiting and go away.

When he opened his eyes again, the apartment was dim and empty, and the door was closed.

Owen unfolded himself from his sitting position. The rush of blood to the limbs made him sway. He had been far under this time, farther than he'd expected when making his escape from Llannat's questions. He shouldn't have brought anything with him out of a trance that deep except a renewed sense of calm, but this time a faint disquiet still remained: perhaps an echo of Llannat's worries, but more likely an echo of his own—for he knew, with a conviction beyond knowing, that his older brother Ari still needed an Adept to look out for him.

# IV. Raamet: Gefalon
## Nammerin: Namport

EVEN IN the Mageworlds, Jessan reflected, a spaceport remained a spaceport. There was something about building a city on the widest, flattest piece of ground available that made places as different as Embrig and Namport unmistakably members of the same family. Galcen Prime was different, of course—Galcen Prime was always different—but Prime had ruled a world long before it went on to rule most of the civilized galaxy, and in any case Galcen South Polar had more than enough wideness and flatness to make up for the lack.

Gefalon on Raamet was another example of the breed. The sun beat down on a city built out of rock, in the same bleached-out brown color as the arid landscape. A range of blue-green mountains in the far distance, with clouds wreathing their snowcapped peaks, suggested that Raamet might elsewhere have better, and cooler, scenery to offer, but no starpilot would risk traveling away from the port to find out. Not on this side of the Net, anyway.

The spaceport itself was mostly landing field, with none of the Republic's high-tech docking facilities. Ships here didn't even set down on tarmac. The lines marking off the vast area into sections had been etched directly into the packed and hardened earth. Jessan wondered how often it rained in Gefalon, if it ever did—and how many Mageworlds warships over how many years of conflict it had taken to bake the desert ground into a surface as hard as rock.

Gefalon had been one of the Magelords' staging bases in the old days, and the landing field looked big enough to hold an entire fleet. Those days were gone, though; the Mageworlders had been stripped of their starflight capability at the end of the war. The few ships currently in port were all registered in the Republic, and had passed through the customs inspection at one Net Station or another.

Jessan and Beka—*No,* he reminded himself, *Doc and Tarnekep Portree*—sat at table in an open-air diner just outside the spaceport landing field. A roof of corrugated metal provided shade, and at the brick grill in the center of the diner a bored cook tended small bits of anonymous meat threaded onto sticks.

The local beer was unspeakable. But the local wine—or so the interpreter sharing Doc and Tarnekep's table had advised them—was even worse. As for the water, Jessan's medical training made him chary of drinking anything remotely resembling that liquid in an unfamiliar and primitive port.

*But we have to drink something in this climate,* he thought with resignation, *unless we want to add dehydration to the rest of our problems. So beer it is.*

Jessan refilled his glass from the pitcher in the center of the table. Tilting back his chair, he watched with half-closed eyes as Captain Portree negotiated for a cargo with a Raametan from somewhere on the other side of the mountains.

According to the interpreter, the small, dusty-looking man claimed to be Raamet's foremost dealer in medicinal herbs, barks, and minerals. His claim, Jessan reflected, might even be true. If so, the Mageworlds had come down a long way from the height of their power, when their medical and biochemical technology had been preeminent in the galaxy.

"Take it or leave it," Tarnekep was saying, while the interpreter murmured his running translation a sentence or so behind. "But I can't guarantee a delivery date for your material. The quantities you're talking about aren't enough to fill a quarter of my cargo space. I'm not going to go straight on to—what's its name?—straight on to Ninglin with most of the hold empty; I'm going to hit a couple of closer systems first. Anything that's perishable, if it's not too bulky, I've got stasis boxes for—or I can carry it frozen, which is a lot cheaper because it doesn't eat up power like the box does. You still interested?"

The herb merchant replied in a rapid patter of sentences that the interpreter relayed in accented Galcenian. "I am interested. But it is not me you will be collecting payment from. My associates on Ninglin may not wish to give you the full fee if shipment is delayed."

"What delay?" Tarnekep demanded. "You didn't have a carrier lined up before I got here. If I walk away, you may have to wait another month or so before you find another. I'll settle up with your buddies, don't worry. Is it a deal or not?"

The merchant shrugged and said something brief and final-sounding. "A deal," relayed the interpreter.

"Good," said Tarnekep, and held out his hand. "Done?"

The merchant met the captain's grip and uttered what might have been his only word of Galcenian. "Done."

Tarnekep nodded. "Have the stuff here before dark so

we can get it loaded," he said as he drew his hand away. "I'm lifting ship first thing in the morning."

After the Raametans had left, Tarnekep picked up his untouched glass of beer and drained it, grimacing a little at the taste. He set the glass down on the table and regarded the two empty chairs.

"I wonder," he said thoughtfully, "which one of our friends is the spy."

"You have a nasty suspicious mind, Tarnekep Portree," Jessan said. "Slandering a couple of honest businessmen like that. They're probably wondering the same thing about us." He took a sip of his beer and added, "My bet's on the interpreter."

"Too easy," said Portree. "I think the interpreter's just for show. That little worm of a dealer, now—he understands more Galcenian than he lets on."

"You could be right," Jessan said.

"I know I'm right," Portree told him. "Did you see his eyes? He was listening to me, not to the interpreter. But it doesn't matter—as long as he's got a legitimate cargo bound for Ninglin, I don't care who he tells about how much I charge to carry it. Think of it as free advertising."

"Out of what we're charging him for that run, we could put up a holosign over every bar in Gefalon."

Tarnekep shook his head. "You're too soft, Doc. I was earning my living at this job while you were still giving physical examinations to lonesome recruits. Traders like us are all the intersystem carriers the Mageworlds have these days."

"The only game in town." Jessan took another sip of beer, and his dubious expression was not entirely for the taste of the pale yellow liquid. "That's not going to make us particularly loved by any of our customers, mind you."

"I'm not asking them to love me," Tarnekep said. "Just to pay up when I hand them the bill."

Jessan considered the statement for a moment. "Prompt payment is usually a good idea," he conceded.

"Damned right it is." Tarnekep scowled at the pitcher of beer. "And it looks like our friend and his interpreter have gone off and left us with the tab for the bar."

"Oh, dear," Jessan said. "Do we have any local cash at all?"

"Zero point zip. We're going to have to turn one of our Ophelan bank drafts into something negotiable before we can settle up and get out."

Jessan finished his beer and stood up. "I can handle the money changing," he said. "You hold down the table so the manager won't think we're trying to skip town without paying."

"That's right," said Tarnekep. "Stick me with having to drink some more of this stuff."

Jessan nodded toward the grill. "Order some of the lizard-on-a-stick instead. It can't be any worse."

"You really think it's lizard?"

"Who knows? You can tell me when I get back."

"Hah." Tarnekep looked up at Jessan. As always, the red plastic eye patch made it hard to read the expression on the captain's face. "You take care, Doc, wandering around dirtside with all that money on you. I'd hate to lose a perfectly good copilot."

The sun was coming up over Namport, and Klea Santreny was tired. She picked her way along the dirty streets in her uncomfortable shoes—her working shoes, cheap and flimsy and overdecorated, with open toes and with heels too high and narrow for the sticky black Namport mud. Even though she stayed on the duckboards as much as possible, she would have to clean the shoes when she got home, no matter how tired she felt.

*One more chore to do before I can sleep,* she thought wearily. *If I can get to sleep at all.*

She hadn't slept much yesterday or the day before: the nightmares were back again. She'd had bad dreams for as long as she could remember, dark and confusing stories with no beginning and no end, but never as often or as dark as lately.

*I don't even remember what I dreamed yesterday. But it was bad, I know that much.*

Tonight, though, had been even worse. Sometime around the third trick of the evening, she'd starting seeing things again. The pictures weren't real—she'd figured out that much by now, but the knowledge didn't help. The pictures were thoughts, other people's thoughts, come loose somehow and crawling into her head: images of faces that weren't in front of her, drifting patches of color, a stab of pain in someone else's leg, the occasional word. . . . *Bitch. Slut. Whore.*

Klea hadn't thought anything could be worse than the pictures. She'd actually begun getting used to those, or at least she'd started learning how to sort them out from her own thoughts. But the images kept getting sharper, and the words kept getting louder, and now the feelings weren't just the ones on the surface anymore. She'd wondered sometimes what the customers at Freling's Bar really wanted when they bought themselves a few minutes' use of her body in one of the rooms upstairs; lately she was finding out. A stiff drink—a real drink, not one of the fakes she had while she was working—helped blur the thoughts a little, but not enough.

*If it's like this again tomorrow night I don't know how I'm going to stand it.*

She laughed unsteadily. "If today's as bad as yesterday, kid," she said aloud, "you may not *last* until tomorrow night."

One of the neighborhood's early risers was passing by in the other direction, on his way to whatever crack-of-dawn job forced him awake and out onto the streets. He caught what she was saying—she hadn't made any effort to lower her voice—and increased his pace.

Emotions touched her as he went past: a suffocating wave of disapproval . . . electric blue tickles of fear . . . a dark image of the warehouses by the spaceport.

"No," she muttered—under her breath, this time. "No, damn you. I'm not coming from the port. And I'm not going there either."

She'd worked in Namport for five years now, long enough to know that for a hooker, the bars and the narrow streets around the edges of the spaceport were the last stop. She shivered.

*If I don't quit acting crazy I will be working there. Freling isn't going to want a crazy woman hanging around his bar, and if he knows I'm cracking up he's going to spread the word.*

*I've got to get some sleep.*

She was approaching the street of old, close-packed houses where she had her apartment. On the corner of the block, a bit closer to her, was one of the few places open at this hour: the little hole-in-the-wall grocery where she did most of her shopping. She quickened her stride, stumbling a little as the high heels of her shoes slid in a patch of mud that some earlier pedestrian had left on the sidewalk.

Outside the shop, she paused for a second on the woven grain-straw mat, steadying herself with a hand on the doorframe as she wiped the clots of mud off her shoes. She caught a brief glimpse of herself in the shopwindow as she did so: hollow cheeks, shadowed eyes, and a bright red dress that only made it all worse.

*I look like a hag.*

She ran her fingers through her brown hair in a futile attempt to improve the sweaty, tangled curls. The colored lights in the shopwindow bounced off the mass of bangle bracelets on her arm. The sudden painful glare made her head spin; she clutched the doorframe even tighter until the dizziness faded and her head came back to something like normal. Still shaking, she pushed the door open and went in.

At this hour, the shop was empty except for the owner at his usual place behind the front counter and a tawny-haired young man in a worn beige coverall. The young man was one she'd seen a few times around the neighborhood, usually in the late evening or the very early morning; he was looking at the shelves in back, and she supposed he must be another person who worked nights and slept—or tried to—during the day.

The shopkeeper smiled and nodded at her as she entered. But the gesture was an empty one: just beneath the surface of his mind the small ugly thoughts twisted and squirmed, while his pleasant expression never changed.

*Liar,* she thought, biting her tongue to keep from saying the word aloud, and forced herself to nod back. Her money was as good as anyone's, no matter what she had to do to earn it, and Ulle would keep his opinions to himself as long as she had something to spend.

*Nobody's hurt by what he doesn't say,* she told herself. *Nobody except you, anyhow, and that doesn't count.*

She picked up a basket from the stack by the counter and began to fill it. A box of water-grain cereal for porridge—a bundle of fresh greens for stewing—a brick of frozen marsh-eels that probably wouldn't taste too bad when she added them to the greens—and then she was at the racks of bottles in the back of the store.

"Can't have marsh-eel soup without beer," she said. She was talking to herself out loud too much these days, she knew that; but it helped her keep track of which thoughts were hers. "Beer for the soup, and aqua vitae for the cook."

She put a couple of bottles of Tree Frog beer into the basket. The square purple bottles of aqua vitae were on the top shelf; she was going to have to stretch to get one. The thought of doing so made her aware that her legs weren't as steady as she had thought. Better not to try at all than to reach for a bottle and fall down while Ulle was watching.

She could feel the shopkeeper's gaze like hands on her back, following the movements of her hips under the tight red skirt. Vertigo struck again without warning; her head reeled, and the bottles of beer and instant-heat cha'a in front of her wavered and blurred, overlaid with a grotesque, distorted image of her own body seen from behind. Reality and hallucination ran together like water, and she watched the dress peel away from her flesh, showing Ulle her naked back and buttocks.

Klea's gorge rose. She gripped the edge of the shelf in front of her and swallowed hard. The image faded and the nausea went with it, leaving her soaked in cold sweat.

"Damn," she whispered hoarsely. "Damn, damn, damn . . . kid, you have *got* to get some sleep."

She drew a long, shaky breath and reached again for the aqua vitae. It was no good—her knees started to buckle under her and she knew she was going to fall.

A hand caught her under the elbow, supporting and steadying her. "Let me," said a strange voice—ordinary, except for a faint trace of some accent she didn't recognize. "No point in confirming Gentlesir Ulle's worst suspicions, is there?"

It was the man in the beige coverall. As soon as she was solidly on her feet again, his hand fell away from her arm and he reached up to take the bottle of aqua vitae.

"Here," he said, putting it into her shopping basket. "It's not going to help you any, though."

The comment washed away any impulse toward gratitude she might have had. "I don't need a sermon, thank you very much."

He smiled briefly, but his eyes—hazel under dark

lashes—remained serious. "Good. I'm not in the sermon business."

"You couldn't prove it by me."

"Look," he said. "Drinking purple rotgut until your skull pops isn't going to keep you from seeing things and hearing voices. I know."

*How does he know . . . ?* The shock of hearing her madness spoken out loud by a stranger made her sway and grab the shelf again. "Who the hell are you, anyway?"

"A neighbor of yours," he said. "And somebody who can show you how to take care of your problem."

She laughed roughly. "Right," she said. "Tell me another one. That line's so old it has moss on it."

She turned her back on him and strode to the front counter, angry now at having the unexpected kindness spoiled by one more ploy like the ones she heard every night at Freling's Bar. The anger buoyed her up, pushing her out of reach of Ulle's nasty little thoughts and keeping her going all the way down the street and up the stairs to her third floor walk-up apartment.

Klea had already locked and bolted the apartment door behind her before she realized the most truly odd thing about the stranger: for the first time in days she'd gotten no assault of unwanted feelings and images, in spite of the fact that he'd stood closer to her than anybody ever got who hadn't paid in advance for the privilege.

*But he could hear* my *thoughts, oh yes he could, even when I wasn't talking to myself like a crazy lady. Maybe he wasn't just trying to get a freebie from the local hooker . . . maybe he does know how to stop what's going on with my head . . . maybe . . . maybe . . . damn.*

"Kid," she said, "I think you've screwed it up again. One more for the list."

There wasn't anything she could do about it now. Moving slowly and carefully, she put the water-grain on the shelf by the stove, the bundle of greens in the cool-box, the marsh-eels in the freezer, and the bottle of aqua vitae on the table beside her bed. Then she stripped off her working clothes, stuffed them into the bag with the rest of her dirty laundry, and pulled on a plain white nightgown.

She took a clean glass out of the cabinet and carried it over to her bed, where she filled it as full of purple liquor as her unsteady hands would allow.

"And here's to *you*, Klea Santreny ... if the first one doesn't do it, we'll keep on trying until we get it right."

In spite of Tarnekep's worries, Jessan was able to convert the bank draft into Raametan cash without any trouble. A sign at the gate of the landing field advertised a nearby establishment specializing in currency exchange; the street directions, in ungrammatical Galcenian plus three alphabets Jessan didn't recognize, suggested that it handled a wide range of customers.

The establishment itself, when Jessan located it, turned out to be a kiosk on a street corner. The shabby, wrinkled man on the other side of the counter appeared to be running the operation without the aid of any comps or comm links. The only specialized equipment that Jessan could see was a metal cash box. Without much optimism, the Khesatan unfolded his bank draft and spread it out for the money changer to look at.

"Can you change this?"

The shabby man squinted at the seal on the bank draft, then held it up to the sunlight to check the watermark. "Ophelan," he said. He spoke Galcenian with an accent even worse than the interpreter's. "Is real thing."

"I know it's real. Can you change it?"

The man nodded. "Cost you twenty percent."

"That's ridiculous."

"Is best rate in town. No find better."

"I've got half a mind to try," said Jessan. "But I haven't got the time. Twenty percent it is."

The shabby man opened the cash box and tucked the bank draft under a clip with a sheaf of similar papers. He peeled off several dozen greyish blue chits marked on both sides with what Jessan supposed were Raametan characters and slipped them into an envelope.

"Here," he said, holding out the envelope to Jessan. "Don't spend all in same place."

"I'll try my best to spread the money around properly," Jessan assured him. Tucking the envelope of Raametan money inside his shirt, he made his way back to the open-air diner.

Tarnekep was still there, an untouched glass of beer at his right hand and an empty skewer on a plate in front of him.

"It's not lizard," he said as Jessan sat down. "Lizard tastes better. Have you got the cash?"

"Right here with me," Jessan said. "Now, if we can just figure out which are the large bills and which are the small ones ..."

"Most of the worlds this close to the Net use Ninglin notation," Tarnekep said. "The Prof had a bunch of comp files on the Mageworlds back at the base, and I transferred them to ship's memory before we started this run. I haven't had time to look at any of the language stuff, but I think I can count from one to twelve well enough to handle the local money."

"Fine," said Jessan. He took out the envelope and gave it to Tarnekep. "You figure out the bill."

"No problem," Tarnekep said. He riffled through the contents of the envelope and pulled out a chit, and then two more chits with a different set of symbols on them. He kept on talking as he did so. "This should do it ... by the way, we've got a passenger for the first leg of the run to Ninglin. Fellow wants to ride along and get off at Cracanth."

"Is that legal?"

Tarnekep raised an eyebrow. "Do we care?"

"I don't want to give our conscientious friends back at the Net an excuse to lock us up and forget the code."

"Don't worry. What our friends don't know won't hurt them—and besides, nobody cares if we haul passengers between planets, just as long as we don't try to sneak them back across the Net. It's part of the local trade, and the pay is good."

"I'm sure it is," Jessan said. "But is it safe?"

"Maybe." Tarnekep smiled. Jessan recognized the sharp, challenging expression that meant the captain had already weighed the risks and decided to ignore them. "And maybe not. But I didn't come here because I wanted to play things safe."

# V. *Warhammer*: Hyperspace Transit
   to Cracanth
   Nammerin: Namport

T HE PASSENGER showed up at first light the next
morning. He was tall for a Raametan, and
neatly dressed in clothes no more than three or four years
out of fashion on the other side of the Net. He'd brought
along a leather carrybag and a battered metal footlocker,
but no other luggage.

Jessan met him at the foot of *Warhammer*'s ramp. "I take
it you're the gentlesir who's riding with us to Cracanth?"

"That's right," the man said. "Vorgent Elimax. Who're
you?"

The passenger's Galcenian wasn't up to educated
standards—far less the equal of the captain's elegant
native-born speech—but Jessan felt certain Elimax had
learned it somewhere within the boundaries of the Republic. The thought did not rouse in him any disposition to be
trusting.

"People call me Doc," he said. "Come along and I'll
show you to your cabin."

Jessan waited until Elimax had picked up the carrybag and the footlocker, then turned and started up the ramp without waiting to see if the man followed. He led the way to the 'Hammer's passenger quarters—actually one of the unused compartments in crew berthing—and opened the door with a touch on the lockplate.

"Here you are," he said. "The bunk doubles as an acceleration couch. Stow your gear in the compartment over there, then strap yourself in and stay strapped until we make the jump to hyperspace. After that you can unstrap and make yourself at home."

Elimax looked at the bare grey walls of the compartment. "How long will it take to get the Cracanth?"

"Long enough for you to get tired of the trip," Jessan told him. "You have a taper in the bulkhead over there, and a holoset with a bunch of canned entertainment vids. The head's behind that door. Don't use it unless the gravity's on."

"What about meals?"

"I'll bring you a tray from the galley when it's time."

Elimax frowned. "Don't I get to look around the ship?"

"No," Jessan said. "This is a working freighter, and we're not set up to carry passengers. If we let you run around loose, you might do something stupid like falling into the hyperspace engines by mistake. Then you'd be dead, and the captain would be angry because he'd have to suit up and scrub out the mess."

Klea woke, sweating, in a lightless room.

*This is all wrong. It shouldn't be so dark.*

She sat up in bed. The aqua vitae weighed her down, swaddling her like a heavy blanket. She still couldn't see anything.

*My eyes are open. I think.*

She brought a hand up to her face, moving slowly under the pull of the aqua vitae, and touched her eyelids.

*Open. I'm blind.*

A kind of sluggish panic rose up in her at the thought. She reached out for the aqua vitae on her bedside table.

The bottle wasn't there. Neither was the table, nor—her groping fingers told her—the bed itself. She didn't know what she was sitting on, except that it was hard and level; or where she was, except that it was dark.

*Maybe I've already gone crazy. Maybe this is what crazy looks like once you get there.*

Off in the distance, or at least in what felt like the distance, a light flicked on and began to burn with a steady glow. Relief flooded through her, and she sat for a while just watching. Gradually she became aware of sound in the darkness, a murmur of voices somewhere out there with the light.

She stood up and walked toward the sound. The light grew closer and became a cool whiteness, suffusing an area where dark, hooded figures gathered in a circle. The voices came from them, hushed words passing back and forth in a language she didn't understand.

At first she thought that the dark ones had no features— only a black opening under their hoods. Then she saw that what she had believed empty was in fact a mask, a featureless visage molded from hard black plastic. In the circle of watchers, no one would ever need to recognize a neighbor's face.

*Watchers . . . why do I think they're watching something when they can't even see me?*

As if in response to her thought, the black-robed circle seemed to expand and take her in so that she stood with them, seeing what they saw themselves: in the open space at the center of the circle two of the masked ones fought one another, gripping short black staves in their gloved hands. The air shone around them like an aurora, in flares and surges of many-colored light that somehow combined to make the clear white glow she had seen from far away.

Klea knew, somehow, that the two who fought had been doing so for a long time. No anger came from them, only mingled feelings of exhaustion and pain. Yet she knew that this fight would continue until one of them was dead.

*Where* am *I?* she thought. *What* is *this?*

As soon as her mind framed the words, she realized that the question was a mistake. The ones in the circle hadn't noticed her before; all their attention had been given to the two who struggled so wearily. But they had marked her now; the low murmur of voices rose to a strident, angry babble, and the masked and hooded figures began closing in around her.

"No!" she cried out in the darkness. "No—stop! I have to get out!"

The hooded figures pressed closer. Then, abruptly, they were gone, all but one who stood with her in silence, washed by a lingering pale remnant of the circle of light.

She knew him, she *knew* she knew him. She reached out a hand and pulled the mask from his face.

Hazel eyes looked back at her. It was the young man from the grocery store on the corner. Her fingers loosened on the mask, and it fell from her hand without a sound.

She wet her lips. "Where are you . . . ?"

He shook his head violently. "There's no time. Run. Save yourself. I'll try to keep them from getting you."

WIthout warning the colored lights were back again, and the man from the grocery was gone. Only the faceless ones remained, watching her from eyes hidden beneath dark masks. In silence they moved closer, tightening the circle around her.

*I told you once already: go!*

The voiceless shout came out of nowhere, but it had the snap of command to it. She turned and ran.

The masked ones followed. She lengthened her stride,

but it was like running in a nightmare—she couldn't get away, and the blackrobes were gaining on her.

The nearest one grabbed her arm, and she awoke.

In the dark interior of the captain's cabin Beka lay half-asleep, listening to the ship around her. *Warhammer* had jumped into hyper shortly after leaving Gefalon Spaceport at local dawn, and the deep roaring of the realspace engines had been replaced by the steady, almost-inaudible hum of the hyperdrive. The ventilation system sighed gently, and the myriad electronic devices that kept the *'Hammer* functioning underlaid everything with their own subliminal background music.

Even more than the soft, regular breathing of Nyls Jessan, lying deep asleep beside her, the sound of *Warhammer* in undisturbed hyperspace transit gave Beka a feeling of security. Dirtside troubles couldn't touch you in hyperspace; even other starships had to catch you before you jumped or wait until you came out again. *"In hyper, the only problems you've got are the ones you bring along with you"*—her father had told her that years ago, when she was still a gawky adolescent barely big enough to reach all the controls on the *'Hammer*'s main panel.

*I didn't know what he meant back then. But I do now.*

It was one of those problems that kept her from relaxing completely, even in sleep. The passenger from Raamet had looked like a good deal when he showed up in the off-port diner: a lot less mass than a regular cargo, in return for a lot more cash. He probably was a good deal, too. Even Mageworlders—if Elimax really was a Mageworlder, which Jessan claimed to doubt—could have legitimate reasons for traveling between planets.

*Just the same,* she thought as she drifted off, *there's a stranger on my ship. And this isn't the time to be careless.*

The beeping of an alarm brought her back awake in an

instant. She sat up and saw a telltale flashing orange on the far bulkhead.

"Damn," she muttered. She flung the sheet aside and strode across the cabin to press the security plate next to the telltale. A section of the bulkhead slid aside to reveal an array of monitor readouts, a duplicate of the "ship's status" display in the 'Hammer's cockpit.

Most of the readouts showed a steady, normal green. One section, however, was bright orange— "Damn," she said again.

"What's up?" said Jessan from the bunk behind her.

"Better get dressed," she told him. "There's non-atmospheric gas in the air over in crew berthing. And somebody down there is fiddling with the lock on the door."

"The passenger," Jessan said. "Shall we go tell him this isn't going to work?"

"Why disillusion him? Did you bring the Prof's pocket holoprojector along on this trip?"

"It's right here in the toys-and-entertainment drawer."

"Get it out. When our passenger shows up, we'll be ready."

Klea lay shaking in bed for a moment, amid a tangle of sweaty sheets. Her left arm was twisted and caught in a fold of the cloth. Outside the window of her apartment, the late-afternoon sky was darkening on toward night. Soon it would be time for her to go to work.

The man in the store had been right, she concluded wearily. The aqua vitae hadn't helped, and she might as well not have slept at all. She got up, turned on the heat under a saucepan of water on the stove, and went to take her shower.

In the tiny bath cubicle, she soaped and lathered herself well, making her body clean before the evening's work. The hot water washed the dried sweat of her nightmare away along with the soapsuds. When she was done, she turned off the water and stretched out an arm for her towel.

The movement brought a twinge of pain; her left arm was sore where she'd dreamed that one of the black-robes had grabbed her. *I must have twisted it in the sheet,* she thought.

She looked at her forearm, small-boned and narrow-wristed, with the pale scars of long-ago cuts across the flesh where the bangle bracelets usually lay. Yes, she had a bruise coming, all right. The purple blotches were already showing up on her skin like so many fingerprints, and she was going to have to wear a long-sleeved blouse tonight. No sense in giving Freling's customers the idea she liked getting beaten up—enough of them thought of that all on their own.

When she came out of the shower, the water in the saucepan was hot. She made a cup of *ghil*, then dumped a handful of water-grain into the steaming cup to soak while she finished dressing. *Ghil*-and-porridge was farmer food, but it was nourishing and cheap, and she'd grown up on it.

After she was dressed, she ate breakfast, then washed out the cup and saucepan in the sink. She was putting the dishes in the rack to drain when she staggered suddenly under the weight of a dreadful apprehension—a formless, heavy darkness that came pouring down on her like water out of a bucket.

*. . . help . . . lost . . . pain . . .*

She gripped the edge of the sink and willed the alien feelings to go away. She didn't know who she was eavesdropping on—in this part of Namport, almost anybody could be that miserable without even trying—but the voices and feelings were starting earlier than usual. That meant tonight was going to get bad.

*Damn,* she thought. *I don't know how much longer I can stand it.*

She looked back at her bedside table. There was still some aqua vitae left in the bottle.

*I've never had a drink before going to work before.*

She laughed under her breath, a harsh sound without humor. *You've never gone crazy before, either. Do you feel like trying?*

"Not tonight," she muttered. She pulled out the stopper and put the bottle to her mouth, taking a long swallow, and then another. "Not if I can help it."

By the time the aqua vitae was gone, the darkness had subsided. She put aside the empty bottle and walked out of the apartment, heading down the stairs and off toward Freling's Bar. The last rays of sunlight were shining outside, and high above Namport the bright star of a ship in low orbit glittered. A ship in orbit meant that portside would be jumping.

The road to the spaceport lay just ahead. *Fast money,* Klea thought wistfully. *Easy. Nobody just off a ship is going to care whether you're seeing things or not.*

"No."

She turned her back on the port and walked as fast as she could in the other direction, without caring where her footsteps took her. She knew the route to Freling's Bar so well by now that she could walk it in her sleep, anyway—she almost had, more than once.

This time, in her haste to leave the port district behind her, she must have taken a wrong turning. By the time she noticed her surroundings again, she had come to a part of town that she didn't recognize. The streets here were narrow and shadowy, mere alleyways crowded between tall buildings that could have been warehouses or manufactories or even offices for all Klea could tell; the grime-smeared names and logos painted on their looming walls gave her no clue. All of them were dark-windowed and deserted.

Klea begun to feel afraid, and this time she was sure it

was her own emotion, not someone else's. She could get her throat cut in one of these alleys, and nobody would know until tomorrow morning when people started showing up for work. She cast a nervous glance down the nearest side street, half-expecting to see the smiler with the knife already waiting.

Instead, and worse, she saw the body of a man, lying on his back in the mud.

*Let him lie there,* she told herself. *He's probably just another drunk.*

But she hadn't seen any bars in this district, or even a store where a down-and-outer might get enough cheap booze to put himself out for the night. She turned and headed down the alley toward where the man was lying.

When she reached him, a tremor of shock ran through her. This was no derelict, or even an unknown victim of the violence she had feared for herself. It was the young man who had spoken to her in the corner grocery—and once again in the midst of her nightmare—now sprawled unmoving at her feet, his tawny hair matted and slick with blood.

Klea squatted beside him, balancing awkwardly on the spindly heels of her working shoes to keep the mud from soaking the hem of her dress. From this close up, she could see his chest rising and falling under the beige coverall. He was still alive, but he looked like he needed serious help.

She glanced over her shoulder and frowned. She couldn't even see the mouth of the alley. *Wait a minute . . . how did I spot him from where I was standing? That big garbage bin is in the way.*

*You're seeing things these days, remember? So this time you saw something that turned out to be real.*

"Hang on," she whispered. "Just hang on. I'll call Security and they'll take care of you."

The man's eyes snapped open. Fever-bright, they glittered in the reflected light from the city around them and the last rays of sunlight before full dark. "No! No Security."

He'd raised his head a bit in his agitation; now he let it fall back and closed his eyes. "No Security," he said again, his voice barely audible. "Just take me home and I'll be all right. Please."

"If you say so. Where exactly do you live?"

There was no answer.

*Damn,* thought Klea. *Now what do I do?*

It wasn't any of her business. She should just call Security and walk on.

*But he was in my nightmare, trying to help me. . . . He said in the store that he could help me. . . .*

It was too confusing. The aqua vitae she'd drunk earlier was fuzzing up her brain, making it hard to decide things. And Freling would be wondering where she was by now.

"Hell with Freling," she muttered, put an arm under the man's shoulders, and hauled him to his feet.

He was light, and the years on the farm had left her stronger than she looked. Bracing him on her shoulder and hip, she guided him to the street, then started walking him back to her apartment. She didn't need to work tonight. The rent was paid to the end of the week.

In the captain's cabin aboard *Warhammer,* everything was quiet. A metallic clink came from outside the vacuum-tight door. The "sealed" light above the lintel cycled from red to green, and the door slid open.

Another moment, and Vorgent Elimax slipped through the open door in a quick sidestep. The low lights of the chronometers and readouts reflected from the respirator he wore over his nose and mouth. Elimax looked for a moment at the two people asleep on the bed: Doc on his back, breathing softly, and Tarnekep Portree lying stretched out beside him, the left side of the captain's face resting on the tall Khesatan's shoulder, and one arm flung across his copilot's chest.

Elimax raised his blaster. The ugly snarl of the weapon filled the cramped space as he sent two high-power beams on tight focus into the heads of the sleepers.

In the silence that followed, another sound erupted—the buzz of a single-shot needler, fired at close range. Elimax crumpled forward; his blaster fell to the deck.

Beka stepped out of the shadowed corner where she'd stood watching, and switched off the miniature holoprojector clipped to the bulkhead. The sleeping images on the bunk—unchanged in spite of the blaster bolts that had charred the pillows beneath them—winked out and left only rumpled sheets behind. She slipped the holoprojector back into the cabin's tiny entertainment locker, and brought the lights up to full.

"A useful device, that projector," commented Jessan from the other side of the cabin. As he spoke, he pocketed the single-shot needler that had brought down Vorgent Elimax. "And better than anything I've seen on the regular market. I'm surprised the Professor never tried to sell it anywhere."

"He didn't need the money," said Beka. She bent over Elimax's body, checking the unconscious passenger for concealed weapons and stripping off his respirator. "He put together that sort of thing just for fun. Elimax, on the other hand—I wonder what he was after. Was he an independent piece of lowlife trying to get a ship of his own any way that he could, or was he working for someone else?"

"We could always ask him when he wakes up."

"I like that idea," Beka said. She started to smile. "I like that idea a *lot*."

Jessan looked down at Elimax and his mouth tightened. "Better move him out of the cabin, then. Things could get messy before we're done."

By the time they had the passenger bound hand and foot to a chair in the *'Hammer*'s common room, he was already starting to twitch. Jessan pulled the last strap tight and stepped back.

"You keep an eye on him," he said. "I'll go get the Professor's question-and-answer kit."

"Nyls—wait." She caught him by the wrist as he turned to go. "If you don't want to do it, I can always ask the questions myself."

"The old-fashioned way?" Jessan shook his head. "That's no good. We need answers we can trust."

"If you're certain."

"It's your brother Ari who doesn't like using chemicals," Jessan said. "Not me."

"Good." She let her hand fall back to her side. "Go get whatever you need."

Jessan left. Beka watched Elimax mumbling and jerking against the restraints as he came up through the final stages of the needler's effect. By the time his eyes were open and fully aware, she had drawn the double-edged dagger from its sheath up her sleeve and was testing its point against the pad of her index finger. A slight tilt of her wrist, and the light from the overhead glow-panel glanced off the blade directly into Elimax's face.

He flinched. Beka smiled down at him.

"Hello, Elimax," she said. "Somebody should have told you that the ventilation systems on this ship aren't cross-connected any more."

"But you're dead—I *saw*—"

"Don't believe everything you see," Jessan said as he came back into the common room. He carried a black metal case in one hand. "An important lesson, but one I fear you're learning a little bit too late."

He took a position at the common-room table just out of Elimax's field of view, and set the case down within easy reach. "Are you ready, Captain?"

"Absolutely," Beka said.

She set the point of her knife under Elimax's chin and put enough pressure behind it to dimple the skin and force his head up against the back of the chair.

"My friend," she said, "it's like this. You tried to kill me, and I intend to find out why."

Elimax attempted to shake his head, and stopped the movement when she pressed in harder with the tip of the knife. "I have no idea what you're talking about."

"I don't believe you," Beka told him. "I believe my monitoring systems, and they tell me it was Sonoxate gas you released into the ventilation system. Sonoxate's a proprietary brand—Nine Worlds Chemical makes it for dirtside Security forces—and not only is it expensive, it's sold exclusively on the Republic side of the Net."

She pulled the knife away and pointed at Elimax with it, moving the blade gently back and forth at the eye level of the bound man.

"And then there's your lockpick," she went on. "Already set up to work with the standard cipher keys for a *Libra*-class freighter. It was your good luck that the door mechanisms are about the only things on this ship I haven't modified. But I'm afraid your luck wasn't quite good enough, because that lockpick tells me you weren't waiting for just any ship to turn up in Gefalon Spaceport. You were waiting for mine."

Free of the knife's pressure, Elimax shook his head violently. His voice was a hoarse croak. "No!"

"Yes," said Beka. "Somebody hired you, and I intend to find out who. Now, I'd be perfectly happy to work on you myself until you're ready to tell me things—but Doc, here, doesn't care for that idea. He says he's got some chemicals that'll do the same thing, only faster and with less blood to clean up afterward. I want to see if he's right."

She looked over at Jessan. "Okay, Doc. He's all yours."

Jessan opened the black box. The click of the latch was

sharp and distinct in the silence. Elimax strained his head sideways, trying in vain to see what Jessan was doing. His eyes were wide and dark with panic, and his breath came in ragged, choking gasps.

Then Elimax screamed. The scream ended in an ugly ripping noise like nothing Beka had ever heard before, and a fountain of red burst out through the front of his chest, soaking his shirt and running down into a puddle at his feet.

Beka swallowed hard. "What the hell did he *do*?" she demanded hoarsely.

"Blew his own heart out," said Jessan. "And no, I don't know how he did it."

"Damn. I wanted him alive."

"We've still got six minutes of brain function left," Jessan told her. His hands were already moving as he spoke, pulling more items out of the black box—items she didn't recognize but didn't like the look of at all—and fastening them to the dead man's head and throat. "Whatever questions you have, start asking them now. You won't have a second chance."

# VI. Nammerin: Downtown Namport; Space Force Medical Station

THIRTY-SEVEN HOURS before he left Nammerin for good, Ari Rosselin-Metadi took the regular Med Station bus into Namport. He got off at the next-to-last stop on the outbound run—an arcade of moderately expensive stores near the spaceport proper—and walked the rest of the way to his destination.

Strictly speaking, Namport's old quarter wasn't off-limits to Space Force personnel, but nobody in authority had ever seen any point in making it easy to get to, either. It was a district where old buildings crowded together along muddy streets, and worn canvas shop awnings cast blue-grey shadows over the wooden sidewalks; and the community's rougher elements found in it their natural home.

Nobody bothered Ari, however, and he found the place he was looking without much difficulty. A flatsign over the door, still relatively new, identified the establishment as FIVE POINTS IMPORTS in bright red letters picked out in gold paint. Munngralla, the big Selvaur who owned the shop, had lost no time in getting started again after the loss of his previous store in a fire; the odd bit of arson was just one of the hazards of doing business as the main on-planet operative for the Quincunx. This neighborhood was much the same as Munngralla's old one, or possibly a trifle more prosperous, and the contents of the new shop were almost identical with the old.

Ari pushed open the door and went in, threading his way between tall stacks of locally woven grain-straw hats and dangling strings of musical seashells from Ovredis. Munngralla himself was working at the rear counter, saving Ari the trouble of waking him up from a midday nap.

Waking up a Selvaur was not something to be undertaken lightly. Like all of his kind, Munngralla had a thick, scaly hide covering his massive body from head to foot. His front teeth were a carnivore's pointed fangs, and the pupils of his yellow eyes were vertical black slits. At almost seven feet tall, not counting the crest of emerald scales atop his rounded skull, the big saurian was one of the few people in Namport who could look Ari directly in the eye.

Nevertheless, even honorary membership in a gang of smugglers and black market traders carried with it certain social obligations, and Ari had been properly brought up. Neither his late mother, the Domina, nor his father, the General—and most especially not his Selvauran foster-father, Ferrdacorr son of Rrillikkik—would have allowed him to commit the social and business gaffe of leaving Nammerin without first paying a farewell visit to the local boss.

The Selvaur came out from behind the counter to envelop Ari in an embrace that might have crushed a smaller man.

*Welcome!* he growled, in the deep, rumbling tones of

Selvaur speech. *You could have come here in uniform,* he added. *Everything you see out here is legal.*

Ari forced his own voice down into the bottom reaches of its range. Not many humans could manage the hoots and rumbles of the Forest Speech, but Ari had been blessed with both the voice and the ear—and he'd grown up on the Selvauran homeworld of Maraghai.

*It's safer for both of us if I show up in civvies,* he told Munngralla. *You don't need a rep for talking to the Space Force—and I don't need to give the service a rep for dealing with you.*

Munngralla chuckled, a low booming sound that caused some of the more fragile bits of bric-a-brac to rattle slightly on the shelves. *Neither of us needs trouble like that.*

He was telling the truth. Five Points Imports, regardless of how much legitimate business it did, was primarily a front. The Quincunx boasted that it could supply a customer with anything—from the merely hard-to-get, like tholovine, to the strictly illegal—as long as the customer was willing to meet their price.

*Come here to say good-bye, have you?* Munngralla continued before Ari could draw breath for his carefully thought-out speech of leavetaking.

"You're not supposed to know that!"

Munngralla snorted. *Don't make me laugh, thin-skin. We've got our sources.*

"Why am I not surprised?" Ari said. Then he dropped back into the Forest Speech. *And you know better than to call Ferrdacorr's fosterling a "thin-skin"—so don't go making *me* laugh, either.*

Unlike his membership in the Quincunx, Ari's clan status among the Selvaurs was anything but honorary. He'd spent more of his childhood and adolescence among the saurians than he had with his human family. And once Ferrda had realized just how big and strong Jos Metadi's firstborn son was going to grow, Ari had gotten the same education as any other youngling among the Forest Lords.

He'd earned his full adult status the traditional way—by stalking and killing barehanded a *sigrikka*, one of the great predators of Maraghai—and still carried the scars of that fight on his back and arms. As far as Selvauran law and custom were concerned, trifling details of species and skin thickness made no difference: Ari was a Forest Lord like any other. And he was not inclined to let pass without comment anything that might imply otherwise.

That, also, was good manners among the Forest Lords. Munngralla made the breathy *hoo-hoo* that served as both approval and wordless apology, then changed the subject. *Where are they sending you?*

"You mean you don't know that, too?" Ari sighed. "Never mind. I've got duty on RSF *Fezrisond*, off in the Infabede sector."

*Infabede. We have people there.*

"Not on shipboard, I hope." Ari held up a hand to stop Munngralla from replying. "Don't say anything. I mean it. I can stretch my oaths to the service and the Republic far enough to keep quiet about things that happen off-base and out-of-uniform. But if you've got stuff going on any closer to me than that, don't even think about telling me, because I'll have to turn you in."

*Don't try to teach an old wrinkle-skin his business, youngling,* said Munngralla. *You need the Brotherhood out there in Infabede, you'll have to make the contact yourself.*

"I don't expect to need anything."

*You did before,* Munngralla pointed out. *On Darvell.*

"Darvell was a fluke."

*Darvell was a mess,* corrected Munngralla. *Not your fault, though. We heard about how you took care of our problem there for us.*

"I'm surprised anybody in Darplex is talking," said Ari. He switched again to the Forest Speech—always better for talking about a good fight. *They got their noses pretty well bloodied that day, and I can't imagine them wanting to brag about it.*

*News gets around. And the word from higher up is that the Quincunx is grateful.*

"What was I supposed to do? Leave the bastard alive so he could keep on using the Brotherhood's name as bait for a Security trap?" Ari bared his teeth. *Come on—Ferrda taught me better than that.*

*Looks like he did,* said Munngralla. *And like I said, we're grateful. If you're ever in the sort of trouble that your buddies in uniform can't help with, come to us.*

"I'll keep you in mind," Ari said. "Meanwhile . . . this is my last day here, so I came by to let you know I'm gone."

Munngralla's crest flared briefly in surprise. His local contacts must not have mentioned that Ari would be leaving quite so soon. *Somebody's working fast,* he said. *The little Adept—is she going tomorrow, too?*

"No. She's staying here."

*Funny. I thought . . . never mind. You tell her, she isn't Quincunx, but she's not bad, for a thin-skin. She can call herself a friend of Munngralla's any time she wants.*

"Right," said Ari. "I'll pass the word along."

He stopped talking for a moment, to cover the sudden tightness in his throat. *I'm supposed to be glad I'm leaving,* he thought unhappily. *I ought to hate this place, after everything that happened while I was here.*

But his feelings had never answered to reason before, and they didn't answer now. He'd been stationed on Nammerin during some of the most desperately unhappy months of his life, a time when not even the chance to strike out against a deserving target had been able to lift the weight from his spirit for very long. Nevertheless, Ari discovered, he was going to miss Nammerin. He'd lost, and found, too much on this world ever to forget it.

*Good hunting,* he said to Munngralla finally, the formal leavetaking of one Forest Lord to another.

*Good hunting to you on the star-trails, brother,* Munngralla replied. *And remember what I told you about asking for help.*

Ari didn't see Llannat Hyfid until much later that evening. The Space Force contingent at the Medical Station had spent the earlier part of the day decorating the junior staff lounge with balloons and colored streamers. Now they had set up a rudimentary bar at a table in the rear, and were bidding a high-spirited farewell to Ari and the other departing officers. Tree Frog beer was very much in evidence as usual, in both the Export Dark and the Moonlight Pale varieties. Ari contented himself with a large tumbler of aqua vitae instead.

Drink in hand, he made his way through the crowd to the corner where the commanding officer of the Med Station was standing. The CO had brought along his pet sand snake to the party, wearing the creature in a series of loops around his shoulder like a bizarre piece of decorative braid. From time to time, the snake would dip its wedge-shaped head downward, put out a long, forked tongue to taste the CO's beer, and then curl up again.

The CO himself appeared pensive and faintly melancholy, but Ari felt no particular worry on that account—such a look was the station commander's usual expression. "Rosselin-Metadi," he said as Ari approached. "We'll miss you around here, you know."

"I'll miss working here," Ari said honestly. The sand snake flowed down the CO's arm, flicked its tongue lightly over the bright purple liquid in Ari's glass, and then withdrew. Ari chuckled and drained the glass. "Shipboard duty is going to take some getting used to after this."

"Shipboard duty is what the Space Force is all about," the CO said. "Everything else is just the fancy trimmings."

"That's what my father says."

"Trust him, Rosselin-Metadi. He's usually right."

"Yes, sir." Ari looked down into his tumbler. Only a faint sheen of lavender remained on the thick glass at the bottom. "At least I'll be able to put my blaster back into the arms locker where it belongs."

The CO shook his head. "I'm afraid not. The authorization and the orders are part of your permanent file."

"Damn," said Ari without thinking. He felt his face reddening slightly, but pushed on. "I'm sorry, sir . . . but I'm going to be heading up the medical department on RSF *Fezrisond*. How am I supposed to do that if I'm carrying a piece of hardware that makes me look like Black Brok, the Terror of the Spaceways?"

"Force of personality?" the CO suggested mildly. "You'll do fine, Rosselin-Metadi. I wouldn't worry."

Ari was silent for a moment, warmed by the unexpected compliment. He looked about the room and noticed that Llannat Hyfid had joined the party while he and the CO were talking. Tonight, for some reason, she'd chosen to wear the formal black tunic and trousers of a full Adept. The silver-and-ebony staff she'd carried away from Darvell shone with a soft luster against the dark cloth.

*She's never worn formal blacks around here before*, Ari thought, frowning. He wasn't certain what she'd meant to show by her choice of clothing, but he found it disquieting.

"Excuse me," he said to the CO. "I have to talk to Mistress Hyfid."

He made his way to the bar to fill his glass with more of the purple aqua vitae, then went over and joined Llannat.

"Thanks for coming," he said.

"Any excuse for a celebration," she said. "But good-bye parties aren't exactly my favorite."

"Mine either. At least this one looks like it's going to behave itself and not turn into a free-spacer's wake."

"Don't tempt fate by talking. The night is still young."

"I thought Adepts didn't believe in fate and luck and things like that."

"We don't. But the universe has patterns, and currents that flow through it ... and the farewell bash my shipmates gave me before I went off to the Retreat was a real classic."

"The weather got a trifle drunk out?"

"More than just a trifle. I still had a hangover when I got to Galcen."

"You?" Ari shook his head in disbelief. "I've never even seen you get a little bit looped."

"That was a long time ago," Llannat said. "It helped me turn off the voices I was hearing inside my skull. Not the safest way in the world to do it, but the best I could manage on my own."

She gave him a crooked smile. "Believe me, Ari, I needed to learn everything the Adepts could teach me."

*A good enough explanation of why the Guild has her loyalty now,* he thought. *Maybe that's why she wore her blacks tonight.*

He wrenched his mind back to the matter at hand. "I have to tell you something. But not in here. Too many people listening. Will you take a walk with me outside?"

Her face brightened—a change that always reminded him of sunlight breaking through clouds. "Of course."

Outside the converted storage dome that served as a staff lounge, the medical service compound was quiet and dark. A light mist was falling, making the protective force-dome glow a faint pink overhead. Ari walked along beside Llannat, enjoying for a little while the simple pleasure of her company. She had an interior calm that he had always envied; now, as often happened, it seemed to flow into him from her presence.

He sighed. "I'm going to miss all of this."

"Nammerin, you mean?"

*Not exactly,* he thought. *But* . . . "Yes."

"I—we'll miss you, too." She halted, and Ari perforce had to stop with her. "You said you had something to tell me."

"A message," he said. "From Munngralla."

"Munngralla." Her voice was expressionless; in the darkness he couldn't see her face. "What does he have to say?"

"That you're not Quincunx—"

She snorted. "Not much chance of that."

"—but you're not bad, for a thin-skin."

"Such flattery. I don't think I can stand it."

"He also says that you can call yourself a friend of Mungralla's any time you want."

"Now, that's more useful. Having someone like Munngralla owe you a favor is like having money in the bank." She paused again. "Is that all?"

"Most of it." He clenched his fists, grateful that the night hid his features as well as hers. "I'll miss you, too, Llannat. It's so easy to lose touch with people, in the service—everybody is always moving on. I don't want that to happen again this time."

"It will," she said. "It always does. The friends I had when I left for the Retreat stopped writing to me before the year was out."

"You aren't leaving me behind that easily, I'm afraid," he told her. "I'm not a very good letter writer, and I hate making voice-message chips. But I won't let that stop me."

"It's going to be harder than you think."

Something had changed in her voice, reminding him suddenly that Adepts didn't see the past and the future in the same way as ordinary people did, and the difference shook him.

"What do you mean?" he asked. "How is it going to be harder than I think?"

"I don't know," she said. "Sometimes I hear myself saying these things, and I haven't the faintest idea what I'm talking about. But there's trouble coming—we knew that a long time ago, back before we went to Darvell. And it's going to be bad."

She sounded frightened, which scared him. He'd seen Llannat Hyfid face down a Magelord without flinching, and leap over a wall into hostile territory without turning a hair. He didn't like to think about what she might find frightening.

"I thought that Darvell *was* the bad trouble that was coming," he said. "You mean there's more?"

"I think so."

"Don't worry," he told her—a futile exhortation, but still one he couldn't help making. "As long as I'm still alive, you'll hear from me. It may take a while sometimes, but don't give up."

"I won't," she said. "I promise."

She reached out and touched his chest lightly with the tips of her fingers. It was the faintest of contacts, and yet he seemed to feel it warming him all the way through the stiff cloth of his uniform tunic. He could hear her breathing, too, fast and slightly uneven.

"Ari—" she began.

Before she could finish, the door of the staff lounge opened and disgorged Bors Keotkyra. The junior officer lost no time in hurrying across the compound toward them.

"Hey, Ari! You've got to come back inside right now. They're about to start making the speeches, and you don't want to miss your engraved holocube with a picture of the main gate of the Medical Station in it."

Llannat's hand fell away, and Ari heard her sigh. "I suppose he doesn't," the Adept said. "Go on back in, Ari—I need to get to my room and grab some sleep before tomorrow morning anyhow."

Llannat Hyfid awoke early the next morning, well before breakfast. Ari would be leaving the Medical Station right about now, and she had duty starting in a little over three hours. She didn't have the time to say good-bye to Ari at the spaceport and then make her way back to base. But she had been charged by Master Ransome with watching over Ari Rosselin-Metadi as long as he was on Nammerin, and she would stay with him until the shuttle lifted for orbit.

She lay with her eyes closed, clearing the distracting thoughts from her mind. Going out of the body had its dangers, and back at the Retreat the students had always worked with a teacher or practiced in pairs—"one to walk and one to watch," as the saying went. But an Adept in the field might not have the luxury of a companion, so the apprentices had learned the basic techniques for working alone as well.

*"Find a safe place where you won't be disturbed."* She remembered the way Owen Rosselin-Metadi's voice had echoed slightly off the cool stone walls of the practice room. *"Lie down if you can—if you're able to get a mattress or a pallet under you, that's even better. Then, when you're ready, stand up and walk away from yourself."*

She'd had a difficult time of it at first. No matter how hard she tried, she and her body had remained obstinately and indissolubly one. Again, memory brought her the sound of Owen's voice, this time asking a question: *How long have you fought against doing this by accident?*

*"Years,"* she had said without thinking, and was surprised to realize that it was the truth. *"It was the first thing to start happening to me. I used to feel myself coming*

*apart like that, and it scared me out of my wits. What hap-
pens if I can't get back?"*

*"Don't worry about it,"* Owen had said. *"Breaking completely away from your body is harder to do than you
think. And while you're practicing, I'll be keeping watch
for you."*

Reassured as much by his presence as by his words,
Llannat had gradually learned how to do on purpose what
she had resisted for so long. Now, in her darkened room in
the BOQ, she let her corporeal and noncorporeal selves
drift apart. She looked down for a moment at the Llannat
who lay on the bunk as if sleeping, then passed out of the
room through the unopened door.

The Med Station bus was hovering on its nullgravs at
the main gate. Unseen and insubstantial, she entered the
vehicle. Ari was already there, sitting with his eyes shut in
a seat close to the rear window. Several more people from
the Med Station boarded the bus. A bell sounded, the door
slid shut, and the bus floated smoothly away from the
main gate.

Ari slept, or seemed to sleep, most of the way into
Namport, opening his eyes just as they passed through the
gates of the shuttle field. Still bodiless, Llannat followed
him from the bus to the main building. Inside the building,
flatscreens full of arrival and departure information covered most of the available wall space. Ari checked the display on one of them and nodded with satisfaction, then
found a chair and sat down.

Almost half an hour later, the speaker system crackled
and blared out, "Shuttle to RSF *Corisydron*, outward
bound from Nammerin to the Infabede sector, now boarding."

Ari stood, stretched, and walked out onto the shuttle
field. Llannat followed, seeing but unseen, all the way into
the shuttlecraft itself. Ari shoved his carrybag into a storage compartment and claimed a seat.

Llannat heard the premonitory rumble of the shuttle-craft's engines warming up and knew it was time for her to go. It wasn't a good idea to leave planetary orbit while walking out-of-body; only the most skilled of Adepts could work at that much distance from the physical self.

*"It's all metaphor,"* Owen had said. *"Once you're out of the body, place and time don't really exist. But the human mind can only take so much metaphor without breaking. So don't go off-planet, don't cut the cord that ties you to your body, and don't start wandering around in time. Those are all good ways to get lost and never come back."*

She gave an insubstantial sigh. Then, even though she knew Ari could not see or hear her, she put out a hand and touched him on the shoulder as he sat waiting for the lift-off.

"Take care of yourself, Ari, please," she said. "There's no one else who can do it anymore."

Klea Santreny looked down at the man asleep in her bed. She'd cleaned the blood and dirt off him and put bandages and sprain-tape on all his visible injuries, but she still wasn't sure that she'd done enough.

*It's been a night and a day,* she thought. *If he doesn't wake up by himself real soon, I'm going to have to do something drastic, like drop him out back by the garbage cans and then tip off Security that he's there. They'll take him to a medic as soon as they pick him up.*

Over in the kitchen nook, the oven beeped to remind her that the brick of marsh-eels had finished thawing. She left the bedside and retrieved the eels, now spread out on the plate like a tangled skein of thick knitting yarn. The greens were already stewing on the cooktop; she tilted the eels and their broth into the pot and gave the soup a stir. A cloud of steam billowed up from the bubbling liquid, filling her nose with the rich unfolding scents of warm greens and cooking eelflesh.

She'd always been a good cook—*a good cook and a hard worker,*" that's what her father had said the summer after her mother had died, and she'd seen all her brothers nodding agreement. That was when she knew she was never going to get away from the farm, not to go to upper school in Two Rivers like she and Mamma had planned, not even to marry into some other family. Dadda was stingy, too stingy to hire help when he had a daughter old enough to cook and mend and clean, and her brothers were just the same and more of them, so she'd looked down at her lap to hide her face and said, "Thank you, Dadda," and the next morning before light she'd hitched a ride with a water-grain hauler bound for Namport and never gone back.

*And this is where it ends up,* she thought. *Some choice. Wearing myself down bit by bit in a backwater farmhouse, or turning up dead some morning in a portside alley.*

"Don't blind yourself," said the stranger's voice from the bed across the room. "If you keep telling yourself that those are your only choices, then those are the only choices that you'll ever make."

By now she wasn't surprised to find that the young man could listen to her thoughts. Turning, she saw that he was sitting up in her bed, the sheets wrinkled around his hips. He was still pale, with dark smudges under his hazel eyes, but his expression was alert enough to make her uncomfortable.

"So you're awake," she said.

"It seems that I am." He glanced around the apartment. "At the risk of sounding like something out of a holovid script—where am I?"

"My place," she said. "I brought you here. You'd been beaten up or something, and you looked like you needed help."

"Thank you."

"Is that all you're going to say about it?" she asked. "What the hell happened to you, and why was I dreaming about you the night before? And who *are* you, anyway?"

He sighed. "My name's Owen, and I think I'm an upstairs neighbor of yours. You're dreaming about me for the same reason you're seeing things and hearing voices. You have a latent sensitivity to the currents and patterns of Power flowing through the universe—only your sensitivity doesn't want to be latent anymore."

" 'Currents and patterns'?" she said. "I heard an Adept talking that way on the holovid news one time, when I was a kid. Is that what you are?"

"A kid?" He actually smiled for a moment. "I've got an older brother who accuses me of permanent irresponsibility, if that counts."

"No," she said. "An Adept. You talk like one."

"Just an apprentice in the Guild, I'm afraid."

She wet her lips. "Did you—"

"See things and hear voices?" He shook his head. "No. Not like you're doing, anyway. I more or less grew up with it—the hard part was learning that most people couldn't see things the way I did. But I've met enough late-bloomers at the Retreat that I can recognize the symptoms."

"The Retreat?"

"The main home of the Adepts' Guild," he said. "On Galcen. Apprentices go there for training."

"Galcen's a long way from Nammerin," she said. "And starship tickets don't grow on trees. You're very kind, Gentlesir Owen, but somehow I don't think this training thing is going to help me very much."

"I'll figure out a way to wangle you a passage to Galcen," he told her. "It's only fair, since having me move in upstairs probably helped force your latent sensitivities to the surface. In the meantime, I'll teach you what I can—

enough to keep Ulle's nasty little fantasies from disturbing you while you're shopping, at least."

"You really can do that?"

He looked embarrassed at the gratitude in her voice. "It's not much," he said. "If you want proper training, it's barely the first step on a long road."

She didn't care. "But you can do it."

"Yes."

For the first time in months—for the first time, really, since the morning five years ago when she'd sliced her left arm open with one of the kitchen knives and then found out she didn't even have the guts to let herself die—Klea felt a stirring of hope. The new sensation went to her head like a shot of aqua vitae on an empty stomach; not until quite a while later did she realize that Owen had left unanswered the most important of her questions.

No matter who had left him for dead in the alley, and no matter why they had done so, her upstairs neighbor clearly had no intention of explaining any part of it.

# VII. GALCEN: PRIME BASE
   NINGLIN: RUISI PORT

GENERAL JOS Metadi looked at the miniature hand-blaster lying on his desk and frowned. At sixty-two percent, the blaster's energy level was lower than he usually liked. It wouldn't last through any sort of prolonged encounter with that kind of charge. Most people wouldn't have worried—nobody expected a holdout gun to take them through an extended firefight—but Metadi hadn't survived as much as he had by being careless.

He pressed a button on the desktop. Part of the smooth black surface slid aside. The little niche thus revealed held a half-dozen of the small square power packs the Space Force used in its ubiquitous clipboards and datapads. He took one out, then broke open the hand-blaster to remove the low-charge pack still inside. After switching in the fresh pack, he put the old one into the desktop to recharge and pushed the button again. The niche slid closed as Metadi tucked the miniature blaster back into its grav-clip up his sleeve.

That taken care of, he turned his attention to the stack of printout flimsies that had been waiting for his attention ever since he came into the office. His new aide, Commander Quetaya, had already sorted through the morning message traffic and weeded out all those items that could be handled effectively at some lower level. The messages that remained, Metadi knew from long experience, would concern problems so touchy, secret, or complex that they couldn't be solved, only worried about—and that, by somebody of the very highest rank.

*As if I didn't have enough to deal with already....*

Metadi let his gaze drift from the pile of flimsies to the holocube beside them. Three of the four side faces of the cube contained images of his children: Beka at her coming-of-age party; Ari in dress uniform; Owen in the plain garments of an apprentice Adept. The fourth side, and the one currently closest to the General, held the holographic likeness of a slender, fair-haired woman in Councilor's robes and a tiara of plain black metal.

*You drive a hard bargain, my lady. If I'd known thirty-odd years ago where your job was going to lead, I might not have had the nerve to take it.*

The Domina Perada Rosselin of Entibor looked back at him from the holocube and said nothing. More and more, these days, Metadi found himself conversing with his late wife as if she were still present. He supposed it meant he was growing old—or maybe he was just running short of people he could talk to.

*The family's all gone now,* he told the holopic, *and the house is so empty you wouldn't recognize it. Ari's off somewhere between Nammerin and Infabede, Beka's poking around on the far side of the Net—stirring up trouble, if I know the girl!—and Owen ... these days I never know where he is or what he's doing.*

Metadi shook his head. *Everything Owen finds out goes straight to the Guild anyway. If I want Errec to know something I'll tell him myself and get the story right the first time.*

He pushed back his chair and stood up. "The hell with it," he said aloud. "Metadi, what you have to do is get out of town for a while."

In the next room, the General's aide was hard at work dealing with yet another stack of message flimsies. Unlike Jervas Gil, who had been so ordinary in his appearance as to be effectively invisible most of the time, Rosel Quetaya was trim and strikingly good-looking, with ivory skin and glossy black curls. She looked up as the General strode into her office.

"Commander," Metadi said without preamble, "give me a list of sectors that could use a surprise inspection."

"Yes, sir." The commander set the messages aside and began keying search criteria into her desk comp. "We have an entire range of possibles," she told him after a few moments. "Do you want the units in question merely startled, somewhat astonished, or caught with their pants completely down?"

"I'm not interested in the small stuff," Metadi said. "But if there's anybody out there with serious bodies buried in their backyard, I want things dug up and straightened out while we still have a chance to do it."

"Right. We're talking wrath-of-the-gods time, then." She tapped a few more keys. The comp extruded a slip of flimsy, which she tore off and handed to the General. "This is the short list based on the extended criteria."

Metadi scanned the printout. "Hah. Here's something that could stand looking into. Infabede sector, Admiral Vallant commanding. It says here the last five lieutenants Space Force assigned to staff duty with Vallant all resigned their commissions before the end of their tours."

Quetaya nodded. "I asked for unusual turnover patterns when I did the search."

"Good thinking. It could just be that the food on Admiral Vallant's flagship is bad . . . but I don't think so." *And Ari's outbound from Nammerin for the* Fezzy, *which means if there's anything wrong on her he's going to walk straight into it. That boy draws trouble the way a tree draws lightning; I swear I should have let Ferrda keep him on Maraghai.* "Let's go to Infabede and find out."

"Yes, sir," Quetaya replied. "Will you want me to file the movement report?"

"And give everyone in the galaxy word on where I'm going? I don't think so."

Quetaya looked doubtful. "The regulations say—"

"I wrote those regs," Metadi told her. "The first draft, anyhow. Now get me a list of ships currently in close orbit or on the ground at Galcen Prime."

"Yes, sir," Quetaya said again. She turned back to the comp. A few keyclicks more, and a second slip of flimsy appeared. "Departure schedules for all available ships."

The General scanned the list. "There," he said, his finger stabbing toward a name. "RSF *Selsyn-bilai*. Stores ship outbound for Infabede with a fresh loadout of supplies. She'll do. Now get me a secure line to the base CO, so he won't have fits when I turn up missing." The General chuckled. "No sense slipping away undetected if we start a galaxy-wide manhunt in the process. That would ruin our incognito for sure."

Quetaya looked up from punching a routing code into the comm link. "Incognito?"

"That's right," Metadi said. "Visiting brass hats never hear about the down-and-dirty stuff, the sort of things that get handed over to junior officers and enlisted types and then forgotten about. I want to poke around in Vallant's territory for a few days before I officially turn up."

"Someone's bound to recognize you," Quetaya protested. "Your picture's all over the place."

"People don't see the face, they see the uniform. And if Warrant Officer Bandur down in Engineering happens to

look a lot like General Metadi in the holonews broadcasts
... well, it's a big galaxy, and Bandur sure would like to
be drawing the General's pay instead of his own."

"I understand," said Quetaya. "I'll get uniforms and ID
plates ready for you in the name of Gamelan Bandur."

"You do that, and think of a name for yourself while
you're at it." The comm link's buzzer sounded. Metadi
picked up the handset. "Metadi here."

"Good morning, General." The commanding officer of
Prime Base sounded a bit surprised to be hearing from
Metadi at this hour on a secure line. "Any trouble I should
know about?"

"No trouble, Perrin. I'm granting myself some leave. If
anything comes up, handle it."

"Handle it, aye," the CO said. "Enjoy your leave time,
General."

"There's that," Metadi said as he switched off. "Now
let's get moving. *Selsyn* hops out of orbit at 1149.45 Standard, and we have to be aboard her with in-transit orders
cut for—let's make it for the supply depot on Treidel."

As soon as Commander Quetaya had gone to take care
of the uniforms and ID, Metadi reached over and touched
another key on the comm panel. "Metadi here," he said, as
soon as the link opened. "Patch me through to the Retreat.
And go secure."

"Secure aye," said the voice on the other end of the
link.

A series of clicks and beeps marked the progress of the
transfer, followed by a synthesized voice informing him
that he had contacted the Retreat's information center and
inviting him to leave his comm code and a message.

"Private message for Guild Master Errec Ransome,"
Metadi told the voice.

"Please enter authorization code for direct messages to
that recipient."

Metadi punched in the code sequence for Ransome's

private message queue. For a moment, he considered using the personal code that would, within minutes, fetch Errec Ransome himself to a direct voicelink from anywhere on Galcen, then decided against it. He'd used that sequence only two times in the past five years—once when the news came in about Beka supposedly crashing *Warhammer* outside Port Artat; and once before that, on the night that Perada had died.

*No point in scaring whatever poor kid's got the job of monitoring the Retreat's comm system this morning,* he thought, and left a recorded message instead.

"Errec, Jos here. Don't bother trying to find me for a while ... I won't be around. Talk with you when I get back. Metadi out."

He switched off. Back in his own office, he took his uniform tunic out of the closet and began removing the ribbons and collar tabs. Once his aide brought the proper insignia for an engineering warrant officer, the tunic would do as well for Gamelan Bandur as it had for Jos Metadi. *Selsyn-bilai* was large enough for him to be just another service member in transit—and large enough, also, that the warrants would have their own mess. That way, Warrant Officer Bandur didn't have to worry about getting bumped up into the wardroom, where there was always the outside chance he might run into someone who'd met the General in person.

Some time later Commander Quetaya returned, wearing an enlisted crew member's uniform and carrying an assortment of insignia, nametags, IDs, and orders.

"All cleared," she said. "I sent the clerk on an errand over to Records and did up the orders and the nametags myself."

"Good," Metadi replied. "I knew there was a reason I grabbed you out of Intelligence. Have you decided who you're going to be for the trip?"

She waved a flimsy at him. "According to this," she

said, "I'm a clerk/comptech first class named Ennys Pardu, going to help maintain the systems on Treidel."

"Sounds fine to me. Let's find some ground transport over to the docks and see about getting back into space."

Wearing their uniforms as enlisted and warrant, Commander Quetaya and the General made their way to the transit deck just below the HQ building. From there, they took the next glidepod to the main port, getting off at the Orbital Arrivals and Departures section. Rows of flat-displays along the walls listed the shuttles to and from the various ships currently in orbit, including a shuttle lifting for *Selsyn-bilai*, outward bound for Treidel at 1149.45 Standard.

Metadi and Quetaya made their separate ways through the paperwork drill. Their orders and false IDs passed official scrutiny with ease—the commander had done her work thoroughly—and in short order a warrant officer and a clerk/comptech first class joined the twenty or so other people aboard the shuttle. The craft lifted from Galcen shortly afterward.

The pilot's acceleration was smooth and the orbits were matched with flawless precision, but Metadi felt his palms itching nevertheless. It had been years since he'd been anywhere during a lift besides the pilot's seat or somewhere close by it, and he didn't like the sensation.

They docked first with RSF *Margaraine*, where eight of the passengers shuffled off under that ship's artificial gravity. Then the shuttle broke free again and boosted to another and, Metadi knew, higher orbit. A little later, they linked up to *Selsyn-bilai* with a click of magnetic grap nels and a sigh of air systems matching. Metadi and Quetaya—as well as a lieutenant commander in traveling blues, three spacers-first, and a petty officer clutching a thin-fold tool case—unstrapped and walked through the connecting passageway to the *Selsyn*'s quarterdeck area.

A young lieutenant was on watch, aided by a clerk/

comptech and a runner. As the seven new arrivals entered the space, the comptech ticked each one off on a nearby flat-display.

"How's everything been, Arlie?" the lieutenant commander asked as he emerged from the passageway.

"Nice and quiet," the lieutenant replied. "Going to be a smooth one this time. How was leave?"

"Outstanding. I'll move along and let you get on with things here. Later."

The three spacers-first and the petty officer, like the lieutenant commander, also appeared to be well known to the quarterdeck team. The young lieutenant processed them quickly before turning to the pair of transients—Metadi and Quetaya.

"I don't have either of you on the manifest," he said. "Are you sure you're on the right ship?"

Metadi showed him the orders and the ID. "I'm directed to travel by quickest available means to Treidel."

At a nod from the lieutenant, the comptech ran his scanner first over the top copy of the orders, and then over the ID plate. The scanner beeped twice.

"Everything checks," said the comptech.

"Fine." The lieutenant turned to the runner. "Take Mr. Bandur down to the Supply Department and get him berthed." Then, to Metadi, "Welcome aboard, sir. I'll let the chief engineer know that you're here so he can put you on the watch bill. The skipper doesn't believe in carrying passengers who don't work."

"That's fine with me," said Metadi. "Neither do I."

In a smoky dive in Ruisi, the main port city for Ninglin on the Mageworlds side of the Net, Nyls Jessan stretched out his long legs and leaned back in his seat. When he did so, his shoulders touched the wall behind him. Ever since he'd started working with Tarnekep Portree, he'd found that having a wall at his back made him feel more comfortable than otherwise. Not that he ever truly relaxed these days. He'd lost that easy sense of security months ago, on the night when the Med Station on Pleyver had exploded around him and Beka Rosselin-Metadi had come into his life.

The dive was crowded tonight, mostly spacers from the Republic with a scattering of Ruisans. A local band was on the stage, playing unfamiliar instruments, and a young female Mageworlder was singing in whatever uncouth tongue they used here. Jessan poked at the green paper flower that adorned the glass in front of him. The bartender had folded the many-petaled blossom out of a single sheet while Jessan watched, and then had set it afloat on the slate-colored drink.

*Barbarous planet,* Jessan thought, rescuing the now-soggy flower before it sank and setting it down on the napkin to dry. *Wasting art like that on cheap booze.*

A young woman wearing blue spangles and very little else slid into the empty chair next to him. "Hello, spacer—new in town? Looking for a good time?"

"I had a good time once," Jessan said. "I didn't like it."

The woman shrugged—an interesting effect, considering the spangles—and moved on to another table. Jessan sipped his drink, harsh with the flavor of raw alcohol, and listened to the strange tones and intervals of the alien music.

The song had ended and another had begun before a man sat down in the chair the woman had vacated. "You brought the ship?" the stranger asked without preamble.

*Good,* Jessan thought, careful not to show his relief. *The code phrase worked.*

He nodded. "She's down at the port."

"That's all right, then." The man sat back in his chair. He was shorter than Jessan, dark and wiry, with a thin black mustache and sharp, watchful eyes. "Can you understand what they're singing?" he asked, nodding at the stage.

"No."

" 'My name is nothing extra, so that I will not tell,' " the man translated. " 'I'm a stranger in the world that I was born in.' " He paused. "They hate us, you know."

"So I've heard."

*Us*, the man had said. So he was admitting to being—or claiming to be—a citizen of the Republic. To Jessan's ear, at least, he had the accent, which was good. From the moment Jessan had left the ship, he'd been afraid of meeting someone who expected him to speak a language he didn't understand.

Logic had told him not to worry. The assassin on board *Warhammer* had spoken Galcenian, even in the last extremity, and the recognition routines he'd surrendered to Jessan implied a meeting of strangers. But logic did little to calm nerves that were still on edge from that macabre interrogation of a man already dead. Jessan had asked as many questions as he could during those last six minutes of brain function—watching the readouts change when he encountered truth, unscrambling the signals from the induction loop around the assassin's throat to turn subvocalized thoughts into words. But six minutes wasn't enough, and he knew it.

*It's always the things you don't have time to ask that come back around and kill you.*

Without warning, the lights went up and the music stopped. Jessan blinked in the sudden glare and saw a half-squad of troopers standing at the door. Another uniformed man slipped in through the rear exit to block that way out. Talk stopped at all the tables and nobody moved.

"Damn, it's the Pemies," the dark man muttered. "I hope you have good identification."

Jessan nodded, keeping his attention on the troops. According to the comp files back on *Warhammer*, the Pemies

were locals, hired by the Republic to keep the peace and
maintain order under the appointed governor of the planet.
*Not exactly a setup that I'd appreciate if somebody tried
it back home on Khesat. And I can just imagine the sort of
recruits they get.*

The Pemies left one man at the front door and another
at the back. The other four split up into two pairs and went
from table to table looking at identification cards. No one
put up any resistance. Finally one set of troopers came
around to where Jessan was sitting. The stranger pulled
out a card and laid it on the table. Jessan extracted his own
ID—taken from the assassin aboard *Warhammer*, and
altered to show Jessan's picture in place of the dead
man's—and held it up. The two Pemies squinted at it for
a moment.

"You there," ordered one trooper in heavily accented
Galcenian. "Stand." His mate took a step back, dropping
his hand to the grip of his gun—a chemical-energy weapon,
Jessan noticed, and not one of the blasters that were univer-
sal on the other side of the Net.

Jessan put the ID down on the table and stood, slowly.
Chemical-energy weapons were clumsy and noisy and
carried only a few charges, but they could kill you just as
dead as a blaster.

"Raise your hands."

He raised them."

"Turn around."

Jessan turned to face the wall, feeling his shoulders
prickle at the loss of its protection. Hands reached to his
belt and removed his blaster from the holster; then the
same hands patted him down and took his sleeve gun as
well.

"You have a permit for these?"

"It's on the table."

"They must be checked, in case they are wanted in a

crime. Come tomorrow to headquarters if you want them again."

Jessan turned back to the two Pemies. His blaster and sleeve gun were already tucked under the first trooper's belt. "May I please have a receipt for my weapons?"

Before the trooper could answer, a man sitting at a table farther into the room leaped to his feet. He dashed for the back door, hitting the Pemi there in the stomach with his shoulder. The man went down. One of the men standing in front of Jessan drew his weapon and fired—the explosion sounded tremendous in the closed room. Then all the Pemies were sprinting for the back door on the track of the fleeing man.

"Come on," said the stranger. Jessan could barely hear him above the ringing in his ears. "Let's get out of here."

They left by the front door. "What was that all about?" Jessan asked, as soon as they were out on the darkened street and heading in the direction of the spaceport.

"The Pemies keep down subversion and unrest, and investigate crimes against the peace," the man answered. "I can't imagine why people don't want to talk to them. Now suppose you show me the ship."

"Okay," Jessan replied. "I've got it."

Silently, he wondered if he should demand to be paid right away, and then vanish. Exactly when the payoff would take place was one of the things he hadn't gotten around to asking the assassin during those last six minutes.

*I hope I don't blow the game by asking for my money too late. Or too soon.*

They continued on, grabbing one of the local jitneys—wheels, no nullgravs, and a noisy engine—for the rest of the journey to the port. During the ride Jessan kept his features calm and his manner schooled to only casual interest, but inwardly he continued to fret.

*That raid was a little too convenient Maybe the whole thing was staged to get a look at my ID, or to make sure*

*I got searched and disarmed before we headed back to the ship. Mustache here certainly knew I was going to show up—if not tonight, then some other night.*

Jessan allowed himself a faint smile. If the stranger was expecting to deal with an unarmed man in a deserted ship, he was going to have a very unpleasant surprise.

The Space Force Headquarters Building on Galcen presented viewers with an imposing facade—the design had won its architect several distinguished awards—and those members of the public with business inside the structure usually found its upper reaches full of activity. Most visitors to HQ never ventured as far as the sub-basement equipment bay at the rear of the building, an echoing, extremely unaesthetic concrete space where delivery vehicles came and went, minor civilian employees staged their hovercars during bad weather, and the crumpled and shredded trash from the rest of the building was collected and sorted for recycling.

Security Operatives Ryx and Tarrey had the responsibility this week for checking out Space SB-2 at regular intervals. It was a dull job, usually reserved for people on the chief's scutlist—no danger, nothing to screw up, and no chance for glory—but someone had to walk along rattling the doors and being a presence.

At the moment, though, the only visible activity in the bay was the regular progress of the automatic garbage handler, a big, slab-sided machine more than twice the height of a man. The handler floated on heavy-duty nullgravs a few inches above the floor, while its long robotic arm picked up the trash bins along the side of the bay and dumped their contents into its hopper for sorting. The bins would be filled up again later by the host of inside-collection robots that emptied smaller containers on the floors above. Everything that Headquarters discarded eventually made its way down into Space SB-2.

"Makes you think, doesn't it?" said Ryx, who tended to wax philosophical on occasion. "All those important people and conferences and things upstairs, and it all comes out as trash in the end."

Tarrey grunted. "Most stuff does."

The two operatives watched as the handler's robotic arm picked up a bin, tumbled its cargo of trash into the gaping hopper, then set back down the empty bin. A second and a third bin were lifted, dumped, and replaced. The arm swung out to pick up a fourth—

"Hey! Waitaminute!"

Ryx dashed across the empty bay to punch the Emergency Stop button on the side of the handler. His partner followed, looking puzzled.

"What's up?" Tarrey asked. The garbage handler had frozen in place, its arm poised with the last bin half-discharged above the hopper. A few small bits of paper and cardboard were still fluttering down.

"I thought I saw something going into the vat."

"Yeah. Yesterday's cha'a cups."

"No. It was too big for that. Come on, give me a boost up the ladder."

Ryx clambered up the emergency access ladder on the side of the handler. He peered down over the side of the hopper, swallowed hard, and pulled out his comm link.

"Section, this is patrol two-zero. Evidence of crime detected, lower level section delta, Space SB-2."

"What's up?" Tarrey yelled from below.

"Crime scene," Ryx yelled back to him. "Seal the whole area." Then, into the common link, "Request major crime task force, forensics, and pathologist. Apparent homicide."

Fumbling in his jacket, he pulled out the pocket holocorder security operatives at HQ were required to carry while on duty. "Time to start preserving the visual evidence," he muttered, and pointed the holocorder down at what he'd seen inside the hopper.

His discovery hadn't gone away. The holocorder's view-finder brought it into sharp and unwelcome focus: the body of a woman in Space Force uniform—a Commander Quetaya, by her nametag and collar insignia—with the gold braid of a high-ranking officer's personal aide looped around one shoulder and the charred circle of a tight-focus blaster burn in the center of her forehead.

# VIII. Ninglin: Ruisi Port
## Galcen: Prime Base; the Retreat

THE JITNEY clattered and bumped over the Ruisan streets, trailing a cloud of noxious fumes behind it in the night. At the gate of the port, Jessan and the stranger—who still hadn't given his name—paid the fare and climbed out. The jitney turned and sputtered back off toward the middle of town, its noise and smell gradually fading into the blackness beyond the lighted gate.

There was a guard at the port entrance, another Pemi. Jessan flourished the stamped gate pass that proved he'd come from within the port area and so had a legitimate reason for going back inside.

*Now,* he thought as he refolded the gate pass and slipped it back into his pocket, *let's see what our friend Mustache has by way of papers.*

The dark man produced an ID card. Jessan looked at it sidelong, trying to catch a glimpse of the name. He was in luck: he could read the printed capitals without squinting.

The stranger claimed to be Lars Olver, a merchant shipping specialist licensed to do business on Ninglin.

*That's probably not his name. And it's certainly not his job.*

After Olver, or whoever he really was, had put his ID away, they passed through the gate. One of the port shuttle buses was waiting inside—bigger than the jitney, and longer, but just as noisy and bad-smelling. Like all the ground transport Jessan had seen on this side of the Net, the shuttle relied on chemical reactions and wheels to get around.

*I knew that the Republic destroyed the Mageworlders' military capacity after the end of the War,* he thought uncomfortably. *But they never told us back in school exactly how thorough we were when we did it.*

Eventually the shuttle bus wheezed to a stop. Jessan and the stranger got off and hiked the rest of the way across the tarmac to where the *'Hammer* perched on her landing legs. Jessan paused for a moment at the foot of the lowered ramp. The door at the top was open, but the faint blur of a security force field shimmered across the entryway. That would be the danger point, as soon as the barrier came down.

Rather than chance getting shot from behind, he gestured at the stranger to precede him. Lars Olver hung back and in the end they went up together.

*He doesn't trust me any more than I trust him,* Jessan thought as they reached the top of the ramp. *And he's right. But I won't nail him until he tries to make the payoff.*

Jessan punched the code combination into the cipher lock, and stepped through as soon as the force field went down. Lars Olver came with him, like a slighter, darker shadow.

"Through that way," Jessan said, pointing to the forward part of the ship. "And . . ."

The sentence curdled in his throat. A black wave rose up in front of his eyes and his legs began to give way beneath him.

*A needler,* he thought fuzzily. *Stupid of me; I should have checked. . . .*

He didn't even feel the deckplates when he hit.

RSF *Selsyn-bilai* had made the jump to hyperspace, and was already out of comms when the high-pri message came out to all units orbiting Galcen: the body of General Metadi's aide, Commander Rosel Quetaya, had been found inside a garbage hopper at Prime Base. The commander had been dead for approximately twelve hours. Any pertinent information should be sent directly to Space Force Intelligence.

"But I'll bet you my next pay raise that whoever was responsible is long gone by now."

Brigadier General Perrin Ochemet's square, copper-brown face reflected his disgust. He'd once considered his assignment as the CO of Prime Base to be the crowning accomplishment of a long career in the Space Force Planetary Infantry. That had been this morning. Now, with the Commanding General out of the loop and with Metadi's final order—*"if anything comes up, handle it"*—burning its way into his brain, Ochemet was beginning to wonder if he should have opted instead for a quiet billet with a reserve training squadron.

He returned to the infantry captain in charge of security at Prime. "Gremyl—any luck contacting the General at his house upcountry? It takes about an hour to get there in a fast aircar; he could have been in transit earlier."

"No joy on that," Gremyl said. He was a thin man with an outdoor tan fading to pale after more than a year of base duty. "There isn't even a record of him leaving the base. You wouldn't happen to have his last call still on file, would you?"

Ochemet shook his head. "No. When Jos asks for a secure line, he means it. No recordings, no traces, nothing."

"Too bad," said Gremyl. "I'd love to see a voice-stress analysis on that message."

"Sorry."

"Oh, well. You've known him for quite a while. When you talked with him, did he seem like he was under the influence of anything? Drugs, beglamourment, any kind of duress?"

"No," said Ochemet. "He sounded just like he always did. It's not unusual for him to make himself scarce for a week or two, although most of the time he leaves word with someone about where he's going to be. But I think we have to assume that Metadi's absence and Quetaya's death are somehow related—especially in the light of the security records from outside the General's office."

Gremyl looked interested. "What do they show?"

"Nothing," said Ochemet. "They're blank. Erased."

The security chief pursed his lips in a soundless whistle. "Somebody's hiding their tracks, that's for sure. Let me have the records. Maybe Technical can find a bit of sound, or an image trace."

"You've got them," the CO said. "Meanwhile—we'll have to handle this as a kidnapping and/or a possible assassination. But I'm not going to go public with all of it just now. Give the holovid reporters all you want to about the commander, but fudge the time of death a bit. As far as anybody on the outside is concerned, the General took off for leave at an undisclosed location some hours before she was shot. No point in telling the other side how much we know. Or how much we don't know."

"You think it's a conspiracy, then?"

"Has to be," said Ochemet. "Do you think that just one person could have snatched Metadi?"

"Before today I'd have said that just one army couldn't manage it," Gremyl said. "But it looks like somebody did. We'd better get the Adepts' Guild in on this."

"You people in Security trust them?"

Gremyl shrugged. "As much as we trust anybody—"

"Which is to say, not much."

"—but the Master of the Guild was Metadi's copilot on the old *Warhammer*. He may know something we don't."

"If you're thinking along those lines," Ochemet said, "there's always Metadi's last aide . . . Jervas Something-or-other, from Ovredis. Gil, that was his name."

"Where is he right now?"

"Mageworlds patrol," said Ochemet. "Commodore of the fleet, no less."

"He must have impressed the hell out of Metadi during his tour on Galcen," Gremyl said. "But he's no good to us—the Net's a long way off, even in a fast ship. It looks like the Guild or nothing."

"I suppose so." The CO still looked doubtful. "But if the situation goes on for longer than a couple of days, I want somebody we can trust handling the liaison." He picked up the comm link and punched a button. "Ochemet here. Get me a list of all the Adepts who also hold commissions in the Space Force."

"You won't find many," Gremyl told him. "Most of ours who cross over usually resign their commissions first. Just as well, I suppose. Anything else makes for mixed loyalties."

"We'll see who Personnel turns up," Ochemet said. "Meanwhile, we might as well pay a call on Errec Ransome and tell him his old war buddy has gone missing."

Jessan woke to the feel of a sheet underneath him and a pair of hands kneading the muscles of his naked back. His first, half-hallucinatory impression—that Lars Olver had given him to the Pemi who'd searched him earlier—

faded as his mind cleared and tactile memory returned. He was lying on the bunk in *Warhammer*'s main cabin, and the hands belonged to Tarnekep Portree.

The lacy cuffs of Portree's Mandeynan-style shirt tickled Jessan's skin. He turned his head sideways and opened his eyes.

The cabin had a blurred, unstable look, and he didn't see Lars Olver anywhere. He closed his eyes again.

"... got away," he muttered against the pillow. "My fault ... should have checked him for that needler."

"Don't worry," said Tarnekep's cool tenor voice. "You're friend with the mustache is still with us. I have him stashed where he can't cause any trouble if he wakes up before you're on your feet."

Jessan rolled onto his side and looked at Tarnekep. The starpilot was dressed for visitors—full Mandeynan rig, from lace cravat to high leather boots. The red plastic eye patch made it hard to interpret his expression, but Jessan thought his companion's angular features seemed paler than usual.

"What happened?" Jessan asked. "Did you stun him after he got me with that needler of his?"

Tarnekep shook his head. "Not exactly."

"What do you mean ... 'not exactly'?"

"He never shot you at all," said Tarnekep. "That was me."

Jessan struggled to sit up. "*You* shot me?"

"No. Not shot. I used the rest of that cylinder of Sonoxate gas our late passenger Vorgent Elimax had in his luggage. Flooded all the passageways and open spaces with it after you left, then sat in the common room for hours wearing one of those damned respirators, waiting for you to get back."

He nodded. The movement made his head reel. "Good idea. I wish you'd told me first, though."

Tarnekep bit his lip. "I'm sorry," he said. "For all I

knew, you were going to meet somebody who would tie you up and introduce you to the joys of active interrogation—and there would go our cover on Ninglin. But what you don't know you can't tell, so I made certain we had a surprise waiting that you didn't know about."

"I suppose you're right. But next time, could you pick a surprise that won't leave me with a head full of dirty grey fuzz? This stuff feels worse than a hangover."

"You didn't look very good, either," said Tarnekep. From the way his mouth tightened on the description, it was an understatement. "That's why I brought you in here."

"Bad reaction," Jessan said. He tried to stand up but sank back down onto the bunk, his head spinning. "Muscle cramps and vertigo . . . we haven't got time for this. If you check the medikit in the locker over there, you'll see a row of hypo ampules."

"Got it," Tarnekep said a few moments later. "I see them."

"Okay—I need the third one from the left."

"Orange label, coded six-zero-three-D?"

"That's it."

Jessan took the ampule Tarnekep handed him and pressed it against the vein in his arm. He felt the usual brief stinging sensation, and forced himself to breathe slowly and evenly while the medication did its work.

When he stood up again his head was clear and the bulkheads no longer wavered when he looked at them. The cabin air was chilly against his flesh, however, and he realized belatedly that all his clothes were lying in a crumpled heap next to the bunk. He thought about putting back on the garments that Tarnekep had removed, but decided against the effort. Instead, he crossed over to the clothes locker and took out a green velvet Khesatan lounging robe lined in gold spidersilk—a bit overstated for his taste, but appropriate enough for the persona he cultivated these days.

"That was the first time I ever tried breathing Sono-xate," he said, slipping his arms into the full sleeves. He wrapped the broad silk sash around his waist and tied it neatly. "Just how far under did it put me?"

"Far enough," said Tarnekep. The pilot's face, Jessan noted, was still pale, and his whole bearing was tense and edgy. "If I'd known about that six-zero-three-D thing I wouldn't have wasted so much time."

"Don't worry; the stuff in that ampule wouldn't have worked until I was conscious anyway." Jessan selected a needler and a wide-beam stunner from the collection of small arms in the locker, and slid them into the pockets of his robe. "Gentlesir Olver is probably awake himself by now. Give me a moment to get the Professor's little box of horrors out of storage, and we can soothe our nerves by asking him a few questions."

Tarnekep Portree palmed the lockplate beside the cabin door and the panel slid open. Out in the common room, Jessan sniffed at the air but failed to detect any trace of the gas that had felled both him and Lars Olver.

"You won't smell it," Tarnekep assured him. "The stuff is practically odorless. Anyway, I flushed the ship to atmosphere right after I scraped you up off the deckplates and took care of your friend."

The captain waved one hand at the unconscious form of Lars Olver, strapped securely into an acceleration couch in the common room. The buckles had been pulled well out of Olver's reach, effectively imprisoning him.

"He's no friend of mine," said Jessan. "I never saw him before tonight. Just as well, I suppose. It makes asking the questions a bit easier."

He ducked briefly into the unused crew cabin that served these days as extra storage, and came out again with the black medikit from the Professor's asteroid base.

"All right," he said to Tarnekep. "Let's do it. Will you want me to bring him round, or shall we wait until he comes to on his own?"

"We don't need to wait." Tarnekep strode over to the couch and slapped the bound man twice across the face, first with the palm and then with the back of his open hand. "He's awake."

The captain moved away from the couch to a chair beside the common-room table. He turned the chair around and sat with his long legs straddling its seat and its back coming up to the frothy lace ruffles on the front of his shirt. Light from overhead glittered off the topaz stickpin in his spidersilk cravat. He pulled his blaster and leveled it at the prisoner.

"Okay, Doc," Tarnekep said. "If he dies like the last one, he's all yours. Until then, he's mine."

The man's eyes were still closed, but Jessan thought he saw a faint shiver of reaction on the otherwise immobile face. Tarnekep pressed on, regardless.

"There's no point in shamming, Olver. I know you can hear me. So make it easy on yourself and everybody else and tell me who you thought you were meeting today."

Olver's eyes remained shut, but after a long pause he spoke. "I met someone I was told to meet."

"You aren't helping yourself any by dodging the question," Tarnekep said. "Here's a different one—who are you?"

"I'm Lars Olver," the man replied stubbornly. "I'm a shipping agent, and I was trying to meet a man about a cargo."

"You're lying," the captain said. "You screwed this one up big time. Your name is Ignaceu LeSoit, you're a killer for hire from the other side of the Net, and you just tried to kill *me*."

The bound man's eyes snapped open. For a long moment he and the captain looked at each other, and Jessan

saw his expression change: from stoic despair to a shocked
and even more hopeless recognition.

Jessan felt a stirring of unease. *He already knows Captain Portree. And the captain knows him.*

But Olver—or LeSoit, as it seemed his name was—
remained silent. Tarnekep hefted his blaster meaningfully.
"Come on, LeSoit. Have you forgotten that much about
what happened the last time?"

LeSoit shook his head.

"You told me back on Mandeyn that you owed me one,"
Tarnekep said. "Remember that, Ignac'?"

"And you said we were even." LeSoit's voice was
hoarse and he was sweating. "New deal, new hand."

Tarnekep favored the bound man with a thin smile.
"Right—and you lost. Pay up."

"That's no good. You're the one with the blaster, and
I'm fresh out of chips."

The captain regarded LeSoit with a speculative expression. "Maybe you'd be interested in a different game, and
a chance to win some of those markers back."

"Captain," said Jessan uneasily. "Are you seriously considering—"

Tarnekep turned a dangerously bright blue eye in his direction. "I did something of the sort at least once before,
remember? And with a damn sight less to go on."

"I recall the occasion," Jessan said. "I believe the alternative I offered was shooting me out of hand. That might
be the safer course this time."

"I thought about shooting him," said Tarnekep, "back
while I was waiting to see if you'd wake up. But right
now I'm disposed to be friendly."

LeSoit moved his head slightly to a position where he
could take in Jessan and Tarnekep together. "These days I
made a point of not working for my friends," he said. "It
makes professional decisions a lot simpler."

"Ah," said Tarnekep. The answer appeared to please the

captain, Jessan wasn't sure why. "Tell me one thing, Ignac': did you know who you were setting up to get hit?"

LeSoit shook his head. "The captain of the *Pride of Mandeyn*, is all. Nobody gave me a name, and I didn't ask."

"Good enough," said Tarnekep. He slid his blaster into its holster and stood up. "Okay, Doc, you can let him loose."

"Are you sure?"

"Yes, I'm sure."

Jessan shrugged. "Your call, Captain. Don't say I didn't warn you."

He went over to the couch and undid the buckles, leaving their former prisoner to remove the webbing himself. LeSoit pushed himself awkwardly to an upright position— the captain had not been gentle with the restraints—and sat rubbing the life back into his arms.

"Well?" said Tarnekep. "Are you in on the game?"

LeSoit nodded. "With pleasure—Captain Rosselin-Metadi."

Space Force Headquarters at Galcen Prime was a good six hours by aircar from the Retreat, in the high mountains to the far north and west of the spaceport city. The nearest inhabited area of any size, the town of Treslin, didn't have landing facilities for anything larger than small atmospheric craft. Neither did the Retreat itself, which let out the chance of cutting travel time by taking a suborbital shuttle.

Nevertheless, neither Ochemet nor Gremyl considered telling their unpleasant news to Master Errec Ransome any other way than face-to-face. From a security viewpoint, they didn't really have a choice. As long as they intended to keep the General's disappearance secret, no other means of transmission could be considered safe. "I know four or five ways to get around a secure line," Gremyl said, "and I'm not an expert."

Nor could they call Master Ransome to Galcen Prime for an emergency conference. Metadi would have done it, and no question, but Ochemet and Gremyl knew their limitations. The Master of the Adepts' Guild might have obeyed Jos Metadi's summons for old times' sake, but the Space Force had no authority over him.

They flew into the sunset out of Prime, and soon overtook the night. For a while they talked of the situation back at Headquarters, and what the forensic reports might reveal about Quetaya's death, but eventually they exhausted all the possibilities for conversation and sat in silence. Gremyl handled the controls of the aircraft—the need for secrecy had kept them from bringing along a third man as pilot—while Ochemet slept briefly.

The lights of towns and cities underneath them thinned out as they drew closer to the mountains. Ochemet stretched his arms and legs as far as the safety webbing would allow, then reached over to pick up the comm link.

"We'll be passing over Treslin in a few minutes," he said. "Time to let the Retreat know we're coming." He keyed on the link. "Retreat Field, Retreat Field. This is tail-number two six zero one Delta, request landing instructions, over."

"This is Retreat Field," came the prompt reply. "You are cleared for landing on strip one-seven. Wind south five, visibility three in rain. How copy, over."

"This is two six zero one, roger, over."

"Retreat Field, roger out."

The link clicked off. "Well," said Ochemet, after a pause. "They don't have much to say, do they?"

"In more ways than one," Gremyl said. "I'm not getting anything on the landing guidance frequencies."

"I don't think there are any up here," Ochemet said. "Sorry about that, but Retreat Field is one of the oldest on

Galcen. Goes back to before they started building aircars with nullgrav-assist—they can handle anything that flies in atmosphere, not just the new stuff."

"Haven't they ever heard of upgrading their systems?"

"You don't know how the Guild thinks," Ochemet said. "They keep to themselves, and they don't trust outsiders very much. Old history at work, I guess; they've been respected for a long time here on Galcen, but the Guildhouses on the outplanets and some of the Middle Worlds were having local troubles right up to the start of the Magewar."

Gremyl sighed. "So they don't believe in making it easy on visitors. Oh, well—if this were a field action somewhere in the boonies, we wouldn't even have visual beacons to go by. I can handle it."

A few minutes later the green and white flashing beacon of Retreat Field appeared. Gremyl put them down near the squat concrete control building, landing in the short space needed by a nullgrav-assisted aircar. The unused strip stretched far out beyond them, one of several on different compass bearings. Ochemet supposed that the multiple strips were a relic from truly ancient days, when even the direction of the wind made a difference to the aircraft.

*Something else odd about those strips*, he realized after a few seconds. *Nobody using them is going to pass over the Retreat, whether they're landing or taking off.*

Out of curiosity, he called up the Treslin area on the aircar's charts, and saw without real surprise that the entire area of the Retreat was marked as restricted airspace. He nodded to himself and wondered how long the restriction had been in place. Somebody in the Galcenian government, or maybe somebody even higher, must have owed the Adepts' Guild a really big one, in order to do a favor like that.

Ochemet and Gremyl stepped out of the aircar into a cold, drizzling rain. They hurried over to the control build-

ing. The main door slid aside to let them into Retreat Field
Operations—a large room filled with an impressive array
of sensor and communications equipment, staffed by one
Adept sitting at a desk next to a galley-sized pot of cha'a.

The Adept was a youngish man in a plain black coverall, with eyes that looked older than the rest of his face. A
long staff of polished wood leaned against the wall beside
his desk. If the rank insignia on Ochemet's uniform startled or impressed him, he didn't show it, but his greeting
was cordial enough.

"Welcome to Retreat Field, General—"

"Ochemet. I'm the CO at Prime Base, and this is Captain Gremyl, my chief of security."

The Adept inclined his head politely. "General Ochemet, Captain Gremyl. Is there some way I can be of
service?"

"Not you, precisely," said Ochemet. "Is there a shuttle
between here and the Retreat?"

The Adept looked amused. "Most of the time, we
walk."

"How far away is it?" Gremyl asked.

"About three hours in good weather."

"Right now it's raining," Ochemet pointed out. "And
we need to speak with Master Ransome on an urgent matter."

The Adept was serious again. "In person?"

Ochemet nodded. "Yes."

"Then wait here with me until my relief shows up, and
we can ride back together. It'll be about an hour."

"Any other choices?"

The Adept shook his head. "Not really."

"We'll wait," said Ochemet. "It's been six hours already, another hour won't hurt."

*"With pleasure—Captain Rosselin-Metadi."*
Beka froze.

*Damn you, Ignac'. Do you* want *to die?*

LeSoit hadn't moved or looked away. He sat watching her intently, and she forced herself to relax.

*You don't have to kill him yet. Find out what he's doing here first.*

She didn't look at Jessan. She didn't need to; she could feel the tension in him from where she sat. One word, one signal from her, and Ignaceu LeSoit would be in no shape to betray her secret to anyone but the dead.

"Good guessing, Ignac'," she said finally. "When did you figure it out?"

"Just a few minutes ago. While you were talking." He paused. "I thought they'd killed you when the *'Hammer* crashed outside Port Artat."

Beka raised an eyebrow. "They?"

"The ones who wanted you dead." Another pause. "I'm working for them these days."

"Are you indeed?" Jessan's voice was level and uninflected, a sure sign that the Khesatan was in a dangerous mood. "How interesting. Captain—"

"No," she said flatly, without looking around. "If I want him dead I'll kill him myself. But first I want to know what's making him so eager to sell out his friends."

LeSoit smiled faintly. "I thought I told you, Captain Rosselin-Metadi. I don't work for friends anymore."

"If you're expecting money—"

"Better to kill him," Jessan cut in before LeSoit could answer. "In the long run, it's cheaper than paying blackmail."

But LeSoit was already shaking his head. "I don't need your money, Captain Rosselin-Metadi."

"You know my first name," she said. "Doc isn't going to shoot you just for using it."

"Beka, then. I thought you were dead, you understand."

"So you told us." Jessan again, with a knife-edged calm

in his voice. "That doesn't explain what you're doing here."

"Following a trail," LeSoit said. "I didn't want to know who sabotaged the *'Hammer*—that's what I thought had happened, when I heard the news about the crash—because all I'd find was people like me, doing the job somebody else hired them to do. I wanted to know who was paying."

"Why?" she asked.

"I was going to kill him. Or her, if it came to that. I'm not particular."

"I can see you aren't," said Jessan. LeSoit's admission seemed to have mollified the Khesatan somewhat. "I can even sympathize with your position. The question is, why haven't you done it yet?"

LeSoit shrugged. "There's a lot more rungs in the ladder than I expected, and I need to be certain I've reached the top. I won't get more than one shot, and I don't intend to waste it."

*Brilliant plan,* thought Beka. *Absolutely brilliant. Are all men suicidal idiots, or just all the ones in my life?*

"We're not going to waste it," she said aloud. "Or you either. You're playing in my game now, and the stakes are higher than you know."

# PART TWO

# I. Galcen: The Retreat; Prime Base
## Ninglin: Ruisi Port

THE HOVERCAR from the Retreat arrived at the Field just as General Ochemet was finishing his third cup of cha'a. The Adept stood up, collected his staff from its place by the wall, and turned over the desk and the cha'a pot to his relief. Then he, Ochemet, and Gremyl sprinted through the rain—harder than a drizzle now, and stinging like cold needles—to the hovercar.

The road up to the Retreat was narrow and full of switchbacks, and hugged the edge of the mountain all the way. There were no markers, and no warnings of cross-winds and sudden updrafts. Even the Adept, who presumably knew the terrain, had to concentrate on taking the car up what Ochemet strongly suspected was a path originally carved out of the mountainside in Galcen's prespaceflight days.

When they arrived at the Retreat itself, Ochemet's suspicion became a certainty. The road ended outside a stone wall stretching up to a high tower, with a massive ironwood gate set into the wall at the bottom. More walls led off into the darkness to either side, and tower upon tower loomed from the fortress within. Ochemet had seen citadels like this before—smaller ones, carefully preserved relics of Galcen's far-distant past, before the warring kingdoms of the Mother of Worlds became a single republic and sent out ships to explore the stars. The Retreat was as old as those, or even older, but Ochemet could have told just by looking—if he hadn't known the truth already—that this was no museum, no cultural landmark with holographic dioramas and guided tours, but a living fortress that held and protected its own.

Their escort must have given some kind of signal, because the great double doors of the gate moved slowly open to let the car glide through into a flagstoned outer courtyard. A glowcube set into the wall on one side of the yard illuminated a small inner doorway with its blue-white light. A figure in a dark cloak stood at the top of the steps leading up to the door, and Ochemet realized with a slight shiver that this was Master Ransome himself, his hood thrown back onto his shoulders and his black hair slicked down to his skull with rain.

*Nobody told him we were coming,* Ochemet protested inwardly. Then he gave an impatient snort. *These are Adepts, remember? They don't need comm links.*

Master Ransome strode over to the side of the hovercar. The Adept who was driving open the front door to let the Master of the Guild slide into the seat beside him. The car turned smoothly around and was moving back out through the gate of the Retreat before Ransome spoke.

"Gentlesirs, I've been expecting you," he said. "I think that we should return to Prime Base together."

Master Ransome said nothing during the ride back down the mountain to the airfield. Ochemet kept silent as well, watching the driving rain out the window of the hovercar.

Only Captain Gremyl and the junior Adept bothered with anything like conversation—mostly dealing with the technicalities of handling atmospheric craft under less than ideal conditions. Ochemet was content to have it that way: the fewer people who knew about the mess at Prime Base, the better.

He still wasn't entirely happy about the decision to bring in Errec Ransome, and the Guild Master's motionless, unspeaking presence in the front seat of the groundcar did nothing to reassure him. *We need him because he knows Metadi better than anyone else we've got,* Ochemet told himself. *They were privateers together, back before the Domina grabbed Jos out of Innish-Kyl and put him in charge of the war.*

But the strength of that connection also contributed to Ochemet's discomfort. Errec Ransome had a self-control that was legendary these days, but Ochemet had heard stories of his earliest career—and especially of his time as copilot of *Warhammer*—which made the CO of Prime Base unwilling to be nearby when that control finally broke.

*Ransome already knows that something serious is happening ... I wish I knew whether he saw it coming because he's an Adept or because the Guild has an intelligence branch that's a whole lot better than it ought to be.*

The weather at Retreat Field had not improved while they were gone, but Captain Gremyl managed a clean takeoff in spite of the antique strip. Once the aircar was riding in safety above the clouds and the buffeting wind, with the long flight back to Prime stretching out ahead, Ochemet knew he couldn't postpone the inevitable any longer. He cleared his throat—but Errec Ransome forestalled him by speaking first.

"You have a problem," said the Guild Master. "And you hope that I can help you solve it."

Ochemet reminded himself not to get too impressed by Ransome's pronouncement. *Nobody's going to think you traveled all the way from Prime Base just to breathe the fresh mountain air. Of course you've got a problem.*

"We need your knowledge of a friend," he said to Ransome. "General Metadi's aide is dead. A pair of civilian employees found her body in a garbage hopper down in the sub-basement areas of HQ. What's complicating the matter is that Metadi himself chose this morning— yesterday morning, now—to pull one of his unplanned vanishing acts."

"Ah," said Ransome. "I warned him the habit was dangerous. But what exactly do you require of me in this case?"

Gremyl spoke for the first time since taking off. "You know Metadi: you crewed under him during the War, and you've been a friend of his family ever since. Maybe you can tell us where we ought to start looking for him."

In *Warhammer*'s common room, Beka felt the tension beginning to dissipate. LeSoit and Jessan still eyed each other warily, but the situation no longer looked like exploding into violence on a second's notice.

*So now they'll give me, oh, two or three whole minutes to wade in and haul them back from the brink.* She sighed inwardly. *And I used to think that having my big brother on board made for a hard crew to handle. That was before the galaxy decided to get generous and give me Nyls Jessan and Ignac' LeSoit.*

She stood up and stretched, exaggerating the movements enough to catch and hold their attention. "This conversation is making me thirsty—how about you? The galley's over there," she said to LeSoit, "and we still have some cha'a in the pot."

LeSoit swung his legs down from the acceleration couch onto the deck. "I think I'll take your offer."

He headed off in the direction she had indicated. She turned to Jessan. The Khesatan stood with his hands in the pockets of his lounging robe, leaning against the bulkhead with an air of casual elegance. Somebody who didn't know him—and who didn't know what he was carrying in those pockets—might have thought he looked relaxed.

Beka wasn't fooled. "You can let go of the artillery, Nyls. We're all on the same side here."

"If you say so, Captain."

"I say so. And this may be the break we needed."

"Maybe." But Jessan's expression remained doubtful.

LeSoit came out of the galley with two mugs of cha'a. He handed one to Beka and took a seat at the other side of the table. He wasn't as relaxed as he pretended, either; his knuckles were white with the tension of his grip on the mug's plastic handle.

Beka glanced down at her cha'a. "I see you remembered I like mine black."

LeSoit shook his head. "Not really," he said, with a half-smile. "Just the way I take it myself, is all. Besides, I didn't know how you'd react if I added something to your drink."

"I trust you," said Beka. "Doc, now, he gets paranoid sometimes, so it's not a good idea to make him suspicious. Not healthy, if you know what I mean."

She took a sip of her cha'a. "But enough talking. Let's get down to business. Tell me—what are your former employers expecting from you?"

"Promptness, confidentiality, and success," LeSoit replied. "But I suppose you want the details, too."

"That's right."

"Okay—I'm supposed to lift ship and take the *Pride* back to where I'm working out of these days. And not just the ship; I'm supposed to bring your dead body along, too. My boss wants to see it for himself." LeSoit's mouth twitched slightly under his thin mustache. "Something that you did must have really annoyed him."

Beka shrugged. "Who knows? I've ticked off a lot of people over the past couple of years. Does your boss have a name I might be able to hang a picture onto?"

"Hatchet-faced son of a bitch from Rolny," LeSoit said. "Name of D'Caer."

"*Ebenra* D'Caer?"

"That's him."

Beka felt a warm glow of gratification spreading through her at the words. *So the bastard is still alive and kicking!* She laughed quietly.

"I'd say I annoyed him," she said. "You've climbed that ladder of yours as far as it goes, if you're working for Ebenra D'Caer."


The morgue at Prime Base was a windowless room in the depths of the base hospital. Stark white light from the panels overhead washed the color out of everything and made the place look even bleaker than it was—although the reality, Ochemet had to admit, was bleak enough.

Uncharitably, he hoped that Errec Ransome found the place as distasteful as he did. They had come here at the Guild Master's insistence, after first showing him the sub-basement area where Commander Quetaya's body had been found. Now, along with Captain Gremyl, Ransome and Ochemet stood looking down at the transparent walls of a stasis box. Protected by the box's field, the late commander seemed like a grotesque parody of a patient asleep in a healing pod.

Stasis had kept her body from deteriorating since its discovery, but the pallid grey skin and the charred meat around the blaster wound were just as ugly as ever. Ochemet had seen far worse things in the vicious fighting that had marked the final pacification of the Mageworlds, but the commander's fate distressed him nonetheless.

Something like this should not have happened to an efficient, conscientious officer on a peacetime base under his command.

Errec Ransome, meanwhile, gazed down at the stasis box for several minutes without speaking, placed one hand on the clear crystal lid, and closed his eyes. What he learned in that manner, or how he learned it, Ochemet couldn't tell—the Adept's expression never changed.

After some time, Ransome opened his eyes and drew his hand away. He turned and addressed Captain Gremyl. "Are you certain of the identification of this body?"

"It matches the recorded data in every respect," said Gremyl. He touched a spot on the lid of the box. The crystal in that area darkened to become a display screen. "See for yourself. That's Quetaya's service file on top, and the info from our examiners on the bottom. We're looking at the same stuff all the way down to the gene-types."

Ransome nodded. "I see the matches. Very solid."

"Is there anything that you can tell us?" Ochemet asked.

"Very little," the Guild Master replied. "Only that her death was unexpected, and nothing caused her any distress except for the shot that killed her."

"That tallies with what pathology's got for us," said Gremyl. "No cuts, bruises, or struggle marks; no sign that she was sexually interfered with in any way."

"Quick, clean, and professional," Ochemet agreed. "I'm glad of that for her sake—but I don't like what it implies about Metadi's disappearance."

"Nor do I," said Errec Ransome. "But I would know, I think, if Jos or any member of his family had died. As for this—" He laid his hand again on the stasis box, and was silent for a moment before going on. "As for this—you are looking at the work of the Magelords."

Ochemet felt a chill run down his arms and the backs of his legs. "I thought we had destroyed them all."

Ransome shook his head sadly. "If only that were true."

He struck the box lightly with his closed fist. "No, this *is* their work, or an essential part of it. And as for Jos—I can tell you right now there's no point in looking for him on Galcen, because he isn't here."

"Are you sure," said Ignaceu LeSoit, "that D'Caer is as high as it goes?"

"Oh, yes," said Beka. "I'm sure about that. He's the one who gave the orders. And anyway," she added, "the ladder doesn't go up past him anymore."

LeSoit gave her an appraising look. "Blew the top off of it, did you?"

"With some help, yes," she said. "Doc was along for that one, by the way—so don't go getting the idea that he's just another pretty face."

"You flatter me immensely, Captain," said Jessan. He took his hands out of the pockets of his lounging robe and slid into one of the vacant chairs. "And here I thought you only loved me for my beautiful eyes."

*Thank goodness,* Beka thought, *he's starting to come around.* She was careful not to let the relief show, however; she only grinned at her copilot and said aloud, "Beautiful eyes, hell. It's your naturally devious mind."

"One does one's humble best," he said. "Gentlesir LeSoit—you asked the captain if she was certain D'Caer was as high as the ladder went. Why?"

"Look around you, man," said LeSoit. "We're in the Mageworlds, in case you hadn't noticed. Local politics around here is about as nasty as politics can get, but no matter who ends up on top they all have one thing in common—they really, really hate the Republic."

Beka said, "We already knew D'Caer had ties to the Mageworlds. But he was taking orders from Nivome the Rolny, and Nivome is dead."

"I heard about that," LeSoit said. "It was the talk of the profession for a while there, Tarnekep Portree and his raid on Darvell, after the Rolny vanished with half the city in flames behind him. Portree was dead too, they said, flown into a star. But when D'Caer heard that the *Pride of Mandeyn* had passed through the Net he went crazy, shouting and throwing furniture. We did the best we could to nail you on almost no notice."

Beka sipped at her cha'a. It had cooled sufficiently for her to swallow it by now, so she drained the mug and set it down on the scarred plastic tabletop. "Well, your best wasn't good enough."

"Be glad of it," said LeSoit. "I certainly am. If I'd recognized your body afterward, I'd have been a bit upset myself." He was quiet for a few seconds, and then added thoughtfully, "Not as upset as D'Caer would have been just a little while later, though."

Jessan stretched his arms and yawned. "This has been a long day, Gentlesir LeSoit—I suppose we should provide you with some means of contacting your presumably former superiors, so that no one will suspect you failed in your mission?"

"While you listen in on the conversation, just in case?"

"Exactly," said Jessan. "And a three-second delay in the transmission. No offense intended."

LeSoit didn't seem insulted by the idea. "None taken. And you're probably right about checking in; D'Caer must be frothing at the mouth by now." He smiled. "But I don't think I've failed. Not a bit."

General Ochemet sat in his office back at Prime, nursing his third cup of strong cha'a since seeing Errec Ransome off to the Retreat. Someone else was flying the aircar this time, fortunately—the Guild Master's visit to HQ hadn't been kept a secret—and Ochemet was free to deal with the regular problems that Prime Base brought to his attention every morning, as well as with the other, overriding problem of Jos Metadi's absence.

The office door slid open and Captain Gremyl came in. The security chief looked as tired as Ochemet felt. But he carried a bundle of printout flimsies in one hand, and his expression was more cheerful than it had been since Commander Quetaya had turned up in the sub-basement.

"What do you have?" Ochemet asked.

It couldn't be Metadi, he knew that already, or Gremyl would be looking downright triumphant instead of . . . vindicated, Ochemet decided. Gremyl looked like a man whose guesses had started paying off. The security chief's answer confirmed Ochemet's suspicions.

"It was a bit of a long shot," Gremyl said. "I decided to take Ransome at his word and assume that Metadi was somewhere off-planet. I also decided to assume—for a while, anyhow—that he left from Prime Base, and not from South Polar or from civilian-side Prime or from some private shuttle pad that we don't know about."

"He might have done just that, you know," Ochemet pointed out. "Either on his own or not."

"We can probably rule out South Polar. I made discreet inquiries with our people down there as soon as we found out Metadi had gone missing. And the other two possibilities imply a whole bunch of stuff I don't want to tackle just now."

"We may still have to," Ochemet said.

"Maybe," said Gremyl, "but the odds just got a whole lot better that we won't."

He laid the printout flimsies on Ochemet's desk—names, columns and columns of names, all but a few of them marked through with a stylus. "We've got lists here of everyone who's on record as leaving Galcen from Prime Base in the past three days, and lists of everyone who arrived on-planet in the same time period. And here's where it gets interesting. Only six people can't be confirmed at one end *or* at the other."

Ochemet flipped through the lists, scanning the names

of people and ships. "I see what you mean. Six people who have back trails we can't check on because the ships they came from are in hyperspace and out of comms—"

"Right. And we can't get in touch with any of those six right now because the ships they're currently on are also in hyperspace and out of comms."

"Not too surprising," said Ochemet. "They're the Space Force. That's where they're supposed to be."

"Right," Gremyl again. "Not surprising. If something actually were surprising, I'd probably rule it out as a deliberate false trail anyhow. So where are we now?"

He tapped the top sheet of flimsy with his fingernail. "Notice that two of our unverifieds happen to be traveling on the same ship."

"Mmmh. Two different origins, though."

Gremyl pulled another, much-folded sheet of flimsy out of his tunic pocket. His expression this time, Ochemet decided, was definitely triumphant.

"Watch this," he said, unfolding the flimsy and spreading it out next to the others. "I happen to have in my office a list that's five years old of everyone in Space Force—a dead file in a comp that isn't tied up to anything else, just used for confidential storage. I found it one day by accident right after I took over in Security, and decided to keep it on hand for information's sake.

"You never know," he continued piously, "when something like that might come in useful. So I checked my little list against that other list, and I didn't find any entries for either Warrant Officer Gamelan Bandur or Clerk/Comptech First Class Ennys Pardu—and with those ranks, they have to have been in the service five years ago."

Ochemet looked at the second sheet of flimsy with its few lines of print, the blunt record of a comp search that had found matches for only four names out of six. "Fakes."

"Fakes," confirmed Gremyl. "One male, one female."

Ochemet shook his head in protest. "But the commander is dead, remember? We know where she is."

"Maybe," said Gremyl. "Oh, I don't mean that she isn't dead—but think about what Master Ransome said about the Magelords. I understand that the Mages were real big on using genetic replicants for intelligence work."

Ochemet said, "That was in the old days. We destroyed all their biolabs at the end of war, along with everything else."

"You mean we hope we destroyed all of them," Gremyl said. "But I'm willing to bet a few workers and midlevel technicians slipped past us. And that's enough to start a nice little black market in illegal replicants on some planet where Republic law doesn't run. As for the customers— who knows?"

Ochemet chewed on that thought for a while. "Right," he said finally. "Let's assume that it really is Metadi on board RSF *Selsyn-bilai*, Metadi and somebody else who's posing as Commander Quetaya posing as CC First Ennys Pardu. The *Selsyn* is already in hyper, so there's no way we can call them back or catch them from here. What do you recommend?"

"We can't catch them," Gremyl said, "but we know where they're going. I recommend sending a fast ship full of combat-ready troopers to Infabede from the Ontimi sector, with orders to intercept the *Selsyn* as soon as she drops out of hyperspace."

"Not particularly subtle," commented Ochemet, "but it'll do. I suppose you already have a ship in mind?"

"As it happens," said Gremyl, "yes."

Ochemet looked at the lists of printed names for a few moments longer, and then nodded. "Very well, Captain— make the signal."

## II. The Net: RSF *Karipavo;* RSF *Ebannha*

"**C**OMMODORE. COMMODORE, wake up."

Gil felt a hand on his shoulder, shaking him out of a comfortable sleep. He turned over and opened his eyes to the dim red light of his cabin's off-shift illumination.

"I'm awake," he said, swinging his legs over the side of the bunk. "What is it?"

His aide, Lieutenant Jhunnei, was standing in front of him, holding a mug of steaming cha'a. She pressed the mug into his hand before speaking.

"We've picked up a contact," she said. "Quadrant N-seven-outer, moderate sublight speed. Appears to be artificial. Not responding to hails."

Gil cradled the mug in his hands, breathing in the warm vapor that rose off the surface of the liquid. He knew from his own experience as aide to General Metadi that waking the commodore wasn't something to be undertaken lightly;

there had to be more to the contact than Jhunnei's demeanor let on.

"Where's she coming from?" he asked.

"Straight out of the Mageworlds."

"Ah," said Gil. That explained a lot of things, including why Jhunnei had brought the news herself. "Thanks, I'll be in CIC directly."

"Yes, sir." Jhunnei turned and departed, the door seal sighing gently shut behind her.

Gil took a sip of the cha'a—it had the unmistakable flavor of something that had been brewing in a hotpot for entirely too long—then put the mug down while he pulled on a set of undress coveralls with the stars of his rank embroidered on the collar. He added a pair of the soft boots that went with the coveralls, and a knit cap. The Space Force had long since discovered that crews were more alert, and electronic systems more efficient, when the air was on the chilly side, so the big ships were always about forty degrees below blood temperature.

Gil picked up his mug of cha'a, took another swallow, and headed for the door. Just as he reached it, the General Quarters alarm sounded. Mug in hand, Gil picked up speed in the direction of the Combat Information Center. He'd drink the rest of his cha'a when he got there.

In CIC, the main battle tank displayed a holographic representation of the situation in progress. A dot of red light shone in the center of the tank, surrounded by three smaller blue dots: single-seat fighters in open formation, none of them fouling the others' ranges, and all of them, he was sure, locked on target and ready to fire.

Gil found the 'Pavo's executive officer standing midway between the tank and the comm board. "What do you have, Erne?"

"We've got a ship, all right," the XO told him. "Constant course and speed. No delta-vee. She's not radiating anything—stone cold with all systems shut off by the looks of it. The CO of RSF *Ebannha*, Captain Inifrey, is the on-scene commander."

Gil nodded in the general direction of the blue dots. "Those his people out there?"

"That's right."

"You have an approximate origin?"

"We've been working on it," said the XO. He gestured, and the tactical action officer came over to join the group. "I'll let Patel fill you in."

"Right," said Gil. He turned to the TAO. "Tell me what you know."

"Working back from where she is right now," said the TAO, "and assuming constant course and speed, the vessel's point of origin was definitely in the heart of the Magezone, some while before the war really got started."

Before Gil could answer, one of the comms techs looked up from the board. "*Ebannha* signals he's detailed a boarding and salvage party," the tech said.

Gil nodded. "Roger, keep me informed."

The captain of RSF *Karipavo* strode over, his own cha'a cup in hand. "Update?" he inquired of the XO.

"We're not really sure," the XO responded. "All we have right now is a spaceship not responding to signals."

"What's your situation, Captain?" Gil asked.

"We went to GQ as soon as I got word there was a stranger," the '*Pavo*'s captain replied. "We're manned up and ready. At the best it gives us a good chance for a drill, and at worst—" A fourth blue dot winked into existence inside the main tank as the holo updated in realtime. "Looks like *Ebannha*'s boarding party just got there," *Karipavo*'s captain said, interrupting himself.

"Boarding party is on station," the comm tech said. "Shall I put their transmission on audio?"

"Yes," Gil said. "I'd like to hear this."

The tech pressed a button, and the voice of the boarding

party's talker came over the speakers in CIC, the words slurred by the slight fuzziness of a decrypted transmission.

". . . and commencing scan at this time. Standard spiral, aft to fore."

"Stand by ready two," replied another voice on the same circuit—*Ebannha*, talking to the boarding party. "Copy."

The fourth blue dot in the tank began to circle the unknown ship, moving forward, while the three single-seat fighters maintained their watchful positions.

"Are you getting the pictures?" the first voice said.

"That's a roger."

"Do they match anything in the library? I don't recognize this class."

"Searching, wait, out," the second voice replied. The transmission broke off, then returned. "Tentative analysis," it said, "first approximation only. Vessel matches known exterior configuration of Mage Deathwing raider."

"Roger, understand possible Mage Deathwing."

"Compare structure, identification ninety percent." The second speaker's tone shifted abruptly. "Watch yourself out there. Those guys were *mean*."

"Roger, watching my ass," the boarding party's talker said. "Spiral scan complete. Unless otherwise directed, I intend to dock with unknown."

"Classify unknown hostile," *Ebannha* responded. "Positive ID Mage Deathwing."

Gil looked about for Lieutenant Jhunnei. He hadn't noticed his aide's presence when he entered the CIC—like all good aides, she had a talent for blending into the background—but he wasn't surprised now to find her waiting nearby.

"That's your signal, Lieutenant," Gil said. "Transmit to CO Republic Space Forces, flash precedence, Commodore's Situation Report, contact made with Mage Deathwing raider. Enemy intentions unknown. Amplifying info to follow."

Jhunnei was over at the comm board almost before he'd finished speaking. Gil turned back to the watch officer and the *'Pavo*'s captain.

"There," he said. "That should definitely wake them up back on Galcen. And if they don't have an amplifying report from us within about fifteen minutes, half the civilized galaxy should be underway for our location."

"How much harm can one ship do?" the watch officer asked.

"These are Mages we're talking about," said the *'Pavo*'s captain. "Who knows what they might be capable of?"

"That's right," Gil said. "No one's ever been aboard a Deathwing. Not until today."

Ensign Tammas Cantrel had no illusions about why he'd been picked to command *Ebannha*'s boarding party. He'd had plenty of experience at boarding merchant ships for inspection before they crossed the Net—and if things went horribly wrong, the loss of a single ensign wasn't going to hurt anybody very much.

He maneuvered his ship, a *Pari*-class short range surveyor-scout, over the forward end of the hostile target until he could match the other vessel's course and speed. *"Hostile target" doesn't half cover it,* he thought. *I'm about to become the first person on this side of the Net to see the inside of a Deathwing raider and—maybe—live to tell the tale.*

*I think I could do without the honor.*

Cantrel glanced over at his mate in the copilot's seat, Chief Hull Mechanic Wyngar Yance. "Did you catch any anomalies on visual, Chief?"

"I got a couple," Yance replied. "If we're assuming lateral symmetry on these things, that is."

"Might as well assume it," Cantrel said. "Gross symmetry anyhow—it certainly looks like they've got it. I picked up a depression on the centerline aft that looks like a docking port of some kind. What about you?"

"I'm seeing a shadow under the ventral ridge that isn't matched on the other side."

"Right," said Cantrel. "So what do you think we've got?"

"Best bet's an empty dock for some kind of small craft, and an open airlock."

"Meaning the crew might not be at home?"

"I sure hope they aren't home," said Yance fervently. "I'm too close to retirement to get into a gunfight on board someone else's ship."

*You and me both,* thought Cantrel. *A whole career away from retirement is too close for something like that, if you ask me.*

But the Space Force hadn't asked him, so he squared his shoulders. "We're ready," he said to Communications Technician Elligret Saben. "It's time to tell 'em we're going in. I'm going to try for the airlock, see if that's what it really is, and come in the front."

Saben looked up from the comm console, where she'd been trying broad-frequency hailing. "Still no reply from the target," she said. "Regular starpilot's grave over there—no emanations of any kind."

" 'Starpilot's grave'?"

"What the merchant spacers call a drifting wreck," she said. "Most of those guys, they don't want to leave their ships until they have to be carried out feet-first—and some of them don't ever get to leave, period. Me, I plan to spend my pension money dirtside somewhere, thank you."

"So we've got a target that looks like it's been dead for a while," Cantrel said. "Or might it be in some kind of deliberate shutdown for silent running?"

Saben shrugged. "Could go either way, sir."

*Just what we needed,* Cantrel thought. *I love playing the stick that springs the trap, I really love it.*

"Times like this," he said aloud, "I wish we had an Adept."

He turned to the boarding craft's engineer. "Falkith, take us to the anomaly I've identified on your screen. Chief, come with me and suit up. We're going for a walk."

"I wish you didn't sound so enthusiastic about the idea," the chief complained as he unstrapped and walked over to the pressure-suit locker. "I can think of lots better ways to make it into the history books."

"So can I, Chief. But they didn't ask me for suggestions."

Under Falkith's direction the boarding craft changed vector slightly, and ended up floating just above the dark patch that the chief had thought might be an open airlock. Waiting in pressure suits inside their own airlock compartment, Yance and Cantrel watched the light over the outer door cycle from red to green. Finally the lock clicked open.

Cantrel went out of the airlock first, a lifeline tied around his waist, jumping across to the Magebuilt craft. Once his magnetic boots had made safe contact, he made the line fast to a grabpoint on the raider's surface and signaled the chief.

"Come on over. Got your recorder working?"

Yance's voice came to him over the comm link in the helmet of his p-suit. "Roger, it's up. Let's do it."

Yance joined Cantrel on the skin of the raider. Then—with the chief walking a little behind the ensign to make a visual recording of their transit, and with the data being relayed to *Ebannha* in realtime via the boarding craft—they walked along the Magebuilt vessel's surface to the opening that the chief had identified as a possible airlock.

Yance aimed his recorder at the airlock. "There it is."

"Small opening," Cantrel said, for the benefit of the

watchers back on *Ebannha* and the boarding craft, who wouldn't have a clear idea of the scale. "Probably personnel only."

He drew a deep breath. "Well, time to go in. I wouldn't like to get caught in one of those, though. And I seriously hate the idea of coming through a lock with unfriendlies on the other side."

"You and me both," said Yance. Abruptly the chief pointed at something. "Hey, look at that."

"I'm looking," said Cantrel. He saw at once what Yance was talking about: the outer door to the airlock was not just standing open, it had been wedged. "What do you make of it?"

"Damned if I know, sir."

"Me neither. Just make sure you get lots of pictures." Cantrel directed his light into the lock chamber, playing the beam all about. "What the—take a look at this, Chief. Someone's wedged the inside door open, too."

"I'm recording, sir. But why the hell would anybody want to do a dumb thing like that?" Yance sounded outraged as well as puzzled; for any spacer, deliberately opening the ship to vacuum ranked as a deadly sin.

"I wouldn't know, Chief. But this job is getting stranger by the minute."

Yance brought the recorder in close to pick up the details of the inner door. "I didn't like it when this was just a Mage ship," he said. "And I definitely don't like it now."

*You can say that again,* thought Cantrel. *This whole setup stinks so bad that you can smell it in vacuum.*

"We're not getting paid to like it," he told the chief. He unhooked his energy lance from its carrying clips on the back of his p-suit and moved on into the open lock. The handlamp on his suit sent a beam of white light ahead of him into the blackness inside. "We're getting paid to board it. Let's go."

\* \* \*

Back on RSF *Karipavo*, Gil divided his attention between the situation display in the battle tank and the flatvid screen showing realtime pictures from the boarding party. The open airlock of the Magebuilt ship gaped like a dark mouth; to the cold eye of the recorder, Ensign Cantrel was a small and uncertain figure standing on its outer lip.

"Poor kid," said Lieutenant Jhunnei quietly at Gil's elbow. "It's a hell of a thing to know that you're expendable."

Gild nodded. "No argument on that, Lieutenant. But we're in the same position, after all."

"Who are, sir?"

"All of us in the Mageworlds screening force," Gil said. On the flatscreen, the ensign unclipped his energy lance and stepped over the rim of the airlock into the dark. "Because if anything bad manages to make it across from the other side of the Net, it's our job to buy the civilized galaxy as much time as we can."

"Understood," said Jhunnei. "In the interest of staving off the day, shall I have the comms tech start compressing the data for a direct hyperspace feed to Galcen?"

"Why not?" Gil said. "They must have gotten the first report by now, and it's going to have them all hugging the comm links and waiting for more, from the Commanding General down to the tech on duty. No point in disappointing them."

The interior of the Magebuilt raider was strangely familiar—the result, Cantrel supposed, of expedients forced upon its builders by the physical realities of starflight—but at the same time subtly alien. He could recognize individual details and pieces of equipment when the beam from his handlamp fell on them, things like airtight hatches, accessways, or emergency gear for dealing with the spacer's twin demons of fire and decompression, but their location was never quite what he expected it to be.

The chief apparently felt the difference, too. "Screwy setup in here."

"Blame it on the Magelords. Which way do you figure is the bridge?"

The chief glanced at his inertial tracker. He pointed. "Forward section of the ship is that direction. If the Mageworlders were sensible about their shipbuilding, the bridge should be up there somewhere."

"That's a pretty big 'if,' " said Cantrel. "But I suppose it beats a random walk. We'll explore forward."

Slowly, with numerous false starts and jogs, they made their way through the maze of the ship. Some of the areas they passed through seemed to make no sense at all, such as the chamber containing nothing but a circle of white tile in the middle of the deck, but others had the same eerie mundanity as the passageway near the airlock. They passed through a ship's galley, hazardous with floating cutlery, and shone their handlamps into a compartment where sheets and blankets lay stretched inspection-taut across neatly made bunks, while odds and ends of personal gear—pillows, boots, a writing stylus and its datapad—hung weightless in the endless cold of space.

Finally, the chief indicated a closed door. "If the inertial tracker isn't lying, then the bridge must be in through there. Because if the bridge isn't in there, we've just run out of places."

Cantrel was examining the edges of the door. "More funny stuff," he said, gesturing at Yance to come over and make a visual record. "It looks like things got pretty desperate here for a while—we've got a small craft missing, and the crew had to open up both airlock doors at once to get something out through the hatch—but I still haven't seen anything that looks like battle damage."

"Mechanical failure?"

"Maybe," said Cantrel. "But what kind of mechanical failure forces an abandon-ship and then leaves everything behind intact? Maybe they had some kind of poison in the atmosphere, so they tried to vent to space—but that didn't work so they took off in that shuttle or whatever that they were carrying. Or maybe it was some Mage-type thing we won't ever figure out."

He abandoned speculation for the moment and went back to inspecting the door. "This thing's locked tight, as far as I can tell. Do you think we'd have trouble cutting through it?"

"Not unless ruining something that we may want later counts as trouble."

Cantrel sighed. "That's what I was afraid of. Okay, you push here and I'll pull. Maybe it'll move."

The two men tried to shift the door. The effort soon had Cantrel sweating inside his p-suit, but that was the only noticeable result. The door remained shut.

"Well," he said, "so much for that idea. Now I *really* wish we had an Adept along. One of those guys could probably open the door for us just by looking at it real hard."

"She's locked up, all right," said Yance. "But every ship I've ever been on had some kind of emergency access to the bridge, in case of power failure. Stands to reason this one would, too."

"If you can count on reason with a Magebuilt raider." Cantrel paused. "Where do you think it is?"

"It has to be inside one of these bulkheads if it's here at all," Yance said. "Let's see how much stuff we can take out without having to break anything."

The two worked silently for a while, removing slabs of bulkhead paneling. In the weightlessness of deep space, the scraps of metal and plastic floated around them.

"Hah," said Yance after several minutes had passed. "Look at this."

Cantrel moved closer and looked. The last panel to come off had revealed a slot in the interior bulkhead, at about chest height. "Probably for some kind of key," he said, "and if you try to fool with it, it'll explode and kill you."

"That would be a really dumb thing to have on a ship," said the chief. "The first spacer-recruit who comes along on bulkhead maintenance duty is going to turn you into space dust."

"These were Mageworlders," Cantrel said. "I remember reading about the reason why nobody ever boarded one of their warships and came back alive: the damned things tended to blow up. Folks like that would have killed off all their stupid recruits in basic training. Besides," he added, "I don't see anything here that looks like it would fit into the slot."

Yance still held the slab of paneling in one pressure-gloved hand. "I know where *I'd* put the emergency key," he said, and turned the slab over. Clipped to the inside surface was a flattened stick of plastic, slightly thinner and narrower than the slot in the interior bulkhead. "I'll bet this is it."

Cantrel reached out and pried the stick of plastic out of the clip. He brought it close to the lip of the slot in the interior bulkhead, and then paused. "We're still sending data in realtime back to *Ebannha*, right?"

"Right."

"Good." he said. "Then it won't be a total loss if we've guessed wrong and this is the self-destruct mechanism instead of the emergency bridge key. They can always make us part of the training vid on how not to open Magebuilt doors."

Holding his breath, he pushed the card into the slot and waited for the explosion. Nothing appeared to happen. After a moment he let his breath out again. "Oh, well, another bright idea shot all to pieces."

"I don't know about that," said Yance. "Let's try pushing the door one more time."

"Can't hurt, I suppose."

This time, when the two men applied pressure, the door began to slide back into the wall to their right. As it slid, it revealed clear armor-glass viewscreens up ahead, with the stars visible through them, and a couple of thickly padded pilot's couches bolted to the deck.

"It's the bridge, all right," said Cantrel. "Looks just like home."

"Only so many things you can do with a spaceship," Yance pointed out. The chief was already moving into the small compartment, making a visual record as he went. Suddenly he froze. "Sir," he said. "I think you'd better look at this."

Cantrel came forward and joined Yance where the chief stood looking at the pilots' seats. The couches weren't empty. The pilot and copilot of the Deathwing raider were still with her, strapped into their seats, their bodies preserved by the endless cold and vacuum of space since the day when somebody had stood beside them and cut their throats.

"That's nasty," said Cantrel, swallowing hard.

"Look what's nastier."

The chief pointed, sending a bright swash of illumination from his handlamp onto the raider's viewscreen. Someone had left a message there, scrawled on the armor-glass with some kind of dark, blurry marker. Cantrel stared at the writing for a long minute before he realized what the chief had been driving at: the angular, unfamiliar characters had been smeared across the viewscreen with a finger dipped in blood.

## III. Galcen: Prime Base
### Nammerin: Space Force Medical Station; Namport
### Ontimi Sector: Planetary Infantry Barracks, Kiin-Aloq
### Infabede Sector: RSF Fezrisond

In Command Control at Prime Base, the main battle tank showed RSF *Ebannha* as a bright blue triangle standing off at a safe distance from the red dot that signified the Deathwing raider. Much closer, *Ebannha*'s boarding craft and the trio of single-seat fighters made a cluster of blue dots around the Magebuilt ship. *Karipavo*, the relaying vessel, wasn't in the tank at all.

Brigadier General Ochemet watched the lights in the realtime display and waited for the "amplifying info" that Commodore Gil had promised. The first twinges of what felt like becoming a truly spectacular headache throbbed in his temples. It was bad enough to have Commander Quetaya dead and General Metadi missing—in the company of what Security Chief Gremyl, at least, thought was a replicant imposter; now they had to have trouble on the Mageworlds border as well.

Over at the comm console, a flatvid screen beeped and came to life. "More real-time data, sir," said the tech on duty. "Sound and pictures from *Ebannha*'s boarding party, relaying via *Karipavo*."

Ochemet moved closer to the flatvid. The pictures there were dark and grainy—partly the effect of data compression and expansion, partly the effect of coming from a small built-in camera on somebody's pressure suit—but they were clear enough for him to follow the progress of the boarders. When Ensign Cantrel and Chief Yance reached the locked door, Ochemet tensed. He'd been a junior officer in the Planetary Infantry during the mopping-up stages of the last war, and had witnessed firsthand the Magebuilt ships' practice of self-destructing rather than permit intruders.

"Orders used to be to blow those things up with stand-off weapons," he commented to the watch officer. "Deep space or on the ground, it didn't matter."

Unfortunately for the two from *Ebannha*—and, halfway across the civilized galaxy, for Ochemet's ever more insistent headache—current standing orders called for boarding and inspection of all vessels passing through the Net. Ochemet watched the flatscreen with ill-concealed anxiety as Cantrel and Yance began yanking sheets of paneling off the raider's bulkhead, and relaxed only slightly when the key that they found there did nothing more than release the slide mechanism for the bridge door.

The flatvid picture shifted to the interior of the bridge. Next to Ochemet, the watch officer bit back a startled oath as the seated figures of the Deathwing's pilot and copilot filled the screen. Even with the poor image reproduction, there was no mistaking exactly how the two Mageworlders had died.

"*That's nasty,*" said the flattened, off-key voice of Ensign Cantrel over the relays; and Yance's voice replied, "*Look what's nastier.*"

Again the picture shifted. This time the bad light and the relayed transmission failed to show clearly what had drawn the boarders' attention. A few seconds later, Cantrel's voice came over the link again: *"We're looking at writing on the main viewscreen. I don't know what the language is. But it looks like whoever killed these two left a message."*

An even fainter, more distorted voice came through— somebody back on the boarding craft, apparently: *"What makes you think that, sir?"*

And Cantrel's reply: *"Because he used their blood to write it with, that's why."*

Ochemet, listened, frowning. A Magebuilt ship emptied to vacuum and set on a course for the Republic side of the Net would be unusual enough; this latest discovery made the derelict into something that might require serious investigation.

"What do you think?" he asked the watch officer. "Mutiny? Somebody going space-happy after too long in hyper?"

The watch officer shrugged. "So he cuts their throats and writes 'No more fried sausages for lunch, ha-ha!' in blood on the viewscreen, then takes off in the ship's shuttle? It could happen, I suppose."

Ochemet sighed. "We can't get away with blowing this one in place," he decided with considerable regret. His life was complicated enough right now without adding an abandoned Deathwing raider to the list of his problems. "But I'm damned if I want to see that ship brought any closer to Galcen than it is right now, either. We'll send an investigating team out to the Net instead."

The comms tech spoke up again. "We've got a text-only message coming through from *Karipavo* now, sir, along with the feed from the boarding party."

"Put the message up on screen three," Ochemet said. He moved closer and read the paragraphs as they scrolled. They turned out to be Commodore Gil's recommendations for handling the abandoned raider—which, Ochemet was pleased to note, largely paralleled his own decision. Only the final paragraph was unexpected: *"Since we are dealing with a Magebuilt ship on the border of the Magezone, I strongly recommend that there be an Adept with the investigating party."*

"An Adept," Ochemet murmured, half to himself. "Where do we get an Adept?"

He could, he supposed, ask Master Ransome for the loan of one, but Ochemet was reluctant to put himself and the Service into the Guild Master's debt. *Bad enough we're having to deal with him over the other problem.*

But thinking about Commander Quetaya's death brought to mind the list Captain Gremyl had made up a few days earlier, of fully-trained Adepts holding Space Force commissions. As the security chief had predicted, there weren't many. But there'd been one, an ensign in the medical service before going to the Guild, who was still with the Space Force as a lieutenant-equivalent and stationed on not-too-distant Nammerin. She was also—according to a recent and highly classified entry in her personal file—the only member of the service to have actually seen and fought with a Magelord since the end of the War.

*Which makes her the closest thing to a current expert we have,* Ochemet thought. *She's already under orders for Galcen, so we can redirect her on arrival. It'll mean doing without a liaison officer to work with the Retreat on the Metadi/Quetaya situation, but I can do that job myself if I have to.*

*We need Mistress Hyfid out in the Net.*

With Ari gone, Llannat found Nammerin a dull place. From time to time she was aware of Owen's continuing presence as he went about whatever errands Master Ransome had given him—but one rebuff was enough, and she didn't try to make contact again. She carried out her usual duties with routine professionalism, watched reruns of "Spaceways Patrol" on the staff-lounge holoset, and listened, with all the patience she could muster, to Bors Keotkyra's unending line of cheerful talk.

"So how's Ari doing on the *Fezzy*?"

Llannat swallowed the last bite of her salad and set the empty plate down on the table beside the lumpy couch. In the holoset's picture tank, the final credits for the lunch-hour replay episode of "Spaceways" dissolved and re-formed themselves into a commercial for Nutli's Instant Super-Enriched *Ghil* ("warm, stimulating, and guaranteed nutritionally adequate!").

"He's probably doing all right," she said finally.

Bors looked curious. "I thought for sure you'd have heard from him by now."

"Me?"

"Hey," said Bors. "You two were always running around together while he was here. I'm surprised he hasn't kept in touch."

"He's old-fashioned in some ways," she said. "If he says he'll write a letter, he means ink and paper and an envelope and postage money for the bulk mail, not compressed-text or a voice chip. And bulk mail travels slower than glaciers."

As she spoke, she found that she could see the letter clearly in her mind: the stiff paper, the ink, and Ari's strong, broad hand wielding the pen, filling the page with graceful lines of Maraghite script. The image had the sharp edge of reality to it; she knew at once that the letter indeed had been—or perhaps would be—written. Then the mental picture winked out, replaced by a sudden, insistent conviction that she ought to be someplace else.

She'd experienced those feelings before, and had learned not to ignore them. "Sorry, Bors," she said before he could ask any more questions, and left the staff lounge at a near-run.

Outside in the Med Station compound, she let her feet

carry her where they thought best. Their destination turned out to be the communications dome, which housed the planetary and system links and the big, heavy hyperspace comms. The duty comms tech looked up, startled, as she came in.

"I just got a message for you," he said.

She nodded, not particularly surprised. "What kind of message?"

"Orders."

"Orders?" It was a possibility she hadn't even considered. "Why me? I'm not due to rotate out of here for another year."

The tech shrugged. "They don't look like rotation orders, if that means anything. Here, you want to carry them to the skipper? He'll need to sign for 'em anyway."

"Sure."

Llannat took the folder and opened it to scan the brief message on the single sheet of flimsy. There wasn't much to read—just her name, a string of accounting data, and a couple of sentences in Standard Galcenian. Taken together, they pulled her away from Nammerin and sent her, via the quickest available means, to Space Force Headquarters on Galcen for assignment to general duty.

She shook her head, confused. "Damned if I know what they think they're up to."

The CO of the Medical Station was equally nonplussed when she brought him the orders for signing. "It's an odd one, that's for sure. I'd have expected you to get detailed to the hospital or the clinic, not the general-assignment desk."

He scrawled his initials on the sheet of flimsy. "You'll have to run this through Disbursing and Admin before you can be certain, but if I read the accounting codes right, you aren't being authorized any leave en route, and the travel and proceed time is consistent with some extremely high-priority seating."

Pausing, he regarded her gravely for a moment. "It isn't any of my business, of course, but it looks like someone wants you on Galcen immediately if not sooner, and doesn't want to say why. If I didn't know better, I'd guess this had something to do with the time you . . . no, on second thought I won't even try to guess. I don't have need to know, or the clearances."

He pushed the folder back over to her. "Go start checking out of the station. RSF *Istrafel* departs the Nammerin nearspace training area tomorrow, en route direct to Galcen Prime, and you'll want to be on her."

Down in Accounting and Disbursing, where the clerk on duty transformed the string of accounting data into actual readable orders, the results came back as the CO had predicted.

The clerk looked impressed. "You must really rate," she told Llannat. "You're getting patched through as fast as they can get you in. According to these codes, you can bump full commanders if necessary to obtain a berth back to Galcen."

"Thanks," Llannat said. "I just wish I knew what was going on that was so important. The last time I left Nammerin in this much of a hurry, I was being kidnapped."

"At a guess, someone punched in the wrong number when they were writing these things up. It happens."

Nevertheless, orders were orders. Still puzzled, Llannat stood next morning by the Med Station gate, her orders in one hand, a small carrybag in the other, and a larger case holding the rest of her possessions by her feet. The short black staff with its silver tips hung from her waist.

The shuttle bus from Namport arrived on humming nullgravs, and the latest group of spacers needing groundside medical attention came off. Llannat threw her bags into the luggage compartment and climbed onto the bus. The morning was wet and cloudy, but not at the moment raining; she looked out at the low grey sky and the heavy green-and-brown landscape, and wondered if Master Ransome was behind this latest development.

*It doesn't feel like his work, though ... the general-assignment desk and the high-pri orders. That reads a lot more like the Space Force trying to be subtle about something.*

Halfway to Namport the rain started again, streaking the bus windows. By the time she reached the Space Force shuttle field, the rain had become a solid downpour—an appropriate good-bye to the planet, she decided, and one unlikely to foster a state of false nostalgia.

Llannat ignored the rain, since only newcomers tried to keep dry, and put her large bag onto the cargo handler for RSF *Istrafel*. She kept hold of the folder and the carrybag, and went into the main building to wait for a shuttle to orbit. By midmorning one was announced, and before the sun had made its meridian passage she was aboard *Istrafel* and heading for hyper.

Halfway across the Republic, on Kiin-Aloq in the Ontimi sector, Captain Natanel Tyche, SFPI, was also in receipt of a new set of orders. Unlike some of the orders Tyche had gotten in the course of his career, these proved upon inspection to be quite simple.

He was to take an entire company of planetary infantry, fully armed with a war loadout, and make contact with RSF *Selsyn-bilai*, currently in hyper and bound for the Infabede sector. Once aboard the *Selsyn*, he was to take custody—discreetly!—of Warrant Officer Gamelan Bandur and Clerk/Comptech First Class Ennys Pardu, then contact Space Force Headquarters on Galcen for further instructions.

Tyche wondered what Gamelan Bandur and Ennys Pardu had done. *Can't be anything obvious,* he thought. *Galcen wouldn't get involved in local stuff. Espionage, maybe—but why send a whole combat company just to make an arrest?*

He shook his head, realizing that he might not ever know the answer to his questions. In terms of clearance and access he would outrank even the commanding officer of the *Selsyn*. In practical terms, however, that rank meant nothing—not when the entire evolution was classified at such a rarefield level.

*That's what you get for deciding on the diplomatic/ military career path,* he told himself. *It's "go there" and "do that" and never hear the whole story on anything.*

He walked on down to the Infantry barracks to confer with the commander there. The commander was doing paperwork in his office when Tyche knocked on the open door and strolled in.

"Hello, Ehlin."

" 'Lo, Tyche." The Infantry commander regarded him warily. "What brings you here?"

The two men knew each other, but without being more than casual acquaintances. They saw one another in the officers' club from time to time, and they at least nominally served in the same outfit—Tyche wore the uniform of the Republic's Planetary Infantry when he wore a uniform at all. But since he was usually seen in mufti, and since he tended to be missing for weeks at a time and never talked in the club about anything more controversial than sports and gardening, the rumor on base was that he was in Active Measures.

"I've got an exercise coming up," Tyche said to Ehlin, "and I'm going to need a company of your best. Who's up?"

"Third of the Seventh is on deck."

"I'll take them. Can you add a heavy-weapons platoon, suitable for shipboard actions?"

Ehlin looked startled and a little curious. "Shipboard actions . . . what are you planning?"

"Sorry," Tyche said. "You know I can't tell you that."

"Just thought I'd ask," said Ehlin, without surprise. "I suppose you can't tell me where or for how long either?"

"That's right. This is going to be a live-fire exercise, though, so have 'em fully armed, armored, and charged."

"Right."

"Thanks." Tyche passed over a sheet of printout flimsy. "Here's a copy of my authorization, just so you can keep your files up to date."

They saluted, and Tyche left. The moment he was gone, the barracks commander punched his comm set. "Have Master Sergeant Onekke step into my office, please."

While Ehlin was waiting, he punched the order number from the authorization into his desk comp to check on its reality with central files. He wasn't surprised to see that the orders giving a reinforced company to Captain Natanel Tyche for an undetermined period were entirely genuine.

Ari Rosselin-Metadi had bought the writing paper and the antique pen while he was waiting on Mandeyn for RSF *Fezrisond* to make orbit. Given his sister's adventures in Embrig's port quarter, he'd stayed away from the bars and gaming houses along the Strip, and had gone decorously shopping for stationery instead. After all, he'd promised Llannat that he would keep in touch, and courtesy demanded something more private than a voice chip and less ephemeral than a sheet of printout flimsy.

He didn't have a chance to use the writing materials for some time. The *Fezrisond* came out of hyper in Mandeyn nearspace not long after he'd made the purchase, and he'd had to scramble to get back to the port in time to claim a seat on one of the shuttles to orbit. After that, he'd been busy reporting in and relieving the former head of the *Fezzy*'s medical department—who was planning, or so she said, to retire to the countryside and take up spider farming—and generally settling into his new position of responsibility.

*There were adjustments, of course,* he wrote to Llannat in the Maraghite script he'd learned during his fostering. *On both sides. And for a while I was getting up early and staying up late and having nightmares about filing systems and emergency response times in between. But things are calming down, finally, and I have a few minutes to myself once in a while.*

He looked up at the overhead in his quarters and wondered what he should write next. Privacy was always a consideration; bulk mail was harder to tamper with in some ways than voice chips or compressed-text, but easier in others. And while Maraghite script was enough to keep out casual eavesdroppers, it wouldn't deter anybody who was serious about learning what the oldest of the Commanding General's offspring had to say.

*The* Fezzy's *a good ship,* he wrote after some thought. *Not as relaxed a junior officers' wardroom here as we used to have back on Nammerin, though. It probably has something to do with RSF* Fezrisond *being Admiral Vallant's flagship. That might keep things from getting too casual.*

The chronometer-alarm in his desk comp beeped at him, and he put the letter aside unfinished. Time now to get into his dress uniform, instead of his working coverall, and report to the admiral's office for his long-delayed official welcome-aboard interview with the man in charge of the Infabede sector.

Fortunately for the fit and symmetry of Ari's uniform, the heavy blaster and its holster now reposed in the *Fezzy*'s weapons locker. On reporting aboard, he'd been told that the Form 8845 ("officer's personal weapons, permission to carry") in his permanent file was superseded by the admiral's standing order prohibiting officers from carrying sidearms.

Ari had been glad enough to hand over a weapon that tended to make him even more conspicuous than his size alone usually did. He'd followed the standing order without demurral, while reflecting with some inner amusement that it was a good thing his baby sister had never shown much enthusiasm for the Space Force. Beka carried a blaster on her hip and a dagger up her sleeve and her ship had guns, and she would probably start a small war rather than give up any one of them.

The interview with Admiral Vallant took place in the admiral's office, a locked room at the end of a maze of corridors. Ari, who hadn't yet succeeded in memorizing *Fezrisond*'s deck plan, found himself twice caught in dead ends before reaching his goal.

*Not good enough,* he thought. *Emergencies can happen absolutely anywhere. The head of the medical department needs to know where everything is* before *the trouble starts.*

Resolving to spend his free time after dinner in a closer study of the ship's internal layout, he palmed the security plate by the side of the closed door. A spy-eye on a flexible rod emerged from a recess above the door, and the synthesized voice of an annunciator intoned, "Please state your name, rank, and business."

"Ari Rosselin-Metadi, lieutenant commander, interview with the admiral," Ari told the annunciator.

He omitted the salute and the formal phrases that he would have used in speaking to Admiral Vallant directly. The spy-eye and the annunciator were nothing but screening devices, and not themselves his superiors in any way. If the annunciator had employed some version of Vallant's own speaking voice, the question would have become somewhat more complicated—but this one still used the bland, sexless tones that had come with it from the factory.

The door slid open. Ari stepped through, ducking as usual out of force of habit to avoid bumping his head. Ad-

miral Vallant—a small, dapper man with dark eyes, his
black hair tending to silver at the temples—sat waiting at
the desk inside. Ari drew himself up to his full height.

"Lieutenant Commander Ari Rosselin-Metadi, reporting
as ordered, sir."

"At ease," said the admiral. He gestured at the tiny office's other chair. "And please do sit down."

Ari sat. Vallant was definitely a short man; even sitting,
Ari was more than head and shoulders taller, and the admiral was plainly aware of the fact. The awareness made
Ari nervous; his size had gotten him into trouble before
with small men who took the mere fact of it as a threat
and decided to attack him first. He'd learned a number of
ways to deal with situations like that, but he didn't know
how well any of them would work if the other party involved was an admiral.

But Vallant was smiling at him cordially. "So, Rosselin-
Metadi—how do you like *Fezrisond* now that you've been
aboard her for a while?"

"She's a big ship," Ari said. "I'm still learning my way
around. But the medical department is first-rate, I can tell
you that much already."

Vallant looked at him sharply. "You came here from
Nammerin, didn't you?"

"Yes, sir."

"Well, this isn't a muddy dirtside station—this is a flagship, and things are different here. My people have nothing less than the best, and I expect nothing less than the
best from them in return. Do you understand what I'm
driving at, Rosselin-Metadi?"

"I think so, sir."

"Good." There was a long pause. When Vallant spoke
again, his voice was thoughtful. " 'Rosselin-Metadi' ...
not exactly a name one expects to find in the medical service."

This, too, was a reaction Ari had learned to anticipate a long time ago. "No, sir," he said.

"Why did you choose it, if I may be so bold as to ask?"

*Of course you can ask,* Ari commented silently. *You're an admiral. You can ask anything you please. And you might even get a true answer sometimes.*

Aloud he said, "I picked the medical service because I wanted more of a challenge."

" 'More of a challenge'?"

"Yes, sir. Breaking things is easy. Putting them back together again is harder."

"I see." Vallant regarded Ari for a moment as if he were going to ask a further question. In the end, however, he said nothing except, "You can go now, Rosselin-Metadi."

Ari went.

Back in his cabin, the letter to Llannat Hyfid remained unfinished. Without bothering to change out of his dress uniform, Ari took out the paper and the pen and added another paragraph.

*I've finally met Admiral Vallant,* he wrote. *He was welcoming enough, but I wish you could meet him too.*

*There,* Ari thought. *I hope that says enough without saying too much.*

# IV. Galcen: Prime Base
## Hyperspace Transit: *Warhammer*

LANNAT HYFID had passed through the massive spaceport complex at Galcen Prime only twice before in her life: once as a medical service ensign on her way to training at the Retreat; and three years later as an Adept bound for Nammerin. Both times she'd had to cross between the vaulted halls and concourses of the civilian side, with their links to the planetary transport grid, and the less elegant sprawl of Space Force's Prime Base. She hadn't cared for the civilian aspect of the port—no one who'd been brought up on the Selvauran world of Maraghai, where human settlements were sparse and few, was likely to find Prime's overcrowded grandeur congenial—and she was glad that this time she wouldn't have to make the switch.

*Here's hoping they've got room for me in the BOQ,* she thought as she collected her carrybag from RSF *Istrafel*'s shuttle and started across the tarmac toward the Space Force ground-to-orbit terminal. *If they're full up and I'm going to be stationed here for a while, I'll have to find an apartment somewhere in the city. It'll probably cost the world to rent, even if I do get a housing allowance, and I'll have to waste more time and money getting to and from base. Maybe there's an auxiliary Guildhouse in Prime somewhere, but staying there wouldn't be a good idea. Somebody might start wondering about the Prof's staff, and then I'd have to answer more questions than I really want to. . . .*

"Mistress Hyfid?"

The speaker was a clerk/comptech second class. He saluted—rather uncertainly, as if he wasn't sure where an Adept in an unmarked medical service uniform rated in the Space Force's grand scheme of things—and held out a plain brown envelope.

"Orders, ma'am."

Llannat stared at the envelope in confusion. *Orders? But I already* have *my orders.*

Just the same, she reflected, standing on the tarmac with her mouth open wasn't going to clear up the situation. She'd better say something before the CC/2 decided that her mind wasn't tracking. She set her carrybag down on the pavement and returned the salute.

"Thank you, Petty Officer," she said, and took the envelope.

The sheet of flimsy inside carried the same identifier as the orders that had brought her to Galcen. The subject line beneath the identifier read "ORDMOD"; the modification that followed changed her destination from General Assignment, Prime, to a berth on RSF *Naversey* (CS-1124), "for duty as assigned."

*Something funny is definitely going on,* she thought. *A CS is a fast courier . . . they put hotshot pilots on those, not med service Adepts.*

Still puzzled, she picked up her carrybag and headed into the shuttle terminal. Somewhere on one of the flat-displays along the terminal walls was a listing that would tell her in what part of Prime Base *Naversey* was docked; or—if the courier ship wasn't in port—which of the available ships could take her to wherever *Naversey* happened to be.

*Look on the bright side,* Llannat told herself. *You may not have to go apartment-hunting in downtown Prime after all.*

Beka Rosselin-Metadi was dreaming.

She knew she was dreaming; she'd been a free-spacer for almost ten Standard years, and captain of her own ship for nearly three, and she hadn't been home to Galcen since she was seventeen. So if she was standing in the reception room of her family's house in the Northern Uplands and wearing a gown of sea-foam green, this had to be a dream. Memory alone had never been so vivid, although she'd remembered this night often during the years since.

She wore her yellow hair in elaborate braids high on her head, and carried a long knife in a sheath up her sleeve. The weight of a blaster on her hip pulled at her belt, and the sea-green dress swirled around it with a sound like the breathing of a ship's ventilation system.

In the entryway behind her, the front door slid open and closed again. Perada Rosselin, Domina of Lost Entibor and Councilor for Entibor-in-Exile and the Colonies Beyond, came into the reception room. She had on a plain gown of black moiré spidersilk, and in her ice-blond hair she wore the unadorned tiara of twisted iron wire that was all the Magewar had left of the regalia of House Rosselin.

"You did very well tonight," the Domina said. "Your father and I are quite proud of you."

Beka-in-the-dream scowled. "My feet hurt." She kicked off the narrow green satin slippers. They hit the floor, first one and then the other, with a faint *slap-slap*. "I hate standing in receiving lines."

"Receiving lines are a necessary evil," said the Domina. "I know you didn't have the time to dance much, but you'll get plenty of chances from now on."

"Dancing." Beka-in-the-dream made the word sound like an obscenity. "With Dadda. With Ari. With Owen, unless he's gone off by himself to listen to the grass grow or something. With two or three of Dadda's friends from the Space Force and a couple of your friends from the Council and a handpicked junior officer from a good family who's so scared of Dadda that he can barely think."

The headlong rush of words left her out of breath. She inhaled with a gulp, and continued before the Domina could say anything. "With Councilor *Tarveet*. Mother, why did you have to invite him to my party?"

In her dream, she heard the Domina sigh, and saw the worry line between her mother's finely arched brows. She didn't remember noticing either one the first time, when all this had really happened.

"You may not like Tarveet—"

"I don't!"

"—nevertheless, he controls an important bloc of votes, and I can't afford to offend him."

"But you don't even like him!"

The Domina pressed her lips together. "I don't have to like him," she said after several seconds had passed. "I do have to work with him."

"Well, *I'm* not going to work with him." Beka-in-the-dream folded her arms across her chest and made a face. "He makes me feel like a slug crawled on me. When I was six he patted me on the head and said that I was 'sweet,' and now that I'm officially all grown up he pats me on the arm and tells me that I'm 'charming'—and I've killed better men than him without even stopping to look back."

Time and place shifted around her as she spoke, and she and her mother weren't in the house in the Uplands anymore. They were standing in a room, an upper room, she was sure of it, paneled in heavy dark wood. The acrid smell of blaster fire hung like smoke in the air around her, and the floor was awash in blood. Nor were they alone—an older, elegantly dressed gentleman was with them. Blood stained the white spidersilk of his shirt, and he carried a black staff in his hand.

"My lady," he said, nodding to Beka-in-the-dream. Then, to her mother, he bowed low and said, "I have failed you, Domina, and my fate is in your hands."

"Death," the Domina said, her voice level, and turned back to Beka. "There's always someone like Tarveet. You just have to put up with it if you want to get anything done."

"Who says I want to get anything done?" Beka-in-the-dream demanded. "I'm not on the Council, you are—so why should I have to be the one who dances with Tarveet?"

The older man had straightened from his bow. "You will walk with me for a while, my lady?" he asked Beka. Then, without pausing for answer, he turned to the Domina. "You will walk with me first—perhaps we will find an exit."

"Listen to me, Beka," said the Domina, seeming not to hear him. The frown line between her eyes had deepened, as though either the conversation or House Rosselin's iron tiara had given her a headache. She took off the tiara and put it on the scarred plastic tabletop in *Warhammer*'s common room—they were on the spaceship now, and the older man had vanished somehow in the transition. "Galactic politics is a serious business. People hold grudges for a long time over trivial offenses, and the friends and enemies you make now will be important to you later."

"I don't care," said Beka-in-the-dream. "And why should I care about politics, either?"

"You're the Domina-in-waiting," her mother said. "The

heir to Entibor. Who else is going to fill our Council seat once I decide to give up politics for good?"

For a moment, Beka was speechless, looking at the Domina. Perada's face had changed—younger, plainer, with sharper cheekbones and thinner lips, and a red optical-plastic eye patch covering one bright blue eye. Council robes were wrapped around her like a shroud, binding her too tightly to move or even breathe, and the iron tiara was burning the flesh of her skull. But the look on her face was still Perada's—careful, polished, and calm.

At last Beka found her voice again.

"Entibor is gone," she said, but her mother's expression never changed underneath the burning crown. Desperately, Beka pressed on. "It's dead. Slagged. Defoliated. The whole world is nothing but a great big planet-sized melted-glass paperweight. I've been in shops where they sell it in chunks for souvenirs. How does a place like that rate a seat on the Council when some of the outplanet colonies have been petitioning for admission ever since the Mage-war ended?"

The Domina had gone very pale, but her voice and her expression were patient as ever. "Entibor still speaks for its colonies. You know that. And there are upwards of five billion planet-born Entiborans resident on various worlds of the Republic. Don't you think they deserve representation by one of their own?"

Beka-in-the-dream picked up a cup of cha'a from the table and took a drink. It was hot, scalding her mouth and throat on the way down.

"Mother," she said. Her own voice wobbled on the verge of tears. "You make it sound like I *belong* to all those people, like a—like a hovercar or a desk comp or something."

"We do belong to them," said the Domina. "They need to feel that something is still left of what used to be, that the War didn't take it all. Things like that are important."

"Not to me they aren't!" Tears of frustration burned in her eyes. "I hate politics, I hate fancy parties, and I hate being nice to people I can't stand. And I'm not going to spend the rest of my life playing nursemaid to a bunch of people with their heads stuck in the past!"

She ran out of the common room before her mother could say anything, heading for the pilot's compartment— but it wasn't *Warhammer*'s bridge that was on the other side of the sliding vacuum-tight door, it was the back stairs of the house in the Uplands, leading to the rooftop terrace where the stars shone down, cold and far away and bright.

Her brother Owen stood at one end of the terrace, watching the night. Beka-in-the-dream hadn't seen him leave the party, but here he was, already home and changed out of his good clothes into the plain beige garments he wore every day as an apprentice Adept. The light from the high, distant moon bleached the color out of even those, leaving him a motionless study in different shades of grey.

She ran to him and grabbed him by the upper arms, shaking him out of whatever reverie held his attention.

"Get me out of here, Owen," she said. "Now."

He blinked, looking startled. "What?"

"Get me out of here," she repeated. "I've got to get away from Galcen before they shut me up inside a glass box with 'Domina of Entibor' written on the lid. I'm not Mother—I'll go crazy if I try to live like that."

She shook him again, harder. "I mean it, Owen. I have to get out."

Owen moved away from her grip without apparent effort. "How do you plan to live?" he asked. "Since you don't want to be the Domina someday . . . ."

She yanked open the drawstring of silver cord that held her evening bag closed, and pulled out the plastic data-wafer with her flatpic on it. "See this? It's a full-range commercial starpilot's license, and it's mine."

"You told Mother you were only going to take the sims for 'pleasure craft, limited.' "

"So I punched the wrong button when I got into the simulator. Anybody who's learned piloting from Dadda is good enough to hold down a berth on a regular ship, and you know it."

His face, in the pale light, told her nothing. She slipped the license back into her evening bag and went on.

"The only thing that's going to slow anybody down about hiring me is my name. I'm going to need your help if I want to get a fair chance ... like you helped me that time with the slug in Tarveet's salad."

Owen's mouth curved upward briefly. "I remember that one. And nobody noticed until he was halfway through eating it."

"Even way back then, you were good at fooling people. I'll bet you're a lot better at it now."

She heard a breath of laughter. "Go get your hair out of those fancy braids and put on your grubbiest coverall," he said. "We can take the aircar as soon as Mother goes to sleep."

He paused, and his face changed again, becoming older and more serious, with tired eyes that had seen more than they should. "The night before you die," he told her, "you'll dream about this, and remember."

Beka gasped and woke up, tangling her right arm in the sheet as she tried to reach for the knife she wore strapped always to her left forearm.

"Easy," murmured Nyls Jessan's voice in her ear. "It's all right, you're awake now."

The sounds of the ship's ventilation systems faded into the background, and Jessan's hands were warm against her skin as he straightened out the twisted sheet. When that was done, the Khesatan propped himself up on one elbow and lay watching her.

"You're still shaking," he said. "Was it that bad?"

"Pretty bad." Her voice was shaky, too. *Just be glad this is only you and Nyls, my girl. If Ignac' ever had any idea of how scared all this was making you, he'd dig in his heels and refuse to go along.*

Jessan's grey eyes were concerned. "Look, if you feel bad about how we decided to play it, just say so and we can think of another way."

"No," she said. "I'm fine about that. It was mostly my idea anyhow." She shivered in spite of herself, and pressed closer to Jessan's warmth. "This was about something else."

He put his free arm around her; as always, she felt her trembling ease off with the physical contact. "It really must have been bad," he said. "Another couple of seconds, and I'd have had to declare the sheet a casualty of war."

"Thanks for saving it." She leaned her forehead against his chest. He smelled of soap, with a faint salty overlay of clean perspiration. "I was dreaming about the night I left home. I don't know why."

"Point of no return, maybe?"

"Maybe." She didn't look up. "I never saw my mother again after that. Alive, that is, except for the holovids when she was making a speech or something."

"Ah."

"I didn't even make it home to Galcen for the funeral."

"Not your fault, surely." His arm tightened around her shoulders. "You've said before that you were in hyperspace and out of comms during that whole affair."

She shook her head, not meeting his eyes. "It wouldn't have made any difference if I'd been dirtside at Prime and caught the whole thing in the holoset at a spaceport bar. I still wouldn't have had the nerve to go home."

"I don't know ... I'd say you had enough nerve to do anything you wanted to."

"Not enough for that." She bit her lip for a moment; her

breath steadied, and she went on. "They'd have caught me then for sure, and I'd never have gotten back out."

" 'They'?"

"The ones who wanted to make me into the next Domina of Lost Entibor," she said. "If the old one's broken, you just slide in the replacement, like fixing a dead light panel. You don't bother asking the new one whether it wants to be a light panel at all."

Jessan leaned his face against the top of her head. His breath sighed gently through her hair. "I far prefer you as a disreputable starpilot."

"You're probably the only person in the galaxy who does."

"But I have *excellent* taste."

She laughed in spite of herself. "Oh, Nyls. What would I do without you?"

"Sleep alone, I hope. . . ." He paused. "But don't worry—I won't go away."

"Good," she said. She put her arms around him, feeling the smooth muscles of his back under her hands. "I need you here."

He bent his head further, pressing his lips against the hollow of her neck and shoulder. "Now?"

"Now."

Later, she lay with Jessan's head on her shoulder and contemplated the light panels over her bunk. Finally she sighed. "Time to take our places for the next act," she said. "We'll be coming out of hyperspace before very long."

Jessan rolled away from her. "True, alas."

She got out of bed and began dressing in Tarnekep Portree's dirtside rig. In the small mirror on the bulkhead, she could see Jessan moving about the cabin behind her, getting his own clothes together. A free-spacer's plain shirt and trousers took less time and attention than the ruffles and lace of a Mandeynan dandy; he finished well before she did, and sat on the edge of the bunk watching her.

She fastened the topaz stickpin into place in her cravat, and put on the red optical-plastic eye patch. "Will this do?"

Jessan stood and gave her an appraising scan. "As the basis for some artistic makeup work, it'll pass."

"Fine," she said. He was already moving toward the cabin door. She lifted a hand to stop him. "One more thing, Nyls."

He halted a step short of the doorway. "Yes?"

"The asteroid base. It used to be that just the Professor and I knew the coordinates, but the Professor is dead."

"Yes."

"And I may not be in any shape to pilot *Warhammer* on our way out of here."

This time he only nodded. His grey eyes were dark.

She went on. "The coordinates are in a locked file in the navicomp, keyed to my ID. And to yours, now. If you need to, you can take *Warhammer* home without me."

RSF *Naversey* (CS-1124) turned out to be already in port and on the ground, halfway across the Space Force side of the complex, with a departure time marked on the schedule display as "late and holding." After one glance at the blinking red letters, Llannat picked up her carrybag and ran for the transbase hoverbus. The rest of her luggage would have to fend for itself. She had a feeling close to certainty that the "hold" on *Naversey*'s departure was intimately related to her own unexpected change of orders.

Her luck was in. Or, as Master Ransome would have said, her actions were meshing with the patterns of the universe: the bus was pulling away from the shuttle terminal as she came running out, but the driver saw her and stopped for her to leap into the open door and swing aboard.

"Landing Field Ten West?" she asked breathlessly, still standing with one hand around the bus's overhead grab bar. "Or do I need to change buses somewhere?"

"This one'll get you as close as anything can," said the driver. "But you'll have to walk the last bit, or else catch a ride out on one of the cargo sleds."

"That's all right," Llannat said. "Thanks." She slid into a seat near the front of the bus and rested her carrybag on her lap. The hoverbus swayed gently on its nullgravs and moved on out into the ground traffic of Prime Base.

*This is getting odder by the minute,* she thought. *What use could the Space Force possibly have for a med service lieutenant-equivalent that's so important they need to rush the new orders out to me on the shuttle field, and— probably—put a departure hold on a courier ship?*

The answer, of course, was: none. If the Space Force needed an officer-grade medic in a tearing hurry, Prime Base and South Polar had plenty of those and to spare.

*Which means it's not a medic they're after. It's an Adept.*

Llannat thought about that idea for a while. It raised a number of possibilities, all unnerving.

*Galcen has all the Adepts anybody could need, up at the Retreat. But none of them are in the service.*

*And face it, you're not exactly the Guild's most impressive member, either.*

*But you* are *somebody who's faced down a Mage, and gone into the Void and come back out again alive, and survived Tarnekep Portree's raid on Darvell. . . .*

The bus sighed to a stop at the edge of Landing Field Ten West, a wide expanse of flat tarmac with the silhouettes of grounded spacecraft showing like foothills in the distance. She stood up, thanked the driver again, and left the vehicle. Carrybag in hand, she started hiking toward the ships.

A hoversled loaded with boxed cargo came humming up behind her before she had gone very far. She waved a hand, and the yard worker steering the hoversled slowed it to match her pace.

"Going to *Naversey*?" she called out.

"No—*Lysith*. *Naversey*'s on my way, though, if you're headed for her. Hop on up with the boxes."

"Thanks," said Llannat. She rode the rest of the way out to the row of spacecraft.

Most of the ships in this section of the port were couriers. They looked big as they rose up above the tarmac, but were minuscule in comparison with vessels like the huge starcruisers that never got closer to the ground than high orbit. The courier ships reminded her of smaller-scale versions of Beka Rosselin-Metadi's *Warhammer*, mostly engines and cargo space, with barely room aboard for the crew.

CS-1124—the number was displayed on its side in large block characters—had its ramp down and its hatch open. One of the crew members, probably the copilot, stood at the top of the ramp, leaning against the side of the open hatch and gazing out over the spaceport. When the cargo sled for *Lysith* swerved toward *Naversey*, the crew member straightened suddenly.

*They're waiting for somebody, all right.*

"Thanks for the ride," Llannat said to the yard worker. She hopped off the sled and walked, as quickly as possible without actually running, over to the foot of the ramp. Dropping her carrybag to the tarmac, she held out her orders to the copilot with in her left hand while saluting with her right. "Llannat Hyfid, reporting as ordered."

"Roger," the copilot said. He motioned her on up the ramp and punched the comm button beside the door. "Last one's aboard."

"Raise ramp," replied a scratchy voice over the link.

Llannat grabbed her carrybag, then hurried to join the copilot. "Follow me," he said as the ramp eased up and the exterior door slid shut behind them with a sigh of hydraulics. "We've got to strap in."

"What's going on?" Llannat asked him as they walked forward through the narrow passageway. The carrybag in her hand bumped against the bulkhead as she went along. Compared with RSF *Istrafel* the courier ship was insect-sized; it could have fit into one of the big cruiser's cargo bays with enough room left over for a scoutcar and a couple of hoverbikes.

"That's what everyone's wondering," the copilot replied. "Sealed orders—hurry up and wait—you know the drill. Here we are."

Courier ships in general lacked the space for refinements like private cabins. The main compartment on this one had been rigged to carry passengers; in place of cargo pallets, it held a half-dozen acceleration couches bolted to the deckplates. All the couches but one were occupied.

*Talk about your odd lots,* Llannat thought as she shut her carrybag into the compartment's baggage locker and strapped herself into the empty couch. *We look like somebody picked us out by poking a stylus blindfolded at the personnel rolls.*

Vainly, she tried to make sense of the strange assortment: a pair of warrant officers whose collections of medals, ribbons, and patches marked them out as both extremely senior and thoroughly experienced; a full captain in the medical service; and two reserve officers whose uniforms were new and unrumpled enough to have been purchased just this morning.

One of the reservists—the younger, stockier one, with staff tabs on his shoulders—looked angry. The older, thinner one, whose service ribbons indicated that he'd last

seen active duty during the pacification of the Mageworlds, merely looked resigned. *Seems like a couple of
people had their commissions reactivated,* Llannat thought.
*If the Space Force grabbed them like it did me, no wonder
they're not happy.*

The copilot went on forward, and Llannat settled back
against the cushions to wait for lift-off. After a minute or
two the deck tilted as the forward nullgravs lifted the
ship's nose skyward, and a few seconds later the heavy
force of launch pressed her back into the cushions.

*Naversey*'s pilot certainly wasn't doing this one the slow
and careful way, Llannat reflected. The acceleration was
heavier than any she'd experienced since Ari's sister Beka
had lifted from Nammerin with the Space Force hot on the
trail behind her, and it didn't let up until the discontinuity
that marked a jump to hyper.

Llannat unstrapped and sat up.

On the couch next to hers, the stocky reservist with the
staff tabs on his shoulders sat up as well. "What the
hell," he said, "is going on? I *demand* that someone tell
me."

His older counterpart smiled faintly. "Since we're traveling under sealed orders," he said, "I presume you'll have
to wait for enlightenment with the rest of us."

At that moment, a flatscreen on the forward bulkhead
flickered to life, with the words STAFF BRIEFING in white on
a shadowed blue background. They faded to the words TOP
SECRET, which faded in turn to a picture of a senior officer
sitting at a desk.

"Ladies and gentlemen," he began. "Two days ago, the
Mageworlds Fleet made an unusual discovery: a derelict
Magebuilt spacecraft. You have been assigned to board
and examine her. . . ."

The officer's picture dissolved to a long-range view of
a Deathwing raider. The superimposed aimpoints showed
that this particular visual had come from a fighter's gun

cameras. "When you go aboard the vessel," the voice continued, "you will already be in possession of every piece of information we have on Magebuilt ships. Your mission will be to find out what we *don't* know. . . ."

"The hell with that," said the younger staff officer. "For this they pulled me away from the office? I have important work to do."

# V. Mageworlds Zone: Eraasi Nearspace; Eraasi Port

**F**AR ABOVE the planet Eraasi—once the heart-world of the Magelords' interstellar hegemony, now stripped of its preeminent status—*Warhammer* popped out of hyper and into realspace.

Nyls Jessan, in the pilot's seat, glanced across at his current partner. The dark, wiry man whom Beka had called Ignac' LeSoit was a pro, all right; he didn't blush or flinch under Jessan's frankly suspicious gaze. The corners of LeSoit's mouth, however, were tight, and his eyes were clouded.

Jessan suppressed a sigh. "All right," he said aloud. "I don't like this a hell of a lot more than you do. But it was the captain's idea, and we handle it the way the captain says."

"She doesn't have any common sense, you know," LeSoit said. He might have been discussing the weather. "She never did."

"So everyone tells me," said Jessan. "In my opinion, common sense is a vastly overrated commodity."

LeSoit made a noise of disbelief. "Sounds like something *she* would say. Where the hell did she pick you up, anyhow?"

Jessan thought about taking offense—it was not, he considered, Ignaceu LeSoit's place to be asking questions like that—but he decided not to bother. The process of turning a living Tarnekep Portree into a realistic bloodstained corpse in a stasis box had been an unpleasant experience all around.

"She needed a copilot," he said. "And the Space Force didn't want me anymore . . . there were a few insignificant legal problems, nothing to concern a gentleman in your profession . . . so here I am."

"So there you are," LeSoit agreed. He watched the starfield for a moment, and then said, "Your captain isn't a person it pays to take lightly. Someone could get hurt."

"Dear me. Is that a caution against trifling with the gentlelady's affections?"

"You could take it that way."

"How interesting," said Jessan. "Allow me, then, to reassure you. The small matter of lethal weaponry aside, I am not, in fact, dangerous to know."

"That's good," LeSoit said. He smiled under his thin mustache. "Because if you'd come up with the wrong answer there, I was going to kill you."

There was silence for a moment in the *'Hammer'*s cockpit. Then Jessan gave a short laugh. "If Captain Rosselin-Metadi could hear this conversation, she'd probably want to strangle us both . . . so I won't bother saying that if you make one false move down there on Eraasi, I'll shoot you myself and save the captain some trouble." ▪

"Right," said LeSoit. The hired gun remained tense; but this time his smile was almost genuine. "It's always a good idea to get things like that straightened out in advance. I really don't like surprises."

Beka Rosselin-Metadi was Tarnekep Portree was a bloodstained corpse in a clear glass box with DOMINA OF ENTIBOR written on the lid. She was awake she was asleep she was alive was not alive was dreaming. . . .

*Ebenra D'Caer.*

*. . . the night before you die, you'll dream about this and remember.*

*Ebenra D'Caer.*

*. . . dream, and remember.*

*Ebenra D'Caer.*

She dreamed, and remembered:

Ovredis, and the elegant rooms and marble staircases of a banker's country estate. Again she wore a dress of seafoam green, and the knife this time was strapped to her thigh, out of sight under the frothy skirt. Mistress Hyfid, small and dark, kept watch at one elbow, and the Professor maintained a grave and avuncular presence at the other. The three of them didn't look like hunters, but they were.

*And Ebenra D'Caer was prey. . . .*

She was no longer Beka Rosselin-Metadi, or even the one-eyed starpilot Tarnekep Portree. She was the Princess Berran of Sapne, young and sheltered and impressionable. She didn't know any better than to go alone to a private chamber with Gentlesir Ebenra D'Caer of the Rolny D'Caers.

The delicate antique door swung shut behind them on its filigreed hinges, and Ebenra D'Caer lost no time. His voice continued spinning out the line of practiced compliments that had drawn the Princess of Sapne away from the crowded reception rooms, while the fingers of one hand began teasing her bodice down over the curve of her breast.

Beka looked past his bent, distracted head and met

Jessan's eyes. The Khesatan stepped forward out of concealment and struck down D'Caer with a single well-directed blow.

*And we had him then, oh yes, we had him. . . .*

*Ebenra D'Caer.*

*. . . dream, and remember.*

She remembered:

The docking bay of the asteroid base, and a phantom Ovredis of light and illusion, built up from the Professor's holodisplays and Mistress Hyfid's beglamourment of Ebenra D'Caer's drugged and receptive mind. She was once again the Princess of Sapne in a sea-green gown, with the weight of a tiara in her braided hair, but the Professor had made her leave the long double-edged knife behind.

Ebenra D'Caer took her by the arm and stepped close. She saw the tiny blaster in his other hand.

"Summon your vehicle," he said; and, in a low voice, "No tricks, Your Highness, or I will hurt you. Badly."

The Professor's illusions shifted, and a hovercar seemed to purr toward them. If she looked closely, she could see that the vehicle was only a mock-up, a shell about which the Professor and Mistress Hyfid could weave their expert illusions—but D'Caer's eyes were wide and dark from the drugs Jessan had given him, and fogged by the Adept's influence upon his mind.

*We had him then; he was ours to wring dry and dispose of any way we wanted to. . . .*

She was the Princess of Sapne, and she was afraid. She let D'Caer guide her to the hovercar and slide after her into the passenger compartment. A touch of his hand on the control panel, and the privacy screen between passengers and chauffeur darkened into place. He was smiling.

"Shall we resume where we left off, my dear?"

She felt his hand grasping at her breast, kneading it, and then he was pulling at the neckline of her gown, dragging the sea green fabric away from her flesh. His mouth was on her nipple, sucking hard enough to leave bruises on the bare skin, and his other hand was reaching up below her skirt.

*But it was worth it. Because we had him, and he didn't know it. And I could have killed him afterward, any time I wanted to. . . .*

*Ebenra D'Caer.*

*Dream, and remember. . . .*

She remembered:

The deep corridors of the asteroid base, where the Professor's robotic servants had turned into jailers for the captive D'Caer. She was no longer the Princess of Sapne, nor was she Tarnekep Portree; she was Beka Rosselin-Metadi, fresh out of a healing pod in a hospital on Gyffer, with the newly regenerated flesh of her right side making her wince whenever she moved too fast.

She had Nyls Jessan with her when she went down to the maximum-security cell. Her legs were still wobbly; when nobody else was watching she let the tall Khesatan take her arm and support part of her weight. She'd paid in blood for the success of the raid on Darvell—and not a little of that blood had been her own.

*We did it, though. We blew the top off the Citadel and pulled out Nivome the Rolny and carried him away in the 'Hammer like so much cargo. A quick stop back at the base to pick up Ebenra D'Caer, and then we could take our matched pair of assassins home to Dadda. . . .*

She checked the status readouts on the flat-display by the cell door. "All secure, no change, subject docile."

"Better bring up the force field just the same," Jessan said. "You never can tell."

She didn't have the energy to argue. A quick touch on the security panel, and the force field shimmered into place. Beside her, Jessan drew his blaster and held it ready. She touched the panel again and the door slid open.

The cell was empty.

It was Magework; she knew it without needing to look further. Ebenra D'Caer had been working for the Mage-lords all along, and his masters had come to fetch him out of his asteroid prison while the Professor wasn't there to guard it.

*I should have shot him when I had the chance. Now it's all to do over. I have a debt to collect from Gentlesir Ebenra D'Caer.*

*Dream, and remember:*
*Ebenra D'Caer.*

*Warhammer* came down from Eraasi orbit to the space-port in the late afternoon, local time. A yellow sun shone on the folded hills beyond the port, long rays slanting across through broken clouds with no hint of rain in them. The air was clear and cool, and full of a golden light.

With a rumble of displaced air, the *Libra*-class freighter broke through the high wisps of cloud, airfoil body provid-ing lift to assist the engines as the freighter decelerated and turned to the strip heading from orbit. Finally the *'Hammer* settled on her nullgravs into the landing block on the hardstand assigned by Eraasi Inspace Control.

Through the cockpit viewscreen, Jessan saw the distant figures of two men standing at the edge of the port field beside a wheeled cargo skipsled.

"Ours?" he asked LeSoit.

"Can't imagine who else they'd be for. Port's dead empty."

Jessan unstrapped his safety webbing and stood up. "I'll go lower the ramp and get ready to open the main cargo hatch. You'd better come along to do the talking."

"And to stay where you can keep an eye on me?"

Jessan raised an eyebrow. "You weren't planning on let-ting me out of *your* sight, were you?"

"Now that you mention it, no."

By the time they got the *'Hammer*'s ramp all the way down, the skipsled and its passengers had almost reached the ship. "Go," murmured Jessan, and LeSoit stepped out onto the ramp.

Jessan himself stood out of sight inside the open airlock, one hand resting on his blaster. By now he was convinced—almost—that LeSoit was as much an ally as the gunman claimed, and as Beka believed. But almost was only that, and from here he could hit the Raise Ramp button and still have time to shoot LeSoit before the airlock closed. He didn't particularly think he'd have to, but it never hurt to be ready.

The sled drew near and braked. "Yo, Ignac'!" one of the riders called out in badly accented Galcenian. "You have it?"

Jessan saw LeSoit's shoulders tense slightly. "Yes."

"Right—we're here to collect."

"I'll open the cargo bay." LeSoit stepped back into the airlock, glancing at Jessan as he did so.

Jessan nodded. "You get down to Main Cargo," he said quietly, "and I'll push the buttons from up here."

A few minutes later, there was a loud *clunk* followed by a metallic groaning noise. Part of the *'Hammer*'s ventral section broke away from the shell of the vessel and lowered itself on hydraulics to the landing block.

Jessan watched in the bulkhead monitor as LeSoit rode the platform down. When the elevator reached the ground, the gunman waved the cargoskip toward him, guiding it by hand gestures up onto the platform. As soon as the skipsled stopped, Jessan pressed another button.

With a loud whine of electromechanical motors, a large box—a little longer than the height of a man—came down from the cargo bay in a bridle of wire rope. The box was finished in dull black plastic, and stood nearly waist-high when it settled onto the sled. LeSoit unfastened the shackles that held the ropes in place; Jessan pressed the button again; and the wires rose back up into the belly of the ship.

LeSoit joined the two Eraasians on the skipsled, and the vehicle pulled back off the elevator. In the concealment of the airlock, Jessan drew a deep breath. He'd taken all the precautions he could, but this next bit—leaving his sheltered niche and joining LeSoit and the others out in the open—was still a good place for a double-cross.

*It can't be helped,* he thought resignedly, and hit the buttons to raise the cargo elevator and to close up the ship after he left. The elevator began sighing its way back into place, and Jessan started down the ramp to the waiting skipsled. He climbed onto the sled with the others as the *'Hammer*'s ramp swung up to seal the ship behind him.

Once aboard the sled, he relaxed somewhat. LeSoit had greeted him with a casual nod, as if he were an expected presence, and neither of the two Eraasians appeared startled by the appearance of a second person from aboard the ship.

"You riding along with Ignac'?" one asked.

Jessan nodded. "My contract said payment on delivery. So I'm delivering."

The Eraasian laughed. "Right. Hang on—here we go."

The skipsled trundled noisily toward the gate. "Not much port traffic lately, from the looks of it," LeSoit commented to the driver.

"You called that right," the driver replied. "Been duller than watching paint dry around here."

They drove through the gate—the guard waved the skipsled past without stopping it—and pulled over to a loading dock where two more men waited with a wheeled cargo truck. From the neat tailoring of the duo's jackets and trousers, and their general unrumpled and unsmudged appearance, Jessan pegged them as the ones actually in charge of the reception party.

After some maneuvering, the driver of the skipsled got

it loaded into the back of the truck. LeSoit and the other cargo wrangler raised the rear gate into place. The cargo wrangler joined his partner in the truck's cab, while the other two men stayed in back with Jessan, LeSoit, and the sled.

With a grumbling roar and a cloud of chemical fumes, the truck lurched forward and bounced off down the road. Jessan braced himself against the black box—until he'd hit the Mageworlds, he reflected, he'd never really appreciated the smoothness of a nullgrav-assisted ride—and watched the pavement unreeling behind him.

The two neatly dressed Eraasians noticed his interest. "Ever been here before?" one asked.

Jessan suppressed the urge to panic. The question was clearly meant for a friendly inquiry. "No."

"You'll like it," the man said. "Not like some of these *garnach* places."

Jessan nodded—he didn't know what a *garnach* place might be, but didn't want to betray his unfamiliarity with the local slang by asking—and went back to watching the road. No telling when he might have to make it back to the ship on his own, and if he did he'd have to do so by landmarks. So far, everybody he'd met on Eraasi spoke Galcenian, but the signs and route markers were written in a language and script he'd never seen before.

Eraasi Spaceport, or at least the parts of it visible from the road, appeared better off than any Mageworlds city Jessan had yet seen. The architecture looked subtly alien, as if the standard dimensions for all the various structures and fittings differed fractionally but invariably from those on the other side of the Net, but the older buildings were well kept up, and there was even a noticeable amount of new construction.

By the time the truck pulled up at another loading dock on the far side of town, Jessan's legs ached from the vibration through the bed of the vehicle. He stretched and looked about. The truck was parked at the end of a long alley between two high buildings made of artificial stone—whatever the material actually was, its surface had the kind of studied ugliness only attained by deliberate effort. The air reeked of garbage and chemicals, and the narrow strip of sky visible above was beginning to redden with the coming of sunset.

The two cargo wranglers got out of the front of the truck and lowered the rear gate. With much lurching and bumping they backed the skipsled and its burden off the truck bed and onto the concrete loading platform. LeSoit tugged open the double doors leading into the building and the sled grumbled through, with Jessan and the others following close behind.

The loading dock opened onto an aboveground cargo bay full of exposed metal ductwork. Old-style incandescent glowbulbs, unshaded, gave the space an ugly yellow light. The driver guided the sled across the bay's raw concrete floor to an open metal lift-cage.

Working without nullgravs, it took several minutes of heaving and pushing to get the black box off the skipsled and onto the lift. They were all breathing harder by the time the Eraasian who disliked *garnach* places rattled down the cage door and pushed the button to take them upward. The lift rose slowly, creaking its protest against the weight, out of the basement and up through a concrete shaft, passing closed doorways onto a dozen floors—Jessan counted them—before groaning to a stop.

The wire cage door clanked open and the outer doors of the lift slid apart, revealing a long, spacious hallway paneled in rich blond wood. Soft lighting came down through what appeared at first glance to be skylights; a second look made it clear, to Jessan at least, that the apparent windows overhead were actually high-quality camouflaged light panels. A nullgrav pallet jack waited for them on the deep-pile carpet—looking, in its current surroundings, like an abstract sculpture by a particularly whimsical artist.

*Current Republic technology,* thought Jessan as LeSoit brought the jack into the lift and slipped it underneath the heavy black box. *And a lot of money, too. Our friend D'Caer isn't exactly living in poverty-stricken exile.*

LeSoit touched the controls on the jack. The box rose upward until it floated a handspan or so above the floor of the lift. With the nullgrav unit taking the weight, the gunman was able to push the box one-handed down the hallway to the pair of double doors at the end. Jessan, still wary, stuck close beside him, while the four Eraasians walked alongside the box, two on the right side and two on the left.

"You know where we are?" Jessan asked LeSoit. *Might as well ask questions while I can. The locals all think I'm from off-planet anyway.*

"I ought to; I work here," LeSoit replied. "Boss man's office is up ahead."

They went through the double doors into an executive suite. LeSoit guided the box past a bank of lifts and through a door into an elegant pastel room holding only a well-groomed young man, a pedestal-mount chair, and a freestanding comp unit.

The young man looked up as they arrived. "Any trouble?" he asked in Galcenian—only faintly accented, this time.

LeSoit shook his head. "None."

"Very good," the young man said. "Please take off the cover. Gentlesir D'Caer wishes me to make a visual inspection of the subject before we proceed any further."

"No problem," said LeSoit. He nodded to Jessan. "Come on and give me a hand here."

Working together, Jessan and LeSoit unlatched the holdfasts on the box's black plastic shell.

"Okay now. One, two, three, lift."

They raised the shell and moved it aside, revealing a clear crystal stasis box mounted on a base of gleaming white metal. Inside the box lay a young man dressed in Mandeynan finery, one eye obscured by a bright red optical-plastic patch. His thin lips curled upward in a tight sneer.

D'Caer's receptionist nodded. "That's Tarnekep Portree, all right."

Portree's one visible eye was closed, and his ruffled shirtfront was covered with blood—bright red, kept from clotting by the stasis field. His arms were crossed on his chest, with the hands clenched into loose fists, and his left forearm half-obscured the blaster mark on his white spidersilk shirt.

The receptionist nodded again. "You've done well," he said to Jessan and LeSoit. "Gentlesir D'Caer will be pleased."

He touched a button on the side of his comp. "It's here."

The inner door opened, and Ebenra D'Caer emerged—still as plainly but expensively dressed as he'd been on Ovredis, and still as predatory and hungry about the eyes. Jessan worried for a moment that D'Caer might recognize him as Princess Berran's scapegrace brother, the Crown Prince Jamil of Sapne, but the man's attention was all for the bloodstained body lying in the stasis box.

LeSoit reached for the controls of the pallet jack. "Do you want this moved inside the office?"

"Don't bother," D'Caer said. "I'll take it."

If his solitary incarceration on the Professor's asteroid base had improved his manners any, it certainly wasn't showing. Before LeSoit or Jessan could protest, he took the controls and smoothly maneuvered the box into the inner office. The door swung shut behind him and closed with a gentle click.

The receptionist turned to Jessan. "Now, about your

payment. Do you wish cash, or will an Ophelan bank draft be acceptable?"

Jessan didn't answer him. "I don't hear anything from the office," he said to LeSoit.

LeSoit shrugged. "Inner door's soundproofed—you wouldn't anyway."

"Right," said Jessan. "So let's do it."

He spun on the balls of his feet and drove the heel of his hand into the nose of the man who stood beside him. The man crumbled. A blaster sounded with a low snarl; LeSoit had fired once, then twice more. Jessan didn't bother going for his blaster; he pulled the needler he kept up his sleeve and shot the receptionist with that instead.

When the firing stopped, he and LeSoit were the only two left standing. Jessan slid the needler back into concealment—a one-shot weapon, it wouldn't be any good again until he could recharge it—and pulled his blaster from its holster.

Over on the other side of the reception room, LeSoit was looking down at a body lying by his feet. It belonged to the cargo wrangler who had greeted the gunman by name at the spaceport field. The Eraasian had a chemical projectile weapon clutched in his hand. LeSoit stepped on the man's wrist and pulled the weapon away.

"Nasty things," he remarked, dropping it on the desk beside the slumped body of the receptionist. "Noisy, slow, hardly any shots in them, and they leave a really messy wound. I'd rather get burned any day."

The gunman began to make a circuit of the room, shooting each of the crumpled men in the head as he came to them. Jessan watched the slow, methodical killing for a moment without saying anything, then turned to the inner door.

Blaster at the ready, he grasped the lever and pulled. Nothing happened.

"Damn it all," he said. "The bastard's got it locked."

*E*BENRA *D'C*AER.
*Dream, and remember: Ebenra D'—*

Beka dropped back into realtime with a shudder, the transition as abrupt as the crossover to stasis had been.

Loud clicking noises sounded in her ears. Nyls and Ignac' unlatching the plastic cover, that would be.

Her eyes were open and staring at the dark; she closed the right eye, allowing the left to stay open underneath the one-way optical plastic of the eye patch. A moment later the cover came off the box completely, but all she could see through the eye patch's red haze was a stretch of ceiling.

"No, I'll take it."

The words came in a distorted metallic whisper, picked up by a comm link hidden in the base of the stasis box and relayed by the tiny speaker close to her left ear. Nevertheless, Beka recognized Ebenra D'Caer's voice.

*Soon now,* she thought. *We have some unfinished business, you and I.*

Her crossed arms hid more than the rough edges of Jessan's makeup job: the long, double-edged knife lay naked in her grip, its handle tight in her fist, its blade extending backward underneath her right forearm. When the moment came, she would be ready. Maybe there would even be time to ask D'Caer a few questions first. That would make Jessan happy, if they could get some word on what D'Caer was doing on this side of the Net, and why the Magelords had bothered to keep him alive and happy after they'd taken him out of his asteroid prison.

The seal around the top of the casket broke open with a sigh, and a sleeved arm reached into her field of vision to swing the crystal lid aside. She couldn't see Jessan anywhere, or LeSoit either. But in the next moment D'Caer himself loomed close above her, leaning over the box, his face dyed red by the plastic filter through which she watched him.

"So here you are," D'Caer said. "I'll bugger you dead, you bastard, for what you did on Pleyver and Darvell. But first—"

He bent closer. She held her breath, so that no rise and fall of her chest would betray her before it was time.

*Where the* hell *are Nyls and Ignac'? One of them should have dropped the son of a bitch by now. If something went wrong while I was out . . .*

"Let's see what you're hiding under that eye patch," D'Caer said, and reached to pry up the piece of crimson plastic.

*. . . then it's up to me.*

The hand came down on her face, darkening her view— Ebenra D'Caer was standing as close now as he ever would. She punched her dagger hand out and upward.

The blade hit something soft, and a gush of hot liquid spattered across her nose and mouth. She didn't stop moving. Throwing her arm over the side of the box, she pulled and rolled her way out, scrambling over the high side to land heavily on the floor.

She glanced down. Her right hand and the knife she held in it were both covered with blood. And her vision was clear—the eye patch was gone, ripped off by D'Caer's fingers.

*So D'Caer knows that Tarnekep Portree has two good eyes.* She laughed under her breath, a ragged, crazy sound. *One way or the other, it isn't going to matter very long.*

She hadn't stopped moving after she landed, first dropping the dagger and drawing her blaster from its holster, then rolling out from behind the cover of the stasis box on its pallet jack. Now she came to her feet in the smooth movement the Professor had taught her, finishing in a combat crouch with both hands supporting her blaster.

A single raking glance showed her that she was in a large office far above the streets of Eraasi Port. The walls were mostly window, with only the evening sky visible outside. The floor beneath her feet was covered in a lush black carpet, and in its center stood Ebenra D'Caer, both hands clutched to his throat, his breath coming in whistling gasps.

She realized that her half-blind stroke with the dagger had nicked D'Caer's windpipe. A wound like that would make it hard for him to answer questions.

*It doesn't matter. He hasn't got anything to say that I'd cry hot tears over missing.*

"Hello, Ebenra," she said, and relaxed her position to stand with the blaster held loosely in one hand. "Remember me? When I was Tarnekep Portree running cargo through the Net, you tried to have me killed."

D'Caer's eyes were wide and dark, but he hadn't given up fighting. She saw how he was edging toward the massive desk that filled most of the room behind him. If he could get to the comm panel, he might even manage to summon help in time to keep himself alive.

*Can't have that,* she thought, and shot him in the knee.

D'Caer collapsed sideways against the desk. His right hand left his neck to grasp his leg where the blaster beam had seared a pathway through muscle and bone alike. A thin spurt of blood leapt in an arc from his neck.

*Nicked an artery, too. Fast, but not fast enough.*

"When I was the Princess of Sapne, you tried to rape me."

She took a step closer and shot him in the arm. His hand fell from its grip on his leg. More blood followed it away.

Another two steps and she was standing over him, looking down as he bled on the deep carpet. He stared back at her, his eyes pain-dark but alive and hating. Incredibly, he was still trying to rise, scrabbling with his left hand for a fingerhold amid the welter of buttons and controls built into the top of the enormous desk.

"And when I was just plain Beka Rosselin-Metadi," she said, "you killed my mother."

She lifted her blaster, set its muzzle carefully against Ebenra D'Caer's forehead, and pressed the firing stud. Then she held the blaster steady while the skin and flesh of his face burned down to the skull beneath.

She was still standing there when Jessan and LeSoit finally broke through the door behind her.

"It's finished," she said without turning around. "Get whatever you want out of his private files, and let's go home."

*Warhammer* lifted from Eraasi without the formality of receiving departure clearance. The clearance had been requested in the proper form and denied without explanation; Eraasi Inspace Control squawked angrily when the denial was ignored, but no other retribution manifested itself on the way to orbit.

Beka leaned back in the pilot's seat. She was still wearing the clean shirt and trousers in which she had walked out of D'Caer's offices and onto the streets of Eraasi Port; the fresh clothing had come into the building with her, hidden inside the metal base of the stasis box.

"This whole thing," she said to Jessan, "has been so easy it's almost indecent."

"Speak for yourself," said Jessan with feeling. "You weren't stuck on the other side of that damned door, trying to break through a deadbolt lock and a solid metal core panel with only a pair of blasters."

She chuckled. "You needn't have worried. I would have opened the door for you if you'd knocked." Her hands moved over the *Hammer*'s controls, rotating the ship into position for a straight run to the jump point. "Still no trouble from the surface. I wonder if Eraasi Security will have a warrant out for me by the time we hit the Inner Net?"

"Hard to tell," said Jessan. "Depends on whether they're mad at us because of the mess we left in D'Caer's office, or mad at us because we forgot to pay somebody the right bribes. It doesn't matter, really. We can send your father a 'mission accomplished' signal as soon as we drop out of hyper."

"You've got a point there," Beka said. She clicked open the comm link to the common room. "Hey, Ignac'—it looks like we're going to get away clean on this one after all. Where do you want us to drop you off?"

"Back on Mandeyn," came the prompt reply over the link. "Or Suivi Point, if Mandeyn's too far out of your way. I think I've worn out my welcome on this side of the Net."

"Suivi it is," Beka said. She turned back to the control panel. "Navicomp data is in," she murmured, more for the benefit of the log recordings than to Jessan. "Coordinates are locked. Ready. Commence run-to-jump at this time."

She fed power to the panel, pushed the throttles forward, and guided *Warhammer* along its trajectory. When the hyperspace engines had kicked in and the stars had blazed and died outside the viewscreen, she watched the readouts for a few minutes to make sure that everything was functioning properly, then switched on the autopilot.

"Autopilot engaged," she said, to Jessan this time, and unfastened her safety webbing. "Let's go see how Ignac' is doing."

Back in the *'Hammer*'s common room, LeSoit had already unstrapped and gone to work, with the comp screen down from its bulkhead niche and a mug of cha'a on the table at his elbow. He looked up at Beka and Jessan came in.

"You were right about grabbing the boss's personal files," he said. "There's stuff here that I didn't even guess about."

Beka got a mug of cha'a from the galley nook and came back over to the table. "Any word on why the Magelords wanted D'Caer back in the first place?"

"He was coordinating imports," LeSoit said. "And not just the odd bit of luxury goods, either. Take a look at this."

He highlighted several lines on the screen. Beka leaned closer, looked, and whistled.

"Essential parts for hyperspace engines," she said. "And resonating chambers for starship-size energy weapons." She glanced over at Jessan. "The Mageworlds are re-arming."

Jessan moved closer and bent to read the screen over LeSoit's shoulder. "How long this has been going on?"

"No idea," said LeSoit with a shrug.

Jessan raised an eyebrow. "And here I thought you worked for the man."

"I was his bodyguard, not his accountant."

Beka sighed. *Good thing I only have to put up with this as far as Mandeyn. At least they're not on the verge of killing each other anymore.*

"Where's all the stuff coming from, anyway?" she asked, then peered again at the screen and answered her own question. "Ophel and Suivi Point via Darvell—no surprises there."

"Well, here's one for you," said LeSoit. He brought up a different page. "Another source of spare parts and matériel is the Republic itself. And somebody in the Space Force is coordinating and supplying."

"Space Force," said Jessan. "Hell. How high up?"

"High," LeSoit said. "Very high. We're talking sector commander or above."

"Name?"

LeSoit shook his head. "Sorry. Not in this file."

"Hell," Jessan said again.

"It's not our worry," Beka said. "We'll pass the bad news along to Dadda and let him deal with it." She gave Jessan a challenging glance. "Or don't you think that he can?"

"I have every confidence in the General," he assured her. "But treason in the Space Force ... I never expected that."

"Idealist," said Beka.

"Everybody's character has its little flaws. So what are we going to do about our cargo?"

"That load of medicinal herbs from Raamet?" Beka asked. "I'll probably sell them myself for whatever I can get, and send the shipper a bank draft. It's not delivery to Ninglin, but it's the best that I can do."

"And more than most would bother with," Jessan conceded. "How long before we drop out of hyper?"

"No time soon," Beka said. "Scheduled arrival at the Inner Net is in three hundred forty-four hours. I don't know about you guys, but I'm going to go stand under the shower sonics until they shake the smell of D'Caer's office off me, and then I'm going to catch up on my sleep. Riding in stasis is interesting, but I wouldn't exactly call it restful."

"Have a good time," Jessan said. "Don't use up all the vibrations. And don't worry about us. We'll amuse ourselves out here somehow." The Khesatan looked at LeSoit speculatively. "You wouldn't happen to play cards, would you?"

"Odd that you should ask." LeSoit reached into the inner pocket of his jacket and pulled out an unopened deck imprinted with a stylized flower and the legend "Painted Lily Lounge—Embrig—Mandeyn."

"Those are a long way from home," said Jessan, sliding into a chair across the table. "But then, who am I to talk?"

LeSoit broke the seal on the deck with his thumbnail, pulled the cards out of the box, and began to shuffle. "I've been saving them for luck."

*Warhammer*'s hyperspace transit to the Inner Net was largely uneventful. Once Beka and Jessan had finished going through the stolen data files and compiling them into a report for her father, there wasn't much left to do except sleep, eat, and—in Jessan's case—play game after game of double tammani with Ignac' LeSoit.

The two of them were still at it when Beka passed through the *'Hammer*'s common room on the last ship's-morning of the transit. She had her long hair tied back in Tarnekep Portree's beribboned queue, and for the first time since leaving D'Caer's office she wore the Mandeynan's ruffled finery and scarlet eye patch.

"Places, everyone," she said to the card players when they looked up. "We should hit the Inner Net and get pulled out of hyper in about ten minutes."

She continued on through to the cockpit and strapped

into the pilot's chair. A moment later Jessan appeared. He slid into the copilot's seat and put on the earphone link to the communications panel.

"Anything new this time?" he asked after they'd finished running through the checklist for dropout.

Beka shook her head. "Not really. We wait for them to hail us, and then we request a direct link to the Commanding General. They'll probably try to give us the runaround instead; have you got any code words you can whisper into their shell-like ears to get us through?"

"You don't have to worry about that part," said Jessan. "It's covered."

"Good," Beka said. "Then we're all set."

She watched the chronometer. "Getting pulled out—now!"

The orange No Jump light on the panel came up as soon as the 'Hammer's hyperspace engines felt the artificial flux of the Net—generated by the matrix of Net Stations in emulation of the natural fields that surrounded worlds like Pleyver. Beka pulled off the hyperdrive and set in the realspace engines.

The stars reappeared, but not in the pristine silence of a regular drop from hyper. The control panel flared into a blaze of red lights, readouts scrolled up monitor screens, and the strident outcry of an alarm buzzer split the air.

"Damn—somebody's radiating fire control out there!" Beka hit the switch that brought Warhammer's shields up to full strength. "Nyls, where the hell are they?"

Jessan was already busy on his side of the panel, his hands playing the buttons and dials like a keyboard. "I can't tell. Wherever they are, though, they aren't locking on to us."

"Then who—"

Beka stopped. High in the viewscreen ahead of her, a globe of blue-white light flared into existence, then faded to a dull red and vanished. She swallowed.

"That was an explosion," she said. "A big one. Nyls, do you think this is some kind of Space Force training exercise?"

"No," Jessan said. "If there's an exercise of some sort going on, it's live-fire. I'm picking up a lot of stuff on the frequencies associated with energy beams."

"Bastards," muttered Beka. "They're not supposed to be doing that sort of thing on the regular jump lanes. . . . Get on the hyperspace comm relays and listen in to what's happening."

Jessan was frowning. "I'm already on them, Captain." He paused. "We have total silence in the hyper bands."

"How about crypto? Or the data links?"

"Nothing. No transmissions. As far as I can tell, hi-comms are completely silent."

"Damn. You think our receiver's gone down or something?"

"It was working fine when we left Eraasi," Jessan said. "I'll check the lightspeed comms."

The alarm buzzer shrieked again.

"Lock on!" Beka's hands danced over the controls, putting on down vector and feeding power to the dorsal and ventral energy guns. "Active homers, heading this way!"

The guns didn't respond.

"*Damn,*" she said. "We've still got the seals up from that blasted customs inspection on our way in." She switched on the link to the common room. "LeSoit! Get down to the main panel and unseal the guns!"

"On my way, Captain."

Beka spiraled the ship in an effort to throw off the homers, and diverted more power from the engines to the shields. Jessan was still working over the controls and readouts on his side of the board.

He looked up. "Captain—I think I have something."

"Put it on."

A voice came over the console speaker: standard Galcenian in the measured cadence that Space Force training and custom reserved for desperate situations:

"Any station, any station, this is RSF *Nomestor.* I transmit in the blind. I transmit in the clear. Under attack by unknown spacecraft. I say again, under attack by unknown spacecraft. Request assistance. I say again, request assistance."

"Dammit, *Nomestor,* what's your posit?" muttered Jessan. He looked at Beka. "Captain, request permission to respond."

"Do it. Maybe he can tell us what's going on."

Two heavy thuds came from aft.

"Missiles," she said. She glanced at the damage-control board. "So far the shields are holding."

LeSoit's voice came on over the intraship link. "Gun seals removed, Captain."

"Good," she said. "Take the ventral gun. I'll gang them both to your panel."

"Orders?"

"Fire only in response to attack. We don't know who's hostile out there and who isn't."

On the other side of the cockpit, Jessan was talking over the exterior comms. "RSF *Nomestor,* RSF *Nomestor*—this is Republic Armed Merchant *Pride of Mandeyn,* standing by to assist you. State your position. I say again, state your position. Over."

*Nomestor* didn't respond. "Any station, any station," the distant voice repeated, "this is RSF *Nomestor.* I transmit in the blind. I transmit in the clear. Under attack by unknown spacecraft. Request assistance. I say again, request assistance. Any station, any station . . ."

The transmission broke off, and the carrier wave vanished with it.

Jessan cursed under his breath in High Khesatan and began to run the board again. "I'm getting a lot of chatter," he said after a moment. "Mostly reports of enemy action and requests for assistance, and pilot-to-pilot transmissions between fighter craft. All comms lightspeed."

"All lightspeed?" Beka slammed her clenched fist against her thigh in frustration. "What the *hell* is going on out there?"

"Damned if I know, Captain." Jessan was frowning. "We're getting comms in languages I don't even recognize. Plus some scrambled and some crypto."

"Anyone close on sensors?"

"No. Lots of junk metal floating around at temperatures above ambient, though."

She dug her fingernails into her palms. Drifting scrap meant broken hulls and dying ships. *No way to find them, nothing to do, not even anybody to shoot back at . . .*

"Any clue where those homers came from?" she asked.

"Probably missed their target and picked us up instead," replied Jessan. "I don't think it was anything personal. There's firing going on, but judging from attenuation and parallax it's over by the control stations for the Inner Net."

"It may not stay over there, though," Beka said. "And we can't jump as long as the Net is up."

She contemplated the orange glow of the No Jump light for a few seconds longer, then made her decision.

"I'm going to make a realspace run for the far side. Nyls, take the dorsal gun and help Ignac' keep us safe." She laughed unsteadily. "Dadda always said this ship could outrun anything it couldn't outshoot. Now's when we get to find out."

Hours passed. The No Jump light continued to burn as the *'Hammer* pushed onward in realspace. Beka sat alone in the cockpit, listening to voices from ships and stations she had never seen. The occasional time-tick on a message only increased her frustration: all the transmissions had been made long before.

Then the alarm sounded again, and the electronic-warfare

board on the control panel began to flash. She flipped on the intraship link to the gun bubbles.

"Nyls, Ignac'—heads up! Someone's lighting us up with fire control—" She glanced at the board again. "—and it doesn't match *any* Republic source in the data banks."

A target appeared on the display of the position plotting indicator. "And there she is. Unknown, inbound." And, as a scattering of small, up-Doppler targets appeared under the other vessel: "Homers. Aimed at us, this time."

She pulled more power away from the engines—in the frictionless vacuum of space the *'Hammer* wouldn't lose any speed—and fed it to the shields. "Keep me safe, guys," she said over the intraship link. "This looks like it could get rough."

The other ship fired its guns, transforming in an eyeblink from a barely visible dot moving against the starfield to a dazzling array of light.

"Son of a bitch!"

Beka swung ship and fed power astern to brake and travel in a new direction. The other ship's weapons—slow plasma bolts, with a target offset calculated on her previous course—missed, but barely.

"Bastard's got pulsed-port weapons and more power in 'em than *anything* in Jein's," she said over the link to the guns. "And it's not a Republic ship. Whose?"

"Magebuilt," came Jessan's voice in reply. "Has to be."

LeSoit spoke up from the other gun bubble. "Well, now you know what all those resonators and engine parts were for."

"I could have waited to find out," said Jessan. "For years, preferably."

Beka ignored the back-and-forth in the gun bubbles and concentrated on matching course with the Magebuilt vessel. She poured on all the power she could, trying to outrun him. Bit by bit, the sensors on the control panel showed her pulling ahead.

"Come on, girl, you can do it," she murmured to the ship. On the PPI scope, the dots that were the homers stopped their relative motion toward her and began to show down-Doppler. "This is where you get to shine."

*Warhammer* did indeed have better engines than the pursuing ship, even if her guns were smaller. When the hostile had vanished off the scope astern, Beka turned back onto her original course—a straight-line realspace drive, clean enough to serve as a run-to-jump anywhere but the Net.

Then the No Jump light winked out.

"The Inner Net just went down," Beka said quietly over the intraship link. "Stand by for hyperspace entry."

She fed a last burst of power to the realspace engines, then cut in the hyperdrive and jumped for the Outer Net.

*NOTHING IS the same anymore*, thought Klea, as she moved through the figures of the exercise that Owen called the ShadowDance. *Everything is changing. Even me.*

She hadn't been back to Freling's Bar since the day she'd found Owen battered and only semiconscious in the alley and had brought him home. The apprentice Adept, if that was what he really was, had returned to his upstairs apartment before the end of the week; but he'd left behind an envelope with her name on it. After she saw how much money the envelope contained, she climbed the stairs to knock on his door.

Owen's apartment, when he let her in, was tidy and clean, but almost as bare as her own had been when she first rented it. She held the envelope out to him.

"You didn't have any business leaving all this."

He made no move to take the envelope from her extended hand. "I think my life is worth at least that much. To me, anyway."

She let her hand fall back to her side. "What am I supposed to do with all this money?"

He shrugged. "It's not a lot, really."

After a moment she realized that he meant it. She tried a second time to explain. "It's enough to pay the rent for a month."

"I know," he said. "You need time to learn, and you'll never have it while you're scrabbling to find the rent money."

"Hooking for it, you mean."

He shrugged again, unshocked. "Whatever."

She gave up arguing with him. The next day—or, to be exact, early the next morning—when Owen returned from his nighttime job, she was waiting outside his apartment door.

"You said you could teach me," she said. "Well, here I am. Let's see how much I can learn in a month."

That had been almost three weeks ago, and she already knew that she wasn't going back to Freling's when the month was over. What she was going to do instead, she didn't know yet; she told herself that she would make her plans later, after she'd learned all of whatever it was that Owen had to teach. Meanwhile, she practiced her Shadow-Dance routines the way he'd taught them to her on the first day, and came faithfully to his upstairs apartment each morning for another lesson.

Sometimes she brought food with her as well, to supplement the frozen or dehydrated quick-meals that were Owen's idea of cooking. On this particular morning, she'd brought a fresh loaf of grain-meal bread and a packet of thin-sliced tusker-ox sausage from Ulle's corner store. The bread and sausage were in a straw basket on the counter in the kitchen alcove, waiting for her to finish the lesson.

At the end of the ShadowDance sequence, she turned to where Owen leaned against the counter watching her.

"Well?" she said. "Better?"

"Better," he said. "Not perfect, but better."

"What happens when it's perfect?"

"It's never perfect," he told her. "But when it's as close to perfect as you can make it, then we go on to the second sequence, and after that, to the third. Meanwhile—are you still having trouble with other people's thoughts?"

"Only sometimes," she said, thrusting aside the prospect of sequence following after sequence all the way to infinity. "And it's not so bad when it does happen."

"Knowing you're not crazy is the first step," he told her. "Discipline is the second."

"Discipline. Is that what this ShadowDance stuff is for?"

He looked pleased, the way her teachers back in lower school had used to look when she figured out something without being told the answer. "Discipline, yes. Among other things."

"What sort of other things?"

"It depends on how you do it," he said. "Watch."

He stepped away from the counter into the center of the room and ran through the first few steps of the routine she had been doing only a few moments earlier.

"Do it like that," he said, "and you have the basic move, just like I've been teaching you."

She nodded. "I see it."

"But you can also do it like this." Almost before she saw it, he had gone through the entire sequence again— not just faster, but harder as well, with an edge to it that she didn't entirely understand. "If you do, whoever happens to be standing in the way is going to be badly hurt."

She thought for a moment about the ShadowDance's other movements; now that she knew what to look for, she could see that all of them had the same ability to do harm.

"Useful," she said finally. "I think I liked the routine better when I thought it was all just for pretty, though."

She half-expected him to disapprove, but to her surprise he smiled again. "The Dance for its own sake is always the best. Which brings us to the third reason for learning it."

"*Another* one? How many reasons are there, anyway?"

"As many as there are Dancers," he said. "Most Adepts find that the moves themselves can function as an aid to meditation."

"A what?"

He laughed under his breath. "It's just a matter of doing the moves very slowly—about one-quarter speed—and not thinking of anything else at all while you're doing them."

Klea considered the idea. Coming from most people, the instruction not to think about anything else would be just another way of telling her to concentrate on what she was doing. But Owen wasn't most people; if he said "don't think about anything else," then that was what he meant.

"It sounds hard," she said finally.

"Do you want to try? I think you're ready."

She hesitated. "What happens if I don't get it right?"

"Happens? Nothing. You try again, or try something else, whichever works better."

"Oh." She looked down at the floor for a moment, then lifted her head and began the Dance. A second later, she broke off in midmove. "Do I need to keep my eyes closed?"

"You can if it helps," Owen told her. "The real trick, though, is to leave them open but not see anything."

After a few more moves she felt the pattern of the Dance grow smoother. Time, always her enemy until now, seemed to float away from under her, leaving only the Dance moving like motes of dust in a sunbeam. Then she was losing touch with the pattern, dropping back into time—and heavy darkness, sudden and unexpected, came down on her like the weight of all the world's despair.

She cried out and gripped her head with both hands.

On board the courier ship, Llannat Hyfid stretched and swung her legs down off the acceleration couch. *Naversey* was in the subdued-lighting portion of the ship's day; the passenger compartment was dark except for the lighted alcove holding the cha'a pot and the water cooler, and the blue safety lights that dotted the floor and bulkheads. Other than Llannat, the only passenger awake was the reservist with service ribbons from the Magewar, who sat with his head bent over a lighted datapad.

At the sound of Llannat's boots hitting the deckplates he looked up from his work. "Still awake, Mistress—?"

He made the title into a question, and she realized that he couldn't see her nametag in the dim light.

"Hyfid," she supplied for him, while squinting to make out his name in return. The tag on his tunic pocket read VINHALYN, in block lettering of an older style than she was used to seeing. She suspected that the tag was a relic of his active service, saved over the years while the rest of his uniform was lost or discarded. "I was asleep, but I woke up again—I've been in transit for so long that my sleep patterns don't know nap time from breakfast."

"Ah," he said. "That explains it. I used to have the knack myself of falling asleep whenever there wasn't anything better to do, but I'm afraid I've been away from the service for too long. So I improve the hour by working, instead."

"Sorry," she said. "Then I won't interrupt you."

"No, no." He cleared the datapad with a touch of the stylus. "Grading papers is marginally better than insomnia, but only marginally."

"You're a teacher?"

He nodded. "To be precise, I hold the Diregis Chair of

Contemporary History at Prime University. Unfortunately for the students in my midweek seminar, I also hold a reserve commission in the Space Force—which I had all but forgotten, but which the service apparently did not."

"The Space Force never forgets," said Llannat. "What do they want with a historian, though?"

"What they want from all of us, I presume," he said. "Expertise. We are all specialists in one thing or another. In my case, the languages and culture of the prewar Mageworlds."

Llannat wondered what Vinhalyn would say if he knew that she herself had once encountered a Magelord. *He'd envy me, if I know these academic types.*

"That's not a very common specialty," she said. "How did you come to pick it in the first place?"

He smiled. "Oddly enough, it was because of the War."

"You were in the Space Force back then?" She could see from his ribbons that he had been, but asking a question seemed like a good way to get the rest of the story.

"Oh, yes. I'm Ilarnan, originally, and we were hard hit in the war's early stages, so like a lot of the young people my age, I joined up as soon as I could. Unlike most of them, I actually got to visit the Mageworlds before my time was over."

"That's what made you decide to be a scholar?"

"Yes," he said. "I was there during the pacification period. The Republic was doing its best to reduce the scientific and industrial base of the Mageworlds to a level where they wouldn't pose a threat to the rest of the galaxy, and the Adepts' Guild was hunting down the Magelords and the lesser Circle Mages for execution out of hand—and it came to me that I was watching the systematic destruction of a culture fully as complex and as civilized as our own, cognate to ours and yet unimaginably alien."

He smiled briefly. "I must apologize for the burst of

rhetoric at the end. It's a speech I've found myself having to make a number of times over the past twenty years or so. I'm afraid my academic colleagues find me a bit of a crackpot on that particular subject."

"So when the Mageworlds Patrol Fleet runs into an abandoned Deathwing raider," Llannat said, "you're naturally on the Space Force's short list of people to haul back to active duty."

Vinhalyn nodded. "Somebody will be needed to translate any documents and records on board the derelict. And the fact that they need my particular skill suggests that the ship is an extremely old one—otherwise a knowledge of contemporary Mageworlds dialects would be enough."

He pointed with his stylus at the couch where the younger reservist lay asleep. "Our rather self-important friend over there is in a similar position. Unless his nametag is lying to us, he is in civilian life a top-ranked data-recovery expert, specializing in the retrieval of information from obsolete or alien systems."

Llannat looked over at their gently snoring fellow-passenger. "Probably got his start in life as a comptech," she said without much sympathy. "And now the Space Force, bless its hard little heart, has shown up to collect on the debt."

"Precisely," said Vinhalyn. "Of the rest of us, our two warrant officers are the easiest to explain—a hull technician and a weapons specialist should be able to cover most of the raider's physical systems between them. The presence of a senior officer in the medical branch is more problematical; that is, until one remembers that prior to the War the Mageworlds had made progress in the biochemical sciences far beyond our own current state of knowledge.

"Which leaves," he concluded, "you."

"Me?"

He nodded. "You're quite a mystery in your own right, didn't you realize?"

"Uh . . . no."

"Yes, indeed," he said. "Since we already have a medic on the team, one must assume that you are here in your role as an Adept, in order to counter any traps or devices the Mages who built and abandoned the Deathwing might have left aboard her. But if that is in fact the case, why should the Guild send a comparatively young and untried Adept when it still has active members with experience from the War?"

"I wish I knew," said Llannat uncomfortably. "All I can figure is that I was easy for Space Force to get hold of— just a little matter of changing my orders at the last minute, and no need to ask Master Ransome for any special favors."

"Quite a plausible theory," said Vinhalyn. "Errec Ransome and Jos Metadi are friends of long standing, but the same can't be said about the Adepts' Guild and the High Command. Mutual mistrust, I'm afraid, is more the order of the day."

She thought about how Ari had always regarded her a trifle askance whenever she chose to wear Adept's blacks instead of her Space Force uniform. "I've run into that myself."

"Just so," the historian said. "The Space Force can't be blamed for drawing as much as possible on its own resources instead of the Guild's, and one certainly can account for your presence among us on those terms."

He paused, then went on in quieter tones. "But someone who carries a Magelord's staff may well bring more to the investigation than convenience alone."

Llannat stood very still, grateful for the dim light that hid her face. "An Adept's staff is for the Adept to choose," she said. "And mine was a legacy from a friend."

"Not the usual practice on this side of the Net,"

Vinhalyn pointed out, "where Adept and staff are all but inseparable, even in death. But in the Mage-Circles a single staff might pass down through several generations—from friend to friend, or from teacher to student, or from vanquished to victor in one of their ritual duels."

He looked apologetic for a moment. "That was, in fact, how I thought you had acquired the staff—in combat of some sort. I hope you'll forgive a scholar's compulsion to find the solution to an intriguing puzzle, whether the answer's any business of his or not."

"I'm not offended," she said. "But you were right about part of the puzzle, anyhow; Space Force probably tapped me for this assignment because I once managed to fight with a—what did you call them?—with a Circle-Mage and lived to file a report on it afterward."

*It's a good thing the Space Force doesn't know the rest of the story*, she thought. *Because if they knew, then the Guild would be sure to find out eventually. And the service might not mind that I was a renegade Magelord's last student—but Master Ransome would throw me out of the Guild in a heartbeat.*

*If he didn't decide to kill me out of hand before I could contaminate anybody else.*

The darkness in Klea's head had weight and pressure to it; it pushed her down relentlessly toward the floor. At the last minute she felt Owen catching her before she hit.

"Klea—are you all right?"

"I don't know. My head hurts."

"Here. Sit down. I'll get you something to drink."

She let him help her over to the room's only chair, a cheap metal foldable with wobbly legs and a dented back. When her vision cleared, she saw that he was busy over in the kitchen alcove, making up a mug of Nutli's Instant *Ghil* with hot water from the tap.

"Offworlders," she muttered. "Don't you people know that you're supposed to use boiling water?"

Owen looked back at her over his shoulder, still stirring. "Does it make a difference? I never can tell." He brought her the mug. "So you've guessed my secret. Was it the *ghil* or my accent that did it?"

She sipped at the lukewarm *ghil*, taking comfort from its familiar gritty taste. The mug had a chip in its rim; she wondered if Owen even had another. *He probably found it in the cupboard when he moved in*, she thought.

"It wasn't much of a secret," she said. "You just never mentioned it. But there aren't any Adepts on Nammerin that I've ever heard of."

"Not these days, anyway," he said. "Are you feeling better now?"

"I'm doing all right."

"Good," he said. "Exactly what happened to you back there in the ShadowDance? Can you describe it for me?"

"I think so." She spoke slowly, searching for the right words to describe an experience that hadn't really felt like something words could describe. "I was doing the movements, like you said, and trying to keep my eyes open without seeing anything. It wouldn't work at first, and then it did—everything sort of slid into place, and I was *there*— and then I wasn't again."

"Nothing unusual so far," he said. "In fact, that's about how it is for most beginners. Go on."

"Well . . . just after I dropped out but before I touched the ground, if you know what I mean—"

Now it was his turn to nod. "I know. What happened then?"

"Then something hit me." She grimaced, remembering. "It was like—like having somebody throw a bag over your head and smash you on the skull with a rock at the same time. Or going straight from feeling-no-pain drunk to hell's own hangover with nothing in between for a cushion."

He winced at the comparison, and Klea thought back to how she had found him lying facedown and bloody in the alley mud.

"That was what happened to you, wasn't it?"

For a moment he didn't say anything, but regarded her with a considering expression in his hazel eyes. "Something like that. Only what hit you was accidental."

"It sure didn't feel like an accident."

"It wasn't aimed at you on purpose, though," he said. "You just happened to be in the way."

"Happened to be in *whose* way?" she demanded. "Whatever was going on, you're not going to stand there and tell me it was part of a plot to do somebody good."

He looked at her for a long time with the same considering expression as before. "You're right," he said finally. "Someone is working to cause trouble. It's the ugly side of what you're learning—like using the ShadowDance as a weapon, only a lot worse—and any beginner, especially one as empathic as you are, is going to be vulnerable."

Klea took a long swallow of the *ghil*. "Are we coming to the part where you make me go away so I can be safe?"

"I certainly ought to," Owen said. "It's a poor teacher who involves his student in something this dangerous."

"Dangerous," said Klea. She gave a short laugh. "I've been a hooker in this town for five years, I've had things happen to me you wouldn't wish on your worst enemy, and you think I don't know about 'dangerous'?"

"Not this kind," he said. "Listen. What you felt was a Mage-Circle at work here on Nammerin."

Klea looked at him. "A Mage-Circle. Like in the holovids about the War?" Only vague memories of her lower-school history lessons kept her from putting the Mages and their Circles in the same mental compartment as her grandmother's tales of marsh-wraiths, or the more improbable episodes of "Spaceways Patrols." "I thought all the Mages were gone."

"They are," he said. "Except for the ones who aren't. You wondered what I was doing on Nammerin. Well, now you know."

"You're working for the Adepts' Guild," she guessed. "Hunting for Mage-Circles."

"Among other things."

She looked down at the dregs of the *ghil* in her mug, and then back at Owen. "But you told me you were an apprentice, not an Adept. If working Mage-Circles aren't a good thing for a student to get messed up in, then why did the Guild send you?"

He sighed. "The easy answer is that any Mages inside the Republic are going to be well guarded against Adepts. So it takes somebody who isn't an Adept to find them."

More images were coming back to her now, memories of the flatpix and old newsholos that had illustrated her history books. Black masks, black robes . . . She'd had nightmares about them for a long while afterward, until she'd figured out that life had worse things to be afraid of than imaginary Magelords.

*And it turns out I was right the first time*, she thought. *Because the nightmares are coming back, and now they're real.*

"There were Mages in my dream," Klea said slowly. "A whole Circle of them. They saw me, and I ran away. You were there, too. And later that night I found you half-dead in the alley."

She looked at him, remembering his bruises and how the blood had caked in his hair, and how her own flesh that evening had carried the marks of injuries inflicted in a dream.

"Was it the Mages who beat you up like that?"

"Yes," he said. "In a manner of speaking. They thought—or at least I hope they thought—that I was just another local with enough untrained talent to make me sensitive."

"Like me."

"Exactly," he said. "Only you don't have just a little potential ability, you have a lot of it. Warning you off with a mental beating, like they tried doing with me, isn't going to work on you either, because you're going to be able to sense what they're up to whether you want to or not. Which is why I haven't sent you off to safety—it wouldn't do any good."

"Oh," she said. "So what are we going to do now?"

"You are going to be careful," he told her. "And I am going to keep on with the work I came here to do."

# VIII. Mageworlds Border Zone:
## RSF *Karipavo*; RSF *Ebannha*

WITH ANY luck, reflected Commodore Jervas Gil, the special investigative team from Galcen should arrive before too much longer. When they did, he could hand over the problem of the Magebuilt derelict to them and get back to his proper job of watching the Net.

Until then, however, he was spending more time than he liked in *Karipavo*'s Combat Information Center. From the CIC, he could keep an eye on the abandoned raider via periodic relays from *Ebannha*, whose boarding party had remained with the empty Deathwing.

*Those guys are probably getting pretty bored with that job by now*, he thought. *If the investigation team doesn't show up soon, we'll have to rotate them out of there.*

The voice of the executive officer broke up Gil's train of thought. The XO was excited about something; his outplanets accent was even more pronounced than usual. "Commodore—we have something odd here."

"Just what we need," said Gil. "Something else odd. As if the stuff we already had wasn't odd enough. What's this one?"

"Looks like a merchantman dropping out of hyper at the Outer Net," said the XO. "We should have gotten word from the Inner stations before he got here."

"And we didn't?"

"Not a peep out of anybody."

*Not a good sign*, thought Gil, and made a mental note to double-check all the Net Control Stations for sloppy procedure. The station crews would complain bitterly about being singled out for attention, but at least they wouldn't be bored. Boredom, Gil had found, was the primary hazard of blockade duty, and an excellent source of stupid mistakes.

The 'Pavo's captain came over to join the conversation. "Maybe our mystery freighter didn't come from the Mageworlds in the first place?"

The XO shook his head. "Not dropping out where he did, with that vector on him."

"Contact Net Station Twenty-three," said Gil. Twenty-three was the closest unit on the Inner Net to the 'Pavo's current position, and the one most likely to have passed the stranger through. "Ask them what's going on."

He glanced at the tactical action officer's monitor screen. "And get an ID on that freighter."

"We're querying him right now," the TAO said. Then, abruptly, "What's this?"

Gil looked closer. The screen was picking up a cloud of garbage around the contact, on a slightly divergent course.

"He's jettisoning his cargo, it looks like," said the 'Pavo's captain. "A smuggler, maybe?"

"Get a boarding party ready for him," Gil said. "And collect some of whatever he's kicking out."

"Muster the duty fighter team," the TAO said to the CIC Watch Officer. "Hail him and halt him."

"Duty fighter, aye."

A crew member at the comms panel looked up. "In combat, we're being hailed."

The *'Pavo*'s captain said, "Who?"

"The merch, would you believe it?"

*This*, thought Gil, *is getting stranger by the minute. Honest traders don't jettison cargo. And smugglers don't stop to trade gossip with a battlecruiser.*

"What's his call sign?" he asked the comms tech. "Can you put him on audio?"

"Audio, aye."

The link by the tactical action officer's watch station crackled and began to speak. Lightspeed comms tended to distort pitch and timbre, but the accent came through—the pure, unmistakable Galcenian of the Galcen-born and Galcen-schooled.

"Any station this net, any station this net, this is Reserve Merchant Vessel *Warhammer*. Patch me through to Commander Patrol Screen, over."

Gil went cold. As far as the galaxy was concerned, both *Warhammer* and Beka Rosselin-Metadi were dead. If this transmission was genuine, then whatever news General Metadi's daughter had for the Net Patrol Fleet was serious enough to make her break her cover identity into irreparable pieces.

"He just keeps on repeating that message, sir," the comms tech said.

"It's got to be some kind of trick," said the XO. "To find out who's in command."

"Not a very bright trick, either," agreed the *'Pavo*'s captain. "Everyone knows *Warhammer* crashed on Artat over two years ago."

"Never mind that," Commodore Gil said. "Give me the comm link." He keyed the handset. "Space Force Reserve vessel, this is Patrol Screen Actual, over."

Nearly twenty seconds went by before a response came

from the unknown, meaning a ten light-second distance between that ship and the '*Pavo*.

"Patrol Screen, this is *Warhammer*. I transmit in the clear. The Inner Net is down. I say again, the Inner Net is down. You have fifteen minutes, twenty at the outside, before hell's own horde of Mage warships is all over you. I only got here first because I'm faster than they are."

"That's impossible," muttered the XO. "We'd have heard when they hit the Inner Net."

"Get on hi-comms," said Gil to the TAO. "Raise anyone on the Inner Net. Do it now."

Then he keyed the link. "Roger, *Warhammer*. Come dead in space. I intend to board you."

"No time for that, Commodore. I've got to get the word back to Galcen."

In the background, Gil could hear the TAO and the CIC watch officer conferring in muttered undertones: "Whoever he is, he sure is fast." ... "Do you think he's planning a run-to-jump?" ... "Where'll he end up if he's running now?" ... "Galcen's on the arc." ... "Then he could be telling the truth."

Gil ignored them. "I can get word back to Galcen faster than you can, *Warhammer*," he said over the link. "Come dead in space and let me board you."

"No thanks, Commodore. Nobody can get the word there faster than I can—and somebody's got to bar the door behind me. Open the Net and let me jump."

Behind Gil, the hushed conference continued, this time in exchanges between the duty comms tech and the '*Pavo*'s captain: "Sir, I can't raise Net Station Twenty-three." ... "Get *Shaja*, then, or *Lachiel*; they've got picket duty in Twenty-Three's area." ... "No joy at all on hi-comms, sir." ... "How's the internal test?"

The link crackled again. "Commodore, it looks like the Magelords have figured out how to jam the hyper-relays. All anybody's got left is lightspeed line-of-sight comms."

"Is that possible?" Gil asked—more of the duty comms tech than of *Warhammer*'s captain, but the voice over the link spoke again anyway:

"It's possible, Commodore. I saw a Magelord take down a whole building full of electronics once. And that was just one guy, working on the run, with no prep."

"Sir," said the *Pavo*'s captain, "we can't raise anyone in the Inner Net."

"Get me Space Force Command on Galcen, then," Gil said.

"No joy, sir," said the comms tech, after a minute. "Looks like that's down, too."

Gil sighed. *Time to start earning your pay, Commodore.*

"Open the Net," he said. "Pass one."

"What?" said the *'Pavo*'s captain.

"You heard me," said Gil. He spoke into the comm link. "*Warhammer*, you have clearance. My respects to your father."

"Roger," replied the voice over the link. "Out."

Gil turned to the captain of the *Karipavo*. "Captain, pass the following signal to all ships in the fleet in lightspeed comms—"

"Hi-comms would be faster!" the *'Pavo*'s captain protested.

"We don't have hi-comms. Do as I tell you. Signal follows. 'Set General Quarters, condition red, weapons free. Mageworlds attack imminent. All vessels in Patrol Screen detached effective immediately. Permission granted to act independently. Net Control Stations, maintain the Net as long as physically possible.' "

"Message being sent now," said the captain.

"Very well," said Gil. "Captain, at your pleasure—come to General Quarters."

At the sound of the General Quarters alarm, vacuum-tight doors throughout the *'Pavo* cycled shut, the gentle sighing of increased air pressure barely audible in the din.

In CIC, going to General Quarters automatically brought up the lights in the main battle tank, but nothing showed in the display except *Karipavo*'s own position. Gil wasn't surprised. If the Magelords were jamming hi-comms as Captain Rosselin-Metadi claimed, realtime updates from other ships in the fleet would have stopped as well.

"Datalink's down," said the CIC watch officer to the tactical action officer.

"Then we'll make do the best we can," the TAO replied. "Set up everybody's last-known positions in manual mode, and update the display as info is available. What's the status on weapons and shields?"

"All normal."

"Very well. Go active on all lightspeed sensors. Maybe we'll get something."

A few feet away, the duty comms tech had the front panel entirely off the bulky hi-comms unit. In company with an electronics tech, he had been poking around inside for some minutes. The captain and the executive officer of the *'Pavo* stood nearby, watching the pair at work.

Gil shook his head. *Check it out as much as you want,* he thought. *You aren't going to find anything.*

Indeed, the electronics tech was already looking up with a frustrated expression. "So far, sir, all readouts and tests are normal," she said to the captain. "We're producing signal."

"Only one problem," the comms tech added. "We can't hear ourselves when we do it."

"Could the receiver be down?" the XO wondered aloud.

"No, sir," the electronics tech said. "When we have a direct connection, everything tests out sat. All internals normal on the receive end. Sir, this is weirder than hell."

At the other end of the CIC, a crew member looked up from the flatscreen monitor for the sensor arrays. "Anomaly on visual, sir."

The 'Pavo's captain strode over to see the monitor for himself. "Where away?"

"Quadrant N-seven-outer, Sector Red One."

*Toward the Mageworlds*, thought Gil. *The closest point of approach to the Inner Net. Captain Rosselin-Metadi's lead was shorter than she thought.*

"What do you have?" the captain asked.

"Multiple contacts, small, spectrum analysis shows real-space engines in use."

The XO came over to join the group at the screen. "Any friendlies out that way?"

"Negative, sir," said the crew member. "And these contacts aren't identifying themselves, either."

"Ah," said the XO. "I see."

He stepped away from the monitor. Then, without haste and without changing expression, he pulled a miniature blaster from the pocket of his coverall and shot the 'Pavo's captain neatly in the back of the skull. Continuing the same motion of arm and body, he brought the blaster around toward Gil.

Gil sidestepped, feeling the heat of a blaster bolt brushing his ear, and flicked the grav-release on his own sleeve-mounted blaster. He missed—but another shot connected, and Gil found himself looking across CIC at the usually inconspicuous Lieutenant Jhunnei, who was holding a blaster of her own.

The compartment smelled of blaster fire and blood. Everybody seemed frozen, shocked into immobility by what they had just seen. Gil knew he only had a few seconds before they gave way to hysteria. If that happened, the battle was lost before it even began.

He slipped the miniature blaster back into its hidden grav-clip, then swept the room with a glance. He had their attention now—good.

"In Combat," he said in a carrying voice, "this is Commodore Gil. I am assuming command."

A shaky chorus of "aye"s arose from the crew. Gil gave an internal sigh of relief as they all turned back to their duties. Jhunnei, meanwhile, was already bending over the XO's body.

"He's still alive, sir," she said to Gil. "What shall we do with him?"

"Sick bay," Gil told her. "Under armed guard." He put the XO out of his mind for the moment and turned to the tactical action officer. "Do you have a course and speed on those contacts out there?"

"Yes, sir."

"Good," said Gil. "Figure an intercept course, and put a spread of active/passive homers in their path. Follow up with crewed fighters."

"Fighter detachment, stand by," the TAO said. "Maintain lightspeed comms."

So far the crisis had been proceeding in the measured increments characteristics of realspace maneuvers. Now the action picked up speed. Contacts from close by—in speed-of-light terms—began showing up in the tactical readouts as the info arrived, each contact tagged with an assigned probability for real-time location based on known position and time of light-lag. In the interior of the main battle tank, red lights started blinking, one by one.

"Get me some speed," Gil said. "And take evasive measures. Launch those fighters."

"What do we have?" the TAO asked.

"We have a dangerous situation. Move us back to where we can support the Net Control Stations. They can't move, and they can't fight. But as long as we can keep the Net up, the Mageworlders aren't going anywhere."

*Somebody has to bar the door*, Gil thought, remembering Captain Rosselin-Metadi's words over the comm link. *The longer we can hold out here, the better chance she has of getting the word through to Galcen Prime.*

"Right," said the TAO. "Course plotted and laid in."

"Evasive/deceptive steering," Gil said.

"Roger," said the TAO.

The status lights on the fire-control side of CIC began flashing. "We're taking the unknowns under fire," announced the tech at the fire control station.

"Report status," said the TAO.

"In range, recording hits."

The TAO turned to the crew member at the comms station. "Any idea how anyone else is doing?"

"Negative," said the comms tech. "No comms with other Task Unit vessels."

"Right. Assume that they also have their comms down."

Gil listened to the colloquy for a few seconds, then turned to his aide. Jhunnei had already sent the XO down to sick bay on a nullgrav stretcher accompanied by several muscular crew members, and was once again standing quietly by and awaiting developments. In a low voice Gil said, "If or when the Net goes down, that'll mean we need to get going. Figure us a contingency course to Galcen."

"Aye, aye," she said.

At that moment a vibration came through the deckplates, and a slight overpressure made Gil's ears hurt.

"Hit alfa, hit alfa, compartment two-oh-two-one-lima," the crew member on the damage control status board called out. "Damage control crew responding from Repair Five."

Gil turned back to Jhunnei. "And get me a course to the nearest friendly or neutral world as well, just in case."

"Already working on one, sir."

"Good thinking," said Gil.

He stepped over to the tactical action officer's station. "Keep us alive and make them dead," he said quietly to the TAO, before raising his voice for the benefit of the watch-standers and the log recordings. "In Combat, this is Commodore Gil. TAO has control."

Then, to the TAO again: "If you need me, I'll be down

in sick bay. I want to ask the XO a couple of questions while he's still in shape to answer them."

By the time Gil strode into the 'Pavo's sickbay, the XO was already plugged into one of the beds. A crew member with a blaster stood guard nearby.

"He's stable," said the head of the medical department, a lieutenant commander from somewhere in the Middle Worlds. "If that's what you wanted."

"I want him awake enough to answer questions," Gil said.

"Well, you've got that," said the medic. "You won't have him for very long, though, unless we get him into a healing pod. That blaster bolt took out some important stuff."

Gil frowned. "How much pod space have you got?"

"Four full-bodies and a couple of partials."

"Not enough to waste. Save the room for our own people—they're going to need it."

The medic looked offended but said only, "In that case, Commodore, I'd recommend you start talking to him right now. He hasn't got much time."

"None of us do, Commander," said Gil. "Thanks to him we may have less."

He felt the deckplates shiver slightly under his feet. The bed holding the XO beeped as the hookups jiggled and the therapeutic and diagnostic systems worked to compensate. The bulkhead speaker clicked on and began to speak.

"Hit bravo, hit bravo. Compartment six-one-twentytwo-lima. Supply from Repair Two."

"You're going to have some more customers in a few minutes," Gil said to the chief medic. "Honest ones this time. Leave me with the XO. I'll tell you when I'm through with him."

Gil put the chief medic out of his mind and moved over

to the bed. He looked down at the XO. The man was already paler than the pillow his head rested on.

"Who are you working for?" Gil demanded.

The XO gave him a death's-head grin. "Why should I tell you? I'm dead anyway."

"Talk, and I might change my mind about letting Doc give you pod space."

"Not after casualties start coming in, you won't. No deal. Go to hell."

*Damn.* Gil drew a deep breath. "If you won't tell me who, then tell me why."

The XO's eyes glittered—whether with pain or fanaticism or both, Gil couldn't tell.

"Because the Mages have to be crushed," said the wounded man. "You Central Worlders run the Republic while the people in the outplanets take all the risk, and you've coddled the Mageworlds ever since the end of the War. Next thing you know, the Council would have been wanting to take down the Net completely and let them into the Republic like regular citizens. . . ."

"Not likely," Gil murmured. "What good has shooting the captain done for the outplanets? The fleet's about the only thing left between them and the Mageworlds."

The XO laughed, a ghastly sound. "It won't be there for long. And the Mages aren't heading for the outplanets. They're going to have a victory big enough to make the Central Worlds finally understand what it's like—and after *that*, what happens to the Mageworlds is going to make Sapne and Entibor look like a pleasure excursion."

"And then the outplanets will be safe."

"Yes."

Gil sighed. *He's mad. Of all the motives for treason* . . . "Who else is with you?"

"No one."

*He's probably telling the truth as far as this ship is con-*

cerned. The Mages can't have found so many crazy people in the fleet that they could afford to bunch them up.

"Did you know that hi-comms would go down?" Gil asked. "Was that the signal?"

"Yes."

"What other surprises have the Mageworlders got for us?"

"Sorry—you won't be finding that out from me."

The XO began to choke. All the lights and telltales on the bed flared red and then went black. The bulkhead speaker clicked on—"Commodore to Combat Information Center!"—while Gil was standing there looking down at the dead man's face.

RSF *Ebannha*'s boarding craft had been umbilically attached to the Magebuilt Deathwing for several days now, and Ensign Tammas Cantrel had long since decided that a boarding craft designed to carry a crew of four was nevertheless too small to hold that same crew for anything longer than a matter of hours. The pilots of the three single-seat fighters composing their escort had gotten rotated on and off the mothership, but Cantrel and his small command had to make do with taking turns at the two claustrophobic bunks located just forward of the engines, tucked in like an afterthought with the galley nook and the sanitary facilities.

Even for one person, a *Pari*-class scout craft was cramped. Ensign Cantrel wasn't outside the normal size range in any dimension, but he'd had to walk sideways to get into the galley, where he was slapping together a sandwich to go with the last of the cha'a in the hotpot. Since he was drinking the last, he'd have to make the next pot. He'd just reached for the pouch of herbals when the comm link in the bulkhead sounded, and he flipped on the link instead.

"Ensign." It was Chief Yance, with a peculiar note in his voice. "You'd better come up to the cockpit."

Cantrel left his sandwich lying on the galley counter. If something important was happening, food could wait. Cha'a, on the other hand . . . He kept his grip on the mug as he sprinted for the piloting position. He was forward and in the control section in only a couple of seconds.

Chief Yance stood by the cockpit windows, looking forward and up at the starfield beyond.

"What is it, Chief?" Cantrel asked.

Yance pointed to a dull red star that hung glowing in space—a star that hadn't been there before. "*Ebannha*'s gone," he said. "She just blew up."

Cantrel stared at the red glow. *Accident*? he wondered numbly. *Rescue . . . depends on what happened. But if somebody doesn't do something fast, there won't be a chance.*

"Get on the comms," he said to Yance. "See if you can patch us through direct to *Karipavo*." He hit the GQ button to rouse the boarding craft's two remaining crew members from the bunks in the rear. "Stand by to cast off from the Deathwing and go looking for drifting lifepods."

Then the starfield near *Ebannha*'s glowing remnants lit up with a quick, bright flash—the color of energy weapons firing in deep space.

"Oh, hell," Cantrel said, as he started flipping switches all across the boarding craft's control panel. "Belay my last. Go silent, go dark, go passive."

The interior lights went out, the life-support system whispered to bare minimum, and in the starlight Cantrel could see the cha'a in his cup float away in a brownish, wavery globe as artificial gravity went down. Outside the cockpit viewscreens, the flashing of energy fire continued, silent and far away.

"Start racking the frequencies," Cantrel told Elligret Saben as soon as she and Falkith arrived on the bridge—

pulling their way along by handholds in the sudden zero-g environment and wondering loudly and profanely what was going on. "See if you can hear anything. But *don't* transmit."

Saben maneuvered herself into the communications seat. She fastened the safety webbing to keep herself from drifting away, then put on the earphone link and began to work.

"What's up?" she asked.

"Somebody just shot *Ebannha* all to pieces," Cantrel said. "I don't know know who or why. But right now, I don't want anyone who's looking for me to find me until *I* tell them where to look."

Saben and Falkith nodded. A few seconds later, Saben looked up from the communications board.

"Getting a signal on the lightspeed comms, sir."

"Put it on."

The comms tech pushed a button. The last notes of the "attention" signal came over the speaker, followed by words:

"Set General Quarters, condition red, weapons free. Mageworlds attack imminent. All vessels in Patrol Screen detached effective immediately. Permission granted to act independently. Net Control Stations, maintain the Net as long as physically possible."

The transmission ended.

"Who was that from?" Cantrel asked.

*"Karipavo."*

Chief Yance nodded in the direction of the expanding ball of glowing gas that had been their home vessel. "Guess *Ebannha* didn't get the word in time."

"Not at lightspeed they wouldn't have," said Cantrel. "And it might not have done any good anyway. Whatever hit them, it hit them fast and nasty."

In the darkness beyond the viewscreens, the brief lightning of energy fire continued, though more sporadically now. Falkith nodded toward the starfield.

"What d'you think's going on out there?" he asked.

Cantrel shook his head. "Who knows? Maybe the fighters are still at it. Maybe the bad guys are shooting lifepods."

"Too bad we don't have guns," said Falkith.

"I feel sorry for the pilots in the fighters," Saben said. "No food supply, no hyperspace engines. Even if they can get up near lightspeed, if nobody comes after them they'll die of starvation or old age before they get to a friendly world."

"I don't know how to tell you this, Elligret," said Falkith. "But we don't have hyperspace engines either."

"Wonderful," said the comms tech. "Because I'm picking up some other stuff now, more lightspeed transmissions like the last one. And there's a war going on out there, all right."

"Keep us posted," Cantrel said. "If our side wins, I want to know about it. Because we sure as hell can't do anything where we are right now."

The four of them waited in the cockpit of the boarding craft, listening as the reports came in one by one over the lightspeed comms: all initial-contact reports, and all—after correcting for distance—originally transmitted at about the same time. The initial-contact reports gave way in some cases to pleas for assistance, and in other cases to silence. Eventually, the signals got too faint to read—lightspeed comms were only good for short range—and there was nothing but the quiet of space, and the stars.

# PART THREE

# I. *WARHAMMER:* THE OUTER NET
## RSF *KARIPAVO:* THE OUTER NET

BEKA WATCHED RSF *Karipavo*'s signal dwindle and fade from the sensors as the *'Hammer* accelerated steadily to jump speed. The No Jump light still burned, but she couldn't afford to stand still while waiting for it to go off. She'd started a straight-line realspace run on a Galcen-bound course right after dropping out of hyper at the Outer Net; she could hit the hyperdrive enable as soon as the Net went down.

*Pinpoint piloting it isn't,* she admitted to herself, *but if it gets me within shouting distance of Galcen I can fine-tune things at the other end.*

The vacuum-tight door of the cockpit sighed open and shut again behind her. Nyls Jessan came forward and slipped into the copilot's seat. She turned to look at him. In the periphery of her vision the No Jump light glowed orange.

"Where's Ignac'?" she asked.

"Still at the guns, in case somebody gets trigger-happy and needs to be scared off."

"Don't worry too much about that," Beka said. "That was your old Space Force buddy Jervas Gil I just got through talking with—smart man, he's got his flagship sitting right on the main jump line from Eraasi to Galcen—and his people have more important stuff on their plates by now than stopping a fast-running merch."

Jessan smiled. "I take it he believed you."

"Damned straight he believed me," she said. "You guys have all the cargo kicked out?"

"That's an affirmative."

"Good, because we've got permission to cross the Net." And, as the No Jump light went out, *"Now."*

She hit the hyperspace controls.

The starfield beyond the *'Hammer*'s viewscreen blazed up and died, replaced by the iridescent grey pseudosubstance of hyperspace. Beka powered down all the ship's nonessential systems, took off all the safeties and regulators, then cut in the overrides.

"Living dangerously again?" inquired Jessan.

She shrugged. "With the hi-comms down it's all ours to lose. Either we overload and blow up in hyper, or we make it to Galcen in record time."

"Better never than late?"

"That's right," she said. "I don't plan on popping out over Galcen South Polar just in time to see the lid blow off."

"No, I suppose not. This definitely puts a crimp in your plan to pay back that herb dealer on Raamet, though. It was his merchandise we ended up dumping to vacuum."

"He'll have to write it off as a bad debt," Beka said. "When the war's over, I'll go back and square it with him."

One by one she cut off all the ship's nonessential systems—lights, artificial gravity, temperature control—and fed the extra power to the hyperspace engines. The *'Hammer*'s frame vibrated with the increase, a complex harmony of many disparate notes. With the overrides disabled, she would be depending on her sense of the ship's internal music as much as on the control panel's arrays of readouts and status lights. A faint discord might warn of trouble even before the problem registered on the sensors; and as long as the song remained constant, she could risk letting a danger indicator or two burn red.

Jessan glanced over at the speed and acceleration readouts. "Just out of idle curiosity—how much faster are you planning to go?"

"I don't know yet," Beka said. "These are new engines, remember? I did a hundred and sixty percent of rated max a couple of times with the old ones, so I'm taking that as my baseline. Nothing lower."

"Mmmph," he said thoughtfully. "Are you planning to fly this thing the whole way by hand?"

"Something like that. Can you fix up something to keep me awake until we get there?"

"If I have to. But it's a bad idea."

She drew breath for a sharp reply, then let it out again. Jessan almost never protested the decisions she made as *Warhammer*'s captain—at least, not that bluntly. When he did, she listened.

"Why?" she asked finally. "We have to make speed, and I'm the only one who knows the *'Hammer* well enough."

"When you push the ship this hard, everything rides on your own judgment. The tireder you get, the less dependable your judgment is."

"Stimulants—"

"Only make it worse. By the time you get to Galcen you'll be so jumpy your eyes aren't even tracking."

She bit her lip. *He's probably right, dammit.* "All right, Doc. What do you suggest we do instead?"

"I'd say, the two of us go watch-and-watch from here to Galcen, four hours on and four hours off. I won't even try pushing the *'Hammer* up to your top speed, but I think I can keep her at baseline velocity while you catch a bit of sleep."

She frowned. "We'll lose time that way."

"Some. But we cut down on the chances of making a fatal mistake somewhere along the line."

She thought about it for a few seconds while the 'Hammer's metal frame hummed and vibrated about her. *Getting there late does nobody any good at all . . . but getting there on time and then killing myself doing something stupid won't do anyone much good either.*

"Okay, Doc," she said. "You win. We'll do it your way."

When Commodore Gil arrived in the control area of 'Pavo's Combat Information Center, everything seemed calm—but the TAO was sweating in spite of the cool shipboard air.

Gil walked over to him. "What's the situation, Patel?"

"The Outer Net's under attack, sir." The TAO pointed at one of the monitor screens. "That's the raw sensor data from up ahead. It's about all we've got, too—no comms with any of the Net ships or the generating stations, and we've lost all of our fighters. The Mageworlders are packing some heavy weapons and they know how to use them."

"How are we holding up?"

"Our shields are working off the backup generators," the TAO said, "and we're still managing to maintain airtight integrity. But those guys have something that punches right through shields. Looks like a homer with a plasma-burst head on it, and they know right where to aim."

"That's not good," said Gil. "I suspected that somebody in the Republic was supplying the Mageworlds with war matériel—but nobody expected them to take the stuff and go us one better."

The crew member watching the sensor readouts looked up from her post. "Net Control under attack, signal fluctuation."

"What's our estimated time of arrival at Net Control?" Gil asked the TAO.

"Ten minutes."

"Do we have any of the Mageworlders in range?"

The TAO shook his head. "They seem to know our range exactly and stay just beyond it."

"Get a signature on those plasma-burst missiles of theirs," Gil said. "Set our secondary weapons systems to acquire them and take under fire automatically. Do we have anyone in voice range, lightspeed?"

"We have Net Control B-Twenty-three requesting assistance, open comms," the TAO said.

"Put B-Twenty-three inside range of our secondaries, then," said Gil. "And tell them we're on our way, ETA ten minutes. Any luck on getting those missiles targeted?"

"We're still trying."

"Keep working on it," Gil told him.

For a few minutes there was no sound in CIC except the back-and-forth of information and orders: "Incoming." . . . "How many?" . . . "Many, all directions." . . . "Max speed, take evasive action. Spiral." . . . "Firing blind." . . . "Engine hit."

Then the crew member at the sensor readouts said, "Friendlies—one five seven relative, speed five."

In the battle tank—being updated now by hand as the bits and scraps of data came in—two specks of light changed from the yellow of unknowns to the blue of friends. There were still entirely too many red-for-hostile dots out there, Gil decided, all approaching the blue marble of the Net generating station.

"Signal those two contacts," Gil said. "I am taking tactical command. Form three-sector screen on Station B-Twenty-three."

"Signal aye," said the comms tech.

"Damage report coming in," announced another crew member. "We have one hundred percent power available, reserve not available, repairs in progress. Hits alfa and bravo sealed and isolated, emergency shields rigged."

*It could be worse*, thought Gil, but without any sense of relief. *It probably won't be very long before it is worse.*

In *Warhammer*'s common room, the emergency glows shed a dim blue light, illuminating the zero-g handholds and attachment points but little more. Ignaceu LeSoit must have come in from the gun bubble as soon as the ship jumped; Jessan, pulling his way aft from the cockpit, was aware of the other man's presence as a darker area within the darkness, a stillness in the still air. LeSoit made no noise at all, not even the whisper of breath that should have sounded now that the temperature-control systems no longer kept up their constant susurration.

"You can relax," Jessan said. "We're not in danger at the moment, unless you count the possibility we might go up like a nova from an overloaded hyperdrive."

"I'll take my chances with that," Le Soit replied from the shadows, a couple of feet from where Jessan had placed him. "The faster we get away from the Mageworlds, the better. Mind telling me where the captain's going to drop us out?"

"Galcen," said Jessan.

LeSoit whistled. "That's a long haul in one jump."

"Hi-comms are down hard all over, and somebody's got to give them the word."

"Civic duty?" The gunfighter laughed quietly in the dark. "That didn't used to be in the captain's line. But things change, I suppose. What's she planning to do afterward?"

"There's a war on," said Jessan. "As far as I know, she's going to join it."

"So much for my plans to jump ship when we hit port," LeSoit said. "I should have known the first time I met her that I'd wind up getting into something like this."

"Resign yourself to a short but merry life full of incredible space heroics," Jessan recommended. "Do you watch 'Spaceways Patrol'?"

"You're joking, yes?"

"Not at all. It's the best preparation I know of for life with the captain once she makes her up mind to do something and damn the consequences."

"I think I liked her better when she was just a tough kid on the run from political speeches and fancy-dress balls."

"There's no accounting for some people's taste." Jessan yawned in spite of himself. "I need to catch a bit of sleep before my watch comes up."

LeSoit sighed, a light breath of sound in the blue-tinged darkness. "I suppose I ought to go forward and offer to take my turn at baby-sitting the autopilot."

"Don't even bother," Jessan said. "We're doing this run by hand at max speed, and you don't know the ship well enough to handle it. She didn't want to put me on the watch bill either, but I managed to convince her."

"I'll bet you did. What am I supposed to do while I'm waiting—play solitaire?"

"If you like," said Jessan. "But I think you'll find it rather difficult in zero-g. I'd recommend sleeping instead."

The glowing dots in *Karipavo*'s main battle tank—blue triangles, painfully few and scattered, for friendly ships; red ones for hostile craft—gave Commodore Gil a clear picture of a bad situation steadily getting worse. The crew members on the control panels and status boards murmured back and forth: "Sensors report five targets inbound, sector green three." ... "Tracking." ... "Locked on."

Lieutenant Jhunnei spoke quietly at Gil's elbow. "We need to get a visual ID before firing."

Gil looked at his aide. Her long, narrow face had a serious expression, one that he found oddly familiar. *Mistress Hyfid looked like that when she told the General there was trouble coming from the Mageworlds.*

Aloud, he asked, "What makes you think so, Lieutenant?"

Jhunnei gave a half-shrug. "Spacer's intuition?"

He turned to the TAO. "Weapons tight in green three pending visual ID."

"Weapons tight aye," echoed the TAO. "Set magnification to plot in main tank."

In the battle tank, the tactical representation winked out and was replaced over the next several seconds by a large-scale ship diagram, built up line by line in blue light as the sensor data came in.

The TAO whistled. "Good call, sir. Those are friendlies, all right. Fighters—Eldan dual-seaters."

"Good," said Gil. Eldans were long-range fighters with short-burst hyperspace capability; less agile in close quarters than single-seaters, they carried heavier weapons and could deliver a powerful blow before dropping back into hyper for their return to base. "Signal them into our docking bay. We need all the fighters we can get."

There wasn't much time for relief; already the crew member at the sensor panel was calling out again, "Hostile craft, many, sectors blue nine and blue ten. Inbound fast."

"Launch missiles when they're in range," said Gil. "And signal *Shaja* to take a blocking position between them and the Net Station."

The fighter-craft image in the battle tank vanished, and the tactical display came up again. Gil watched the diagram shift as the sensors and the lightspeed comms fed information into the *'Pavo*'s comp systems—old data, all of it, minutes old in a situation where seconds could mean everything.

*With nothing but lightspeed comms, getting updates is like pouring syrup on a cold morning*, he thought. *And if we're not lucky it's going to kill us.*

The vacuum-tight door of CIC sighed open to admit a messenger escorting the senior pilot from the flight of Eldans. Shoulder flashes on the pilot's pressure suit said that she was a JG; she carried her helmet in the crook of one arm, and her eyes were dark with fatigue.

Her salute was weary but professional. "Lieutenant junior grade Orialas reporting as ordered."

Gil returned the salute. "Under the circumstances, Lieutenant, we're very glad to have you aboard. Now—tell me what you've seen at your end of things."

"There isn't much," Orialas told him. "My buddies and I were ready squadron on board RSF *Sovay*. Word came down to launch, and we were vectored over to investigate a long-range contact. As soon as we dropped out at the contact point, we got ambushed by a flight of small fighter craft. By the time we finished them off and jumped back to base, *Sovay* was gone."

The JG swallowed and went on. "I don't know who it is we're fighting out there, but they've got some bad stuff to shoot at us with. We ran into a kind of multidirectional energy lance, and a collimated beam weapon that seems to work at lightspeed—it's a lot faster than our plasma pulses, anyway—and some sort of large-aperture pulse weapon that could probably blow an asteroid out of orbit if it had to."

"You've got sensor records on all this stuff?"

She nodded. "They're pulling the datachips out of our recorders down in Space Ops right now. You should be getting profile updates any moment."

"Very good," said Gil. "And what happened after you found out that *Sovay* had been destroyed?"

"Well, we shot at hostile targets until we'd used up all our missiles and our energy weapons were running empty, and then I decided to jump for the Net—didn't have the range or the data for anything else, really, and we figured that if anybody was still alive out here they'd have some more work for us."

"We certainly do, Lieutenant," Gil said. "Have your craft rearmed and prepare to launch as soon as you're combat-ready."

The lieutenant said, "Yes sir," and departed, guided by the messenger. Gil turned back to the TAO.

"Have we got those profile updates yet?"

The TAO checked the board. "Just came in. Interesting stuff, too—especially if you figure the Mageworlders built it all out of smuggled bits and pieces from our side of the Net."

"Nobody ever said they were stupid, Patel. Lock the profile data into our secondaries, and sent it over to *Shaja* and *Lachiel*."

*It might even reach them in time*, Gil added to himself.

The comms tech looked up from the board and said, "Net Station B-Fourteen is no longer transmitting, Commodore. We're unable to reestablish contact."

"Assume B-Fourteen is down, then," Gil said. "TAO—how many stations do we still have?"

"In this sector? B-Twenty-three is hanging out there on visual and still transmitting; and B-Twenty-five and B-Twenty-one both turned up on the last long-range comms sweep." The TAO shook his head in frustration. "Without hi-comms, there's no way to tell about the rest."

*It doesn't matter about the rest*, Gil thought. *Once the last three stations in this sector go, the Mages will have a hole big enough to jump their warfleet through.*

He sighed. "Very well. We'll hold Station B-Twenty-three until relief arrives or the tactical situation alters."

"Fighters report ready to launch," said a comms tech.

"Launch fighters," said Gil. "Vector to intercept inbound Mageships and identify targets for long-range stand-off weapons."

"*Lachiel* reports multiple hits," another tech reported. "Unable to maneuver in realspace. Losing airtight integrity, requests permission to withdraw."

Gil shook his head. "Send to *Lachiel*, 'Permission denied. Take targets under fire as long as you are able to bring weapons to bear.' "

*Sorry about that*, Lachiel. *But as long as they're shooting at you they aren't shooting at the Net Station . . . and every minute we can keep up the Net is a minute longer before the Magefleet can jump for Galcen.*

"We've lost Station B-Twenty-five," said the TAO a moment later, as if Gil's thoughts had been the signal for more bad news. "Net integrity less than fifty percent in this sector. There's nothing to stop them from jumping out."

"They won't jump yet," said Gil. "Not until their whole fleet can go. Hang on."

A bright light blossomed on an internal-view monitor, briefly illuminating the red-lit dimness of the CIC.

"Who just went up?" asked Gil. "Ours or theirs?"

"Our secondaries just took out one of the Mage fighters," said the TAO, after a glance at the status boards. "Son of a bitch was pretty damned close."

"They'll get closer," Gil told him. "How's engineering?"

"Engineering reports minimum standards available; Damage Control reports temporary repairs complete."

"Good," said Gil. "We can move and we can fight."

A crew member looked up from the sensor analysis panel. "They're massing out there, sir," he said to the TAO. "Just out of range."

*They're getting ready to jump*, Gil thought. *They'll head straight for Galcen—they have to; surprise is their big advantage, and if they don't take out Prime it's all wasted—but if anybody can handle this fleet, General Metadi can do it. As long as he gets the word in time . . .*

He looked over at the TAO. "What's the Net integrity now?"

"Down to thirty percent and falling fast. Stations B-Twenty-three and B-Fourteen can't hold up the field between them for long."

"Every second counts," Gil said. "The longer we can hold them, the more time Captain Rosselin-Metadi has to spread the word on the other end." He turned back to the crew member on the sensors. "Where are the Mageships located?"

"Netward of us, sir; none behind or below relative. They appear to be pulling away from active engagement with any targets besides the Net Stations."

"Getting ready for their jump run," said Gil; then, to the TAO, "Send to *Shaja* and *Lachiel*, 'On my signal, fire all available homers at the center of mass of Mageworlds tactical group. Reserve missiles until that time'."

"Lost carrier signal to Net Control Station B-Fourteen," the comms tech broke in.

"Sensors picking up radiation consistent with catastrophic energy release at location B-Fourteen," another crew member reported. "Net integrity fifteen percent ... ten ..."

"Stand by to sortie," said Gil. "We're going to take the war to the enemy. Beam and plasma weapons only. *Lachiel*, remain on station, fire at will. *Shaja*, take posit one-niner-five relative; I'm going to take posit zero-zero-three. Fighters, scan Mage comm frequencies. As soon as someone in the Mage formation starts transmitting, attack that unit—it'll be the commander."

He drew a deep breath. "Stand by, execute."

The deckplates under Gil's feet vibrated as the *'Pavo*'s already-stressed engines responded to the demand for more power. A few seconds later, alarms on the main control board began pipping as the ship's sensors detected the first inbound homers from the mass of Mageworld ships ahead. In the monitor screens, ugly flashes and streaks of light showed where the *'Pavo*'s own secondary weapons systems were sending out energy beams and slower-moving but even more deadly plasma slugs to intercept and destroy the oncoming missiles.

"We're within half-range now," reported the TAO.

"Close enough," said Gil. "Send to *Shaja*, weapons free."

"Weapons free, aye."

"Fire main batteries," he ordered, thinking, *With the Net failing, every second we can buy is vital. They can't fight and make a jump-run at the same time.* "Engage as many targets as possible. Send to *Shaja*, on my signal, fire all homers, empty the tubes."

"*Shaja* rogers for it."

"Send to *Shaja*, fire missiles."

"Fire missiles."

"Missiles away."

Gil let out his breath in a faint sigh. *And that's about all the damage we can do.* "*Shaja* and fighters, guide on me. Return to Net Control blocking stations. TAO—take us back to the Control Station."

"On the way."

"Sir!" exclaimed the crew member at the sensor analysis board. "Net integrity is down to five percent. The Magefleet is starting to move Galcenward."

Gil felt the sinking sensation of inevitability. *It's the jump-run.*

"Stay with them," he said. "Engage as many as possible."

A gory explosion lit up another monitor. A red dot winked out in the main battle tank just as a massive thud, not so much heard as felt, sounded in the *'Pavo*'s CIC.

"Engine hit, sir," reported the TAO. "One of their homers got through."

"Keep going—keep firing," said Gil.

"Keep firing aye," said the TAO. He was bent over the sensor analysis board, reading the data as it scrolled in. "The Magefleet isn't firing back anymore. They're passing us—Net integrity at three percent—they've got a hole—"

His voice dropped and flattened. "They've jumped."

# II. WARHAMMER: GALCEN NEARSPACE
## RSF FEZRISOND: INFABEDE SECTOR

WARHAMMER'S HYPERSPACE transit to Galcen ended up taking close to two Standard weeks. Jessan stood watch-and-watch with Beka the whole time. He barely saw the captain, except for the few minutes every four hours when she came forward to the cockpit for another stint of pushing the hyperspace engines to their limit and a shade beyond. Then Jessan would make his way aft through the common room to their darkened quarters, seal himself into the zero-g sleepsack, and fall into a thick, dreamless slumber. Four hours later the alarm on the far bulkhead would bring him awake with a jerk, and he'd head back to the cockpit for another watch.

With the galley off-line as nonessential, the 'Hammer's crew had to subsist on uncooked space rations, chewing up the dried bricks of unreconstituted food and washing the powdery mouthfuls down with cold-water instant cha'a. Ship's laundry and the sonic shower had also gone by the board in the name of speed. It didn't really matter; Jessan

and the captain slept in their dirtside clothes for lack of
time to change them, and cleanliness, like uninterrupted
rest, became nothing but a fading memory.

On the fourteenth day of the run, Jessan was off-watch
and asleep in the captain's cabin—the deep, unmoving
sleep of someone whose exhaustion has penetrated clear to
the bone. Then, without warning, he was awake, snapping
back to consciousness and pulling himself out of the sleepsack so quickly that he floated across the cabin and into
the far bulkhead before he could recover.

"What the *hell*?" he muttered.

Something was wrong. He couldn't hear any alarms or
warning signals, but he knew that the ship was in trouble
just the same. He made his way to the door, then worked
his way handhold by handhold through the common room,
nearly colliding with Ignaceu LeSoit on his way toward
the cockpit.

"What's up?" asked the gunman. He was pulling himself hand-over-hand along one bulkhead like an experienced free-spacer.

Jessan didn't stop moving forward. "Damned if I know.
But I sure as hell don't like it."

The two of them reached the pilot's compartment together, with Jessan a little in the lead. What he saw didn't
do much to ease his feeling of disaster. Beka had the cover
off part of the console, revealing the diagnostic readouts
beneath, and there were stars outside the cockpit viewscreens. That, he realized, was what had jolted him awake
from a dead sleep: the dropout from hyper.

He cleared his throat. "Beka?"

"Imbalance in drive number one," she said without looking up. "Don't know how bad yet."

"Damn." Jessan pulled himself forward to the copilot's
position. "I'd like to check our comms and get a navigational fix. Permission to put nonessentials back on-line?"

"Go ahead. Do it."

Jessan started flipping switches. The copilot's seat gave a little beneath him as the gravity eased back on, and for the first time in two weeks he was able to sit there properly instead of just occupying a position in space a millimeter or so above the padded surface. A faint thud behind him suggested that LeSoit had let go his handhold and dropped onto the deck.

"I'll be right back," the gunman said.

Beka only nodded. Jessan brought up the rest of the nonessential systems and set the ship's navicomps to working on a proper fix. Finally the captain straightened up from the diagnostic screens and put the cover back onto the console.

The long hyperspace run had left its mark: her hair was dingy and unkempt, and dark smudges shadowed the skin around her eyes. She pressed the heels of her hands against her forehead and sighed.

"Hell and damnation," she said. "Nyls, have you got anything from hi-comms or the navicomps?"

"No, and, unfortunately, yes."

"Damnation," she said again. "How bad is it?"

The cockpit doors slid open before Jessan could answer, and LeSoit's footsteps sounded on the deck. The rich, bitter-sharp aroma of fresh-brewed cha'a struck Jessan's nostrils, and Beka smiled faintly.

"Bless you, Ignac'," she said, reaching out to take the mug LeSoit handed her. "I may live after all."

"Rule one of the spacer's trade." The gunman passed another mug to Jessan and kept the third for himself. "No problem is so bad that cha'a can't help it."

"There's a first time for everything," Beka said. She drank off almost half of the mug's contents without stopping, heedless of the near-scalding temperature, and turned back to Jessan. "What were you going to say about the navicomps?"

Jessan had both hands wrapped around his mug of cha'a

for warmth. Two weeks without temperature control had chilled the ship almost to freezing. "Well, I have good news and bad news."

"I don't have time for jokes."

Jessan shook his head. "No joke. The bad news is that hi-comms are down hard in this sector, too. The good news is that we're only twelve light-days out of Galcen."

Beka scowled. "What the hell kind of good news is that? We might as well still be on Eraasi."

"I'll admit that it's a little too far to walk," he said, "but Space Force patrols this far out. There's a chance we can find someone who'll pass the word along."

"We'd better," she said. "Ignac', you stay up here and start broadcasting 'mechanical breakdown' on the distress frequency. Nyls, you and I have got some work to do."

"How long will it take?" LeSoit asked.

Beka shook her head. "I won't know until we can make a visual inspection of the hyperdrives. After they cool we'll have to realign them at least. Maybe reset the reference coordinates. Maybe more. Damn piece-of-junk Gyfferan engines."

*Warhammer*'s outsized power plant had been Beka's pride and joy for as long as Jessan had known her.

"Was it that bad?" he asked quietly.

"Bad?" She drained the rest of her cha'a, and Jessan saw for the first time that her hands were shaking in the backwash of an adrenaline reaction. "Bad? We almost went nova."

Being the head of a department on a flagship, Ari had discovered, required endless administration—or, as his sister Beka would have put it, hell's own supply of paperwork. He was sitting in his office aboard RSF *Fezrisond*, trying to project the next quarter's consumption of lint-free wipes and disposable bandages, when the buzzer sounded at his door.

"Yes?" he said, still working. "Can I help you?"

The door slid open. A tall lieutenant (junior grade) from the Operations department stood on the threshold, looking uncertain. "Can we talk privately?"

"Sure. Close the door."

Ari placed a small bet with himself. Either the fellow had caught some kind of venereal disease at a port call, or else his wife back home on Wherever was going to have a baby and he wanted to know what the process entailed.

"Well, it's a little embarrassing," the JG said as the door slid shut behind him. "Maybe you could take a look at this rash I've got. . . ."

*Port call*, Ari told himself, mentally paying off his bet.

He had already reached into the storage cabinet behind him for the appropriate medication—the problem was a common one, even here on the admiral's flagship—when he saw that the JG was holding a folded piece of paper in one hand. Ari looked at it and raised his eyebrows. The JG unfolded the slip of paper and laid it on Ari's desk.

Ari picked up the note and read it while the JG continued to babble nervously of rashes and other embarrassing symptoms.

"This compartment is wired for sound," the note read. "We need to talk in a secure space. Meet me at the starboard sensor nacelle in twenty minutes."

Ari crumpled the note and stuffed it into his trouser pocket for later disposal—in some other compartment, since the eavesdroppers, whoever they are, could have gotten to the trash recycler.

"Well," he said, "that certainly is an interesting rash, but I don't think it's anything serious. Keeping the area clean and dry for two weeks should do the trick."

The JG nodded. "You've been very helpful."

"Think nothing of it," Ari said. "See you later."

"Thank you," the JG said, and left.

Ari checked his chronometer. *Twenty minutes*? *Well,*

*why not?* He straightened up his desk, punched the Send button on the work he'd done, and walked out.

It was quiet on the big ship, midway through the forenoon watch. He made his way quickly to the sensor nacelle, after first stopping by his cabin to pick up a Berthing and Workspace Sanitary Inspection Module for his clipboard. He was going to have to do those inspections this week anyway; if anyone asked him why he was wandering around, he'd have a legitimate excuse.

*What am I thinking of?* he wondered. *I'm a lieutenant commander, on board the ship where I'm assigned, carrying out the duties of my position. Why should I have to explain anything to anyone?*

Just the same, he found himself wishing—and not for the first time, either—that Llannat Hyfid could have come with him to the *Fezzy*. The Adept had a knack for sensing these things; maybe she could have told him what was wrong.

*Because there sure as hell is* something *going on, and it's so rotten that I'm even beginning to smell it.*


Twelve light-days out from Galcen, *Warhammer* drifted in vacuum. Tethered to the ship's hull by lifelines, two pressure-suited figures worked over the external hyperdrive components.

"Test pad one," Beka said over the link.

"Test one, aye," Jessan replied. He pushed the button.

"Test pad one sat," Beka said. The voicelink from her suit's helmet picked up the sound of her breath along with the words. "Test pad two."

"Third-party modifications screw up everything," Jessan muttered. "You should be able to do voyage repairs without having to suit up and go out in vacuum."

"Save your philosophy of design for later," said Beka. "Test pad two."

"Test two, aye," Jessan responded, and pressed the next button.

LeSoit's voice broke in over the link from the cockpit. "Captain, Doc—I just picked up a response on lightspeed comms. Looks like Space Force is out here."

"Great," Jessan said. "Respond to them. And say these words, exactly; 'Cosmic daylight break authenticate one five echo.' Repeat it back to me."

" 'Cosmic daylight break authenticate one five echo.' "

"You got it," Jessan said. "Now transmit and let me know how they respond."

"What was that?" Beka asked.

"Remember I told you that getting through the Net wouldn't be a problem? Assuming the skipper of whoever's out here has the clearance, what I just told him should bounce him right out of bed."

"Fine," said Beka. "Now test pad three."

"Test pad three, aye."


Ari reached the starboard sensor nacelle exactly twenty Standard minutes, by his chronometer, from the time his unexpected visitor had passed him the cryptic note.

He wasn't particularly surprised to meet the same JG coming down the passageway from the opposite direction. The young officer nodded to Ari without speaking and gestured to him to follow. In silence, they made their way back along the outboard passage into "fighter country," the part of the *Fezzy* that was reserved for the fighter detachment.

They halted at the door of the pilots' ready room. Ari palmed the lockplate, but nothing happened. He looked at the JG. The younger officer reached past him and touched the lockplate. The door slid open, and Ari followed the JG inside before it could close again.

In theory, as head of the *Fezzy*'s medical department, Ari should have had his ID scan on file in ship's memory with override access to all spaces—but in theory, the head medic's office shouldn't have had snoop-buttons planted in it, and junior officers shouldn't be inviting him to mysterious private meetings.

*Somebody jury-rigged a new ID filter on that lockplate*, Ari thought as the door slid shut behind him. *I hope they remember to switch it back before the next time one of them needs a medic in a hurry.*

The ready room was packed with what looked like all of the pilots and other ranks from the fighter detachment, crammed in so tightly that the ventilation systems were having trouble clearing the air. The senior officer of the det, another lieutenant commander, stood by the forward bulkhead.

"That's it," he said. "I believe that's everyone. All doors secure?"

"Secure, aye," said another one of the fighter pilots.

"Listening device disabled?"

"Disabled."

"Great." He turned to Ari. "Whatever you decide to do, Commander, please don't do anything foolish. You won't leave this space without my permission."

Ari nodded, slowly. "I can see that. Do you mind telling me what this is all about?"

"We're having a mutiny, and you're part of it," the lieutenant commander replied. "You'll have a chance to join us; but be assured that you won't be allowed to hinder us."

Ari forced himself to relax. He was too far away from the lieutenant commander, the JG, and the door to get to any one of them in a single stride; better to wait until he knew who was involved and how they were armed. Judging by the growls and muttered exclamations that arose from the rest of the group, he wasn't the only one hearing the news for the first time.

The JG who'd slipped him the note spoke next, addressing not just Ari but the room in general. "It is my belief that Admiral Vallant is in open rebellion against the Republic."

More exclamations and noises of disbelief came from the crowd, but the JG kept on talking.

"At the moment, we are underway for an unknown location—but getting underway at this time is entirely against the mission of this vessel. Further, Admiral Vallant has placed personal friends or those who owe him favors in command of *every* vessel in this sector. In addition, hi-comms are down, and I have reason to believe that Vallant knew in advance that they would be. The bulkheads to senior-officer country are sealed, and no one other than Vallant's handpicked few are in the engine room, in Combat, or on the bridge."

The JG paused for a moment. When the general buzz of comment died down, he went on.

"We had been ordered to deliver messages, hardcopy, across the fleet. As it happens, I know what those messages contained: ultimata for every planet in this sector, directing them to swear loyalty to Vallant personally or face destruction by his fleet. The ultimata are being delivered at this time. Also at this time, Lieutenant Commander Rosselin-Metadi was to be arrested and held as hostage against the actions of his father, the Commanding General."

"And that," said the commander of the fighter det, turning to address Ari directly, "is why we arrested you. If you're going to be a bargaining chip, we'd like you to be ours."

"Believe me, I understand your position," said Ari. He could tell from the way the JG and the det commander were watching him that they had expected something far more explosive by way of response. *Fine*, he thought. *Let them stay confused until I figure out what's really up.* "But what happens if I don't want to be a bargaining chip at all?"

The det commander looked regretful. "I'm afraid you don't have much choice."

*It's a good thing Beka didn't join the service*, Ari thought. *Telling her that she doesn't have a choice is a quick way to get blood all over the deckplates. Bee never did know how to wait for anything.*

But Ari had learned about patience and subtlety a long time ago, when Ferrdacorr gave him hunting lessons in the forests of Maraghai. He was not going to get drawn into a fight now, when he was outnumbered—and when he didn't know for certain where his true enemies lay.

"I suppose I'll have to believe you," he said aloud. "You know more about the situation than I do at the moment. How many people are aligned with you . . . I mean, with us?"

"Enough, I hope," said the det commander, looking distinctly relieved that Ari had not chosen to put up a violent resistance. "For the moment, though—I'm sorry, but we'll have to put you under guard."

Two hours after *Warhammer*'s initial contact with the Space Force vessel, a ship dropped out of hyperspace near the outer edge of the 'Hammer's sensor range. Beka made it to the cockpit in time to see the comm panel start blinking.

She glanced over at her copilot. "Nyls?"

"Transmitting Space Force identifiers," he said. "Looks like our rescuers are here."

"I don't want a rescue," she said. "I can rescue myself just fine, thank you. I want somebody who can carry the news back to Galcen."

She put on the earphone link for the comms. A quick check of lightspeed communications and the relay stations showed nothing on the frequencies except noise and, far away, a program of dance music from somewhere in Galcen Prime. Over on hi-comms there was still nothing.

"Direct hyperspace communications are still down," she said. "Whatever the Mages are doing, they're doing it here, too. I can't believe people aren't running around screaming and panicking."

"Planetary hi-comms may not have been down this whole time," Jessan pointed out. "Just the transmissions from the Net. That's how I'd do it, with an agent in place to pass along fake reports from the Magezone saying that everything is just fine and dandy and how's the weather back home."

"Say something to cheer me up, why don't you?" said Beka. "We already know the Mageworlders have some-body on our side working for them. And if hi-comms just now went out in Galcen space—"

"Then the Magefleet can't be all that far behind us."

"Oh, wonderful. And here we are, drifting like a rock. Time to start talking, I think."

Beka slid aside an access plate on the top surface of the comm panel. Using her fingernails, she teased the datachip bearing *Pride of Mandeyn*'s ID data out of its socket and laid it aside. Then she pulled a second, older chip from its hiding place in the panel's inner recesses and slotted it back in.

"No more disguises," she said.

She switched over to lightspeed comms, fed as much power to the output as she could without burning out the plate, and began to broadcast. "Space Force vessel, Space Force vessel, this is Reserve Merchant Vessel *Warhammer*, comm check, over."

She paused for a response, then repeated the call.

"They're eight light-minutes out," she said after the second broadcast. "It'll take a while to hear back from them. But I wouldn't be surprised by a rather confused welcome."

"Absolutely nothing surprises me anymore," said Jessan. "Satisfy my curiosity, though—why are we using the old call sign? With you and the *'Hammer* both officially dead, anyone with that ID is going to get listed as a fake right away."

"Maybe," Beka said. "But I'll bet the report gets sent straight on to Dadda anyhow. He knows I'm still alive, and using his call sign is one way to get his personal attention."

"I hope you're right."

"So do I." Beka picked up the link again. "Space Force vessel, Space Force vessel, this is RMV *Warhammer*. Comm check, over."

Again there was no response. Beka checked the navicomps and the chronometer. Then she glanced at the sensor readouts. "Too slow."

A short while later, the comm link picked up a voice signal. She put it onto the cockpit speakers so that Jessan wouldn't have to wonder what was going on.

"Unknown vessel, unknown vessel," the voice was saying. "This is Republic warship one-zero-niner-seven. Request you identify yourself."

Beka took a deep breath. "Here we go," she muttered, and keyed on the link.

"This is Space Force Reserve vessel *Warhammer*," she told the voice. "Request secure link, captain-to-captain."

The lightspeed comms beeped twice as the crypto synchronized. Beka opened the link again.

"One-zero-niner-seven," she said, "this is *Warhammer*. Request you pass to commander, Space Defense Command: attack of Galcen by Mageworlds warfleet imminent, over."

There was a several-second transmission lag as Beka's lightspeed signal crossed the distance between the two ships and the warship's reply came back again.

"This is one-zero-niner-seven actual; who am I talking to?"

She straightened her shoulders. "This is Captain Beka

Rosselin-Metadi speaking. The Inner Net is down; the status of the Outer Net is unknown. I need you to patch me directly through to the Commanding General."

Again the transmission lag and then the voice. "Come dead in space, *Warhammer*, and zero your guns. I intend to board you."

Beka drew in her breath between her teeth. "I do not intend to be boarded. Read my ID signal. This is a Republic warship, and I need to report to the Commanding General."

Another, briefer pause—the gap between the two vessels was steadily closing—and then the other ship's captain replied. "Your ID is not listed. *Warhammer* crashed. Rosselin-Metadi is dead. If you attempt to enter Galcen space you will be destroyed. Come dead in space. Do it now."

"Oh, dear," said Jessan. "This isn't working well at all."

"They've got idiots in the Home Fleet," she said under her breath. "Idiots. What happened with your secret security message? Why doesn't he believe us?"

"Well . . . not everybody has your family's, ah, casual attitude toward the formalities. He could be one of those captains who believes in doing everything strictly by the book. He's being cautious, is all. For all he knows, the codes were broken and this is a Mage trick to get control of his ship."

"Going by the book'll kill you every time," she said. "You're Space Force, Nyls—what's next?"

The Khesatan looked thoughtful. "What's wrong with allowing them to board?"

"I don't like—"

"These are the good guys, remember? Talk with them, show them around—let them get a look at your face, for heaven's sake! Anybody who ever saw a flatpic of your mother is going to think twice about calling you a liar then."

"We haven't got the time for all this nonsense . . . but you're probably right."

She put *Warhammer* into a skew-flip and began to decelerate under main power. Then she unstrapped and stood up.

"You've got the conn," she told Jessan. "Bring LeSoit up here to fill the other seat, and tell your pals we're ready to receive a boarding party."

"Where will you be?"

"In my cabin getting dressed," she said. "If I have to talk us in on the strength of a family resemblance, I'm going to have to look better than this."

**III.** Warhammer: Galcen Patrol Zone
RSF *Naversey*: The Outer Net
Galcen: The Retreat

THE COMMANDER of 1097 didn't seem in a hurry to rendezvous with the 'Hammer and come aboard. Beka rushed her own shower-and-change as much as she dared—getting her long hair back to its natural pale yellow from Tarnekep Portree's nondescript brown was a finicky process, but one she couldn't omit—and then got on the intraship link to the cockpit.

"What's the status on our visitor?" she asked.

"Still not here, Captain," Jessan's voice replied from the bulkhead speaker. "He's doing everything by the book, just like I said—approaching at moderate speed, then standing off and observing through active scanners."

"Damn." She bit her lip. "Patch me through to him, right now."

"Aye, Captain."

Beka waited for the double beep and said, "One-zero-niner-seven, this is *Warhammer*. There are people *dying* to buy us the time you're wasting! Rosselin-Metadi, out."

She slapped the link closed and turned back to the cabin mirror for a final check. Tarnekep Portree hadn't vanished completely—the Mandeynan starpilot had been her alter ego for too long—but she'd done the best she could, swapping Portree's lace-trimmed finery for plain free-spacer's gear and omitting the scarlet eye patch altogether. Her hair hung loose; she scowled at it for a moment, then began separating it into strands for braiding. She still remembered the pattern, or her fingers did, which came to the same thing, and soon she had a coronet of multiple braids arranged in the old Entiboran style.

*All I need is the goddamned iron crown. . . .*

She left the captain's cabin and strode into the *'Hammer*'s common room. Nyls Jessan was already there, leaning against the bulkhead with folded arms and a fine air of unconcern that she might have believed if she hadn't looked at his eyes first.

"Where's Ignac'?" she demanded.

"Waiting at the airlock to receive our visitors when they decide to show up."

"Good," she said. She was pacing by now, back and forth from the acceleration couches to the mess table. "So what the hell is keeping the bastards?"

"Patience," Jessan murmured, "patience. We're in the Galcen control zone now, and there's a certain formality here that you don't find in the frontier worlds—"

Beka snarled. Before she could say anything, the intra-ship comm link crackled open and LeSoit's voice came over the bulkhead speaker. "Boarding party inbound, Captain."

She forced herself to stop pacing and wait. Three minutes later by her chronometer, LeSoit ushered in the boarding party—an officer and two senior enlisted, just like at the Net. The leader of the team, a full lieutenant this time, gave Beka a dazzling parade-ground salute.

"Captain, the commanding officer of my vessel extends

an invitation to you and your second-in-command to meet with him aboard our craft."

"Do I have a choice?"

"Permission to speak freely?" the lieutenant said.

"Granted," she said tightly.

"Then . . . I'm afraid you don't, Captain."

She drew a long breath, then let it out again. "Very well. LeSoit!"

"Captain."

"Take care of the ship while I'm gone."

"Aye, Captain."

LeSoit left for the cockpit, and Beka turned back to the waiting lieutenant. "Let's go."

In the company of the boarding party, Beka and Jessan made their way through the 'Hammer's airlock to the shuttle. After a brief crossing to the Republic warship, they soon found themselves being ushered into the captain's mess. The captain was there before them, sitting at the table with a couple of other officers.

He rose as they came into the mess and gestured them into chairs. "I'm sorry about this," he said as he took his own seat again, "but a face-to-face conference seemed to be best. The open comm circuits aren't really suited—"

"Right," Beka cut in. "Listen to me. The Mageworlders have broken the Inner Net, and they were attacking the Outer Net as we passed through. And that was two weeks ago."

"You made the transit from the Net in just two weeks?"

He sounded dubious. She pressed her lips together and met his gaze without blinking.

"Yes."

"You didn't bother to use hi-comms? And the commander of the Net Patrol Fleet didn't use them either?"

Jessan answered for her this time. "Hi-comms are down," he said. "Test them for yourself."

The captain looked at the lieutenant who had escorted

them over from *Warhammer*. The lieutenant nodded and left.

"We will check, of course," said the captain. He leaned back in his chair and put the tips of his fingers together. "While we're waiting for confirmation on the hi-comms— what exactly is your request? Your initial message stated mechanical breakdown. Do you require transit to an inhabited world? If so, regulations require that you be charged for the passage, unless you can prove yourself destitute."

"I don't need a transit to anywhere, thank you," Beka said. "I'm in the process of making voyage repairs right now. I do need you to carry word of the Mage breakthrough to Galcen."

The captain looked at her. "Let me get this straight. You have traveled here from the Net much faster than possible; you have made initial contact under a false ID; and you want me to put the whole Space Force onto high alert on your word alone?"

Beka clenched her fists. *I've killed people for less than what this son of a bitch doesn't even know he's doing.*

"I *am* Beka Rosselin-Metadi," she said, "and I want you to give me a direct line to my father. Let me talk to the Commanding General, and we'll see whose word is and isn't any good around here. And while you're thinking about it—ask yourself what happens if the rest of my story checks out too."

The pause that followed seemed to stretch out forever. At last Jessan broke the silence.

"A moment, Captain," he said. "I am Lieutenant Commander Nyls Jessan, SFMS, lineal number five eight niner niner six three. I am TAD to Intelligence, on detached duty in the Magezone. I have a Link-level clearance. May I have a word alone with you and your security manager?"

A buzzer sounded. The warship's captain picked up a handset. "Down? Very well. Have Mr. Yeldin report to the captain's mess, and keep on trying." He turned to the other two officers in the mess. "Please escort Captain—ah—Captain Rosselin-Metadi to the wardroom."

Beka and the two officers stood and left. Just outside the door to the captain's mess she almost ran into a third officer hurrying the other way—probably the "Mr. Yeldin" who'd been summoned earlier. The wardroom wasn't far from the captain's mess; Beka had no sooner arrived and been offered a cup of cha'a when the attention signal sounded.

"All officers not actually on watch, muster in the wardroom."

The captain of one-zero-niner-seven arrived a moment later himself, accompanied by Jessan and the other officer, whom Beka presumed was the security manager. The captain gestured to an ensign with supply corps tabs on her uniform.

"Please escort Captain Rosselin-Metadi and Commander Jessan back to their vessel," he said. "Let them take the shuttle alone."

"Thank you, Captain," Jessan said, and they followed the ensign out.

Beka didn't say anything until they were back onto the shuttle and headed for *Warhammer*. Then she turned to Jessan.

"All right, Nyls—what did you tell that guy? He looked like he'd seen a ghost."

"Nothing much," said Jessan. "I just filled him in on a few truths. At the same time, he discovered for himself that he had no communications. The combination proved irresistible."

LeSoit was waiting for them in the airlock vestibule. "Did you see what that bugger did?" he demanded. "He was already on a run-to-jump before you got halfway back—left his shuttle with us, too. I hope he doesn't expect us to pay for it."

Jessan raised an eyebrow. "Pay for it? Surely not. Neither the captain nor I instructed him to abandon the boarding craft—we merely impressed on him the seriousness of the situation."

"Now that you two have gotten the pleasantries out of the way," Beka said, "let's turn to. We have some hyper-space engines to repair."

Llannat was moving through the ShadowDance exercises as best she could in the cramped space of RSF *Naversey*'s passenger compartment when the bulkhead speaker crackled to life.

"All hands secure your personal belongings and strap in. Dropping out of hyperspace in about five minutes."

She was surprised by the announcement; none of the passengers aboard *Naversey* had been expecting dropout for at least another day. Even in a fast courier, one of the speediest ships the Space Force owned, such an early arrival meant that the crew had been pushing things the whole way. And courier schedules were grim enough—the pilot and copilot generally stood watch-and-watch during the entire run as a matter of course—that nobody was going to make one even tighter without a command from above.

*Finding that derelict Deathwing must have put everybody into serious panic*, Llannat thought. *I don't think I've ever seen the top brass moving so fast over something that isn't a shooting matter.*

She made certain that her carrybag was properly stashed in the luggage compartment, went back to her acceleration couch, and strapped herself in. Around her in the passenger cabin, the others were doing the same thing. She knew all her fellow-passengers by surname at least by now, after the enforced intimacy of such a long transit: E'Patu and Rethiel, the two warrants; Lury, the med service captain; Govantic, the data specialist; and the linguist-historian Vinhalyn.

The bulkhead speaker crackled again. "Stand by for hyperspace translation and deceleration."

The announcement was a formality; Llannat knew that the pilot's status board would have flashed an alert signal if anything in the passenger compartment was unsecured. Nevertheless, she checked her safety webbing one more time just to make certain.

"Dropout in ten seconds," said the speaker. "Five seconds. Four. Three. Two. One. Now."

Llannat felt the faint shock of discontinuity that marked the transition from hyperspace to the normal universe. Once out in realspace again, *Naversey* began decelerating smoothly. From here it shouldn't take long to rendezvous with RSF *Ebannha* and the Deathwing.

*I hope they let us unpack and eat a proper meal before we start investigating*, she thought. *I'm getting tired of low-mass space rations. And I seriously need a shower. And laundry. . . .*

"Senior line officer present, please come to the bridge."

Startled out of her reverie, Llannat glanced first at the bulkhead speaker and then at her fellow-passengers, trying to determine who was meant by the summons. She herself was out on two counts—as a member of the medical service, she was support, not line; and as an Adept she was barred from holding formal rank.

*Lury's out, too*, she thought, *and both warrants. That leaves our two reservists. Lieutenants, both of them—this could get sticky.*

By now the others had all worked through the same or similar lines of reasoning, and Govantic and Vinhalyn were eyeing each other speculatively. The younger man started to unstrap the safety webbing on his acceleration couch.

"Excuse me," Vinhalyn said quietly.

Govantic paused. "You heard what the man said. I'm wanted up in the cockpit."

"Not necessarily," said Vinhalyn. "Our pilot called for the senior line officer present—and since I served in the late War, I believe my commission predates yours."

Govantic sank back onto his couch, looking disgruntled. Lieutenant Vinhalyn unstrapped and made his way forward through the vacuum-tight door to the cockpit, leaving an uneasy silence behind him. Several minutes passed, and then the bulkhead speaker came on again.

"Mistress Hyfid, please come to the bridge."

Llannat wondered nervously what the pilot—*and Vinhalyn,* she reminded herself; *nobody called you until he was up there*—would be wanting an Adept for, out here in the middle of nowhere. Obediently, she got out of her seat and went forward. The vacuum-tight doors opened for her and sighed shut again as she entered the cockpit.

*Please come up to the Retreat at once. There is something I have to show you. Ransome.*

Brigadier General Perrin Ochemet had found the cryptic summons waiting on his desktop when he returned from lunch. His eyebrows had gone up. The Space Force didn't need anything from the Guild at the moment, and he certainly hadn't asked. Then he'd shrugged (*Maybe Ransome wants something from us for a change*) and made arrangements for one of the duty atmospheric-craft pilots to fly him into the mountains beyond Treslin, and up to the massive stone pile that was the Retreat.

Unlike the first trip he'd made, this one was almost relaxing. Nothing urgent required his attention at the moment; the only crisis, the disappearance of General Metadi and the death of the General's aide, had been ongoing for a while now with no change—and as Metadi himself was fond of saying, "Anything that lasts more than a week isn't a crisis, it's a situation." Ochemet could lean back against the padded seat and take an afternoon nap with a reasonably clear conscience.

This time, the airfield at the Retreat had a hovercar waiting for him when he arrived. Ochemet rode up the narrow switchback road to the citadel, and found the Guild Master waiting again in the courtyard.

"Well," Ochemet said, as the hovercar purred away to wherever the Adepts at the Retreat kept such things, and the massive ironwood gates swung closed, "I got your message. Here I am. Where is this thing I'm supposed to see?"

"Come with me," said Ransome. He turned and began climbing the narrow stone steps that led up from the courtyard onto the walls. Ochemet shrugged and followed.

Once on the battlements, Ransome led the way to another stair, this one spiraling upward inside a dark, thick-walled tower. They emerged at the top to walk along more battlements to where a second, even higher tower reared up over them, and then climbed yet another spiral stair up to the highest point in the Retreat. Nothing but the dull blue sky of late evening remained above them on this topmost level, not even the banners that might have flown over such a fortress in the ancient days; the Adepts flew no one's banner, and had none of their own.

The sun was setting—in Prime, Ochemet reflected, it would be close to midnight by now—and a chill wind blew down across the watchtower from the icy face of the mountains beyond the Retreat. Master Ransome looked out at the ragged skyline and said nothing.

"Well?" said Ochemet again. "Where is it?"

Ransome shook his head. "I don't know. All I know is that there is something here tonight that you and I will see. And I know that you and I are together when we see it, and that it will be important to us both."

*This*, Ochemet reminded himself, *was why you wanted someone else to handle liaison with the Guild.*

"Do you know what this thing is?" he asked.

The Adept made an impatient gesture. "If I knew, I

would tell you." He smiled briefly, without much humor. "Unless, of course, you shouldn't know it."

"That's not especially helpful," said Ochemet. "And if I wasn't sure that you were on our side, I'd worry." He paused. "I'm waiting."

Ransome was silent for a while longer. Then, still looking out across the darkening landscape, he asked, "What do you know about the Mages?"

The question caught Ochemet off guard. "Not much more than anybody else does," he said after a moment. "A bit more than some people, maybe—I was around for the tail end of the War."

"Then you saw the end of their hegemony and the destruction of their works," said Ransome. "But you know almost nothing of their philosophy."

"I leave that to your people."

Ransome laughed; Ochemet thought he heard a faint note of bitterness in the sound. "My people. Things would be easier for me if they really were. But no one controls anyone else, ever. No one is possessed by another, ever. No matter what the Magelords think."

"If you say so," Ochemet said uneasily. "I wouldn't know."

"No," said Ransome. "I suppose you wouldn't. But have you heard anything . . . unusual . . . from the Mageworlds lately?"

Ochemet thought about the Magebuilt raider that was even now gliding through the Outer Net, and about the team of specialists traveling out to examine it. Their courier ship would drop out of hyper soon; their first report might come as early as tonight or tomorrow. The team—including an Adept. Had she reported to Ransome, Ochemet wondered, and if so, how? For that matter, how did Adepts do any of the things they did?

He decided to hedge. The formal report hadn't yet shown up on his desk, which as far as the regs were concerned made him still officially ignorant. "Nothing's happened lately that hasn't happened before."

Ransome turned toward him. "Don't trifle with me," was all the Guild Master said, his words as soft and mild as ever. Then he turned away again, and was silent.

The tension in *Naversey*'s cockpit hit Llannat like a physical blow; she had to grab at one of the zero-g handholds to steady herself.

*What's wrong? Everything* looks *okay. . . .*

She took a deep breath to restore her equilibrium, then glanced about the cockpit. The starfield that glowed outside the cockpit viewscreens appeared normal, at least as far as she could tell; if there was a problem, it wasn't close enough to see. Vinhalyn and the two pilots were looking at the control-panel readouts instead, and the very air around them was full of the dark colors of dismay.

Llannat cleared her throat. "Mistress Hyfid reporting as ordered. Is there some kind of problem?"

The pilot nodded. "*Ebannha*'s not here."

"Not here. You mean you can't find her?"

"I've already been through this with Lieutenant Vinhalyn," said the pilot; his voice had a ragged edge to it. "I mean she's not here. These are the coordinates we were given; we should be close enough already to pick her up as a bright star on visual. And she isn't here. No visual, no comm signals, no ID signals, nothing."

"Not quite nothing," Vinhalyn said. The academic had a tight-lipped expression quite unlike anything Llannat had seen on his face before. "The sensors are picking up a great deal of hot drifting metal. And hi-comms are completely down—our attempts to contact Prime, or anyone else, have been in vain."

"Hot drifting metal." Llannat shook her head. "What's been going on out here?"

"I don't know," said the pilot. "And I don't like it. I

think we ought to head back to Galcen. But I'm just the taxi driver for this expedition—Lieutenant Vinhalyn has the final call. And he says we ought to consult with you first."

"Me?" She looked at Vinhalyn. "What am I supposed to know that you guys don't?"

The former academic shrugged. "Perhaps nothing. But I learned during the Magewar that it never hurts to ask."

"Right," she said. She looked out at the starfield again, a myriad glowing dots against the black. *So now I'm supposed to make like some kind of oracle ... what do I tell him, that I can't do that sort of thing on order? Better at least give it a try first.*

Closing her eyes, she tried to sense the patterns that flowed through the universe beyond the cockpit. Nothing at first; she had trouble working with the immensity that was realspace between the stars.

*Relax*, she told herself. *Don't push it.*

She let the patterns move for a while without watching them, letting herself float and grow accustomed to this new experience. Abruptly there was a shifting sensation, much like dropping out of hyper, as her awareness flexed and changed, leaving her newly at ease with the scale of things. And, in the next instant, certain of what she was seeing.

*Magework. Magework and dark sorcery.*

Not since the raid on Darvell, when Magelords and Circle-Mages had manipulated the fabric of the universe to fight both her and each other, had she felt the patterns twisted and knotted like this. And nowhere out there was any spark of light. It was all dead. . . .

*No. Not quite.*

"On."

Her voice came out in a hoarse croak. She didn't have any idea how long she'd stood with her awareness turned away from her physical surroundings; her knees would have given way if Vinhalyn hadn't steadied her.

"We need to go on."

# IV. RSF *Selsyn-bilai*: Infabede Sector Galcen Nearspace

By THE time RSF *Selsyn-bilai* reached the dropout point for the Infabede sector, the engineering warrant officer who currently answered to the name Gamelan Bandur was more than ready to see realspace again. A stores ship like the *Selsyn* took its time about getting from one place to another, spending several weeks in hyper for the same journey a courier ship could make in a couple of days. Such unhurried progress irritated a man who had always preferred his starships fast and dangerous. On the other hand, the *Selsyn* had been going back and forth between Infabede and the supply depots of the Inner Worlds for several years now, and the warrant officers' mess was full of very interesting gossip. Bandur had listened, contributing now and then a humorous anecdote from the shipyards of Galcen Prime, and had taken copious mental notes.

Elsewhere aboard the *Selsyn*, he supposed, CC1 Ennys Pardu had been pursuing similar interests. Except for occasional brief glimpses, he hadn't seen the clerk/comptech since they'd both come aboard, but he remembered her efficiency very well. If RSF *Selsyn-bilai*'s record files held something she considered important, stopping her would take more data security than a stores ship was likely to be able to muster. Bandur hoped that she was equally competent at covering her tracks afterward.

On a large vessel like the *Selsyn*, artificial-intelligence routines in a ship's memory handled most aspects of the the dropout from hyperspace, but the engineering spaces kept up full crews just the same, in case of emergencies. Both the realspace and the hyperspace engines underwent considerable stress at the moment of transition, and the systems of a vessel with the mass of a stores ship were orders of magnitude more complex than those of a small cargo vessel.

Bandur had a station in Main Control, monitoring the datalink that transmitted the conning officer's helm and throttle commands from the bridge down to the AI systems in Engineering. The smooth functioning of the *Selsyn*'s machinery and the performance of her transition-detail team impressed him, in spite of his long-standing preference for fighting ships—and in spite of the fact that where shiphandling was concerned, he'd never been an easy man to please.

He listened to the speaker on the IC panel as it echoed the words of the bridge team:

"Stand by for realspace." . . . "Standing by." . . . "On my mark, drop out, mark." . . . "Realspace transition."

On the panel, the power readouts flickered as the realspace engines cut in, and the accelerometer began to show negative during deceleration. Bandur nodded to himself in satisfaction and verified the log entry showing time of dropout.

"Right, then," the chief engineer said. "Secure from hyperspace running."

Shortly afterward the speaker on Bandur's panel came to life again, this time relaying the voices of the junior officer of the watch and the officer of the deck:

"Two contacts, close aboard. Friendlies." ... "Roger, prepare arrival report for transmission." ... "Aye, aye."

He listened, curious. In the old days, even friendly contacts this soon would have been reason for serious alarm; nobody back then had good reasons for waiting around so close to a known drop point.

*Plenty of bad ones, though ... I remember the points just beyond Ophel, where the big Magebuilt cargo ships used to halt and top off on fuel and stores before the long push home. On a good day you could pick off the escorts one at a time as they came through, and after that it was easy pickings. ...*

Bandur shrugged. Times changed; no one knew that better than he did. He turned to his duties, supervising the junior crew members as they secured the hyperspace engines preparatory to opening them for inspection. A few minutes later he was surprised to see the chief engineer walking over to him.

"Secure, Mister Bandur. Skipper wants to see you in his cabin, instantly."

*Now, what the hell. . .?* "On my way."

Bandur spoke to the leading petty officer in his party—"Carry on smartly"—and left Main Control by the vacuum-tight door leading forward. He strode through the passageways to senior officer country without any hesitations or false turnings, and found his way to the captain's cabin. Once there he knocked, then palmed the lockplate. As soon as the door slid open, he took a step forward and came to a careful attention, his thumbs aligned with the seams of his uniform trousers.

"Warrant Officer Bandur, reporting as ordered."

"Very well, Bandur," said the CO—the longest speech

that he'd made to the warrant so far. "Stand easy. Captain Tyche here has a couple of things for you."

Bandur relaxed and looked around the captain's cabin for the first time, just as another officer, this one in Infantry uniform, entered the space.

"Mister Bandur," the newcomer said, "I have orders that you accompany me."

*I don't know what they've got waiting back on Galcen,* Bandur thought, *but if it isn't something really good I'll have Perrin Ochemet's guts for garters.*

"Yes, sir," he said aloud. "Shall I collect my gear?"

The Infantry captain shook his head. "That won't be necessary. Your gear is being collected for you right now."

One of the comm links on the desk beeped. The CO picked it up—it was a hush-circuit, mostly earpiece with a small vocal pickup attached—and kept an eye on Tyche and Bandur as he talked: "The devil you say! . . . Retransmit. . . . *All* circuits? . . . Are you sure? . . . Well, keep trying."

Bandur glanced over at Captain Tyche. "Mind if I ask what's happening?"

Something about the Infantry captain, possibly the way his appearance managed to combine wholesome square-jawed blandness with an impression of knife-edged efficiency, suggested to Bandur that there was more to Tyche than met the eye. *One of the Intel boys*, the warrant officer conjectured. *Perrin must be seriously worried.* He wasn't surprised when Tyche said only, "There's been a modification to your orders. You're to come with me."

The quick pinging of a portable comm link sounded from Tyche's belt. The Infantry captain pulled the device free and thumbed it on.

"I have a party from that long-range recon craft we spotted earlier," a tinny voice said. "They request permission to board and inspect."

"Permission denied," Tyche said into the link. "I say again, denied." He nodded to the *Selsyn*'s CO, who was still on the hush-link and all but ignoring the two men. "Sir, I'm taking this man with me in accordance with my orders."

The CO waved a hand to signify that he understood. Tyche palmed the lockplate for the outer door and gestured at Bandur to precede him through it.

Just as the warrant officer stepped forward to cross the threshold into the corridor beyond, a movement in the cabin behind him caught his eye. Two more men in uniform had entered the space through the inner door. They didn't look like any of the regular crew, though, and they carried sidearms—definitely not standard operating procedure on board the *Selsyn*.

*This is starting to smell like genuine trouble.*

The years had provided Warrant Officer Bandur with a well-developed set of protective instincts. He kept on moving, with Tyche close on his heels. Behind them, the first of the new arrivals was saying to the CO, "Captain, you're under arrest."

The *Selsyn*'s captain started to his feet. "The hell—!"

"By order of Admiral Vallant. . . ."

*Vallant*, thought Bandur with perverse satisfaction as the door closed behind him and Tyche. *I thought there was something going on in Infabede!*

Outside, the bulkhead speaker began an announcement. "All officers please assemble in the forward wardroom. All officers please assemble in the forward wardroom. All officers . . ."

"If you ask me," said Bandur, "that sound like a damned unhealthy order to be obeying right now."

Tyche just looked at him. "You know your way around the ship a lot better than I do. What's the quickest route to the docking bays?"

Bandur consulted his mental map. "This corridor, up a level, then starboard."

Tyche nodded. "You lead, I'll follow."

Beka seated herself in the pilot's chair and belted on the safety webbing. "Places, everyone."

"The shuttle's cast adrift with a beacon on it," came LeSoit's voice over the intraship comm link.

"Good. If the Space Force wants it, they can come get it. Now we find out if our repairs are going to hold."

"Let's not push it," Jessan said. "There's no point in blowing ourselves up before we get there."

"There's a time to be cautious," Beka said without looking at him, "and this isn't it." She pushed the realspace engines to full forward. "Navicomp data check, confirm. Near approach Galcen, check, confirm. Stand by, jump."

She pushed the throttles forward the last bit needed for jump speed, and flicked on the hyperspace engines. The stars winked out and the substance of space went to opalescent grey. She heard a sigh of relief from Jessan in the copilot's seat as the music of the hyperdrive hit its proper note and held true.

"Engines normal," he said. "Run true, dropout calculated on time, twenty minutes real time running."

"Roger. Let's see how things look when we get to Galcen."

"You're expecting trouble on dropout?"

She looked at him. "You saw what was going on at the Net. Where the hell else could an armada like that be headed *except* for Galcen? The Mageworlds can't have built enough ships to take on the entire Space Force at once—they'll have to break our fleet up into portions small enough to defeat one by one. And that means hitting Galcen first thing after they bring down the Net, so that even if we get our communications back together there's no central command."

Jessan nodded. " 'Cut off the head first, then deal with the body piece by piece.' . . . Have you read Chelysi's *Poetics of Armed Strife*?"

In spite of herself, she smiled. "Sorry. The finishing school I went to left it right out of the Galactic Literature in Translation course."

"Well, Chelysi calls that strategy a classic method of dealing with a superior force. But it's still tricky, especially the first strike against enemy HQ. Any little thing can mess up your timetable and lose you the element of surprise."

"Exactly what I want to do," she said. "As soon as we hit Galcen nearspace."

"You don't trust our friend back there to have alerted everybody?"

"I don't trust anyone. Besides, he might have classified the information—especially after all the galactic superspy noises you had to make to get his attention."

"And you intend to break security?"

"That's right," she said. "Wide-beam, in the clear. I'm tired of sneaking around."

"Coming up on time for dropout," Beka said a few minutes later. "Dropping out . . . now."

The shifting not-greyness outside the cockpit stretched and darkened and blazed up into a field of stars. A quick series of beeps told Beka that the ship's sensors had gone into their automatic data-collection routine for the navicomps, pulling in beacon signals, star patterns, and anything else that might help them identify one point out of a vast galaxy.

The navicomps went to work digesting and collating the information. Beka turned to Jessan. "Check to see if we're getting anything on lightspeed comms."

"Nothing so far," he said after a moment. "I think we beat the Mages in."

"That was the whole idea. . . . Do you have any Space Force activity?"

"Negative. I don't see any."

Beka straightened suddenly in the pilot's seat.

"Hit the guns," she said, as the sensor readouts lit up and alarms began shrieking all over *Warhammer*'s cockpit. "Assume that anything not squawking Space Force identifiers is hostile. We've got company."

In the viewscreen ahead, the fabric of reality was rippling and trembling, shaking back and forth between the starfield and the grey pseudosubstance of hyperspace as ship after ship came through. The Mageworlds warfleet had come to Galcen.

Warrant Officer Bandur found himself lying on the deck against the bulkhead, with the hidden sleeve gun he always carried held unconcealed and ready in his hand. It took him a moment to figure out why he was there.

*Ah, yes—I heard a blaster.*

He looked around and found Tyche also prone on the deck and pressed tight against the opposite bulkhead—and for all that he hadn't been armed a moment ago, the Infantry captain was holding a blaster as well.

The two men looked at each other. "Well," said Bandur. "Now we know who *we* are. We're the good guys."

Tyche ignored him and switched on his comm link. "Status?"

"Under attack with small arms," said the voice on the other end. "Maintaining."

"Roger." Tyche hit a second button on his comm link. "Status on Party Two?"

Another voice spoke up. "We're pinned down in compartment two-twelveforty-lima."

"Roger," said Tyche. "Do you have the package?"

"Affirmative. Instructions?"

"Stand fast. Wait for relief." The Infantry captain

glanced over at Bandur. "Get us to two-twelveforty-lima, please."

*Perrin's being damned thorough*, thought Bandur. *I'm a bit surprised he didn't just grab me and leave Quetaya in place for later. But if Vallant's trying something funny in this sector, we'll both be safer off the ship anyway. Maybe somebody slipped Galcen a warning ahead of time. . . .*

He stood up and pointed down the corridor. "This way."

They headed out at a quick walk. Tyche spoke again into his comm link: "I'm en route to Party Two's location. Send a relief party as soon as tactically feasible."

The bulkhead speaker came to life again. "Security alert, security alert. All hands stand fast."

"One of the roving patrols must have failed to return on schedule," Bandur guessed.

"That's what I figure," agreed Tyche. "It also means that whoever's attacking doesn't have the entire ship secured yet." He nodded at the warrant officer's miniature hand blaster. "You have a stun setting on that weapon?"

Bandur shook his head. "Never saw the need."

Tyche's eyebrows went up a fraction of an inch. "I don't know who you really are, and I'll probably never know . . . doesn't matter. In the meantime, keep in mind that right now we don't know for certain who the friendlies are."

"I'll try to remember," said Bandur. He glanced from his blaster over to Captain Tyche. "I suppose you're a friendly?"

"Make it your working hypothesis," Tyche said. "Those sure as hell weren't *my* guys back in the CO's cabin, I can promise you that much."

"Right," Bandur said. "Compartment two-twelveforty-lima is on the far side of this bulkhead. Two entrances: one through the docking bay and another from one level up in Operations berthing."

Two nervous-looking crew members with Space Force standard-issue blasters came through the vacuum-tight door at the end of the corridor, blocking the route Bandur had just indicated.

"Ours or theirs?" muttered Tyche.

"Ours, I think," said Bandur. "Security alert team." He raised his voice enough to carry. "Yo, Raveneau!"

"Mr. Bandur," one of the crew members replied. "What in the *hell* is going on here?"

"We've got hostiles dressed as Space Force on board," Bandur replied. He kept on walking toward the vacuum-tight door, not looking back to see if Tyche followed. "I'm heading out to relieve some good guys. Either come with me or get out of my way."

The crew member Bandur had addressed as Raveneau shifted his weight uncertainly from one foot to the other, his forehead wrinkled in a puzzled frown. "You're not supposed to do that, sir. During a security alert you're supposed to stand fast."

"Then go ahead and shoot me right now," Bandur said, "because I'm coming on through."

"You know I can't do that, Mr. Bandur."

"I don't have time to argue." He'd reached the security alert team by now, and was relieved but not actually surprised when Raveneau and his partner stepped aside to let him pass. "Follow me."

On the other side of the vacuum-tight door, a ladder led upward to an overhead hatch—mechanically operated, which meant it opened onto one of the emergency access-ways. Bandur climbed the ladder. A quick glance downward before he started working the opening mechanism showed the warrant officer that Tyche had come on after him, along with both members of the security alert team.

Raveneau still looked worried. "You sure we won't get into trouble, Mr. Bandur?"

"No trouble," Bandur assured him. "You might get killed, maybe, but not into trouble."

Raveneau's brow cleared. "Okay."

The hatch clicked open. Bandur pushed the hatch cover up until it locked, then scrambled through with Tyche and the two crewmen close behind him.

"This particular pair of spacers won't get into trouble," he commented under his breath to Tyche as the Infantry captain joined him in the darkened compartment above, "but if the skipper makes it, he's going to wish he'd trained his troops better."

Tyche shook his head. "Unless I miss my guess about what was going on back in his cabin," he replied, also under his breath, "your CO isn't wishing anything anymore. Fill me in on what you know."

"Normal transit, normal dropout," said Bandur. "I was at my assigned location when word came to go to the skipper's quarters. Now *you* fill *me* in."

By now they were making their way through another vacuum-tight door into what was labeled as COMMUNICATIONS DEPARTMENT ENLISTED BERTHING (FEMALE). Captain Tyche ignored the indignant exclamations and occasional rude comments from the occupants and said to Bandur, "My orders are to make contact with you."

Bandur grunted. "Mind telling me who you are?"

"Natanel Tyche, Captain, SFPI." The captain's tone made it clear that Bandur wasn't going to learn anything else.

They left the berthing compartment behind them, with the two crew members from the security alert team still following, and continued on forward. From around the corner ahead came the high whining sound of a blaster discharge.

"All right, people," Tyche said. "We're coming in from behind. Don't fire unless fired upon."

They rounded the corner in a rush, weapons at the ready. "All right, you sons of bitches," said Bandur to the group on the other side. "Freeze."

"Hey!" protested Raveneau. "Those are some of our guys!"

"Another security alert team," said Bandur. "At least someone aboard this tub is doing their job."

"Not that it helps us a lot," Tyche said. "Mr. Bandur, secure their weapons."

A voice called up the ladder from the compartment below. "Captain, is that you?"

"Yeah," Tyche called back. "What's the status?"

"No problems."

"Good. Hold your fire. We're all coming down."

The six of them—Bandur, Tyche, the two security alert team members whom they'd caught, and the two who had joined them earlier—climbed down the ladder into 2-1240-L. CC1 Ennys Pardu was already inside, in the custody of what looked like one of Tyche's Infantry troopers, wearing an armored p-suit with the faceplate unsealed. The trooper looked harried; Pardu looked more like somebody who'd managed to tuck the crucial datachips into her regulation undergarments, and who was now content to wait on events.

"About time you showed up, Captain," the trooper said to Tyche. "I was beginning to get worried."

"No need," Tyche said. "How are things down here?"

"Confusing," said the trooper. "I got to the lower docking bay, and I found that it was occupied by armed personnel who had the bad manners to shoot at us. So we headed back here, where *these* gentlemen had the bad manners to shoot at us." He shook his head. "Violence in the holovids causes all this, you know."

"Right, then," Tyche said. "I suspect we'll have a good deal of sorting-out to do later, but the first order of business is still to make it back to the ship. Is the lower bay on the far side of that door?"

The trooper nodded. "Yes."

"Good." Tyche punched one of the buttons on his comm

link and spoke into it. "As soon as convenient, using the minimum amount of force required, take tactical control of the upper and lower docking bays."

"Roger," said the voice on the other end. "Out."

Bandur couldn't see or hear the rest of Tyche's troopers, but they worked fast. Within five minutes, he heard a knock at the vacuum-tight door on the docking-bay side. The door opened to show a grinning staff sergeant.

"Captain, welcome back."

"Good to be back," said Tyche. "I'm going to the ship. In the meantime, at your convenience, there is a second vessel in the upper bay. Capture it."

"Yes, sir!"

The sergeant gave Tyche a flashy salute, then turned and trotted off, making hand signals to the troopers spread out around the bay. Tyche turned to Bandur and Pardu.

"If you would come with me, please," he said. "I've got some questions for both of you."

# V. Warhammer: Galcen Nearspace
## Galcen: The Retreat

ALARMS WERE sounding all over the *'Hammer* as Jessan ran for the dorsal gun bubble and belted himself in. He double-checked the fasteners and made sure that everything in the bubble was either strapped down or sealed tight, including the flaps on his pockets. Give the captain's penchant for high-g, hell-on-the-engines shiphandling, the last thing her gunners needed was a lot of miscellaneous junk floating around the bubbles and getting in the way.

He picked up the earphone link to the intraship comms and put it on. "Gun One in place."

Over the headset, he heard LeSoit coming in like an echo. "Gun Two in place."

"All guns, stand by," came the captain's voice over the link from the cockpit. "Commencing high-speed realspace run. Ships are most vulnerable at dropout—they can't have shields up in hyper. So I'm going to be a reception committee."

* * *

In *Warhammer*'s cockpit, Beka fed more power to the realspace engines. *Good thing it was the hyperdrives that heated up on me,* she thought. *I wouldn't dare push the 'Hammer like this if the realspace engines had been the ones to go bad.*

All over the viewscreen and the sensor monitors, Mage warships were still dropping out of hyper—small raider ships, heavy cruisers and destroyers, enormous black-hulled dreadnoughts shedding fighter craft as they came. An alarm pipped: one of the hundreds of warships had fire-control up and was illuminating *Warhammer.* Beka pushed up the shield on the engaged side and hoped for the best.

The pattern-recognition systems on the system-nav package beeped and chittered. The comps had been working on Galcenian data ever since she'd dropped out of hyper, when she'd keyed in Prime Base and asked the comp to locate it for her. The noises from the console meant that the system had come up with a Found mark.

Beka picked up the lightspeed comm link, dialed in the Inspace frequency, and pushed the output power to max.

*I hope they're listening down there,* she thought. *Because this is all the warning they're going to get.*

"All stations, all stations," she said. "This is RMV *Warhammer.* This is not a drill. Mage warships are in the system. I say again, Mage warships are in the system. Space attack Galcen."

The lightspeed transmissions on the frequency scanner suddenly picked-up. She couldn't follow Space Force code-talk, and lots of transmissions in the particular squeak of scrambled, enciphered, and high-speed compression signals were suddenly coming from the scanners.

Jessan's voice came over the intraship link. "Captain—targets, many, close, not transmitting any identification."

"Take them under fire."

A pulse weapon sent colored light cascading across

space ahead of her as she turned *Warhammer* back toward the area where Mage warcraft were still dropping out of hyper. The sensor monitor on the console beeped at her: more ships were coming through outside of visual range.

*How many years were the Mages putting this fleet together and we didn't even know it?* she wondered. *If I ever find the guy who was passing them Space Force parts and plans, I swear I'll kill him myself and send Dadda his head in a basket.*

"Lock on," she said aloud. "Fire at will."

"Locked on and firing," Jessan replied over the link. As usual in the midst of action, his voice was light and almost casual. "But as far as I can see, we're the only good guys around. You aren't planning to take on the entire Mage warfleet single-handed, are you?"

"That's an idea," Beka replied, keeping a wary eye on the readings from the other ships and spiraling to break sensor lock. There was a lot of stuff out there, and none of it friendly. "But I do want to live past the next twenty minutes—there's somebody in the Space Force I want to track down and kill for this."

"Sorry," said Jessan. "That one's mine."

"Fair enough. Right now, though, we need something that'll mark the Mages' drop point for local defense forces. And firing our energy weapons will do it."

"You do realize that's dangerous."

"The thought had crossed my mind," she told him. The fire-control alarm sounded again. "Lock on."

Energy beams darted forth from Number One Gun, firing at a Mage raiding craft coming past on the end of a dropout. A plume of gases feathered out from the contact as the hit broached at least one of the raider's compartments to vacuum.

"Good shot," came LeSoit's voice from Number Two, just before the ventral gun struck the raider in turn. "But I wish we had some missiles."

"If we live through this I'll buy you one for a souvenir," promised Beka. "Make do with what you've got back there—damage or cripple as many as you can, and keep them from getting too close."

From one of the airless planets in the Galcen system, a pillar of fire rose up into the void, striking and shattering one of the Magebuilt dreadnoughts. A moment later, a yellow explosion flowered on the planet's surface.

"Missile launch, friendly," said Jessan over the link. "Looks like local defense is taking over."

Beka checked the status boards. "Sensors show a Republic dreadnought heading this way, dropping off fighters as she comes; and there's another one maneuvering into position between the Mages and Galcen. Only two, though. That's not enough."

By now the Galcenian outer defense beam-weapons were tracing across the starfield with red and yellow fire. More explosions bubbled out in the vacuum. And still the Mage warships kept dropping out of hyper in wave after wave, while the warships already in the system drove inward toward Galcen.

"I've marked two contacts on my screen," commented LeSoit from the Number Two gun bubble. "You see them?"

"I have them locked on," Beka said. "What about them?"

"They're sure heading somewhere in a hell of a hurry."

"I noticed that," she said. "I'm going to follow them and see what they're after."

She pushed in some down vector to pass astern of a fighter crossing her path, and set the 'Hammer's inertial guidance system to remember the way to Prime. "Come on, baby, show me some of that speed."

Over the intraship link, she could hear LeSoit and Jessan talking back and forth between the gun bubbles: "One crossing to your side." . . . "Got him." . . . "Nice work."

The two of them sounded friendlier now than they ever had; Beka shook her head and turned her attention forward. Up ahead of the foremost Mages, there was something . . . a distortion, a waveriness . . . against the disk of Galcen in the magnified visual repeater.

*Where have I seen that before? Now I remember—the Prof had his old Magebuilt scoutcraft under a some kind of cloak, back when we were sneaking into Darvell.*

She clicked on the intraship link. "They're using hidden vessels—the first wave is already inside Galcen's local defense screen. I'm going to go check it out."

"Do you have a probable course on them?" Jessan asked over the link.

She squinted sidelong at the navicomp; most of her attention was reserved for the shield-integrity and engine-function displays. "Wait one . . . Galcen Prime. They're going to skim the atmosphere."

"What's up there?"

"Could be planning to take out the planetary-defense satellites."

As she spoke, a dozen or more lights on the cockpit console flashed orange. The fire-control alarm started pipping again, followed a second later by the wail of another, louder alarm.

"Lock on," said Beka. "Homers inbound."

She hit a switch on the console. "Commence active jamming. Nyls, Ignac'—fire on homers, but *only* on homers, and only if it looks like they're going to hit us. I don't want those guys in the cloaks to see me coming up on them."

"Fire on homers, aye," said Jessan, and LeSoit echoed him, "Fire on homers."

Beka fed more power to the realspace engines. She could hear LeSoit and Jessan talking back and forth in the gun bubbles: "Watch out!" . . . "I hope that was a homer, because I just shot it." . . . "If it wasn't a homer it was too damned close anyway. Don't worry about it."

She laughed under her breath—*Idiots, the both of them!*—

and kept her eye on the sensor data. Soon enough, the target of the cloaked ships made itself clear, and she cursed aloud.

"What's up, Captain?" asked Jessan.

"Somebody on the Mages' side really thinks ahead," she told him. "Prime and South Polar just launched courier vessels—every one they've got, from the looks of it. The Republic's heavy ships are going to have to stay and fight, but the couriers can run for hyper and get away to spread the word. If those cloaked ships don't hit them first."

Beka fed coordinates from the navicomps into the gun tracking system. "All right, people, I have a target for you. Range long. Marked on your scopes."

"I don't see anything," LeSoit said.

"It's cloaked," she said. "But it's heading for the jump points from Galcen, same as all those couriers. They don't have any guns, but we do. So it's time to fly some cover for them."

The alarm wailed again.

"Damn!" she said. "More homers. Let the shields take them from now on—save your fire for the Mages."

She cut in the overrides.

*I can't push the ship much faster,* she thought. *Not without screwing things up for Nyls and Ignac' at the guns. But I can throw power to the shields and keep those homers from blowing up my engines.*

"Stand by," she said. "Fire at will."

Up ahead, a sleek dark-hulled ship suddenly winked into view. A double trace of energy shot out from it to intercept one of the courier ships.

"Bastard," she said. "Nyls, Ignac'—take him."

"Number One Gun, firing," came the reply as energy beams flashed out; and the echo, "Number Two Gun, firing."

In the next moment Beka felt a series of rapid explosions hammering at the skin of her ship as missiles from one of the Mage ships made contact. LeSoit's voice came over the link.

"Captain, request permission to target incoming missiles."

"Denied. Keep on firing at that ship!"

She hit the controls to turn *Warhammer* on her side so that both the dorsal and ventral guns would have a direct line at the target, and checked the status boards. "Damage control reports we're open to vacuum in the outer holds, but the shields over the engines are up. We'll do."

Ahead of her she saw four couriers in formation, heading for a jump point. Beka put their course and speed into her own navicomps. "Heading for Gyffer, are you?" she muttered under her breath when the data came up. "Nice place, Gyffer. Good shipyards. Don't worry; I'll see that you get away."

The *'Hammer* pushed on closer. Yet another alarm added its note to the cacophony as the *'Hammer* shuddered suddenly and then pulled forward again.

"What was that?" she heard LeSoit calling to Jessan over the link between from the guns.

"Defense satellites don't know we're friendly."

"Never mind the defense satellites!" Beka snapped over the link. "Let the shields take it. Keep on firing at the Mage warships."

One of the couriers blew up; the others began changing course, to take evasive steering. Beka shook her head.

"They'll never get away like that—that's what the Mages want, to keep them from making a run to jump. I'm going to get ahead of them and clear the way."

"Can you do that?" LeSoit asked. "Those damned things are all engine."

"So am I. Keep them safe." She picked up the exterior comm link and keyed it on. "Space Force couriers—this is *Warhammer*, Rosselin-Metadi commanding. I am your cover. Maintain course and speed. Run to jump. Do it now."

*Warhammer*'s guns took another of the suddenly uncloaked Mage ships under fire. The warships were matching speeds with the couriers as the Republic vessels straightened their course and began another run-to-jump. Beka threw the 'Hammer into a spiral to put herself between the remaining couriers and the Mages. The guns of the black ships spat out fire, the energy pulses tracing across the darkness and dimming the stars with their brilliance, and the 'Hammer's guns cut lines of dazzling light through space in reply.

One of the couriers winked out, space distorting around the vessel as it made the transition to hyperspace. Another exploded as a homer took it. Then the third one jumped and was gone.

Beka turned away to look for more couriers to escort. Over the link, the voices from the gun bubbles went back and forth in her ears: "Homers, close!" . . . "Locked on." . . . "Fire." . . . "Four more hostiles inbound."

A power satellite exploded in orbit below them. Far away, one of the Space Force destroyers was breaking up, with beams of energy flashing around the pieces.

"I think our side is losing," said LeSoit. "Time for us to get out of here."

"Hell with that," Beka said. "We still have engines and guns."

A few seconds later an explosion sounded from farther aft, and the loss-of-pressure alarm sounded. The power-level indicator on the control panel showed the weapons systems flat.

"Nyls, Ignac'—report!"

"I'm still here," said LeSoit; and a moment later Jessan said, "No response from the guns, switching to override." A pause. "Secondary power available, clear. We're up."

Energy beams lanced out from the dorsal bubble as he spoke—Beka saw them connect with a Mage fighter. The warfleet's transports must have come through and started dropping off space-and-atmosphere craft.

Then another heavy blow made the *'Hammer* groan and tremble. Beka didn't need to look at the sensors this time.

"Shield hit," she said. "We're hurt."

"How bad?" Jessan asked from the dorsal gun.

"Bad—damage control panels report more compartments open to vacuum, and the rear shields at fifty-percent power. The ventral shield is going up and down erratically. Secondary power for the guns is fading fast, too."

"Another one like that and we're gone," said Jessan. "We can't protect ourselves and we can't shoot. I agree with Gentlesir LeSoit—it's time to get the hell out of here."

"It was worth taking hits to let the couriers get away," Beka said. "But if we stay here now, all we can do now is die like the rest of them."

Her voice caught for a moment in her throat; she mastered it and went on. "Commencing run-to-jump. Clear the way with fire. Here we go."

On the watchtower of the Retreat, the chill of evening deepened. An apprentice came, apparently unsummoned, with cloaks of dark wool for Ochemet and Master Ransome, and then soundlessly vanished again. The night was deep, with a far-off stars showing diamond-bright.

An hour had passed, by Ochemet's chronometer, before Ransome spoke again. His voice sounded weary, and somehow deeply sad.

"We all must follow the paths of our own choosing. I thought for a while that when I walked this part of my path, I would do so in the company of Jos Metadi, who was my friend and captain before. I see now that it is not to be. But you will accompany me."

*Damnedest invitation to the dance I ever heard,* Ochemet thought. He swallowed and wet his lips. "What path are you talking about?"

"The time has come to fight the Mages again—this time to their complete destruction."

"You'll never convince the Grand Council," Ochemet said. "The Mageworlds have been crippled for decades."

Ransome shook his head. "We will be pilot and copilot once more, fighting them."

Ochemet felt cold. Adepts could see into the future, some people said. Adepts didn't make any sense and they never had, said others; they saw everything from some twisted angle that made everything they told you come out like gibberish.

"I'm honored by the idea," he told the Guild Master. "But I'm afraid it's not very likely."

"As you will."

Silence fell again. Later, when he thought back on their conversation, Ochemet would remember the Adept's black-cloaked shoulders stiffening, and his head beginning to turn, an instant before the sudden efflorescence of blue-white light as a new star blossomed in the southern sky.

Now, though, he had no thought for anything beyond his own astonishment and Master Ransome's voice: "That is what you came here to see."

Ochemet was already heading for the stairs.

"That was Number Two Power Sat we just saw go up," he said over his shoulder. "I've got to get back to Prime."

Ransome moved swiftly, and the hand he laid on Ochemet's arm had a weight to it that halted the general in midstride.

"I'm afraid that's impossible," he said gently. "The Retreat has been sealed. We will fight the Mages in a different way than you see now."

The Adept turned and vanished into darkness, leaving Ochemet dumbfounded and alone on the tower, watching the sky while the hours of the night went past. Toward dawn, a meteor shot across the sky in a trail of glowing flame: Power-Sat Two, he supposed, burning up on reentry. Other than that, he saw and heard nothing else.

# VI. NAMMERIN: NAMPORT
## RSF *Naversey*: THE OUTER NET

**K**LEA SANTRENY lay on her back and looked up at the ceiling over her bed. The room was dark, but she couldn't sleep. Too many years of working by night and sleeping by day had made a night person of her. If she lived to be a hundred and twenty—if she somehow managed to do what Owen claimed she could, and transformed herself from a backwater farm girl and working-class whore into Mistress Klea Santreny, Adept—even then she would still find herself restless at midnight.

The weather in Namport wasn't helping any. All the windows in her small apartment stood open, as did the louvered wooden doors to the pocket-sized balcony, but no wind stirred. The thick, humid air felt the same temperature when she drew it into her lungs as when she let it out again; and in spite of the shower she'd taken before going to bed her skin felt slick with body oil and sweat.

Outside, the atmosphere was wet and hazy, without the cooling relief of a true rain. Light from the streetlamps made the sky beyond the windows into a dark grey smear. In the still air, the noises of the city had a distant, muted clarity: the steady background purr of traffic from the center of town; a drift of voices mixed with dance music; the deep boom and long, growling rumble of a ship landing at the port.

Sighing, Klea pushed aside the sheet and got up. She went to the kitchen nook and filled a glass with cold water from the sink. After a moment's thought she took a couple of ice chunks from the cool-box and dropped them in as well. She drank half the water straight off, then carried the glass with her over to the balcony—the air was a little cooler there—and set it on the wooden railing while she stood looking at the night sky.

Between the low haze and the glare from the port, she couldn't see any stars. Thinking back, she realized that she hadn't seen them properly more than a handful of times in the years since she'd left the farm. In the hinterlands, where the farms were miles apart and the houselights went out early, you could look up on almost any clear night and see all the stars you wanted. Not here, though. You had to look at the flat grey-blackness overhead and take it on faith that somewhere past it the starfield glittered. . . .

*Glittered in constellations whose names she could still remember after all these years in the city: the Yoke, the Tree, the Leaping Frog.*

*And now the clustered stars broke apart. The patterns above her altered and took on shapes she'd never seen before. She was looking at the sky of another place—she knew this, somehow—but whether it represented time past, time present, or time to come she didn't know.*

*As she watched, an insignificant star suddenly flared into a ball of blue-white light. Reflexively, she threw up her arm to shield her eyes. . . .*

The glass of water she'd put down on the balcony railing tipped over when her elbow struck it, and a second later she heard it smash against the sidewalk below. Slowly she brought her arm down again to her side. The sky over Namport looked as flat and hazy as ever.

Klea gripped her rough wooden railing with both hands. "That wasn't just somebody's stray nightmare," she whispered.

Her voice sounded tight and shaky, even to her. She had a right to be scared; she could tell the difference between the hallucinatory images that meant she was picking up on the thoughts of other people, and something like this.

"I need to talk to Owen."

But Owen wasn't home yet; he was still at the portside bathhouse, operating the big laundry machine that kept the establishment supplied with clean sheets and towels. She went back into her apartment, brewed a pot of hot *ghil*, and sat at the kitchen table drinking cup after steaming cup in spite of the humid weather.

*Something bad is happening somewhere. Something really bad, and I just watched it begin.*

Llannat was doing the ShadowDance again in the *Naversey*'s passenger compartment. She knew that the others were watching her—either covertly, like the med service captain and the two warrants, or openly, like Govantic the data specialist—but she went through the familiar movements anyway. If things in the Net had happened as she feared, keeping herself calm and well practiced was more important than what people thought.

*Lots of floating metal. Ebannha gone. Nobody answering on comms. Only one thing it could be, and we all know it.*

*The Mages have broken through the Net.*

The voice on the bulkhead speaker cut through her concentration. "All hands, strap in for a high-g burn. We've spotted something promising and we're going to scoot over for a closer look."

Clipping the staff back onto her belt, Llannat made her way to the acceleration couch and strapped herself in. The bulkhead speaker said, "Stand by for acceleration," and a second later inertia pressed her down into the cushions.

*Pilot doesn't believe in messing around*, she thought breathlessly. Her weight increased and increased until she could feel each separate bone in her body. *Five gravities, maybe even six.* The weight stopped for a moment as the pilot executed a skew-flip, came back again as the courier ship decelerated, then ceased.

The speaker crackled on again. "Lieutenant Vinhalyn, Mistress Hyfid, to the bridge."

She unstrapped and accompanied the reservist-historian forward to the *Naversey*'s cockpit. The starfield outside the viewscreens appeared the same, to her untrained eye, as the one she'd seen when the courier popped out of hyper, but the pilot and copilot were looking considerably more sure of themselves.

Vinhalyn, it seemed, had noticed the change as well. "What have you got?"

"Well," said the pilot, "when we couldn't find *Ebannha* anywhere we started doing a helical scan Netward—Mistress Hyfid said 'go on,' and that was about as 'on' as we could come up with—"

"Yes, yes," the historian said. "And?"

"Now we're picking up some more scrap metal on the scans. We thought maybe you could give us some guidance on which bits we should look at."

Vinhalyn glanced over at Llannat. "Mistress?"

*I don't know anything about interpreting sensor data*, Llannat thought. *I got "familiarized" with the readouts in basic training, but that doesn't count for much....*

She stepped forward and looked at the monitor anyway. Several different contacts were showing up, and all of them looked about the same.

"There," she heard herself saying. She tapped the screen with her fingernail. "That one."

"That's outside of the path we're checking," the pilot protested. He indicated two other marks. "I was thinking of these two things, here and here."

She shook her head. "No. You need to check the other one."

"It's only a little out of our way," said Vinhalyn to the pilot. "Take the time and look it over."

"Your call," said the pilot. "Here we go."

He changed *Naversey*'s course to bring them closer to the sensor contact. A couple of minutes later the target showed up in the courier's viewscreens, first as a bright dot, then as a shape that grew darker and lighter in the starlight as it tumbled.

"Fighter," the pilot said. "No emissions. Another damned starpilot's grave."

"One of ours, too," said the copilot. "Poor bastard. Let's get back onto our scan path."

"No," said Llannat. She touched the sensor readout screen again. "What's this new bit of stuff here?"

"Probably just another chunk of scrap metal," said the pilot. "But we might as well check it out too."

This time, when the courier ship came into visual range, the sensor target wasn't tumbling in space. It was stable and undamaged, a sleek, dark-hulled starship with a shape like a flattened teardrop: a Magebuilt Deathwing.

As soon as the sun came up Klea began watching for Owen. She didn't want to go out onto the balcony again; she was half-afraid that if she did, she'd have another uninvited vision like the last one. Instead she listened for Owen's footsteps on the stairs—nobody else in the building had his characteristic light, even tread—and as soon as he had come home, she left her own apartment and hurried up to knock on his door.

He opened it almost the moment her knuckles struck against the wood. "Klea—what's wrong?"

"I saw something last night."

" 'Saw'?" he said. "Are you sure?"

He moved aside to let her come into his apartment as he spoke, and closed the door behind her. The room was just as bare as the last time she'd been in it, and still didn't have any furniture that hadn't come with the lease. Even the sheets and towels, although clean, had a threadbare look to them, as if they'd been purchased secondhand as an afterthought.

Klea sat down on the wobbly chair. Owen leaned against the counter in the kitchen nook and said again, "Are you sure?"

She could tell from the way he spoke that he meant something more than the usual kind of seeing. "It wasn't a hallucination," she said. "I haven't had one of those in weeks, not since you showed me how to keep other people's thoughts from leaking into mine. This was different."

"How did it happen?"

"I was on the balcony," she said. "It was hot, and I couldn't sleep, so I was out there drinking ice water and looking at the stars—at where the stars would have been, anyway, if you could see them—and then I really *was* looking at them, only the patterns were all wrong. Then one of the stars went all bright and too hot to look at, and I was back on the balcony again. But that wasn't what scared me. What scares me is that I know it really happened. Or will happen, or is happening. But I don't know the time, and I don't know where."

He looked at her for a while without saying anything, his expression serious. "That was a seeing, all right," he said finally. "Congratulations. You've got a rare and very inconvenient talent."

"Inconvenient?"

He nodded. "An Adept I once knew used to compare it

to getting anonymous notes in the mail. Reliable enough to be upsetting, but not trainable enough to be useful."

"Can you . . . 'see' . . . like that?"

"No," he said. "I can follow chains of probability and tell you which way they lead, and I can tell you when somebody is or isn't in synch with the flow of things— what most people would call having good luck, or bad— but when it comes to *knowing* something, the way you just did, then I'm as future-blind as the next person."

"Oh," she said.

She sat without talking for a moment, one hand rubbing the old white scars on the other wrist, and wondered why she got to see trouble coming for people somewhere she'd never even been, when she couldn't see it for herself.

*If I'd known what I was heading for when I left the farm, I'd probably have stayed home and done the cooking and mending like a good girl . . . no food and no place to stay and nothing I knew how to do except for the damned farmwork, and then along comes Freling with his "business proposition" . . .*

" 'Inconvenient talent,' " she said. "Yeah."

His eyes were dark and sad, as though he'd caught a glimpse of her thoughts without meaning to. "I'm sorry," he said.

She shrugged. "Not your fault."

She paused, and spoke aloud the other thought that had come to her while she sat there. "The thing is—now that I know that something bad is going on, what am I supposed to *do*?"

The Deathwing for which *Naversey* had come so far was hanging in the courier's viewscreens like a nightmare given shape. In spite of the name, Llannat Hyfid saw nothing avian about the Magebuilt vessel. It made her think instead of some dark, hungry creature of the deep ocean, gliding silently through the cold water and searching for prey.

"There it is," she said.

The pilot nodded. "Whatever you say. Let's hope it's the one we're looking for, and not part of whatever took out *Ebannha*."

"Visual configuration and sensor profile match the data we got from the first investigation," said the copilot. "So it's either our ship, or another one from the same class."

"It's an archaic design," Lieutenant Vinhalyn said. "A raid-and-reconnaissance vessel—similar to the ones the Mageworlders used at the start of the last war, but much older."

" 'The last war,' " said the pilot. "I don't think I like the sound of that. . . . We'll make a standard spiral pass around the thing and investigate. See if we get our silly heads blown off."

The courier ship began the graceful maneuver designed to take it within visual range of all sides of the target vessel. Several minutes in, the copilot spoke up again.

"We're picking up something anchored to the ventral surface—a small craft of some kind."

The pilot was already feeding close-range sensor data to *Naversey*'s on-board comps. "Looks like Mistress Hyfid was right," he said after a moment. "Analysis makes the additional contact a *Pari*-class short-range surveyor-scout. Probably belonged to *Ebannha*'s boarding party."

"Good," said Lieutenant Vinhalyn. "This is where we're supposed to be. Make ready to rendezvous."

The pilot looked uneasy. "We've got a mint-condition Magebuilt Deathwing out there. Are you sure you want to get that close?"

Vinhalyn's lips tightened, and he gave the pilot a withering glance. "A *Pari*-class scout has no hyperspace engines," he said, "and no guns. If this one's crew is still alive, they are surely desperate by now. Take us in."

The pilot shrugged. "Have it your way. Coming in."

Soon *Naversey* had matched course and speed with the Deathwing. The courier ship hovered just above the *Pari*-class survey vessel clinging to the dark ship's hull, their relative motion zero.

Vinhalyn nodded to himself—a quick, decisive motion. "Time for somebody to suit up and get over there," he said. "Mistress Hyfid, will you accompany me?"

"Of course," she said. She didn't look at the waiting Deathwing as she spoke.

Several minutes later, moving awkwardly in their pressure suits, Llannat and Vinhalyn approached the airlock of the survey ship. The lock's outer door stood open, but the inner one was closed; they entered and cycled through to the ship's interior. A quick search of all the compartments on the small vessel showed it deserted, with power levels at minimum. The log recorder's last entry had been made two days before: "Transferring operations to salvage ship."

"Wonderful," Llannat muttered. "They're aboard the Deathwing. I used to have nightmares about those things when I was a kid, just from the holopix in the history texts, until my mother told me they'd all gotten blown to pieces in the War."

Vinhalyn's voice came to her on the suit-to-suit comm link. "Cheer up. If this vessel's crew managed to cross over without destroying both ships, we can probably do the same." She heard the click that meant he was switching in the suit-to-ship link. "Survey ship deserted—crew appears to have transferred aboard the Mage vessel. I intend to follow. If we haven't returned in two hours, use your best judgment."

They cycled out through the survey ship's airlock and clambered down onto the black hull of the Deathwing. Their magnetic boots clicked and shuffled as they made their way across the metal surface to the Mageship's ventral airlock.

It was closed.

"Now what?" said Llannat. She'd never liked pressure-suit work all that much; being this close to deep space and hard vacuum made her twitchy, prone to the irrational fear that the laws of the universe would suddenly decide to repeal themselves and the plates in her boot soles would become no more magnetic than ordinary shoe leather. "How are we going to get in?"

"There should be a secondary access port around here somewhere," Vinhalyn replied. He pointed to a spot a few feet away from the main lock, where a row of angular yellow symbols stood out in sharp contrast to the sleek black hull. "And that looks like it."

He click-shuffled over to the area with the symbols on it and bent clumsily to put one pressure-gloved hand onto the deck. Llannat saw him push down against the hull, then twist—and a small but workable hatch opened in the side of the ship.

"Don't tell me," she said. "That yellow writing says, 'Press here and rotate.' "

"Well, yes," Vinhalyn admitted. The reservist-historian was already climbing in through the hatch, but the suit-to-suit link brought his voice back to her clearly. "Rotate leftward, to be precise. Of course, the important point was that last symbol on the end. . . ."

By now he had disappeared into the small airlock. Llannat, following him through the hatch, said nervously, "What about the last symbol?"

"Ah, yes . . . a very interesting character, linguistically speaking. In the older dialects of Eraasian—which served as the spacefarer's common-talk for most of the Mageworlds—it represents the imperative premonitory suffix."

"The what?"

Llannat and Vinhalyn were standing together now inside a half-size airlock, or at least one that would have been half-size on a Republic ship. The wall of the lock was covered with dials and other old-style monitoring devices, the unfamiliar notation on their glassed-in faces illuminated by the lights of the pressure suits.

"A syllable tacked onto the last word of a warning or command," Vinhalyn said as he frowned over the rows of dials. "In spoken Eraasian, it was used to emphasize an order by raising the possibility of negative consequences: 'Do this or else!' In the written language—especially when we take into consideration the explicit directions to rotate the latch mechanism *leftward*, and the Mageworlders' known predilection for incorporating self-destruct mechanisms into their vessels—"

Llannat glanced back at the now-closed outer door of the lock. "I get your point," she said. "Wonderful language, Eraasian. I'm glad you speak it."

Vinhalyn peered more closely at one of the dials. "It is, alas, an academic knowledge only. . . . Ah. Here we are. No pressure inside the Deathwing, either. This won't be as tricky as I was afraid it would be."

He pushed and rotated another yellow-labeled plate on the Deathwing's bulkhead—Llannat didn't bother asking what this one said; she didn't really want to know—and the inner door of the minilock cycled open. They climbed out into a narrow, slightly curving passageway near the main airlock.

Llannat played the light of her suit around the deck and the bulkheads: a lot of standard shipboard construction—basic solutions to basic engineering problems, she supposed; a lot of notices and labels in the Eraasian script; and a chalked arrow drawn on the metal paneling at about eye level, pointing to the right.

"There we are," she said. "Looks like our boarding party left us a trail."

"Then by all means let us follow it," said Vinhalyn.

They headed down the passageway to the right. Each time the route branched, another chalk-marked arrow appeared to show them the way.

"Where do you think they are?" Llannat asked.

"From the number of Eraasian warning signs and don't-even-touch-this-without-a-proper-clearance notices, it looks like we're heading toward the power plant."

"Oh," she said. She frowned into the darkness ahead of her. "Is that a light over there?"

"It does look like one," said Vinhalyn. "And our destination appears to be Main Engineering Control, or the equivalent for this vessel."

Llannat shook her head, although she knew the gesture was useless inside the concealment of a p-suit's helmet. "I hope our friends aren't getting ready to twist something the wrong way."

"So do I, Mistress Hyfid. . . . Let us proceed quietly now, to avoid precipitating any rash actions."

They went the rest of the way down the corridor in silence, and through the open doorway into what Llannat presumed was the main engine control room of the Deathwing. Several figures in Space Force standard-issue pressure-suits turned to face the entrance as she and Vinhalyn came in.

One of the suited figures had ensign's stripes on his helmet. He came hurrying forward, waving a hand as he did so at somebody else outside Llannat's range of vision.

"Put up the energy lance, Chief," he said. "These two are some of ours."

Then, as if remembering himself at the last minute, he came to a full stop and saluted. "Ensign Tammas Cantrel, late of RSF *Ebannha*, now of—of whatever this thing's called when it has a name. And could one of you people please tell me just what the hell is going on out there in the Net?"

# VII. Galcen: The Retreat
## Infabede Sector:
### RSF *Selsyn-bilai*; RSF *Fezrisond*

WHEN DAWN came to the Retreat, General Ochemet was still standing on the tower wall. The light that washed over the mountains went from pearly grey to pink to a warm yellow glow, without bringing a similar warmth to Ochemet's heart. Prime Base was a long way from the mountains, six hours by aircar at least. Even if he left now—assuming that Master Ransome intended to let him leave, after all but kidnapping him in the first place—he might not get back in time to avert disaster.

Footsteps on the stone behind him made him turn around. One of the senior apprentices had come up onto the tower with a mug and a hotpot of steaming cha'a on a wooden tray. The cha'a in the mug was already cool enough to drink. After his long night's watch Ochemet took it gladly, in spite of his dark thoughts about the Master of the Guild.

He finished the cha'a in a couple of gulps and held out

the empty mug for more. "I need to get back to Prime as soon as I can. What's the news?"

The apprentice shook her head. "Nothing that ı can tell you," she said as she filled his mug. "Master Ransome sends his apologies for not providing a proper breakfast, and he wants you to come with me as soon as you've had enough cha'a."

*He does, does he? Arrogant bastard.* Ochemet put the mug back onto the apprentice's tray beside the hotpot. *Galcen's in danger—he knows it; hell, he admits it!—and he's playing games with me for some reason of his own.*

Still, as long as Ransome controlled all the ways in and out of the Retreat, Ochemet knew that he didn't have much choice. He followed the apprentice down the tower stairs to the lower ramparts, where an Adept was waiting. Ochemet recognized the young man who had met him and Captain Gremyl at the landing field, only a few weeks ago.

"Here he is," said the apprentice. "Now what do I do, Master Tellyk?"

Tellyk gave the apprentice a brief smile. Ochemet supposed it was meant to be encouraging. "Take the tray down to the kitchen. Then go join the rest of your group."

The apprentice hurried off.

Ochemet went with his new guide still farther into the center of the fortress, along hallways and down stairs that grew steadily narrower and rougher in their construction. He guessed that Tellyk was taking him down a considerable way below the surface. The last turning brought them through a heavy door—blastproof, from the looks of it—into a large room full of detector screens and status boards. Adepts in plain black were busy on all sides; monitoring readouts, punching in orders and code strings, talking over comm links in low, earnest voices.

*Operations Control,* Ochemet thought. *State-of-the-art, too. What else do they have in here that I don't know about?*

Master Ransome was there as well, staff in hand, the dark cloak he'd worn last night on the ramparts swirling about his ankles as he strode forward.

"Tellyk," he said. "Are the apprentices away safely?"

The younger Adept checked his chronometer. "The last of them should be leaving about now. The group leaders know the drill; they'll be out of Retreat territory by local noon, and scattered all over the planet by sunset."

"Good," said Ransome. "We'll make certain no one has time to look for them today, or tomorrow either."

Ochemet took a deep breath and broke into the conversation. "I'm glad to hear that your emergency evacuation plans are working properly—" *And how long have you had those in place?* "—but if the danger is that imminent I must go back to Prime Base at once."

Ransome was already shaking his head. "I'm afraid it's too late, General. The Mage warfleet is in the system, and Prime is already in their hands."

Captain Natanel Tyche, SFPI, looked across the dining table at the two people Galcen had sent him to collect. Outside in the *Selsyn*'s docking bay, the sounds of armed conflict continued. Here in the common room of Tyche's long-range recon vessel, however, things were relatively quiet. The ship's interior lights were on dim, and—except for the pilot and the copilot, several compartments away— nobody remained on board to overhear what might be said.

Gamelan Bandur had slipped his hand-blaster back up his sleeve, but he still looked dangerous, a grizzled hard case with service ribbons from every rough spot since the Sack of Ilarna. Most of his attention seemed to be given over to the fighting outside. CC1 Ennys Pardu, on the other hand, was looking directly at Tyche with a challenging expression.

"I know you, Nat Tyche," she said at last. "And you certainly ought to know me."

The face and the voice together jogged Tyche's memory. He and Pardu—whose name was not Pardu at all—had gone through some of Space Force's more specialized training together.

"Rosel Quetaya!" he exclaimed. "What are you doing here?"

"My job," she said. She nodded toward Bandur. "Haven't you figured out yet who he is?"

Tyche shook his head. "Just somebody I've got orders to pick up and take home to Galcen."

"Well, he's the guy who gives the orders," she said. "Commanding General Jos Metadi himself."

Under the circumstances, Tyche didn't think she was lying. He glanced over at Bandur, who was looking amused and—now that Quetaya had brought up the subject— distinctly familiar.

*Damn. She's right. It is him.*

"Nevertheless," Tyche said doggedly, "I have orders from Galcen to pick up both of you and take you back to Prime."

Metadi gestured in the direction of the docking bay. "I'd say your orders just got overtaken by events. Captain, do you have any idea at all what's going on out there?"

"Not much more than you do," Tyche said. "Some people who claim to be acting for Admiral Vallant appear to have seized control of the ship. Now that *my* people have achieved their main objective—" He nodded at Metadi and Quetaya. "—I can start taking care of that problem next."

"You do that, Captain," said Metadi. "And get me a hi-comms link to Galcen. I want to find out what has Perrin so worried he had to send in the Infantry."

"We'll both report, General," said Tyche. "The situation here being what it is."

He punched the button on the bulkhead comm link to the scout's cockpit. "Tyche here. I need a hi-comm link to Prime HQ, top priority."

"Hi-comms, aye." There was a pause. "No joy on hi-comms, sir. They're down hard. Galcen doesn't answer."

"Double-check your equipment and try again. Let me know when you get through. Tyche out."

He clicked off the link. "I don't like this," he said.

"Neither do I," said Metadi. "*Selsyn*'s been going back and forth between Galcen and Infabede for a long time now; the warrant officers' wardroom was a prime source for gossip from all over the sector. Everybody on board knew that something out here was going sour—too many good people had been putting in for transfers or deciding to take early retirement—but nobody said anything about mutiny. In fact, the usual theory was misappropriation of government funds."

"Oh, there was that, too," Quetaya said. She was looking pleased with herself, Tyche noted. "I may not have gotten enough out of the *Selsyn*'s data banks to hang Vallant with, but I certainly got enough to make the rope." She paused. "And it wasn't just funds, it was property. Arms and armaments, to be precise."

"Is he building a private fleet?" Tyche wondered.

"What for?" Metadi said. "He's got all the Space Force in this sector already."

Quetaya, meanwhile, was shaking her head. "No fleet—all the matériel passes on to somewhere else. I can't track it any farther from here."

The bulkhead link clicked on again. "We've run self-tests on the hi-comms, sir," said the pilot's voice. "They check out fine. It's the links and relays that aren't working."

"Keep on trying," said Tyche, and clicked the speaker off. He turned back to Metadi and Quetaya. "It looks like hi-comms are down hard. We may have to wait until we hit Galcen to straighten all this out."

"Are you a betting man, Captain?" the General asked.

"I'm afraid not. In my line of work, it doesn't pay."

"Too bad. I was going to bet you fifty credits that we don't go back to Galcen."

"My orders—"

Metadi snorted. "—aren't worth a damn anymore," he finished. "Perrin Ochemet found something on his desk he didn't want to handle, that's all. Mutiny, on the other hand—that's serious. I intend to deal with it myself, here and now."

*Mutiny works fast if it works at all,* Ari thought. *If this was going to come off, we would have heard something back from the others by now.*

Except for Ari and the JG who had brought him there in the first place, the ready room for RSF *Fezrisond*'s fighter detachment had been empty for some time. The JG had a blaster from the fighter det's weapons locker, but as time passed and Ari made no attempt to break away, he'd transferred his worried expression to the door instead.

*I don't blame him. As soon as the dust clears enough for the winners to count heads, somebody is going to come here looking for us.*

Ari thought about the prospect for a moment and decided that he didn't like it at all. The *Fezzy*'s fighter det might be right about Admiral Vallant, or they might not— after taking his own impressions of the man into consideration, Ari rather thought that they were—but if their coup failed, nobody was going to believe that the ship's head medic had been keeping disloyal company under compulsion.

*In which case, Rosselin-Metadi, you've twiddled your thumbs in here long enough. It's time to say good-bye.*

Standing up, he stretched his arms and legs, then wandered over to the door of the ready room and laid a hand against the lockplate. When the door didn't open, he started working noisily at the edge of the plate with his thumbnail.

"I'm sorry, sir, but you shouldn't be doing that." The voice came from behind Ari. "Just sit back down, all right?"

Ari turned, his hands raised to shoulder height, and looked into the business end of the blaster, pointed directly into his face from not more than arm's length away. He shrugged.

"Oh, well," he said. "It was worth a try."

In the next breath he swept his arms inward, so that his right hand caught the inside of the JG's wrist at the same time as his left hand struck the blaster away to the right. The JG fired, but the bolt whined through the air to one side of Ari's skull and sizzled against the bulkhead behind him. Ari didn't waste any time; he made a quick forward snap-kick to the other man's belly, and the blaster went skittering across the deck as the JG collapsed.

Ari stooped and retrieved the weapon, then went back to prying up the lockplate. He worked quickly, since it wouldn't be long before the man on the deck was good for something besides gasping for air. He didn't think he'd done any permanent damage; nevertheless, his actions might be somewhat resented.

Fortunately, the ready room hadn't been designed for holding prisoners. As soon as he'd pulled the plate loose the door slid open with a click.

He paused for a moment on the threshold. "I wish you and your friends all the luck in the galaxy," he said to the still-helpless JG. "But I don't think you're going to get it."

The door of the ready room slid closed again behind him. He paused in the empty corridor to take stock of his situation.

On the plus side, he was out of custody and the blaster was a Space Force Standard with a full charge, more than enough to shoot his way out of trouble if he needed to. On the minus side, he didn't have any idea where he ought to go next. Heading for sick bay wasn't going to do him much good—anybody looking for him was bound to try there first—and his own quarters probably weren't any better.

*Wherever I go, chances are I'll walk right into a reception committee from one side or the other. And if Vallant wants me for a hostage, then this whole ship is a trap.*

*Which means there's only one place left.*

He turned and began walking quickly in the direction of the lower level of *Fezrisond*'s docking bay. Nobody was around—*Not surprising*, he thought; *all the pilots who aren't off somewhere helping Vallant take over the sector are busy trying to take over the ship instead*—and the lockplate at the underbay entrance hadn't been tampered with. His medical override brought the door open smoothly, and he stepped inside.

The underbay was a dim, low-ceilinged cave where metal ladders rose up like stalagmites from the deckplates to hatches overhead. A number of the hatches had their status lights off, meaning that the corresponding slot in the open bay above was empty. Red or amber lights meant that the craft docked overhead was low on fuel or down for repair. Ari shook his head.

*Green. I need a long-range craft in status green.*

A figure appeared unexpectedly out of the shadows in the depths of the bay, making Ari's breath catch in momentary panic. But it was only a member of the maintenance crew in a grease-stained uniform, heading from one access ladder to another. He gave Ari an amiable grin as he came near.

"Hey, Doc—what are you doing down here in fighter country?"

"Double-checking the emergency medical kits," Ari lied. The blaster was in his right hand, on the side of his body away from the mechanic; he hoped that the half-light would blur the weapon's outline enough to do the rest. *That, and the fact that nobody expects the head medic to be armed and dangerous.* "The pilots are supposed to check the kits themselves, but you know how they are."

"I sure do." The mechanic shook his head. "You wouldn't believe some of the things I've seen them try."

"It can't be worse than the stuff they get up to when they're on shore leave," said Ari. "I'm not going to trust any of them to remember the medical kits either."

"Good thinking, Doc. Which fighters do you want to check out first?"

"I might as well start with the long-range craft."

The mechanic nodded his head back toward the row of ladders behind him. "Right over there."

"Thanks."

*With one, two, three green lights in a row. Oh, yes. . . .*

Ari climbed up the nearest ladder and through the hatch into the body of the docked fighter. It was a bit cramped—most pilots were smaller than he was—but he was able to reach the cockpit and strap himself in. He looked out the forward viewscreen into the airless expanse of the upper bay, with the blackness of deep space showing beyond the open dock portal, and drew a deep breath.

*This isn't the 'Hammer, and it isn't an atmospheric craft either, but you can handle either one of those with your eyes closed. And this one is simple enough that even fighter jocks can figure it out.*

A quick inspection of the controls showed him that most of the deep-space instrumentation was familiar from his time on *Warhammer.* The weapons he could ignore, with any luck, and the stuff for close-in maneuvering; that left only the problem of navigation. With the aid of a standard navicomp, he could plot a jump-run and a hyperspace transit—but he wasn't a professional starpilot and it usually took him quite a while.

Fortunately for him, he reflected, most fighter pilots weren't navigators either. He switched on the cockpit navicomp. The screen lit up, but instead of the usual array of data and calculations it showed him a brief list of preset options:

MANDEYN
ARTAT
KIIN-ALOQ
RETURN TO BASE
OTHER [SPECIFY]

The navicomp had a pickup for voice input built into the side of the screen. He hit the "on" button.

"Galcen," he said.

The screen blinked and a new message appeared beneath the last line of the menu: OUT OF RANGE.

"Nammerin."

OUT OF RANGE.

*Damnation.* "Maraghai."

OUT OF RANGE.

*Blast it, is* everywhere *out of range on these tubs?* He made on more desperate try. "Gyffer."

EXTREME RANGE. NO RETURN POSSIBLE. CONFIRM CHOICE YES/NO?

"Yes."

MAIN SHIP'S MEMORY ENGAGED. WORKING.

*Damn. I hope they're too busy with their treason and mutiny to spot this.*

Ari held his breath.

JUMP-RUN AND TRANSIT PLOTTED AND LAID IN. MAIN SHIP'S MEMORY DISENGAGED. SEQUENCE RUN YES/NO?

"Yes," said Ari, and the fighter's engines came to life.

Tyche heard the underhatch of the recon ship clank open and shut again. Heavy footsteps sounded on the deck-plates, and a few seconds later one of his troopers came into the compartment carrying a sheaf of papers and printout flimsies and a handful of datachips. After juggling awkwardly for a moment to get all his prizes into one hand, the trooper came to attention and saluted.

"Docking bay and all embarked craft now secure, sir!"

"Very good," said Tyche. "What is the status of the armed intruders aboard the *Selsyn*?"

"We've got them pinned down in the CIC. *Selsyn*'s own security forces hold the bridge and the engineering spaces."

"Good," said Tyche again. "Coordinate with *Selsyn*'s people and take CIC as soon as possible." He indicated the flimsies and datachips. "And what are these?"

"Hardcopy messages and log chips from the captured scout, sir," the trooper said, and placed them down on the common-room table with a flourish.

Tyche picked up the hardcopy and glanced through it, conscious as he did so of Metadi and Quetaya watching him. The first few pages were more than enough; he could feel the blood leaving his face as he read. He put the loose bundle of papers back on the table and pushed them over toward the General.

"You'll want to look at these, sir," he said. "This isn't just a mutiny we're dealing with. Vallant has sold out to the Magelords, and this is a war."

*The Mage warfleet is in the system, and Prime is already in their hands.*

In the deep-buried Operations Center of the Adepts' Retreat, General Ochemet stared at Master Ransome in shock and disbelief. "I ought to have been there," he said finally. "You had no right—you tricked me into coming here, and then held me against my will."

His voice grew sharper as his anger mounted. "And just whose side are you on, anyway?"

The accusation brought a sudden quiet to the crowded room. Master Tellyk, standing at Ochemet's elbow, gasped

and reddened, but Errec Ransome's face remained as pale
and cold as if it had been cut from marble.

"I belong to the Guild," he said. "And the Guild has
fought against the Magelords since the beginning."

Ochemet stood his ground. "So has the service, damn
you. I should have been with my people when the attack
came."

The Adept's expression softened a little. "Even if you
had been there you couldn't have stopped it. The Mages'
warfleet is too massive, and Galcen's close-in defenses
were overwhelmed. Also—we were betrayed."

Ochemet drew a sharp breath. "What are you talking
about?"

"Magework," said Ransome. "Magework and sorcery.
Here on Galcen, working to bring down the Republic and
the Guild both."

"Are you certain?"

"I've been certain for a long time," Ransome told him.
"But the Galcen Mage-Circle was well hidden and seldom
active. I didn't have the means to search it out. Now,
though—now they are acting openly, and we will destroy
them. Come."

The thought of doing something, anything, to strike
back at the attackers was tempting, but Ochemet still har-
bored suspicions of his own. "What do you need me for?"

"Local knowledge," Ransome said. "In Jos Metadi's absence, you have access to all of Prime Base."

"Which you tell me has already fallen." Ochemet shook
his head. "No. Pick a story and keep to it."

Ransome made an impatient gesture with one hand. "In
the long run, it doesn't matter who holds Prime. What
matters is that we find the Mage-Circle at work there and
destroy it. After that, the civilized galaxy may have a
fighting chance."

"A nice thought," said Ochemet. "If I decide to believe
you, that is." He folded his arms and looked Errec

Ransome up and down. "At the moment, frankly, the distinction between the Master of the Adepts' Guild and an ordinary traitor doesn't seem all that clear."

"Think whatever you want," said Ransome. "But choose. Stand here and do nothing, or come to Prime with me."

The Adept turned and strode off. After a moment, Ochemet sighed and hurried to catch up with him.

They plunged still farther into the depths beneath the Retreat, through dimly lit passageways carved from cold stone. From time to time they overtook and passed other men and women—Adepts, Ochemet supposed, though instead of dressing in black and carrying wooden staves, these wore pressure gear and carried flight helmets.

At length Ochemet and Ransome came out into a huge, vaulted docking bay filled with armored atmospheric craft, nearspace short-range fighters, and stargoing reconscouts. The far end of the cavern lay open to the sky, and Ochemet saw that light was growing there as the sun rose over the uplands. All about him was the organized confusion of a well-trained strike force making ready to launch.

"You didn't put this setup together yesterday." Ochemet had to shout to make his voice heard over the din. "How long have you known that the Mageworlds were planning to attack?"

"Nothing was known," said the Adept. "But while the Mageworlds existed, the threat of treachery existed. And we prepared ourselves to meet it."

Still talking, Ransome led the way through the crowded bay to a nondescript aircar with a civilian number stenciled on its side. "For a long time the Magelords watched me. I could only work through agents, or not at all. But now—while they are distracted and busy with bringing their plans to fruition—now I have a little time when I can act unseen."

Ochemet nodded mutely and followed Ransome into the

aircar. The Adept strapped down in the pilot's position and donned a set of earphones.

"Ready to launch," he said over the voice pickup.

A blue guide light floated down from the ceiling in front of the aircar and began clearing a way forward through the tangle of large and small craft. Ransome brought the aircar along after the light at a sedate glide, coming eventually to a runway laid out in the stone of the cavern floor. The guide light hovered in front of the aircar for a few seconds longer and then went out.

"So now it begins again," Ransome said, and pushed the throttles of the aircar all the way forward.

Engines roaring, the aircar hurtled down the runway, then out through the bright blue opening to soar among the crags. Looking back, Ochemet noticed that the cavern's mouth actually lay below the level of the highest peaks.

"That's a clever setup you've got there," he admitted. "If anyone was watching, your launch point's going to be lost in all the ground clutter."

Ransome gave him a quick, impatient look. "It had better be. With Prime gone and South Polar's fighter craft destroyed on the ground, what you saw back there is all that Galcen has."

# VIII. Galcen Nearspace
## The Outer Net
## Galcen: Prime Base

"FROM SPACE, the heart-world of the Adepts is truly a beautiful sight. I count myself fortunate that I have lived to experience this day."

In his flagship orbiting above Galcen Prime, Grand Admiral Theio syn-Ricte sus-Airaalin paced back and forth before the row of viewports overlooking the blue and green planet below. The autoscribe pinned to his collar caught the words as he spoke and stored them for inclusion in his next report to the no-longer-hidden Resurgency on Eraasi.

sus-Airaalin was a lean, wiry man—not tall, by the standards of the Adept-worlds, but above average for an Eraasian of the old stock—with black hair going prematurely grey. He wore plain brown fatigues tucked into leather boots, with shoulder and collar insignia of dull metal. Nothing about him glittered or caught the light; even the short ebony staff clipped to his belt had only the simplest of silver binding.

He continued talking to the autoscribe. "We have come this far successfully, after breaking through the artificial barrier at the Gap Between—successfully, but not without cost, in ships and in time. We can ill afford to lose more of either."

Frowning, he glanced over at the twin chronometers set into the bulkhead between the viewports. One chronometer gave the elapsed time since the operation began; the other showed how far ahead or behind schedule they had fallen. At the moment they were behind, and uncomfortably so. Resistance at the Gap had proved stronger than expected, forcing the warfleet to spend valuable minutes in breaking through the screen of enemy ships, minutes which had become hours in the transit.

"With respect to our goal of achieving total surprise: such a result has not been possible. I mean no ill-reflection upon the Circles; our Mages have given of themselves without stinting. Hyperspeed communications among the Adept-worlds were interdicted on schedule as we were promised, and have not yet resumed. Nevertheless—and I *will* remind all of you that I warned the Resurgency of this before!—at least one ship broke through and carried the warning to Prime."

sus-Airaalin frowned again, remembering how Galcen's inadequate home-defense forces had been waiting for the warfleet at the dropout point. More delay . . . the handful of vessels had held off the attack on their planet by more hours, and worse, had kept the jump points out of his hands long enough for couriers from Prime and South Polar to launch and make the jump into hyper.

"We have always counted time as our friend, but with the assault on the Gap it has become in one stroke our enemy. The Circles cannot suppress hyperspeed communications much longer, even if I should call upon them for the ultimate sacrifice, and news of the attack on Galcen Prime is undoubtedly spreading throughout the Adept-worlds at the speed of a fast ship.

"We must, therefore, bring the heart-system under control by whatever means necessary, and carry the attack to the enemy forces while they remain scattered and headless. Divided, they cannot equal the strength of our fleet; but should they ever recover themselves enough to unite against us, I can make no promises concerning our further success."

The vacuum-tight doors to the observation gallery sighed open to let in a messenger. sus-Airaalin thumbed off the autoscribe and turned away from the viewports to receive the newcomer with proper courtesy.

The messenger saluted. "Admiral, our forces on the ground report that Galcen Prime is now secure, and the major regional centers are coming under control. Fighting is continued but sporadic, and local defenses are weak."

"Very good. My compliments to our commanders, and to the troopers. Has General Metadi been identified?"

"No word on that, sir."

"Find him," ordered sus-Airaalin. "If he's out of our hands, he's dangerous. And if somebody tells you he's dead, see the body for yourself."

"Yes, sir."

An alarm bell started ringing, its tocsin running on in counterpoint beneath the annunciator's repeated warning: "Unknown fighters, inbound . . . unknown fighters, inbound . . . unknown fighters . . ."

The Grand Admiral stiffened.

*Metadi,* he thought for an instant, and felt a moment of profound apprehension before the true nature of the attacking force made itself felt to his extended senses. Not Jos Metadi's troops, but those of the other, greater enemy.

*Ransome. The Adept Master. The Breaker of Circles.*

Theio syn-Ricte sus-Airaalin unhooked the silver-and-

ebony staff from his belt, and felt the unseen fire running
up and down its length. There had been no particular happiness for him in smashing through the barrier at the Gap
Between Worlds, or in taking out the system ships in Galcen nearspace—but Errec Ransome was an enemy it
would be a pleasure to destroy.

"Summon the others," he told the messenger. "Tell them
to meet me in the meditation room. We have work to do."

The passenger compartment of RSF *Naversey* was an
awkward place in which to hold a debriefing, especially
with the four survivors from *Ebannha*'s boarding craft
added to the those already aboard. On the other hand,
*Naversey* had air pressure and shipboard gravity, which
meant that everyone could dispense with their p-suits and
magnetic-soled footgear.

Llannat sat at Lieutenant Vinhalyn's right, her staff lying across her lap. She'd had to leave the weapon behind
for her suited expedition into the Deathwing; she hadn't
realized how much its absence had upset her until she had
come back.

*I'm going to have to think about that. But not now.*

She looked across the central aisle of the passenger compartment at Ensign Tammas Cantrel, seated on the foot end
of an acceleration couch. The ensign was a painfully young
man, with dark circles under his eyes and lines on his face
that had no business being there. A stubble of beard on his
jaw made an awkward contrast with what must have once
been a prized and carefully tended mustache.

". . . so nobody was answering us on the hi-comms," he
said, "and after a while we decided that if we wanted to
make it home we were going to have to use the Deathwing. We were tracing systems on the main engines when
you folks showed up."

"Tracing systems?" said Llannat.

Cantrel nodded. He was holding on to a mug of hot

cha'a with both hands as if it were a lifeline. "Engineering by feel, more or less. We knew what a hyperdrive is supposed to do, and we knew—the chief knows, anyway—how the drives on our ships do it. So we were trying to figure out if the Mages got their ships into hyperspace the same way we do; and if they did, we were going to make their engines take us there."

E'Patu and Rethiel, the two warrant officers who'd come with *Naversey*, looked at each other. "You know," said E'Patu, "working blind like could have killed the lot of you."

"I know," said Cantrel. He took another swallow of his cha'a. "But even at one-eighth rations we only had a couple of months before we starved to death. I figured this way we could at least die trying."

"Under the circumstances," said Lieutenant Vinhalyn, "I think I would have done the same thing."

Llannat took a deep breath. "I think we still ought to."

The others—both *Naversey*'s original complement and the boarding party off *Ebannha*—looked at her with varying degrees of surprise. She took a firm grip on her staff and continued.

"There's a war out there. The Mageworlders have broken through the Net. I don't know where they were heading—"

"Galcen," put in Govantic, the data specialist. "I'll bet it was Galcen. With hi-comms down, they've got surprise—and they aren't going to waste it on the small stuff."

"A good point," Vinhalyn said. "Mistress Hyfid?"

"Right," she said. "With things in the shape they're in, we can't just drop out of hyper over Prime and expect the Space Force to be waiting. Not in an unarmed courier. But with the Deathwing, we can fight if we have to."

"We'd have people from both sides shooting at us," said Lury, the senior medic. "Not a real good idea."

"With the Deathwing we could shoot back," Llannat

countered. "And we could bring *Naversey* and the *Pari*-class along for escort."

"It'd be an interesting job," said E'Patu. "Dangerous as hell, though. The safe move would be to transfer everybody to *Naversey* and jump for some point closer in."

"No," said Llannat. Her persistence was starting to surprise even her; but she was in the grip of a new and pressing certainty. "Not in an unarmed ship when there's a war going on. We'd get shot to pieces the moment we dropped out of hyper. I say we ought to take the *Deathwing*."

Govantic was starting to look interested. "It'd be fun, all right—I've only gotten a chance to play with Magebuilt comp systems once before, and that was a ground-based setup that got left behind on Ophel after the War."

"Archaic Magebuilt battle and navigation systems," promised Llannat. "More fun than a twelve-hour session of *Deathworld* in a holovid arcade . . . and Lieutenant Vinhalyn reads Eraasian. If the old-time Mageworlders put instruction manuals on their ships, he can translate them for us. We won't be working blind at all."

It was three hours after leaving the Retreat in the aircar that General Ochemet saw the first signs of dirtside fighting. All morning the incongruously bright sky had been laced with the contrails of atmospheric fighters weaving about high above Master Ransome's low-flying craft, but this was the first time Ochemet had spotted something that he could make out with his bare eyes.

Looking down on the road below, he saw a column of armored fighting vehicles strung out like the beads of a broken necklace. Black smoke poured from their hatches, and here and there in the dirt around them lay small crumpled figures.

A mile or two farther on beyond the wreckage, Ochemet saw another line of armored vehicles approaching from the other direction. He didn't recognize the design, which meant they weren't anything the Republic had available on Galcen. The unfamiliar vehicles came on in open skirmishing order, infantry mixed among the armor, making their way at an easy walking pace away from Prime.

*The Mageworlders have got the cities,* Ochemet realized. *Now they're moving out to secure the countryside.*

It wasn't going to be hard. He didn't like the thought, but he knew it was true. Galcen had always relied on the Space Force for defense, and the Space Force had counted on the efficiency of the Republic's hyperspace communications, the links and relays that transferred messages in seconds between the outplanets and the Central Worlds. That wide-spread, multiply redundant system had been the cornerstone of all their strategic planning—a technical achievement that allowed the Space Force to patrol a vast collection of worlds and still muster in strength at a trouble spot.

*We never counted on losing hi-comms,* Ochemet thought unhappily. Nobody in the high command had ever devised a theoretical way to break a system that had so many relay stations and backups and alternate routing patterns. Eventually, the idea had been given up as impossible. But the Mageworlders had somehow managed to do it.

*If we still had our communications grid working, the fleets from Khesat and Wrysten would have shown up last night sometime, and the out-sector forces would be rolling in right about now.*

*Instead, Galcen's in flames and nobody outside the system knows it.*

He looked again at the advancing column of Mageworlds fighting vehicles. The aircar had to be plainly visible from the ground; they were well out of the mountains, with nothing for a backdrop but the clear blue sky.

"Why aren't they shooting at us?" Ochemet wondered aloud.

Ransome didn't bother turning his head. "They aren't shooting at us because they aren't seeing us. Be quiet. I need to concentrate."

They flew on toward Prime. The sun climbed in the sky, and the columns of smoke on the horizon grew closer.

Grand Admiral Theio syn-Ricte sus-Airaalin knelt in the quiet of the meditation room, among the other eight of his Circle. Like them, he wore the mask and the hooded robe, hiding his uniform and his badges of rank. In this one compartment of the great flagship, outside power and position no longer mattered. sus-Airaalin had been First of his Circle long before the Resurgency found him and made him the commander of their secret warfleet.

Before military office and authority had come to him, his lifelong struggle had been solely to keep the heritage of the Circles alive. He'd made enemies enough that way, those who didn't care if they wore chains as long as their beds were soft—and others who would have turned the broken Circles into mere political tools, using the Mages as spies and assassins, no better than Adepts.

In the end, he had won: without the efforts of the Circles, the warfleet could never have broken through the barrier at the Gap and gone on to take Galcen Prime. And on this ship, at least, a Mage-Circle functioned as Circles had done in the old days: guiding the attack, providing their fighters with support where support was needed, luck where luck was needed, comfort where comfort was needed.

Here among his own people sus-Airaalin felt the most at home, even during combat. The details of tactics he left to those who were trained in such things, the younger sons and daughters of families with a tradition of service.

It had taken a generation for the Resurgency to bring them together—all the ones who had been clever enough or lucky enough to escape the killing time. Finding teachers for them had taken almost as long. Of those who understood the military arts or possessed the skills of spaceflight, only a handful had survived the great purges at the end of the War. From Raamet to Eraasi, the family didn't exist that hadn't seen one or more of its members taken away by the Adept-worlders, never to return.

And what had happened to the Circles . . . it hurt sus-Airaalin yet to remember. He hoped that now, after his victory, he could persuade the Resurgency to have mercy.

*Or else we are no better than our enemies,* he thought, *and I have worked all my life for nothing.*

A hand grasped his shoulder, shaking him back to present awareness. He opened his eyes.

"Who dares—?" he began, but then he felt the messenger's burden of news pressing against his own spirit, and he understood. He rose to his feet.

"Prepare a shuttle," he told the messenger. "I have to go down to the surface."

Errec Ransome grounded the aircar on a strip of concrete near the Space Force Headquarters at Galcen Prime. The sky overhead had gone from a sharp-edged midday blue to the softer, blurrier colors of twilight, but the invisibility that had protected them during the flight still seemed to be working. A ground trooper in an unfamiliar brown uniform—a Mageworlder, Ochemet presumed—hurried past them without reacting, only a few feet away.

Ransome retrieved his staff from the clips that held it and opened the door of the aircar. Ochemet put out a hand to stop him. "I think it's time you told me where we're going."

The Adept Master shook his head. "I follow the patterns of the universe," he said. "Sometimes I can see where they lead, and sometimes not."

Ochemet looked at the headquarters building, its windows broken by explosives and its elegant walls pitted by blaster-fire. In the marble-paved plaza out front, amid the splashing fountains and expressive monumental statuary that had brought its architect galaxy-wide acclaim, troopers in blast-armor stood guard over several hundred men and women in Space Force uniform, lined up in rows with their hands on top of their heads.

*Prisoners,* Ochemet thought, and the realization filled him with bitterness.

"I suppose this is what happens when you don't know where you're going," he said to Ransome. "Or did you see it and keep on following your damned patterns anyway?"

Ransome's mouth tightened. "You don't know enough to understand your own questions, General. Stay quiet if you don't want to get us both captured."

Ochemet and Ransome entered the headquarters building in silence, stepping through the wreckage of the blasted-open doors and past the half-buried body of a guard. Inside, they walked up the long, curving ramp to the upper level of the grand rotunda. The lifts that should have taken them higher were dead, sliding doors frozen halfway open on empty shafts. At a gesture from Ransome, Ochemet led the way to the emergency stairs, tucked out of sight behind a pierced metal screen and a full-sized Khesatan *ilyral* tree in a marble tub. A bolt from an energy lance had burned away half the screen, but the *ilyral* remained incongruously green and healthy.

Somebody had found the stairs already and taken out the lock with another energy bolt. But the fighting at Prime was long over. Ransome and Ochemet climbed all the way to the top levels of the headquarters building without passing anyone.

Once out of the stairwell and into the office blocks, they saw more of the men and women in unfamiliar brown fatigues: the strangers were shorter than Space Force troopers, on the average, and tended toward dark hair and pale skin. Most of them looked tired; none of them noticed the two intruders, one in the Republic's uniform and one in Adept's black.

The General and Ransome passed the open door of Ochemet's office. The room was unlighted and empty, but otherwise it looked just as Ochemet had left it the day before. Clearly the Mageworlders hadn't bothered searching there yet. They'd get to it soon enough, though; Captain Gremyl's much smaller cubicle, only a few doors down, already had three of them, one sorting through the hardcopy and physical files while the other two conferred in quiet, alien voices over the desk comp.

Ochemet held up a hand. "Wait," he said—only the movement of the word, without voice.

Ransome frowned, but stayed.

Ochemet went on through the door into his office. If the room hadn't been disturbed, there should be a fully-charged blaster in the lower right-hand drawer of his desk. General Metadi had always insisted that his senior officers keep sidearms within easy reach. At one point Ochemet had considered the order unnecessary, not to mention somewhat paranoid, but no longer.

The desk was on emergency self-power, but it answered to his ID scan. As soon as the lock clicked over he pulled the drawer open and took out the blaster. He felt marginally better once he had the weapon in hand.

The top of his desk held the usual pile of printout flimsies—he'd left a stack behind unread when he'd hurried off to the Retreat, and more messages and paperwork had accumulated while he was gone. He tucked the blaster in his belt and started riffling through the messages, looking in vain for any hint of preparation for the Mageworlds attack. Near the bottom of the stack, he found a sheet tagged "Personal for CO," with a time-stamp only minutes after his departure. It was a situation report from one of the nearspace patrol ships. He broke the seal and read through the message in silence and growing dismay:

> Vessel identifying itself as RMV *Warhammer*, captain identifying herself as Beka Rosselin-Met-adi, reports that the Net is broken, hi-comms are down, and a Mageworlds warfleet is inbound. Request instructions.

Knowledge pressed down on Ochemet like a weight, and he closed his eyes. *There was time,* he thought helplessly. *If I'd known, there were things we could have done. There was time.*

He looked up, the flimsy crumpling in his hand, to see Ransome beckoning impatiently from the open door. *He knew!* For a moment he felt like using the blaster on the Adept, but he mastered the urge and followed Ransome once more.

They went down that corridor and then another. Finally Ransome halted before a closed door labeled 44–55 (CUSTODIAL).

"There's nothing in there but the top-floor cleanup robot and a couple of emergency pushbrooms," Ochemet protested in a hoarse whisper.

Ransome ignored him and opened the door. Inside was a dark room, far larger than the closet that should have been there, with a white circle painted on the concrete floor. In the circle a group of eight people, masked and hooded in black, knelt facing inward. None of them turned or looked up when the door slid open and Ransome and Ochemet entered.

"Mages?" Ochemet asked in a whisper.

"Yes."

"What are they doing?"

"It doesn't matter. They are guilty. Their treason helped to bring down Prime. You have a blaster—kill them now."

Ochemet lifted the weapon and trained it on the oblivious, kneeling circle. His finger brushed the surface of the firing stud. Then he shook his head and reversed the blaster to hold it out butt-first to Ransome.

"Do it yourself."

Ransome didn't reply, or even look at the blaster. The Adept Master stepped away from Ochemet and into the middle of the white circle, brushing past the kneeling figures as if they didn't exist. He lifted his staff above his head in both hands and closed his eyes.

Blue-green fire began to play around the ends of the staff, and Ochemet felt himself growing cold. The Guild had broken the power of the Magelords after the last war—he'd always known that, and thinking of Entibor and Sapne and Ilarna, he'd been grateful. But now he was seeing how it must have been done. Slowly, inexorably, Master Ransome was calling forth more and more of the blue-green light, drawing on reserves of internal power whose nature and extent Ochemet could scarcely imagine, making ready to deliver a single devastating blow.

Ochemet stepped backward almost unconsciously, moving away into the shadows until his shoulders came up against the concrete wall. He wasn't certain any longer what he feared: the Mages in the Circle, or the thing that Errec Ransome would do to them.

Time seemed to slow. Ochemet held his breath. He knew that in the next moment Ransome would strike.

Then, in the instant before the gathered energy came smashing down, another figure appeared in the open doorway. This one was also robed and masked in black, but between the hem and the boot tops showed the ubiquitous brown fatigues. He carried a short staff loosely in one gloved hand, and green fire ran up and down the weapon's length.

"Master Ransome," the stranger said, in rough but passable Galcenian. "What right have you to dispose of my Circles?"

Ransome brought his staff down before him into a defensive position. The witchfire still writhed and flickered along it, casting eerie shadows onto his set and uncompromising face. "Lord sus-Airaalin. What is mine to protect, I protect by all the means I have."

The Magelord—Ochemet supposed that this was indeed a Magelord; certainly Ransome seemed to be addressing him as such—inclined his masked head in a grave nod. "So you do. And your name is known for it in the homeworlds. But I do not recall ever giving you the favor of knowing mine."

"No," said Ransome. "Nevertheless, I know it."

Ochemet, pressed back against the wall in the darkness, thought for a moment that sus-Airaalin would demand the source of Ransome's knowledge. Instead, however, the Magelord strode between two of the kneeling Mages to join Errec Ransome in the center of the white circle.

"Master Ransome," he said formally, "we are too powerful, you and I, to stand by while others do battle for us. Will you fight me here and now, for the mastery of this Circle and for the possession of the galaxy?"

Ransome smiled without humor. In the blue-green light his features looked pale and haggard.

"No," he said, "I won't. I have too much to lose."

"Then yield," said sus-Airaalin, and the light died as he took the staff from Errec Ransome's hands.

# PART FOUR

# I. Gyffer: Port of Telabryk
## Deathwing: The Outer Net

GYFFER WAS a world that lived by its ship-yards and its weapons factories. More of the Space Force's capital ships came from Gyffer's massive orbiting spacedocks than from anywhere else in the Republic. On the surface, other shipyards worked in the construction and repair of smaller dirtside-to-hyperspace vessels like the old *Warhammer*, and arms dealers would sell a starship captain anything from a custom-modified blaster to a new set of energy guns.

The last time Ari Rosselin-Metadi had touched down on a Gyfferan landing field, he and Nyls Jessan had brought in the *'Hammer* after the raid on Darvell. They'd cut it close; the ship's dying realspace engines had been held together with little else besides solder and positive thinking, and Beka—who had known the *'Hammer* better than anybody except Jos Metadi himself—had been in worse shape than the ship. By comparison, making planetfall in a long-range Eldan fighter with low fuel reserves and only the simplest of deep-space navigational gear was an easy bit of work.

*On the other hand,* thought Ari as he cut in the Eldan's nullgravs and lowered the craft gently down onto its landing legs at Telabryk Field, *the 'Hammer had all her papers. They were fake papers, but at least they were in order.*

*This thing, though . . . how the hell am I supposed to explain a Space Force fighter and a Space Force uniform? I'm a deserter, possibly a traitor, and who knows what the local law is going to think.*

Hiding was impossible; Gyffer had its own in-system fleet, and maintained nearspace security as tight as or tighter than any place in the civilized galaxy. Ari had been hailed by a patrol vessel within seconds of his dropout from hyper. More out of desperation than anything else, and in order to buy some time for thought, he'd taken the high line when the ship challenged him—refusing to identify himself and demanding a direct communications link to the nearest Space Force unit.

That, he reflected, was when things had started getting odd. The Gyfferan patrol vessel wouldn't give him a line to the Space Force, or even tell him which vessels were in the area. But nobody challenged him any more either, or demanded that he submit to inspection. Instead, the patrol vessel escorted him to orbit, patched him through to Gyfferan Inspace Control, and handed him off to an orbit-to-atmosphere fighter. Inspace Control had given him landing clearance here at Telabryk, and the fighter had stayed with him, making sure he didn't deviate from his flight path, until he'd grounded.

Ari unstrapped from the safety webbing and climbed wearily down through the Eldan's belly hatch to the tarmac. He hadn't slept for over two days; most of the run through hyperspace he'd done with the autopilot, but the cockpit of a two-seat fighter wasn't designed to be restful, especially for somebody his size. More than almost anything in the universe right now, he wanted a cup of hot cha'a, a bath, and a warm bed.

He didn't think much of his chances for getting them, though. Not until he'd gone through all the explanations, paperwork, and still more explanations involved in letting the Space Force know that he hadn't been deserting or absconding with government property when he left the *Fezzy*. And if Gyffer turned out to be a willing partner in Admiral Vallant's dreams of grandeur, then things could get really awkward.

At least there wasn't anybody waiting on the field to arrest him. Stretching, Ari looked around and tried to take stock of the situation.

Telabryk Field, like most dirtside ports, was a flat piece of paved ground stretching out to the horizon in all directions. Off to local apparent north, Telabryk proper was a dark blue on the horizon, looking at this distance more like a range of low hills than one of the biggest cities in the Republic. The field was emptier now than at the time of Ari's previous visit, when the ships in port had completely hidden Telabryk's urban sprawl.

Scattered here and there on the tarmac were low concrete buildings painted with the insignia of shipping lines, planetary governments, and such other organizations as maintained their own interstellar fleets. General Delivery had a courier ship in; the vessel's garish red and yellow color scheme showed up halfway across the field. The Space Force port complex—a couple of squat, blocky structures barely deserving the name—should have had a full wing of atmosphere/nearspace fighters, but it didn't.

Ari wet his lips nervously. *This doesn't look good.*

Still, his first duty was to report to senior authority. Leaving the Eldan two-seater behind him, he started walking across the field.

When he got to the Space Force complex, things

looked even worse. Not just the fighters were missing; so were all the assorted ground and atmospheric craft—skipsleds, hovercars, aircars, and the like—that should have cluttered the area. Ari circled around to the front of the main building and the big armor-glass doors marked with the Space Force seal. The doors should have parted automatically as soon as he came within their sensor range. By now, though, he wasn't surprised when they stayed shut.

He shielded his eyes with one hand against the glare coming off the field, and tried to see inside the building. No luck—the interior lights were off. Methodically, he tried the complex's other entrances, all the way down to the hinged metal door of the machine shop skipsled-loading platform, which turned out to be as locked as the rest.

Ari leaned against the back wall of the machine shop and let exhaustion wash over him. No wonder Gyfferan patrols weren't patching anybody through to the Space Force: the Space Force wasn't here.

*They aren't just secured for the day, either. They've packed up and left. They're gone.*

Helmeted and pressure-suited, Llannat Hyfid stood in the main airlock of the Deathwing and watched the status light cycling—from yellow to purple, which at the moment struck her as odder and more unnatural than anything else about the derelict ship.

*Not quite a derelict,* she thought. *Not any longer.*

She wasn't certain which had done more to convince Lieutenant Vinhalyn that they should bring the Magebuilt vessel back on line—their need to acquire the Deathwing's potential firepower, or his own overwhelming scholarly curiosity about an artifact from a time long past. The combination, at least, had proved irresistible. Now, after two Standard days of nonstop work, the combined crews of *Naversey* and the boarding craft had achieved their first success. The Deathwing's primary life-support systems were back on line.

The status light flashed rapidly back and forth between yellow and purple for several seconds, then settled on purple and held. A bell-tone sounded. The inner door of the lock cycled open.

Ensign Cantrel checked the readouts on the sensor pack he'd brought over from the boarding craft. "Mark one! The lock's tight and we've got a good atmosphere."

With a gloved hand, Lieutenant Vinhalyn slid aside a bulkhead panel with more of the yellow Eraasian script on it. The space behind the panel was full of dials and gauges.

"These all seem to agree with you," the linguist-historian said after a prolonged inspection. "We'll want some of the techs to double-check them later, but it looks like the old monitoring systems are still working."

"It's safe to breathe in here, then?" asked Llannat.

"Sure," said Cantrel. "I can't vouch for what the air's going to smell like, but the sensor pack isn't registering any known biohazards."

The ensign was already unfastening his own helmet as he spoke. He lifted it off, revealing a face freshly depilated—except for the cherished mustache—and considerably less worn than when Llannat had first met him.

"Now that we've got atmosphere," he continued, "we can start trying to figure out the gravity system. And after that, we'll tackle the engines."

"The manuals," Vinhalyn explained to Llannat, "turned out to be very specific on the matter of proper cold-start sequencing." The linguist-historian had his helmet off by now, and was cradling it in the crook of his arm. "The systems must interlock correctly, or catastrophic failure will result."

Llannat undid the last seal on her helmet and took it off. She rubbed her nose vigorously with the back of her free hand; as usual, being inside a p-suit had given her a half-dozen maddening and unscratchable itches.

"Did the old-time Mageworlders have a problem with their engineering," she wondered aloud, "or did they just like to watch things explode?"

"We may never know," said Vinhalyn, with a faint smile. He turned to Cantrel. "You people were lucky in one thing, though. It appears that whoever abandoned this ship put it through an orderly shutdown first."

"That's what we were thinking, too," said Cantrel. "Except for—well, except for what we found on the bridge. Looking at that, I still can't figure out what happened."

"Yes," said Vinhalyn. "The bridge: That's what Mistress Hyfid and I were intending to investigate. Now that we have atmosphere back, we'll have to do it quickly, too. They're going to start to get high pretty soon."

Llannat nodded, but without enthusiasm. She'd put off the investigation as long as possible—the all-hands job of bringing the first of the Deathwing's systems on line had provided an excellent pretext for delay—but there was no getting out of it now. She was an Adept, and she was going to have to walk into a scene of bloody murder on a Magebuilt ship, with a dewy-eyed innocent like Tammas Cantrel watching her and expecting a miracle.

"This isn't like picking out a live target on the monitor screen," she cautioned the ensign. "These were Mages, and it's a cold trail. We may not learn anything at all."

*And maybe we'll learn something we didn't want to know.*

Sighing, Ari pushed himself away from the wall of the deserted Space Force installation. He wasn't certain where he ought to go next. Even getting off Gyffer looked close to impossible. The Eldan two-seater had been pushed to its limit and wasn't going to lift again for anywhere without refueling and a maintenance workover. He'd left the *Fezzy* in his working uniform, with nothing by way of assets except a Space Force ID card, a Mandeynan quarter-mark coin, and a fully charged blaster.

A quick message to Galcen Prime would go a long way toward solving his problem. On the other hand, he wasn't sure that talking to Gyfferan customs was going to be a good idea. If Admiral Vallant's mutiny had reached as far as Gyffer, the local government might well greet Ari with open arms and march him aboard a courier ship bound straight back for Infabede—or throw him in the local jail as a bargaining chip for their side, whichever side that was.

*I need some local intelligence,* Ari thought, scanning Telabryk Field for anything that looked like a source of information. *And I need it now.*

The gaudy red and yellow colors of the General Delivery building caught his eye, and he felt a surge of relief. General Delivery had its own fleet of courier ships making high-speed runs all over the galaxy, and maintained its own data net for electronic messages. The company's entire reputation was built on its ability to keep the farthest elements of the civilized galaxy in touch with each other and with the Central Worlds.

*If anybody can fill me in on how the land lies the G-Del people can. And they're a Suivi-based firm, so they probably won't tell the locals that they saw me.*

From the Space Force complex to the G-Del block was quite a hike, especially with the heat of the sun reflecting up from the tarmac at redoubled strength. Ari was sweating before he'd covered half the distance to the red and yellow building. This time, though, the doors opened at his approach, and he stepped through into the cool, dry air inside.

Most of General Delivery's Telabryk Field operation was devoted to cargo handling. Employees in more subdued versions of the company colors were sorting through the incoming cargo from the courier, throwing the boxes and envelopes into tubs for delivery to G-Del offices all over Gyffer. Other employees were loading up a skipsled with the outbound mail. A long counter stretched across the front of the big room, separating the workers from the small reception area near the entrance.

The clerk at the counter was a thin man with worry lines between his eyebrows. He glanced up from his comp screen when Ari came in.

"I thought you people left already."

"They did," said Ari. "I came in-system from the Infabede sector a little while ago. I want to send a message to Galcen, fastest means available."

The clerk pointed to another desk comp at the far end of the counter. "Flimsies and keyboard over there to write a letter. Hardcopy's the only thing getting out right now."

"No voicelink?"

"No."

"What the hell's going on?"

"That's what everybody wants to know," said the clerk. He looked at Ari with a sour expression. "I suppose you want me to tell you what happened."

"That's right."

The clerk tightened his lips briefly and then said, "Okay. First thing, about a week ago all the hi-comms went down. Ours and everybody else's. We figured it was trouble in the orbital relays at first, and sent a repair crew up to work them over. The repairs didn't do any good. Meanwhile there's no word getting into the system that doesn't come by ship."

Ari nodded. "I'd heard a rumor about the hi-comms back in Infabede. Didn't have time to check it out, though. So what happened to the Space Force?"

"I'm getting there," said the clerk. "About three days after the hi-comms died, we got a Space Force courier ship on a fast run from Galcen Prime. And I do mean *fast*—

she'd overridden her hyperdrive and damn near went nova on the dropout, and she was squawking her news all over the lightspeed bands on her way into the system, just in case she didn't make it."

"News from Prime?" Ari tried to conceal his growing apprehension. He'd been expecting to hear word of trouble in the Infabede sector, not of some unspecified disaster at the heart of the Central Worlds. "How bad?"

"If it's true," the clerk said, "then it's as bad as it gets. The pilot of the courier said that the Mageworlders were attacking Galcen in force—how the hell they'd managed to get a fleet through the Net he didn't say—and that with hi-comms down and no help coming Prime was about to go under. That was at about midnight local. By dawn, Space Force was gone."

*Standing orders of some kind,* Ari realized. *Somewhere in the CO's files was an eyes-only folder labeled "What To Do In Case We Lose Galcen Prime," and now they've gone and done it.*

"Do you think the story was true?" he asked.

"If it wasn't, those pilots nearly fried themselves for nothing," said the clerk. "And none of our regular cargo runs from Galcen have shown up since the courier came in."

"But you're still sending hardcopy mail back?"

"We're sending," the clerk told him. "It may not get past the sorting depot on Cashel, but we'll do our best. As long as you realize that under the circumstances, timely delivery isn't guaranteed."

"Right," said Ari.

His Mandeynan quarter-mark probably wasn't enough to pay for a hardcopy message anyway. Just the same, he had to do something with the news from Infabede. After a moment's thought, he went over to the other desk comp and began keying in a letter:

View all traffic from COMREPSPAFOR INFA-
BEDE with suspicion. Ari Rosselin-Metadi, LCDR,
SFMS, sends.

He pulled out the sheet of flimsy and took it back over
to the clerk.

"Here," he said. "This is what I was going to send to
Galcen. Make up your own mind what to do with it. I'm
going in to town."

With the return of basic life-support systems, the interior lighting on the Magebuilt ship had come back as well.
The ship's passageways, while still narrow and mazelike,
no longer gaped like dark open mouths in the beam from
a p-suit's handlamp. In the white light of the glows—not
quite the same color mix as Space Force's Galcen-based
standard, but close enough for comfort—the Deathwing
turned out to be a thing of metal and glass and plastic like
any other starship.

*Almost like,* thought Llannat. The fact that there was life
in the glows didn't reassure her as much as it should have.
*Those lights ought to have burnt out centuries ago. Except
for the fact that somebody turned them all off.*

That was what made her feel cold, even inside the pressure suit: a picture she couldn't shake, of a shadowy figure
going through the empty ship from compartment to compartment, turning off all the light switches like a thrifty
householder bound away for an afternoon in town.

*Somebody was expecting to come back. And they
wanted the ship to be working when they got here.*

She wet her lips—the newly awakened systems kept the
air in the Deathwing bone-dry—and said, "It looks like
most of the compartments we've been through so far are
pretty standard. Berthing, the galley . . . I wonder if their
space rations were any worse than ours?"

"I'm not hungry enough to try them," said Vinhalyn.

"We can omit the desperate measures until they become necessary."

"I'm with you on that," Cantrel said. "Before you guys showed up, I was thinking we'd have to crack open some of the packets in the galley and try them out. Not a fun idea, believe me, when you don't know how to tell the powdered porridge from the stuff that opens up clogged drains."

"I suppose not," murmured Llannat. In spite of the lights and the comforting background hum of a working life-support system, she was finding it hard to shake a continuing sense of oppression. It clung around her as it had from the time she'd stepped aboard, and seemed to intensify as she and Vinhalyn followed Cantrel forward, their magnetic boot soles clicking and shuffling against the deckplates.

Clearing her throat, she said, "Tammas—did you and the rest of the boarding party come up here much?"

Cantrel shook his head. "Not if we could help it. Once or twice to see where a power line went, but that's all. It's too damned spooky in there."

They came at last to the vacuum-tight doors of the Deathwing's cockpit. The ensign pulled a slice of plastic out of his p-suit's cargo pouch and gave it to Lieutenant Vinhalyn.

"This'll get you in," he said. "The key slot's over there. But if you don't mind, I think I'll stay outside."

Llannat watched uneasily as Vinhalyn put the slice of plastic into the lock. She could feel Ensign Cantrel watching the back of her neck—expecting her to work wonders, no doubt, and provide marvels of explanation. But her sense of foreboding continued to grow.

She knew that what afflicted her wasn't the simple prospect of looking at what remained of the Deathwing's pilot and copilot. She'd seen worse things than that as a medic;

she'd done worse things than that herself, when she went with Beka Rosselin-Metadi to Darvell. This was different.

*There's something waiting for me in there.*

The door slid open. The Deathwing's cockpit was still dark; nobody had come by to bring the lights back up after the systems had come on line. Vinhalyn had already stepped inside; she could hear him muttering to himself as he fumbled to locate the switch for the cockpit illumination.

"Aha!" he said after a moment, and the lights came on.

Llannat forced herself to step inside, only to find the scene oddly prosaic for something so bloody—it was work for the Med Service pathologist who'd come out with *Naversey*, not for an Adept.

"We need to put these two in a stasis box," said Llannat. "If we've got one."

"We can rig something, I'm sure," said Vinhalyn absently. He was standing in front of the Deathwing's viewscreens, bending closer to peer at the dark, blurry characters scrawled upon the glass. "This, now—*this* is truly interesting."

"What do you mean?"

"It's a message," said Vinhalyn, straightening up again. "Not to just anybody who might come by, either. It's in the second person familiar, and the writer speaks as an equal to someone who has already been introduced, not to a stranger of unknown rank."

Llannat moved to stand beside him. "What does it say?"

Vinhalyn turned from the viewscreen and gave her a strange and rather wary look. "Roughly translated? Something on the order of 'Adept from the forest world: Find the Domina; tell her what thou hast seen.' "

## II. NAMMERIN: DOWNTOWN NAMPORT
## OPHEL NEARSPACE

IT WAS early evening in Namport, and the street-lamps were coming on one by one. In her walk-up apartment in the old quarter, Klea Santreny twitched aside a flimsy gauze curtain and looked out at the corner below. She was glad to be inside tonight. For the past three days, gutter-choking rains had alternated with steaming heat, turning Namport's mucky thoroughfares into rancid ox-wallows. Tonight was one of the steamers; she could smell the mud from four floors up.

*Nobody ever told me that the big city was going to smell five times worse than the farm ever did. Maybe if they had—*

She turned away from the window. *I still wouldn't have believed it. If there's anybody on this planet who's more stupid-stubborn than I was, I haven't found them yet. Five years at Freling's Bar, and it took going crazy to make me wise up enough to get out. I just wish I knew where it is I'm getting to. . . .*

She hadn't been getting much of anywhere lately, not even in the most literal meaning of the phrase. Ever since the night when she'd seen a star explode against a back-drop of constellations that didn't shine over Nammerin, she'd been restless and uneasy.

Owen had taken her uneasiness seriously. "On a planet with a working Mage-Circle, an Adept has to be careful. And so does an apprentice."

"I'm not an Adept," she'd said. "Or an apprentice either. I'm just—"

"You're not 'just' anything." He'd sounded almost angry—and worried, which unsettled her even more. "You're powerfully sensitive to this kind of stuff, and the Circle knows it. If they decide you're a threat to them, you're in trouble."

With his warnings fresh in her mind, she'd stayed close to home, not going much farther abroad than Ulle's All-Night Grocery. Even that, as it turned out, was enough to increase her sense of something formless and imponderable hanging over the city.

The streets were full of weird rumors: that the hi-comm news feeds from off-planet had been down hard for three days now, and the Namport Holovid Network was patching together old stories from five or six months ago to keep people from noticing; that the Space Force Med Station had closed its gates and canceled all leaves; that Suivi Point had seceded from the Republic and the outplanets were revolting. Even the bad weather was generally conceded to be some kind of plot.

*One more reason to be glad you don't work at Freling's anymore*, she told herself. *This is the sort of night that brings out the real sickos.*

An urgent knocking at the door of her apartment broke into her thoughts. She hurried over to the peephole and looked out. It was Owen, to her considerable surprise; he'd gone off to his job at the laundry more than an hour ago, and shouldn't have been back until morning. She unlocked the door and let him in.

"What's wrong?" she demanded as soon as he was inside.

He didn't give her a direct answer. Instead he waited until she'd shut the door behind him before asking, "Do you want to go to the Retreat?"

She stared at him. "Right *now*?"

"That's right," he said. "The Planetary Assembly is going to shut down the port at noon tomorrow."

"They're going to—where did you hear that?"

"At work. One of the bathhouse regulars is a clerk in the Customs Office. Klea, you're going to have to make up your mind tonight. Do you want to go or stay?"

"Go," she said without stopping to think. Now that she had to choose, the choice was surprisingly easy.

"Then pack what you need. We have to get to the port as soon as possible. It's going to be a mob scene by morning."

She was already stuffing clean clothes and underwear into the ancient day pack that she'd brought with her from the farm all that long time ago. *I kept telling myself I ought to throw it out,* she thought somewhat dizzily; *it's a good thing I never listened.*

"Is there a ship in for Galcen?" she asked aloud.

"I don't know. It doesn't matter. Once we manage to get off-planet, then we can start thinking about Galcen."

"What are we going to do about money?"

He made an impatient gesture with one hand. "Don't worry about the money—I'll take care of it. First we have to find a ship."

She sealed up the pack and slung it onto her shoulders. "Whatever you say. Let's go."

"One more thing first," he said. He looked straight at her, and his hazel eyes were so dark a green they seemed almost black. When he spoke again, his voice took on a more formal cadence. "Kela Santreny—do you come to the Adepts for instruction only, or will you take the apprenticeship that is offered to you?"

"What do you mean, 'take the apprenticeship'?"

"Answer yes or no," he said. "Please. It's important."

She stood there for a minute, feeling her life changing around her like a forest whipped by the wind. *Everything else I've ever done, I could back out of. What I say now is going to make things different forever.* She drew a deep breath.

"Yes," she said.

Owen let out an exhalation of relief. "Good. Now that you're a Guild apprentice, if anything happens to me or we get separated, you can ask for help from any Adept or Guildhouse in the civilized galaxy."

He paused, and glanced about her small apartment as if searching for something. "You'll need a staff."

"What for? You don't have one."

"That's different . . . my teacher on Galcen keeps mine."

He crossed the room to the kitchen nook in a couple of quick strides, and picked up the broom that stood in the corner: a plain, local-made thing, the sort of broom that farmers put together out of *grrch* wood and grain-straw and sold for a quarter-credit apiece when they came to town.

With seeming ease he snapped off the brush and offered the stick to Klea. She wasn't surprised to see that both ends appeared equally smooth and even; anybody who could break *grrch* wood bare-handed could probably make the broken part look like anything he wanted it to.

"Take this," he said. Once again the words sounded like part of a formal ceremony. "Hold it and cherish it as you do your honor. Wield it in truth and justice, and as the patterns of the universe direct it and you together. By the staff an Adept is known; let neither one disgrace the other."

She took the broomstick—the staff, she supposed she

ought to call it now—and held it awkwardly before her in both hands. "What am I supposed to do with this?"

"The ShadowDance, to begin with," he said. "It also makes a decent walking stick. And more things, that you can learn when you have time. But now we have to hurry. If the port gets too crowded the Assembly may decide to close it early."

Above the plane of the Opheline system, far to the Netward of the Central Worlds, the fabric of realspace stretched and shifted as two ships dropped out of hyper. Several tense seconds later, a third ship followed.

In RSF *Karipavo*'s Combat Information Center, the duty sensor analyst looked up from his board and announced to the compartment at large, "*Lachiel*'s made it through."

A ragged cheer went up, and Commodore Jervas Gil, the *'Pavo*'s acting CO, let out a sigh of relief. If three ships were all that was left of his squadron, they were at least his, and he was still their commodore.

"Signal *Lachiel*," he told the communications tech. "Ask if the voyage repairs to their realspace engines are holding up well enough for them to make Ophel."

It would be good for *Lachiel*'s pride, he reflected, if the crew could bring their ship in without assistance—but in the long run it wouldn't matter if they needed the help of a spacedock tug. After the battle at the Net, when *Lachiel* had taken a crippling hit to the realspace engines and lost airtight integrity in over half her compartments, what counted was that the third ship of Gil's much-diminished fleet was here at all.

"*Lachiel* reports that she can make it all right if we take it low and slow," reported the comms tech.

"Very well," said Gil. "Low and slow it is. How are we doing on a hi-comms link to Prime?"

"No joy, sir," said the tech. "Whoever took down hi-comms is still keeping them that way."

"Keep trying," Gil said. "The minute they come back I want to know. For now, get me Ophel on the lightspeed comms."

From this distance out, patching through the connection took several minutes. Gil waited, frowning with barely restrained impatience. Ophel hadn't been his first choice for a dropout point. It was a neutral world, friendly enough but not bound to the Republic by an treaties that Gil knew of; and ever since the First Magewar it had been a major transshipment point for trade back and forth across the Net.

But Ophel was in range of *Lachiel*'s hastily repaired and barely functioning engines, and Ophel's shipyards, the biggest between the Net and the Central Worlds, were capable of handling the refit. Of course, Gil reflected further, those yards meant Ophel would be high on the Mageworlders' strategic priority list when they got around to mopping up after—*Not after*, he corrected himself, *if*—the Central Worlds fell.

"We have Opheline Inspace Control on lightspeed comms, sir," reported the communications tech.

"Put it on audio," Gil said.

"Audio, aye."

A moment later a crackly, attenuated transmission came on over the speakers in CIC:

"Unknown ship, this is Inspace Control, Ophel. Identify yourself. Opheline law requires that all inbound vessels provide their planet of registration and their last port of call; the name and homeworld of their master, captain, or commander; and a summary of their cargo before receiving permission to approach, orbit, dock, or land. Over."

Gil picked up the handset for the lightspeed comms and keyed it on. He paused for a moment, trying to put into order all the things he needed to say. Working with lightspeed comms from this far out was awkward and slow, with a lag time of minutes between a message and its reply.

"Inspace Control," he said finally, "this is RSF *Karipavo*, in company with RSF *Shaja* and RSF *Lachiel*. We request permission to orbit and perform repairs. I am Jervas Gil, captain, Republic Space Force, and commodore of this squadron; my world of origin is Ovredis. I am declaring an in-flight emergency and claiming the right of innocent passage. I regret that I cannot provide details of our cargoes and ports of call; I request a direct connection to the Republic's embassy as soon as possible. Over."

Gil keyed off the handset. Again, there was the long wait. He paced, fretting; then realized he was pacing and made himself stop. Dealing with Inspace Control was going to be only the first of his problems. All three of his ships needed repairs, not just the much-battered *Lachiel*, and he had no idea whether any of Ophel's yards would be willing to do the work.

*One thing at a time*, he told himself. *The 'Pavo's not as banged up as* Lachiel *or* Shaja; *I can probably find a yard that's willing to take her. That'll give me one fully operational ship to work with while I figure out how to fix up the others.*

*And after* that, *I still have to come up with some way to pay for all this—because if there's one thing you can depend on when you're dealing with civilians, it's that absolutely nothing comes free.*

Finally, the speaker crackled again. "RSF *Karipavo*, this is Inspace Control. You have permission to approach and orbit with three vessels."

Gil's tension subsided by a fractional amount. His deepest fear, firmly suppressed during the slow hyperspace transit from the Net, had been that the Ophelines would want nothing to do with him or his ships at all. That would have meant scuttling the crippled *Lachiel*—transferring the crew to *Shaja* and *Karipavo*, destroying the engines, the

weapons, and main ship's memory, then leaving the hulk
to drift—before the squadron could go on. At least he was
going to be spared that much.

Meanwhile, Inspace Control was still talking.

"*Karipavo, Shaja, Lachiel*: Make your orbit in compli-
ance with the following data. . . ."

The voice halted for a second, then continued in a
slightly altered tone—as if, Gil thought, somebody had
handed the talker at Inspace Control an unexpected addition to the standard message.

"Break—new subject. Coded text incoming. Stand by to
capture immediately. This text will be transmitted only
once. I repeat, stand by to capture immediately—"

"Get ready to grab it," Gil said to the comms tech.

He looked over his shoulder for Jhunnei. As usual, his
aide was there, seeming to materialize out of the background as easily as she faded into it the rest of the time.

*I wish I knew how she does that*, he wondered—again,
as usual—and said aloud, "We're going to need the codebook for this one. Have you got it?"

The lieutenant held up the palm-sized scanner/breaker
unit. "Right here, Commodore."

"Good," said Gil. Inspace Control was back to sending
the orbital data now, and the comms tech was handing him
a sheet of printout flimsy.

The coded message was several lines of letters and num-
bers with no pattern to them that Gil could make out.
Jhunnei handed him the codebook, and he ran the unit's
scanner over the message.

The codebook beeped.

"Got it," he said, and looked at the unit's minuscule
screen for the plaintext version.

FOR COMMODORE. REPORT IN PERSON TO
EMBASSY SOONEST. AMBASSADOR SENDS.

Gil hit the codebook's Wipe button and the plaintext vanished. Crumpling up the sheet of flimsy, he dropped it into the nearest recycler and turned to Jhunnei.

"Pack an overnight bag, Lieutenant. We've got an important engagement. Dress uniform with all your medals."

Improvised staff in hand, Klea paused in the doorway for one final glance back at her apartment. This would make the second occasion in her life when she'd abandoned everything in order to look for something better.

"Let's hope I have more luck this time," she muttered under her breath.

"There's no such thing as luck," said Owen. "We make our own choices, for good and for bad."

"Yeah—and my track record as a chooser isn't exactly the galaxy's hottest." She shifted her day pack into a more comfortable position on her shoulders. "We might as well get going before I lose my nerve."

They stepped out into the hallway, and started down the stairs to the street. Halfway down the flight to the second-floor landing, Owen halted. Klea almost bumped into him.

"What—?"

In the dim glow from the light panel at the top of the stairs, she could see him frowning slightly. He held up a hand for silence, but all she heard was her own breath and the sound of her heartbeat in her ears.

"Someone's waiting outside the front door," he said.

"How can you tell?"

"I can sense them," he said. "What people think and do shows up in the pattern of things. It's mostly a matter of knowing where to look."

She nodded—not really understanding him, but supposing that she'd learn more about it eventually in this new life she seemed to be headed for. "So what do we do?"

"We go up onto the roof," he told her. "There's a ladder and a trapdoor, for when somebody has to fix the lift."

"Nobody's fixed the lift for as long as I've lived here."

"So much the better," Owen said. "They won't be expecting anybody to go that way. Then we cross over and go down the fire escape on the other side."

He looked back down the stairs, and then at her again. "You lead; I'll follow and keep an eye out in case somebody comes in after us."

Klea swallowed. "Sure."

The stairs felt a lot steeper and darker going up than they had on the way down. Halfway to the third floor, she turned and looked back. Owen wasn't anywhere in sight; she supposed he was hanging back and keeping watch, like he'd said.

She took a tighter grip on the broomstick staff and kept on climbing. Her footsteps echoed in the empty stairwell. She was on the third-floor landing now—only one more set of stairs and she could wait for Owen by the ladder to the roof.

But out of the shadows ahead of her stepped a man in a black hooded robe, his features hidden by a dark plastic mask. Laughing, he held up a short staff of dark steel-bound wood before him. Red fire ran along its length, and its flame-colored aura limned him in a nimbus of gory light.

"Little girl," he said, "you're only pretending to be an Adept. If you're all that Ransome has left to send, then surely our day is near at hand."

Klea was afraid—more afraid than she'd ever been in her life; not even the worst of the streets had been able to scare her as much as this—but it was a strange, cold fear without the familiar edge of panic in it. The black-robed Mage took a step toward her; she took an involuntary step back.

Then she halted.

*Where am I going? There's only the stairs, and another man at the front door.*

She clasped the *grrch*-wood broomstick before her, and stood her ground. A picture filled her mind, cool and strange, like the fear: Owen, moving through the steps of the ShadowDance.

*The ShadowDance, which could also be used as a weapon—which could also be done with a staff—*

—and she moved without thinking into the Dance's first sequence, bringing up her hands and the staff with them. In the next instant she felt a stinging in her palms as the *grrch* wood caught and stopped a blow.

The shock brought her out of her half-trance in time to see an orange-yellow light, pale but there, tracing down the length of her staff, and the Mage drawing back his arm for another strike. Desperately, she groped with her mind for the next step in the Dance. This time she couldn't find it.

*I'm going to die*, she thought.

But in the moment before the Mage's staff came down, he seemed to stagger and bend backward. His arms flew wide and he dropped his staff. For another second he hung there. She heard a cracking sound, not loud but clear and distinct in the awful stillness. Then he dropped like a broken doll to the floor, and the crimson light around him faded as he died.

Now, where there had been only shadows a moment earlier, Owen stood. The Mage's body lay crumpled at his feet. Klea stared and backed away.

"How did you get there?" she demanded shakily. "I didn't see you anywhere. And what did you do?"

"I broke his neck," Owen said. He was looking down at the body of the Mage with an intent, thoughtful expression—nothing like his usual almost absentminded regard. He glanced up at her briefly.

"I was walking behind you the whole way; you just didn't see me, and neither did he. When his whole mind was set on the fight in front of him, I slipped past both of you and took him from behind. Misdirection, mostly—it's an easy trick, compared to some things. I'll teach it to you later."

Bending down, he picked up the Mage's staff and propped it against the wall so that the metal-bound wood made the long side of a triangle. Then he stamped down and broke the staff in the middle. The two pieces clattered to the floor.

"That's done," he said. "Let's go."

# III. Nammerin: Namport
## Ophel: Sombrelír

NOBODY BOTHERED Klea and Owen on the way to the port. She wasn't sure whether it was because nobody was trying, or because of something Owen had done to confuse the pursuit. She didn't ask; the answer wasn't going to make a difference, so why bother? Another question, though, was nagging at her too much to ignore. By the time they had passed through the gates and had almost reached the main terminal building, she had finally nerved herself to speak.

"I don't understand," she said.

Owen didn't break stride. "Understand what?"

"Why those people—the Mages—want to keep us from leaving Nammerin. If you're dangerous to them as long as you're here, I'm surprised they aren't delighted to see you go."

"Some things are more complicated than that."

Klea sighed. "*Everything*'s more complicated than that these days. I should have stayed on the farm."

"Your life might have been safer that way," Owen conceded. "But mine would have been shorter, if you hadn't been in Namport to find me lying in that alley."

"Not really," she said. She'd had plenty of time to consider this over the past few weeks. "You're tougher than you look; you'd have still been breathing when the garbage truck came through in the morning."

He didn't answer. The terminal building was just ahead of them now, and beyond it the arc lights on their tall poles were casting a stark white light over the landing field. Coming early had been a good idea: there was already a small but noisy crowd gathered outside the doors of the terminal. Out on the field, there was only one ship in port that Klea could see, and no shuttles waiting to ferry stuff back and forth to the larger craft that never left orbit.

"If that clunky little freighter is the only thing in," Klea muttered, "we've got a problem. They'll never let us past the gate."

"Don't worry about it," said Owen. "Stick close to me and don't say anything."

They were at the edge of the crowd. He didn't pause, but headed straight on into the terminal. Klea followed him. By now, she wasn't surprised when people stepped aside to let them pass. Somehow, without changing either his clothes or his features, Owen had transformed himself from a scruffy portside laborer to a person of importance and someone to be deferred to.

*It's like that vanishing trick of his turned inside out,* she thought. *Making himself more visible, instead of less. If he tells people he's an Adept, they'll believe him, even if he doesn't have a staff and a fancy black outfit to back him up.*

She stayed close, hoping that some of the effect would rub off on her—making her look like a proper Guild apprentice, or at least an honest farmer's daughter instead of a ten-times-a-night punchbroad. She blessed the stupid-stubborn pride that had kept her from ever working the port; nobody in this crowd was likely to recognize her and spoil the game.

Inside the terminal, more people thronged the counters and the ship's-status displays. Klea followed as Owen made his way through the press with the same ease as he had outside, and somehow drew the attention of the man sitting behind the main information desk. The official looked them both over and, apparently satisfied, said, "Okay, you're next. What's your business at the port?"

"I need to reach Galcen as quickly as possible," Owen said. Whatever he was doing to impress the official, it was strong stuff; Klea could feel the power of it moving in the air around him and making the hairs on her arms and neck rise up. "I have urgent business at the Retreat."

But the man was already shaking his head. "Nope, nothing going out of here to Galcen. Not for love or money."

Seeming undismayed, Owen glanced out through the armor-glass back wall of the terminal. The window gave a good view of the landing field and the one ship in port. The vessel, a freighter, was already loading for lift-off; crew members and port robots swarmed about its gaping cargo bays.

"How about that one?" he asked. "Where's she going?"

"*Lady LeRoi?* She's heading for the outworlds, and as far's I know she's not coming back."

"What's her next port of call?"

"Flatlands Portcity, on Pleyver," the official said. "But if you're planning on getting to Galcen from there, I wouldn't."

"Why not?"

The man stared at him. "You haven't heard? I thought you Adepts were supposed to know everything. The Mages are back, they've taken Galcen, and they're sweeping everything before them. There's nothing left of the Republic, and as soon as *Lady LeRoi* is loaded up and gone the port is shutting down until the Mages get here."

"I see," said Owen. His voice was as calm and unruffled as before, but Klea could tell that he was shaken: he'd gone paper-pale under the cold white glare of the terminal lights. "Where's the nearest planet-to-planet voicelink station?"

"That's down, too." To Klea, the official seemed to be enjoying his role as the purveyor of such dire news. "So what's it going to be—do you still want to go dicker with the *Lady*'s captain for a ride out of here?"

"Not now," said Owen. "Perhaps later."

He turned to Klea. "Come," he said, and strode off through the crowd without looking back to see if she was following him.

It was late evening when *Karipavo*'s shuttle touched down on Ophel. The embassy had a hovercar waiting at the spaceport, and the Republic's military attaché met Commodore Gil and Lieutenant Jhunnei on the landing field. The attaché eyed their dress uniforms with approval and led the way to the gate.

"Sorry about the hurry, Commodore," he said over his shoulder as he walked. "But we can't afford to waste any time—the ambassador wants to talk with you at once."

Gil nodded. "Understood, Major."

He waited until they were safely inside the hovercar and on the road into the Opheline capital city of Sombrelír before saying anything more. Soon the lights of the port were dwindling away behind them, and Gil felt free to ask, "What word do you have from Galcen these days?"

"Just rumors," said the attaché. "But Ophel's always got rumors. The ambassador will fill you in when you meet him."

Gil took the hint and devoted the rest of the ride to studying the local architecture. The spaceport buildings had been of modern construction in an uninspired pangalactic style. As the hovercar took them into the diplomatic section of Sombrelír, however, they began passing older buildings, fantastic edifices of painted pastel brick and dark wrought iron, along broad, clean streets illuminated by warm amber lanterns. One of the houses had its doors flung open, so that the light from inside spilled out onto the portico and the plaza beyond.

The hovercar purred up to the front steps of the house, where a footman waited. Belatedly, as the attaché handed over the vehicle, Gil understood that this must be the embassy.

Gil and Jhunnei followed the attaché up to the open door. They passed through a gilded foyer into an enormous reception room—Gil estimated that it took up most of the ground floor of the embassy—filled with men, women, and assorted nonhumans, all wearing fashionable evening dress. In one corner a Khesatán harp quintet played gentle, rippling music; in another, long tables covered with white damask held elegantly arranged food on dishes of crystal and silver.

*I don't believe it,* Gil thought. *We came all the way from the Net, after fighting every Mage warship in the galaxy and damn near getting ourselves blown to pieces in the process, and the Republic's ambassador to Ophel is throwing a party.*

At least he and his aide wouldn't stand out too much in this crowd. The Space Force full-dress uniform had enough glitter and panache to let them blend right in—and if the hand-blaster in its grav-clip up Gil's tunic sleeve was nonstandard it was at least invisible. Whatever Lieutenant Jhunnei was carrying didn't show either, though something about his aide's demeanor made Gil certain that she hadn't come down to Ophel unarmed.

Instinct born of long service—and of five years on Galcen as aide to General Metadi—already had Gil turning toward the refreshment tables. Firmly, the attaché steered him in the opposite direction. Gil left the canapés to Lieutenant Jhunnei and followed dutifully toward where the harp quintet played amid a small forest of potted plants.

At Gil's approach, a portly gentleman in full evening dress stepped forward out of the shelter of the greenery. From his medallion and his sash of office, Gil realized that this must be the ambassador himself.

"Thank goodness you're here, Commodore," he said quietly as the attaché moved off into the crowd. At the same time, Gil caught the almost inaudible humming noise that meant a privacy screen was in operation; the generating unit was probably concealed somewhere among the potted plants. "Please tell me everything you know concerning the Mageworlds situation."

Lines of worry and fatigue marked the ambassador's round face. Hastily, Gil began revising his earlier opinions about the nature of the evening. If the ambassador to Ophel was throwing a party, it was for the same reason that Gil and Jhunnei had worn their best and most impressive uniforms: to make certain the galaxy at large knew that nothing had changed, that the Republic was still a force to be reckoned with.

"I don't know anything beyond what happened at the Net," Gil said. "Everything was normal—no sign of military activity in the Mageworlds, nothing. Then a freighter came from the Inner Net with word of a Mageworlds warfleet bound for Galcen, and at the same time we discovered that our hi-comms had gone down."

He paused a moment, considering his next words carefully. "The freighter was a known ship, and her captain was one of our agents. I passed them through the Outer Net on a jump-run for Galcen Prime, and kept the Net up behind them for as long as I could. Then I took what was left of my squadron and came here."

"Only three ships?"

"*Shaja* and *Lachiel* were the only other ships within communications range," Gil said. "Until hi-comms come back up, there's no way to rally the rest of the Net Patrol Fleet, or even find out how many made it through the fighting."

The ambassador regarded him gravely. "Still, if three vessels were fortunate enough to survive, perhaps others have as well. And you yourself are here tonight, which is very good."

"We try our best," said Gil. "What news do you have from Galcen—or do you have anything at all?"

"Rumors," said the ambassador. "Rumors, and nothing else. A merchant coming from Galcen said that he'd left just minutes after hearing over the open net that Prime was under attack. But he was on a run-to-jump at the time, and he might not have been paying proper attention. Certain people in Sombrelír who have—how shall we put it—'connections' on the other side of the Net have been making a lot of wild statements, claiming that Galcen has fallen and the Space Force is disbanded."

"It may be true about Galcen," Gil said. "But about the Space Force—no. As far as I'm concerned, we're still here."

"That's why I wanted you at this reception," said the ambassador. "To refute the rumors. People in the street are starting to look at us askance, and the local holonews reports are beginning to ask some awkward questions."

"We can't have that."

"No," the ambassador agreed. "I've issued a statement saying that I intend to keep the embassy open until my government directs me to do otherwise." He paused. "And what exactly are your intentions, Commodore?"

Gil straightened his shoulders. "I intend to repair my ships and prosecute the war against the Mageworlds to the best of my ability."

"Good," said the ambassador, with a firm nod. "Then

we're agreed. If you like, I can give you letters of marque and reprisal; they should let you increase your options somewhat, regardless of subsequent political events."

"They certainly should," Gil said. "I'll take them."

With the ambassador's offer, the difficulties ahead of him became a fraction less insurmountable. Operating under letters of marque, he could legally attack not just military vessels belonging to the Mageworlds, but their merchant shipping as well—and the shipping of neutral worlds who traded with them. Jos Metardi had started that way, as a privateer out of Innish-Kyl, before the Domina had called on him to build the Resistance a warfleet instead.

"Our immediate problem, though," Gil went on, "is going to be carrying out the necessary repairs."

"Major Karris will work with you on that," the ambassador assured him. "He's got the local knowledge you need. They like to boast about their shipyards here, but frankly, some of the companies are no better than thieves. You'll be wanting one of the orbital docking facilities, I suppose?"

"Yes. All three of my ships are space-only. I've got some shot-up fighter craft that can get repaired in orbit or on the surface, wherever's cheapest . . . that's going to be the main difficulty, in any case."

"The money, you mean?"

"That's right," said Gil. "I haven't got a government contract to offer anybody, so it'll have to be cash-up-front."

He frowned, remembering the task he had set the officers of his little squadron before leaving for the Opheline surface: to itemize and prioritize all the necessary repairs, both for the squadron as a whole and for the individual ships.

"Failing anything else," he continued, "I'm prepared to break up *Lachiel* and sell her for scrap in order to finance repairs on *Shaja* and *Karipavo*. A shame, after all the work *Lachiel*'s crew put into bringing her in, but if we have to, we have to."

The ambassador smiled for the first time since Gil had met him. "I have hopes, Commodore, that you won't be required to destroy a third of your force. There's someone here tonight that I want you to meet."

"I'm at your service, naturally."

"Good, good; we're all in this together." The ambassador gave his sash of office a tug, settling it more neatly across his immaculate shirtfront. "Time for us to find you something to drink and a bite to eat—and let all our guests have a good look at you, of course."

He cast a cautionary glance in Gil's direction. "No need to let anyone know that those three ships are all we've got ... as far as anybody here knows, the rest of the Net Patrol Fleet is undamaged and carrying out its mission."

"Given the lack of hi-comms," Gil said, "for all we can tell, that's the truth. Life must have been a lot easier back when ships and communications moved at the same speed." An idea came to him as he spoke, and he asked, "Tell me, do you have any courier vessels available to you?"

The ambassador shook his head. "Not if you mean assigned Space Force craft. But something could be arranged, I'm sure—Major Karris is very resourceful. Do you require a vessel?"

"I could use one," Gil said. "If I had a good fast ship, I'd send it back with orders to run the length of the Net in microjumps. Doing that, we'd have a chance of making contact with undamaged units who still haven't gotten the word that an attack took place, or with survivors who may be unsure of their instructions."

The ambassador was looking interested. "I see. You think that the Mage breakthrough might be of small scale?"

"Mmm . . . let's just say that I suspect they had to concentrate all their force at one point in order to succeed."

"Interesting. We'll see what we can do about getting
you that ship. Meanwhile, Commodore, let's circulate. . . ."

They began a stately progress throughout the reception
room, pausing at the refreshment table to provide Gil with
a caramel meringue and a glass of sparkling pink punch—
the puff-pastry angelbirds, regrettably, had long since vanished. The ambassador nodded affably to everyone, but
kept on scanning the crowd as if he searched for one person in particular.

Finally, his eyes lit up and he changed course, drawing
Gil after him in the direction of a frail, ancient-looking man
in evening dress of an old-fashioned but impeccable cut.

"Adelfe!" he exclaimed. "How delightful to see you
here! Adelfe, I know you'll enjoy meeting my good friend
Commodore Jervas Gil. Commodore, this is Adelfe
Aneverian, the Hereditary Chairman of Perpayne."

Gil gave his best formal bow. "I'm honored, Chairman
Aneverian," he murmured.

He was also immensely relieved. Perpayne was a proprietary world, officially neutral but in practice a long-
standing friend of the Republic (and a regular trading
partner—but no friend—of Ophel); and Perpayne's Hereditary Chairman of the Board was widely reputed to be the
richest private individual in the civilized galaxy, someone
who could refit *Karipavo* and her sisters out of the loose
change he found in his pockets at the end of the day.

And if the Republic's ambassador to Ophel was intent on
charming Adelfe Aneverian into becoming the source of
money behind the Net Patrol Fleet's continued existence—
why, then, Commodore Jervas Gil was more than willing to
help the ambassador do it.

By the time Klea caught up with Owen, he'd gone beyond the crowd at the doors of the terminal and out of the

port entirely, and was striding down Dock Street fast enough that she had to run if she wanted to stay even with him. What frightened her was that she didn't think he knew where he was going.

She grabbed at his sleeve. "Hey!"

He stopped and turned. From the expression on his face, she would have thought he didn't see her, until he spoke. "What is it, Klea?"

"Look," she said. "I know the news is bad, if what that man said is really the truth—"

"It's true."

"Okay, it's true. That doesn't change the fact that we've got a problem—a whole bunch of problems, starting with a dead body lying on the floor outside my apartment. We can't go back there, and we've got to go somewhere."

She was still holding on to the fabric of his sleeve; keeping her grip, she looked frantically about Dock Street for some place that might provide a temporary haven. The gaudy holosign and bright interior lighting of an open-front noodle shop caught her eye.

"There," she said. She headed in the direction of the shop, pulling Owen after her. "We can sit in there for a while and talk."

The shop had an an empty table close to the street; she took off her day pack and dropped it into one of the chairs. Then she pushed Owen in the direction of the empty seat and stood watching him until he sat down.

"All right," she said. "You told me you'd take care of the money; do you have enough on you for noodles and some *ghil*?"

"Yes," he said finally.

"Good. Then give me some cash and stay right there until I get back."

She took the smudged and crumpled credit chits he pulled out of the breast pocket of his coverall, and went with them up to the counter. Five minutes later, she carried the tray of noodles and *ghil* back to the table.

To her relief, Owen was still there. She set the tray on the table and pushed her day pack off the chair onto the floor, then sat down across from him.

"Eat something," she said. "Nothing is ever quite as bad as it looks when you're hungry."

For a moment he seemed as if he might refuse. Then he shrugged and picked up a fork. "And there's no point to not eating, either ... what is this?"

"Noodles and eels," she said, feeling almost giddy with relief now that he was talking to her again. "Good farmer food. Don't you have eels back on—where *do* you come from, anyhow?"

"Galcen," he said.

The *ghil* in the cup she was holding spilled out over her hand. She let the scalding liquid drip onto the table.

"Oh, damn. Owen, I'm sorry."

He shook his head. "Don't be. It has nothing to do with you. Except that you need to be studying at the Retreat, and with Galcen fallen into the hands of the Magelords there *is* no Retreat, and no Guild either for all I can tell. . . ." His voice broke off, and he seemed to shudder all over. "I should have been there when it happened."

"What good would that have done? I mean, you're hot stuff, but nobody's so hot they can stop an invasion single-handed."

"No," he said. After his silence before, the words came out in a rush, full of pain and urgency. "I wanted to be there—I asked Master Ransome to let me stay at the Retreat over the winter and teach the new apprentices—but he told me to come here instead. He knew—he *must* have known!—how close the danger was, but he sent me off to Nammerin instead of keeping me by him where I could help."

"Maybe he wanted you to be safe?"

"I never asked him for safety," Owen said. He was as pale now as he had been when he first heard the news at the terminal, and his expression frightened her. "For almost ten years I obeyed his word as my teacher and acted to serve the Guild, and the places I went and the things I did were not safe. And then—when the enemy we had watched and followed all that time was getting ready to strike—then he sent me to Nammerin, where he already had an Adept in place, and where in all the time I've been on-planet the Mage-Circle hasn't done anything more than rough me up when they caught me eavesdropping. Something is wrong here, Klea; something is very wrong."

# IV. Asteroid Base
## RSF *Selsyn-bilai:* Infabede Sector

BEKA HAD made longer hyperspace transits than the one from Galcen to the Professor's asteroid base, but never one that seemed as interminable. The few repairs that she could handle without needing to work outside the ship were soon taken care of, leaving her with nothing else to do besides monitor the autopilot, pace the *'Hammer*'s corridors, and try to get some sleep.

She didn't have much luck with the attempt. More times than not she would find herself thrown awake in the middle of ship's night by some unremembered dream, then lie staring up at the dark overhead until at last, driven by desperation, she would get out of bed, dress herself, and start pacing the corridors again.

Finally the *'Hammer* dropped out of hyperspace inside the asteroid field that masked the location of the Professor's hideout—if "hideout" was the proper word for such a place. The chambers and tunnels of the secret base extended far into the depths of the asteroid; Beka herself was only familiar with the upper reaches. How her former co-pilot had acquired the complex, and from whom, she didn't know—though she'd begun, of late, to have her suspicions.

The Prof had been Armsmaster to House Rosselin while Entibor was still a living world; when he came to be *War-hammer*'s copilot and Tarnekep Portree's tutor in the assassin's trade, he had been loyal until death; but before that, he had been a Magelord, and a traitor to his own Circle. And the asteroid base—which perhaps was not and had never been truly an asteroid at all—was Magebuilt from core to surface.

"You'll want to be careful while we're staying here," Beka said to Ignac' LeSoit shortly after she had settled the 'Hammer down onto its landing legs in the base's huge docking bay. Together with Jessan and LeSoit, she was standing at the foot of the 'Hammer's ramp, prior to giving the ship a postflight walkaround. "Don't go wandering about by yourself. If you get lost we might not be able to find you in time."

The air in the bay was thin and cold. The bay itself was a cavern some distance beneath the asteroid's outer skin, accessible only by hair-fine realspace shiphandling. *War-hammer* wasn't the only starship currently occupying a place on the bay's metal deckplates. The asteroid base was home to a score or more vintage spacecraft, from a shot-up Resistance fighter to a blue-and-silver pleasure yacht. The Professor had owned, and at one time or another had piloted, all of them; now Beka supposed that, like the base itself, they were hers.

"How long are we going to be here?" LeSoit asked. Her old shipmate was doing a good job of not seeming impressed by the enormous bay and the collection of antique ships, but she could sense the uneasiness beneath his surface nonchalance.

Beka shrugged. "I don't know. As long as it takes to get

the hull repaired, for sure. After that—it depends on what's happening out there. A shooting war is no place for a merch."

Jessan, standing close by her right hand, looked troubled. "It's your decision, Captain."

She bit her lip. *Hell of a time for Nyls to remember he's got a Space Force commission. What was I supposed to do, drop him off on Galcen so he could get killed like everybody else?*

"Right," she said aloud. "And I'll decide when I'm ready. Meanwhile you can show Ignac' around—fix him up with a place to bunk, and make sure the robots know he's friendly. I'm going to get the repairs started before I go in."

She watched the two men heading off across the docking bay, then turned and made a complete circuit, on foot, of her ship, noting each hole and ding in the vessel's metal skin.

It wasn't too bad, she decided after she had finished the inspection. There wasn't anything broken that couldn't be fixed at the base, and in fairly short order.

*And then we can take Ignac' back to Suivi Point, and Nyls and I can see what kind of cargos are available somewhere out of the way of all the fighting. . . .*

*. . . if there is somewhere out of the way of all the fighting, and as long as Nyls doesn't decide he wants to go commit suicide along with all the rest of his buddies, and . . .*

*. . . hell. I'm not deciding anything until the hull's repaired, and that's final.*

She clapped her hands once, sharply. The sound echoed off the ceiling and walls of the bay. Out of the shadows in the far reaches of the vast space, a half-dozen black-enameled robots moving forward on silent nullgravs to answer the summons.

"Welcome back, my lady," said the first one to arrive.

Inside the dark plastic ovoid of its sensor pod, crimson lights moved and flickered. Its voice had an uncanny likeness to that of Beka's dead copilot; not surprising, since the Professor had built and programmed all the robots at the base. "What are your current needs and desires?"

"Don't call me 'my lady,'" said Beka, out of habit—a pointless order, since the robot, like its builder, would certainly ignore it. "Tell the kitchen to have dinner ready for three at 2040 Standard. A Khesatan, a Suivi Point freespacer, and me; adjust the menu to suit. Make certain that Nyls and our new guest have everything they need—ask them if you're not sure. And have the maintenance robots commence repairs on *Warhammer* at once."

"Yes, my lady." The robot didn't have a waist; if it had, Beka thought, it would have bowed. "What do you wish done with the household illusions?"

Beka hesitated for a moment. The holographic systems that masked the utilitarian metal furnishings of the asteroid base had been another of the Professor's creations—works of art more than decoration, designed and programmed over a long span of years by an eccentric and essentially lonely man.

"The Prof's gone," she said finally. "And he isn't coming back. Leave them off."

"Now that we've got all Vallant's people under restraint," said Commander Quetaya, "the question is, what should we do with them?"

Captain Natanel Tyche shook his head. "That's a question, but it's not the main question. What I wish I knew was what we ought to do with *us*."

In company with Commander Quetaya, Tyche was going through the files in what had been the CO's office on board RSF *Selsyn-bilai*. The *Selsyn*'s captain hadn't survived his initial encounter with Admiral Vallant's troopers, and Commander Quetaya was currently occupying the service-issue stack-chair behind the former CO's desk, working her way through the comp files while Tyche cleared the hardcopy.

"That's up to the General," Quetaya said. "And we already know that he's planning to fight."

"I'd like to know what with, then," said Tyche. "A stores ship and a pair of recon craft aren't exactly what I'd call a fighting fleet."

The office door slid open while he was talking. "Neither would I, Captain," said General Metadi, as he joined the others in the cramped office. "But we have to start with something."

Tyche reddened. The General ignored his discomfiture and went on, "How's the comp search doing, Commander?"

"Nothing useful so far," Quetaya said. "But it's still running. How about the prisoners, sir—anything from them?"

Metadi folded his lean form into another of the stack-chairs and sighed. "Not a hell of a lot. Most of the troopers are the usual article, go where they're told to go and shoot who they're told to shoot. About half of them didn't even know Vallant had mutinied, and most of the rest of them didn't care. If we break up their units and mix them in with our own people, they'll do just fine for us. The officers, though—" His expression shifted to one of genuine disgust. "—they're all Vallant's handpicked loyalists, and we can't keep 'em."

Quetaya nodded gravely. "Do we shoot them or space them?"

"There's no need to be bloodthirsty," said Metadi. "I thought we might strip them down to their undershorts and drop them off on the next inhabited world we come to. Giving some planet a good laugh at Vallant's expense might pay off in the long run anyway."

"What about Galcen?" Tyche asked.

"Nothing good." Metadi looked very tired. "Judging from what our prisoners have to say, the admiral has pretty much ceded Galcen to the Mageworlds in advance."

Quetaya had gone back to working with the desk comp while they talked; now she looked up.

"I think I just got something here," she said. "Key word Purple Cloud. CO's eyes only. Encrypted."

Metadi sat up straight. "Can we break it?"

"Not a problem, sir. Here it comes now."

"What do we have?"

Quetaya was smiling broadly. "Standing orders in event that the Republic loses control of Galcen Prime."

"Those vary sector by sector," Metadi said. "Summary?"

"The orders are fairly detailed," she said. "But essentially they call for all units not exclusively ground-based to leave their assigned positions and rendezvous at a designated point somewhere in Infabede. I'm no starpilot, but it looks like they picked some patch of deep space with nothing to recommend it besides being a long way from anything."

"Harder for the bad guys to find you that way," said Metadi. "Do we have the coordinates?"

"Yes."

"Good," Metadi said. "Then so will every other Space Force unit that's trying to figure out what to do now that they can't call Prime for help anymore. That's one way to get yourself a fighting fleet, Tyche. Collect all the pieces."

Tyche sighed. "I hate to dampen people's enthusiasm, but there's a small problem. Admiral Vallant has a copy of the standing orders in his comp files, too. In fact, he probably issued them."

Quetaya's face fell. "Damn. That means he'll take the rendezvous point first thing."

"Not necessarily," Metadi said. "Think about the kind of man we're dealing with. Vallant doesn't want to win a war; he wants to be King or Dictator or Grand High Something of the Infabede sector. He's going to be concentrating most of his forces on nailing down the planets, not on patrolling the blank spaces in between them."

"So what do you think he'll do?" Tyche asked.

"My guess," said Metadi, "is that he'll hand over the job of watching the rendezvous to somebody he thinks he can trust—a tough guy in a tough ship. Cruiser or better is my guess. Then the admiral's buddy can sit in the middle of nowhere snapping up ships as they drop out, while Vallant takes the rest of his fleet on a grand tour of Infabede, spreading the word about Galcen and making sure all the planetary governments know who's the new man in charge."

Metadi gave his aide and Captain Tyche a grim smile. "In the meantime, people, we have a chance to take ourselves a capital ship while Admiral Vallant is looking the other way. And with a cruiser and a stores ship, anything is possible. Even taking back the galaxy."

"Well," said Jessan to LeSoit, "that's about all you need to know for now. Stick to the top levels and the public rooms, and you should be safe."

The two men were standing in the long entrance hall of the asteroid base. In the Professor's day, the room had been a masterpiece of elaborate real-time holovid programming, a painfully accurate likeness of the Summer Palace of House Rosselin on long-dead Entibor. Now, with the illusions turned off, it was just a spare, undecorated room.

"Don't worry," LeSoit said. "If you want the truth, this place gives me the creeps."

"You aren't exactly seeing it at its best," Jessan told him. "I'd have left the holovids up, myself, but the decision wasn't mine to make. The captain dislikes 'fake scenery,' as she calls it."

"She would," said LeSoit. He paused a moment, then asked, "Do you have any idea what she's going to do next?"

Jessan shook his head. "I wish I did. I'm just as glad she didn't stick around Galcen and try to fight off the entire Mage warfleet by herself—but this kind of indecision isn't her usual style at all."

"Probably means she's working up to something crazy," LeSoit said. "I could tell you a couple of stories. . . . Are you planning to stick around after she makes up her mind to go flying off and get herself killed?"

There was a moment of intense silence.

"If," said Jessan slowly, after several seconds, "by that rather offensive question you meant to inquire about the permanence of my affections for Captain Rosselin-Metadi—"

"Touchy, aren't you? Yeah, that's what I was asking."

"—then the answer is yes."

"Fine. Just as long as there's somebody."

"I'm glad you seem to think I qualify," said Jessan. He regarded LeSoit for a moment and added, "Although, frankly, I'm not certain who you are to judge."

"The captain was a shipmate of mine once," LeSoit said. "She was a good pilot and a damned good friend, and she flat didn't care about being the heir-apparent to Entibor. But I couldn't shake the idea that her family was going to come and fetch her back home again someday, so I took off before I had to watch it happen. Looks like I was wrong, though."

"No," said Jessan. "You weren't wrong—what do you think that business with D'Caer was all about if it wasn't a family fight? But when the family needed her, she came back on her terms, and not on theirs."

When the communications center in the asteroid base was working, it could pull in hi-comms from all over the

Republic, and provide everything from a direct voicelink to a planet on the other side of the civilized galaxy, to the late-night rerun of "Spaceways Patrol." At the moment, however, hi-comms were still down, and the base was too far off the normal transit lanes to pick up anything on the lightspeed bands that wasn't already several centuries old.

While the robots in the docking bay labored over *Warhammer*'s torn hull, Beka spent several fruitless hours in the comm center trying to pull in a signal—any kind of signal—from Galcen Prime. Nothing came, and she bit her lip in frustration.

*They could all be dead by now and I'd never know it.*

"I did everything I could," she said aloud. "I brought them the warning. I made sure their messengers got away to spread the word. I nearly blew myself up in hyper and damn near got myself shot to pieces in realspace. There wasn't anything more I could have done if I'd stayed."

She clenched her fist and struck it against the arm of her chair. *The galaxy's going all to hell around me,* she thought, *and I haven't got the faintest idea what I'm supposed to do next.*

"There's always going back to Galcen once the 'Hammer's repaired," she said aloud. "That's where the fighting is, and Dadda is sure to be the thick of it. But the fleet action is probably all done with by now, and an armed freighter can't do any good in a war on the ground. And if the Mages have everything, dropping out of hyper in the wrong place at the wrong moment could get me in big trouble."

She shook her head. It looked like the safest bet for a small fast merch with only two gunners was to lie low for a while, until the fighting was over. No matter who won, there would always be a dirtsider somewhere with a cargo the 'Hammer could carry.

"I'll be all right. With this base to hole up in, and the *'Hammer* to make my living, I can handle whatever comes along."

The statement was true, but somehow it failed to reassure her. She fell silent again, and sat moodily running the lightspeed comm bands for another half-hour without result. She didn't look up from the board again until the familiar voice of the base's chief robot broke into her reverie.

"My lady, if I may presume to interrupt . . ."

She spun the chair around to face the robot. "Why not? Right now I've got plenty of time on my hands and nothing to do with it."

"If you say so, my lady. The matter concerns the maintenance of your ship."

Her voice sharpened. "There's a problem with the repairs?"

*Damn, if we've got to take the* 'Hammer *to a yard right now, we've had it.*

"No, my lady," said the robot, to her intense relief. "The procedures are simple, and we have all the necessary supplies here at hand."

"Then what's the hangup?"

The robot seemed to pause a moment to collect its thoughts—an illusion, Beka knew, part of the Professor's artful programming. The robots had been his only company for a long time after the Magewar ended, and he had been a perfectionist in small matters as well as in large ones.

"In the course of performing routine maintenance on your ship," the robot said at last, "it has always been our practice to back up *Warhammer*'s log recordings into main base memory."

Beka frowned. "I never told you to do that."

"The order was not yours, my lady."

"The Prof? Damn and blast him, that was a hell of a liberty to take without my permission! What did he want a copy of my log recordings for, anyhow?"

"My series-mates and I were never told such things," said the robot. "But if I may conjecture—"

"Oh, why the hell not. Go ahead."

"Very well, my lady. You were always intended to be the next owner of this complex; whatever went into main base memory from your ship would only be returned to you in time. As indeed it has been. In any case, the latest transfer of data proved especially significant."

Again the robot paused. Beka bit her lip to keep from cursing the Professor's artistry, and said, "Why?"

"As it happens," said the robot, "the data contained several triggering factors. I am therefore required by my programming to deliver to you a message."

"I'm waiting."

But instead of replaying a voice message, the robot made a brief whirring noise. Part of its black enamel surface slid aside, revealing a small storage compartment. There was nothing inside the compartment except a folded sheet of stiff white paper. Beka stared.

"That's the message?"

"I must presume that it is," the robot said. "I have no idea why such a method of transmission would be chosen, when my series-mates and I are quite capable of recording and reproducing a vocal transmission in minutest detail—"

"The Prof had his own ways of doing things," Beka said.

She took out the folded paper and looked at it. A blob of purple sealing wax held it closed; the design on the seal wasn't one she'd ever seen the Professor use. The sealing wax was a characteristic touch, though—old-fashioned but elegant like all the rest of him, from his clothes to his manners.

"You can close yourself up and go away now," she said

to the robot. "You've done what the Prof wanted you to do."

The robot said, "Very well, my lady," and floated off.

Beka waited until it was well out of sight before turning back to the letter. If the Prof hadn't trusted his message to the robots, he'd probably had a good reason. When the robot was gone, she pulled her knife from its sheath up her left sleeve and broke the seal. Bits of purple sealing wax fell onto the floor at her feet.

She slipped the knife back up her sleeve and unfolded the paper. Inside, the sheet was covered with lines of script, in a classic, unadorned Entiboran hand:

My lady:

I write this on the night before our leavetaking for Darvell; I do not know when you shall read it. I will leave it in the care of my robots until such time as they learn from your ship's log that you have resumed your rightful name in the galaxy, and are no longer hiding beneath the cloak of Tarnekep Portree. Such an identity is a good servant but a poor master, and if you no longer require its protection then I will be the happier for that.

The robots will have told you long since that the base and all its contents are yours. So, likewise, are my remaining personal funds, currently on deposit at Suivi Point. Dahl&Dahl will release them to you upon your demand. Make what use you can of them; they are yours to dispose of as you will.

The galaxy is coming to a crisis, and the time will be soon. The Iron Crown of Entibor is yours by inheritance, whether you decide to wear it or not. I will not say you must, or even that you should; you have fought too long and too hard for your own choices, and I will not take them from you now.

Live in honor, child, and be well.

The letter closed with a line of symbols in a script and a language that Beka didn't recognize. It took her several seconds, staring at the page with blurring eyes, before she understood that the alien characters were a signature.

"Damn him," she whispered. "*Damn* him. The only time he ever used his own goddamned name . . .!"

Her hands clenched, crumpling the paper between them. She bowed her head onto her knees and wept.

# V. Galcen Nearspace
Gyffer: Telabryk
Asteroid Base

O<small>N THE</small> observation deck of his flagship,
Grand Admiral sus-Airaalin once again
paced back and forth in front of the row of viewports that
showed him the blue and green, cloud-streaked sphere of
Galcen. On the bulkhead, the twin chronometers kept their
time, reminding him that the first phase of the war was almost at an end. The Circles could not suppress hyperspace
communications much longer, however valiant their efforts; and then—no matter how much physical damage
their work had done to the links and relays—bit by bit the
tattered network would begin to mend itself.

"We have crushed the head of the serpent," sus-Airaalin
dictated to the autoscribe on his collar. "Galcen Prime is
in our hands, together with the commander of its ground
forces; the citadel of the Adepts has fallen to us as·well,
and the Master of the Adepts' Guild has become our prisoner. One thing, however, is lacking: our forces have

failed to locate the Adept-worlders' Commanding General, either among the living or among the dead."

The door to the observation deck slid open. A brown-uniformed crew member entered, carrying a message tablet in one hand. "A report from the surface forces, sir."

"Thank you, Trooper."

sus-Airaalin took the tablet and scanned the lines of script displayed on its surface. He recognized the hand-writing at once as that of his aide; and the news the report contained had him tensing his jaw to keep from making comments not fitting for the crew member to hear or the autoscribe to record.

When the crew member had gone, sus-Airaalin resumed his measured pacing. The period of self-enforced silence had enabled him to master his emotions and his voice, let-ting him speak to the autoscribe in the same collected tone as before.

"The question of Metadi's whereabouts becomes even more pressing in the light of recent discoveries on Galcen. Members of our ground forces, in the process of clearing the Space Force Base at Prime, found references in the se-curity files to the mysterious death of Metadi's aide. And you will remember, I trust, that the position of flag aide to the Commanding General was targeted for one of our rep-licant agents."

sus-Airaalin paused and drew a deep, steadying breath. If the Resurgency did not remember that bit of informa-tion, he did; the call for volunteers had taken some of the best of his Circle-Mages. The replication process was del-icate as well as permanent, and only the strongest minds could survive the transfer into a vat-grown body, followed by the subsequent destruction of the original flesh. The agent who had been chosen to replicate, shadow, and ulti-mately replace Commander Rosel Quetaya had been one of the most promising young members of sus-Airaalin's own Circle.

He was silent for a moment, remembering. Then he continued his report.

"More searching—among the medical buildings, this time—produced a body to match the security reports. Since per your designs the replicant body cannot be distinguished from the target even on the subcellular level, we have no way of determining actual identity with the means at hand. A cross-check of the security records shows that General Metadi has been listed, very discreetly, as missing for some weeks; and at least some of the entries maintain that his aide, or someone using her name, is likewise missing."

The Grand Admiral suppressed a tired sigh. This had been his most secret fear from the beginning: that the strike against Prime, designed to take out the head of the Adept-worlds' fighting ability with one blow, would fail to destroy General Metadi at the same time.

*For while the heart still beats,* he thought, *the coils of the serpent remain as deadly as before.*

But the Resurgency wouldn't be interested in the doubts and misgivings of one whom they, at least, would call victorious. sus-Airaalin continued dictating to the autoscribe.

"I am, therefore, planning to send the body from Galcen Prime home to Eraasi on the first available ship, in the hopes that you can examine it and tell me in whose company General Metadi—wherever he may be—is currently traveling. And if, despite security considerations, I could be informed what our agent's actual orders were, I would be even more grateful."

The Five Hours to Midnight Bar and Grill in Telabryk had an extensive collection of Gyfferan beers and imported liquors. Ari Rosselin-Metadi sat at the shadowy end of the polished wooden bar, nursing a shot of Galcenian brandy and waiting for the bartender to finish drawing a half-dozen mugs of beer for the shipyard workers in the corner booth. In addition to serving as a neighborhood tavern, the Five Hours provided Telabryk with its main hookup into the Quincunx—something Ari had discovered by working his way down a list of possibles that had included the Cinquefoil Lounge, the Pentangle Salad Shop, and the elegant and expensive Restaurant at 555.

By now Ari was resigned to looking for help from the criminal brotherhood. With the Space Force pulled out of the Gyfferan system, and with no money in his pocket beyond the Mandeynan quarter-mark that had bought the brandy, he didn't have anywhere else to go. The credit-and-debit data net was down hard along with hi-comms, so any money in his own account or the family's was just going to have to sit there until he showed up in person at the GalPrime Bank to claim it. As long as the Magelords held Galcen and Admiral Vallant held Infabede, that wasn't likely to be any time soon. Ari was going to need a job, and he was probably also going to need a place to hide.

On a shelf behind the bar, the customary holoset glowed and flickered with the local evening news. The tableau inside the tank showed the massive golden dome of the Gyfferan State House rising above a cluster of lesser government buildings. In the foreground, a reporter stood and spoke in appropriately serious tones about the historic debates currently going on somewhere in the pile of architecture behind her.

". . . and communication with the rest of the galaxy remains impossible. As never before in its history, Gyffer stands alone. The Citizen-Assembly at this very moment is discussing possible courses of action. . . ."

The bartender finished dealing with the booth full of yard workers and came back to Ari's end of the bar.

"We can talk now if you want to," he said. "How's it going, brother?"

"Not good," said Ari. "Frankly, I'm stranded and I'm broke and I'm a long way from home."

"Galcen?"

"The accent's that strong?" Ari wondered aloud. "Yeah, Galcen will do. Maraghai's good, too."

The bartender shook his head. "This is a bad time; word is the Assembly's going to close the port. If you'd come in here a couple of weeks ago, now, I could have slipped you onto a liner bound for Galcen without any trouble."

"And I could have been dodging Magelords right this minute, if what everybody says is true." Ari took another sip of the brandy. "I'm just as glad to be on Gyffer as far as that goes. But I'm going to need a job."

"They're pretty strict about work permits around here."

"I figured they might be. That's one reason I came looking for the Brotherhood."

"We can fix the permits for you, no problem." The bartender looked at Ari—who had realized some time earlier that not even removing all the patches and insignia from his Space Force uniform would be enough to disguise it for very long. "Are there some other reasons the Brotherhood ought to know about?"

Ari nodded. "There's probably some people looking for me who shouldn't get a chance to find me."

"Care to name some names?"

"Admiral Vallant, for one. I jumped ship when I heard he was planning a mutiny. And the Magelords for another."

The bartender pursed his lips in a silent whistle. "You don't mess around, brother! What did you have to do, to make enemies like that?"

*You tell me,* thought Ari, *and we'll both know.*

He was silent for a moment, trying to think of a more appropriate reply. In the quiet, he became suddenly aware that the reporter in the holoset over the bar was speaking now with a faster, more emphatic cadence.

". . . results of the vote. In the interests of security, the Citizen-Assembly has resolved to seize all spacecraft currently in-system and begin arming them for planetary defense. Selected units of the spacegoing reserve forces will be mobilized, and all shipyards and weapons factories will be converted to a wartime footing. According to the Speaker of the Assembly . . ."

With difficulty, Ari wrenched his attention back to the conversation at hand. If the Citizen-Assembly knew he was here, he reflected, they would probably resolve to seize him, too, just to keep him from falling into the wrong hands.

"How did I manage to get such important enemies?" he asked finally. "I was born, that's how. You might as well know—my name's Rosselin-Metadi."

There was another long pause. "I've heard about you," said the bartender finally. "You're the one who took care of our problem on Darvell."

Ari laughed under his breath, without humor. "So this is what it's like to have a reputation. Yes, that was me."

"Then the Brotherhood owes you a lot more than it would any random fellow wandering in," the bartender said. He didn't look too cheerful about the thought. "I'll be honest about it—with the times like they are, I'd just as soon somebody else had been the one to pay up. But a debt's a debt. What kind of jobs can you handle?"

"I'm a medic. I've got a full-range commercial starship pilot's license, but I haven't used it. And I'm pretty good at flying atmospheric craft."

"No good," said the bartender. "You do any of those things, and people are going to look at you. And—no offense, brother, but you're a bit too conspicuous as it is."

"Sorry about that," Ari said. "When I figure out a way to make myself shorter, you'll be the first to know."

The bartender looked thoughtful. "Until then, you still need a job. And—just how particular are you, anyway?"

"These days? Not very."

"Then we're in business. There's at least one place

where a big guy like you isn't going to draw much attention, and that's right here."

Ari took the bartender's meaning at once. "You're looking for a bouncer?"

"Not me, no. This place doesn't usually get any trouble that I can't handle. But there's a place down near the port called the Pilot's Joy that draws a pretty rough crowd. How do you feel about working there?"

"I can't afford to be choosy," said Ari. "I'll take it."

*And so much for saving the galaxy,* he thought as he downed the last of his brandy. *It looks like I'm going to be sitting out the Second Magewar in a house of ill repute.*

sus-Airaalin thumbed off the autoscribe on his collar. What he had to do next was not meant for the hearing of those to whom he made his reports; the Resurgency preferred to learn of results without being troubled by knowing the means. Little wonder, he reflected—some of those to whom he answered were men and women of honor, who wanted only to restore the old knowledge and bring back those things which had been lost, but many of them were not.

*We have let our defeats make us smaller,* he thought regretfully. *We fail to see beyond the moment; we struggle for advantage over one another, and forget the greater enemy.*

sus-Airaalin, at least, had not forgotten. He left the observation deck and strode down ever-narrowing corridors until he had reached the deepest core of the ship. There he found the detention cells, emptied now of their usual complement of quarrelsome, laggardly, or disobedient troopers in order to hold much greater prizes.

One of the cells contained Brigadier General Perrin Ochemet, taken in the same sweep through Prime that had brought them Errec Ransome. sus-Airaalin passed by the door of that cell without bothering to look within. He wasn't interested, particularly, in what stories Ochemet might have to tell; the general was a stolid and unimaginative man. He had fought well and killed several before being captured, but he wasn't likely to know anything that wasn't already covered in Prime's extensive files.

The cell next to Ochemet's was empty, but the third cell in the row was occupied. sus-Airaalin touched the lock and opened it. Errec Ransome lay on the flat metal bunk inside, his black cloak wrapped around him against the cold shipboard air. He sat up awkwardly at sus-Airaalin's entrance, hampered by the manacles on his wrists—bonds of more than ordinary forging, wrought for this one purpose only, to hold and keep harmless the Breaker of Circles.

"Lord sus-Airaalin," Ransome said. His voice was tired but even. If he knew fear at being in the hands of his enemies, he didn't show it. "Has the time come so soon for questions?"

"The time has come for civil questions," replied sus-Airaalin, "and for civil answers. Later we will discuss other things. Where is General Metadi?"

Ransome shook his head. "I don't know the answer to that." His mouth quirked briefly in what might have been an ironic smile. "Believe whatever you want, Lord sus-Airaalin. But sometimes I will tell you the truth."

In spite of the Adept's manacles, sus-Airaalin felt a chill, remembering the words of one who had known Master Ransome well in the days of the last war: *Some people lie to their enemies and tell the truth to their friends. With Errec it's always been the other way around.*

At least, sus-Airaalin reflected, that meant his own relationship with the Adept Master was an honest one—and in its own way, safe. He waited until the silence between them had outlasted the length of their previous exchange, then brought out his next question.

"Where is Commander Rosel Quetaya?"

Again Ransome shook his head. "I don't know that either."

*One more ...*

"The rest of the Commanding General's family—where are they now?"

sus-Airaalin watched the Adept Master closely. An answer to this question, or even a hint of an answer, would make up for any silence elsewhere. The Resurgency wanted the Rosselin-Metadi line destroyed root and branch; the only motive that sus-Airaalin could discern was pure hatred for the General and the Domina, who between them had made the coalition that brought down the homeworlds.

*Wasteful,* thought sus-Airaalin—who had his own reasons for finding the children. The threads they wove into the fabric of the universe were strong ones, such as could make the pattern whole, or destroy it utterly.

But again Errec Ransome was shaking his head. "I'm sorry. I can't tell you."

*Not "I don't know,"* sus-Airaalin noted. *But "I can't tell you."*

*He knows.*

As usual, dinner at the asteroid base was a formal affair, a matter of cut-glass goblets and spotless napery, of milk-white porcelain dishes and tall scented candles.

Nyls Jessan and Ignaceu LeSoit sat on either side of the glittering table. In deference to the setting, Jessan had dressed for dinner in the suit of Khesatan formal wear that the robots had provided. LeSoit, on the other hand, had apparently puzzled the robots at first; Jessan doubted that the devices had anything in their memories covering fancy dress on Suivi Point. In the end, the robots had compromised on ordinary free-spacer's garments, tailored from white spidersilk and black broadcloth instead of cheap synthetics.

Beka was nowhere in sight, and her chair at the head of the table was empty. The robots offered no explanation. Jessan tried not to keep watching the door, and tried not to worry.

He fiddled absentmindedly with the silverware as the robots began wheeling out a selection of dishes in electrum-plated warming trays: baked *crallach* meat in brambleberry sauce; pickled *faan*-fruit; spiced water-grain frumenty. He let the robots serve him with helpings of all of the dishes, then poked at the food idly with the tines of his fork.

Across the table from him, LeSoit methodically pulled a dinner roll apart into small pieces, then left the fragments in a heap on his plate.

"The food's all right," LeSoit said after some time—though Jessan had yet to see him taste any of the dishes the robots had presented. "Where does it all come from?"

Jessan shrugged. "I don't know. Synthesizers, some of it, I think. For the rest, your guess is as good as mine."

LeSoit didn't answer. A robot came and took the torn dinner rolls away, replacing them with a clean plate; LeSoit picked up another roll and started all over again.

After a while the gunman said, "How long do you think we're going to be cooped up here?"

"Until the repairs are done, at least," said Jessan without looking at LeSoit—he was watching the door again instead. The door remained obstinately shut. "Probably until the hi-comms come back up, and we can get some idea of what's going on out there."

"You think the comms are going to come back?"

"What?—oh." Jessan forced his attention away from the door. "I'd say so, yes. Bringing them down was a Mageworlds trick in the first place, and their fleet will need to talk with their own people back home before much longer."

Another robot glided up to the table, this time to pour

wine into the goblets. Jessan sipped at the liquid without tasting it and set the goblet back on the table. LeSoit asked him another question; when Jessan realized that he hadn't heard either the question or the answer that he gave to it, he pushed back his chair and stood up.

"That does it," he said. He crumpled his napkin and threw it down onto the tablecloth. "Go ahead and finish without me. I'll be back after I find the captain."

It took him almost an hour of searching to find her, and then it was in the most obvious of places, the one he had left until last because he hadn't thought she would be there. But when the rest of the base's upper reaches proved empty, he went at last to Beka's room—the bare chamber far down an unused corridor that had once been the asteroid's observation deck.

He set his palm against the lockplate, and the door slid open. Inside, the lights were off and the ceiling panels were down, leaving nothing but armor-glass for a barrier between the room and the stars.

Beka was standing alone in the center of the room. Her back was to the door, and she was looking up at the starfield spread out overhead.

She didn't turn around as Jessan entered. Something about her posture made him feel colder at the bone—some indefinable quality at once familiar and totally alien—so that he was shaken by fear for her. He crossed the room in three quick strides, the velvety floor covering yielding under his feet with each step, then made himself stop an arm's length away.

"Beka?" he said quietly. "Are you well?"

She turned around. "Nyls?"

"Yes."

He had to fight to keep his composure. No trace of the usual go-to-hell arrogance remained on her features—her face was so pale that the starlight made it look like bone, and her eyes were wide and dark, as if she'd been contemplating something she feared more than death itself.

*And the captain doesn't fear hell, death, or damnation. . . .*

He reached out a hand toward her and called her by the nickname he'd learned from her brother Ari. "Bee?"

She caught at his hand with desperate strength and pulled him to her. This close, he could feel the tremors that ran through her body, one after the other. She pressed her face down hard against his shoulder, and he held her without saying anything until the shaking stopped.

"There," he said finally—knowing it sounded inane, but not knowing anything better to say, either. "There . . . are you feeling better now, Captain?"

She pulled back a little and looked up at him. He saw with relief that the frozen terror was gone from her face. She was still pale and intent, but she no longer looked like a stranger in her own body.

"Nyls," she said, "do you love me?"

He blinked, startled. "Yes. I thought you knew."

"Then stay with me, Nyls; I need you."

"Of course. Always."

She seemed to relax a bit more, as though her worst fear had receded a little further. But her face was still worried.

"Then you'll come with me to Suivi Point?" she asked.

"To Suivi, or anywhere," he said, puzzled. "But what is there for us at Suivi Point?"

"For us? Nothing . . . but there's something I have to go there and do. Promise you'll back me, no matter what happens?"

"No matter what happens," he said. "When do we leave?"

"Tomorrow," she said, and now her voice had the familiar snap of command. "Because I have to be ready at Suivi when the hi-comms come back up."

# VI. NAMMERIN: NAMPORT
## THE OUTER NET

"**S**OMETHING IS wrong here, Klea. Something is very wrong."

Klea Santreny stared at Owen across the table in the all-
night noodle shop. His words seemed to hang in the air
like a holosign above the plastic tablecloth—they weren't
going to go away. After a moment, she ventured a cautious
question.

"So your teacher didn't play completely straight with
you. Is that so bad?"

"I trusted him," Owen said. "To work as I did, there's
no other way besides trust. And if my work was based on
lies—"

Klea saw him flinch away from the thought. "But meant
for the best, maybe," she said, trying to offer some comfort. "If he didn't want to see you taken by the Mages, or
something."

She couldn't remember ever trusting anybody enough to
have the loss of faith hurt her as much as this did Owen.

Not since her mother had died, anyhow. She wondered what his own family had been like. He never mentioned them except in passing, and all his shock and horror at the news from Galcen had been for the Adepts' Guild and not for his own blood kin.

"Maybe," he said. "But he shouldn't have done it, no matter what the reason. Singling out one of his students to keep safe no matter what the cost was a great wrong done to all the others. And to me."

He fell into a long silence. Klea watched him nervously, uncertain what to do or say. He didn't appear to want comforting words—and she'd just about exhausted her supply of them—so it seemed the only thing she could do was wait. For quite a long time, as it turned out; she began to worry that they would get thrown out of the shop for holding down a table too long without ordering more food. But she didn't dare leave her seat long enough to buy anything, even if she'd had the appetite for it.

At last, Owen blinked and came back from wherever it was he went when he put himself under that way. From the look in his eyes, she could tell at once that he had made a decision.

"What are you going to do?" she asked. "Is there even anything you *can* do?"

"Nobody stays an apprentice forever," he said, "and I've been an apprentice far too long. It's time I became an Adept."

"Can you?" she asked. "I mean, is it allowed?"

He nodded. "It's every student's right to petition his teacher for the rank of Adept, if the student thinks the rank has been unjustly withheld."

"You can do that from here?" Klea asked. "Without going back to Galcen?"

"There's a way," Owen said. "It's never been used that I know of, but there is a way."

He didn't sound particularly enthusiastic about the idea. Klea looked at him sharply.

"There's some kind of catch, isn't there?" she said.

"Yes," he said. "You only get to try once. And the way I'll have to do it, going out of the body—it's dangerous all by itself."

"Oh," said Klea. She didn't know exactly what "going out of the body" involved, but if it was serious enough to give Owen pause then she felt inclined to regard it with respect. "You're going to try anyway, though?"

"I have to," he said. "I can't work under direction any longer. I need to be free to act as I see fit."

Klea looked down at the tablecloth. As far as she could tell, Owen had been doing exactly that as long as she'd known him—a brief while, in the grand scheme of things, but an intense one. Of course, whatever instructions he'd thought he was working under all this time probably hadn't said anything one way or the other about making a Guild apprentice out of the hooker downstairs.

"Are you going to want any help?" she asked.

"Yes," he said, after a moment's hesitation. "I'll need somebody to stand guard while I'm under, and some place where I can lock the door and not be bothered."

"I'll watch," Klea said at once. "But a locked door is going to be a lot harder to find."

She heard him sigh. "I know. But we can't stay here."

"We can't go back either," she told him. "The whole damned apartment building's probably got Namport Security crawling all over it by now. Or that Mage-Circle you keep talking about. Or maybe even both."

Klea stopped. She could feel herself having an idea—it was crawling out of the back of her mind while she watched, and she didn't think she was going to like it.

She was right. She didn't like it, any more than Owen liked the thought of whatever it was he intended to do.

*I wonder,* she thought as she drew a shaky breath, *if this is what trying to be an Adept does to you.*

"There is one place we can go," she said aloud. "You still have some credits on you?"

"Yes."

She stood up, grabbing the day pack and the *grrch*-wood staff without giving herself time to hesitate. "Then come on."


The engineering control room of the Deathwing was no longer silent. In addition to the constant whisper of circulating air, and the low humming—more sensed than heard—of the ship's electronics and gravity systems, anyone standing in this part of the ship could feel the steady beat of the Magebuilt vessel's realspace engines vibrating in the deckplates like a pulse.

To Llannat Hyfid, hearing the sounds of the vessel increase in complexity as system after system came back on line had been like listening to some immense creature coming out of stasis and into life. Of the Deathwing's major systems, only the hyperspace engines remained inactive, and that wouldn't last much longer.

"We can bring the drive up for jump-testing any time now," said E'Patu, the hull-tech warrant officer who'd been overseeing the physical end of the job. "Everything's as ready as it's going to get outside of a proper shipyard. Just give the word and we'll do it."

He'd been addressing Lieutenant Vinhalyn, but his gaze slewed over toward Llannat as he spoke. As if it had been a signal, she felt everybody else in engineering control turning to her as well—even Vinhalyn, in the careful way he didn't look at her at all.

*I'm not some kind of oracle,* she felt like telling them, but she knew that the outburst wouldn't do her any good. Ensign Cantrel and the rest of *Ebannha*'s people had regarded Llannat with a combination of awe and gratitude ever since they'd learned about her part in finding the Deathwing; and Vinhalyn had a deferential regard for Adepts that was straight out of the closing days of the last war. But she didn't have to like it.

*If you don't like it,* inquired the voice at the back of her head, *then why have you started wearing Adept's gear all the time instead of your Space Force fatigues?*

She didn't have an answer for that one, except that the change had felt like a necessary one, and that it still did.

The brief, awkward pause had started stretching out long enough to be noticeable. Another breath more, and Lieutenant Vinhalyn would decide that the resident Adept didn't have any advice for him this time, and he'd give the order to commence the jump-tests for the hyperdrive.

"No," she said, startling herself. "Don't do it yet."

Now that she'd spoken, Vinhalyn cast a worried glance in her direction. "What's the problem, Mistress? If there's anything we've overlooked—"

"Not that I know of," she said. "It's just—hold off for a little while longer, all right? I need to make one last tour of the ship first."

Vinhalyn looked grave. "I take it you feel that something more is needed before we power up the hyperdrive?"

"That's about the shape of it, yes."

"Then do what you have to, Mistress," he said. "Keep us safe. Let us know when you're ready to start the jump-tests."

She gave him a nod by way of reply, then grasped her staff—her short, silver-bound, Mage's staff—in her right hand and turned to leave the engineering spaces.

*Keep them safe,* she thought. *Right. I still don't know what I'm doing or why I'm doing it. All I know is that it isn't time yet for us to jump.*

But it seemed that she knew something more after all. The thought floated unbidden up to the surface of her mind. *Because there's something here that I haven't found yet. When I find it, we can go.*

She closed her eyes and let her feet take her on the path she ought to follow. She walked, turned, walked and turned again, guided by her inner certainty, until she came to a spot where she no longer felt compelled to go forward. Like a cloud lifting, her compulsion and restlessness departed, to be replaced by a profound feeling of peace.

She sighed, and opened her eyes. All at once, the stench of Magework filled her nostrils. The feel of it pressed in against her on all sides—tangled, knotty, a twisting of the substance of things, heaviest and thickest where the power should flow most cleanly. She was at the center of the ship, where no engineering or control systems ran, the dark room with the inset circle of white on its bare deck. Dim light filled the compartment. She was alone.

*I've been avoiding this place,* she thought. *Ever since I first heard Cantrel talking about it, I've been avoiding it, even taking other paths when the direct route lay beside this compartment. And now I'm here anyway, whether I wanted to come here or not. Because this is the place that I have to be.*

"All right," she said aloud to the listening universe. "Here I am. What do you want?"

And the universe answered. A sudden lethargy filled her, and she nearly collapsed with fatigue. The urge to kneel down in the center of the circle of white was near-overpowering. She struggled to fight it off.

*This is unnatural,* she told herself. *I should leave.*

But she was unable to will her feet to move.

Klea set a fast pace on the way from the shop, walking through Namport's darkened streets without speaking. Owen followed close behind her, also in silence; she didn't think he was more than halfway with her, anyhow. Most of his mind was already off somewhere, making ready for whatever it was that he planned to do. She knew her way well enough that she didn't have to slow down until she reached a moderately prosperous quarter well away from the port, and came to her destination: a brightly lit tavern, flanked on one side by a businessman's hotel and on the other by a theater showing full-presence holovid extravaganzas.

"Okay," she said. "Here we are. Come on inside."

Owen glanced up at the tavern's gaudy holosign—an advertisement for Tree Frog Moonlight Pale. "Here?"

"You wanted a locked room," she said. "If Freling's isn't good enough for you, then you're on your own."

He looked back at her. She could see that he was uncertain, and it occurred to her that uncertainty wasn't an expression she'd seen him wear all that often. Finally he said, "I don't mind. But you—Klea, are you sure you want to do this?"

"Whether I want to or not doesn't matter," she said impatiently. "You need a place and this is it." Shrugging off her day pack, she thrust it and the *grrch*-wood staff into Owen's hands. "Hold these for me and come on."

She turned away and headed for the tavern. A few seconds later she heard Owen following her. The door sensors beeped at their approach and the glass panel slid open. They passed through the antechamber and the inner doors into a climate-controlled dimness a long way from the muggy air outside.

A large man in a loosely cut suit came up to them out of the shadows. "You've been away for a while."

"Yeah," Klea said. "I wasn't—" She glanced back at Owen, and lowered her voice so that only the bouncer could hear. "I wasn't feeling too well."

She let her voice rise again. "This sexy guy says he feels like an all-nighter."

"Right. See Freling, then."

The bouncer faded back into the darkness near the door.

Klea led the way deeper inside the tavern. Up on a long runway, a naked woman was dancing with a big, grey-scaled Selvaur. Over to the right, lit by pale blue lights whose illumination didn't extend all the way to the ceiling, a long wooden bar stretched the length of the room.

Klea walked up to the bar and sat down. Owen, after a second's hesitation, took a seat beside her.

She didn't have to wait long before Freling showed up—a large, florid man in a long apron. He reached up to the shelf behind the bar to pull out a glass and a bottle, and poured a shot of purple aqua vitae for Klea without being asked.

"Been a while," he said.

She ignored the drink. "But I'm back."

"Could I see your health card? I don't want to get busted by the medicos."

Klea's heart sank. *Oh, hell. I should have remembered. That damned card is back at the apartment with my working clothes, and it hasn't been updated for a month anyway.*

She drew a deep breath preparatory to embarking on a string of excuses that were bound to be futile—Freling was a real bastard when it came to anything that could get him in trouble with the law.

*Show him your card.*

The voice in her head was clear and recognizable. *Owen?*

*Show him the card!*

*Right.*

She made a pretense of reaching into the pocket of her shift for a square of plastic that wasn't there, and then held out the nonexistent card to Freling for inspection.

"There you go. All fresh and clean."

Freling squinted at the card. By now she could almost see it herself, the official seal and her flatpic only slightly obscured by the dim blue light.

"Looks fine to me," he said. "What'll it be, then?"

She slipped the not-there card back into her pocket. "My hot lover here wants an all-night special."

Freling turned to Owen. "That'll be two hundred room rent, plus fifty for special fees. Cash up front."

Klea held her breath, unsure of how Owen was going to react to the demand. She needn't have worried; he looked at Freling for a moment with no expression whatsoever, then reached into a pocket of his coverall and pulled out a wad of cash. He dropped the money on the bar without bothering to count it.

Freling picked it up and counted it instead, his lips moving as he thumbed through the stack of chits. When he was done, the money vanished somewhere under his apron, and he nodded.

"Room five," he told Klea. "You still remember the way?"

"I haven't forgotten. Come on, lover."

She stood up and took Owen by the hand, leading him to a darker corner of the room, where a wide stairway led upward into the dimly glowing dark. Little lights along the side of the stairway showed the treads and risers, or else the stairs would have been invisible.

"All right," she said to Owen as soon as they were out of earshot of the room below. "You've got your locked door."

Llannat couldn't move. The compulsion that had brought her to the dark room at the heart of the ship was upon her again, this time forcing her to stay. She wanted nothing, at this moment, so much as she wanted to be out of this place, with its overwhelming stink and feel of Magework and sorcery. But her feet would not let her go.

*This is where I'm supposed to be. Where the Magework is thickest. If there's another message for me, it's in here.*

Once again she was surprised by her own thought, and

even more surprised to realize that it was true. The first message left for her on the Deathwing had been upsetting enough—she had no doubt but that she was the Adept the message had addressed, in spite of the gap of centuries. Now she understood that the ship itself was a message.

*Magelords live a long time, and they make long plans. And they're particular about who's going to have something after them; Vinhalyn told me about that. Made it sound like they hand down projects and power, and—and* things *the way my family used to hand down shoes.*

*And this ship was left out here for me.*

Only one thing remained for her to do. If messages were waiting for her in the very air and steel of the ship, then she would have to go and find them. Reluctantly, she sank down to her knees in the circle. Laying the short ebony staff on the white deckplates in front of her, she closed her eyes and tried to relax enough to enter the meditative state.

It was hard, much harder than usual. The smell and feel of Magish sorcery permeated the room; with every slow, even breath she seemed to be drawing the stench deeper into her lungs. Trying to work through it was like trying to breathe water—she kept breaking through again to the surface, her heart pounding and her lungs heaving in panic.

*"Fighting it never works."*

The old piece of advice came back to her—one of the first things the teachers said to a new apprentice at the Retreat. Owen Rosselin-Metadi had been the one to say it to Llannat, back when she was still a green ensign who thought that the only way to deal with what her sudden talent was doing to her was to suppress it all as much as she could.

And now she was doing the same thing again, trying to fight against the way the room really was, and to make it as if what had happened there had never been. No wonder it wasn't working.

She quit trying to ignore the Magework that pressed in so closely about her. Instead she allowed her mind to drift, unforced, and let the room enfold her however it would, as a part of the necessary shape of this portion of the universe. Gradually, as her tension ebbed, she felt her pulse slow and her breathing become more regular—and then, as easily as slipping into warm water, she slipped away from regular thought and into the meditative trance.

She had no idea how long she knelt there before she knew that it was time to open her eyes, pick up her staff, and rise to her feet. But when she did so, she was in another place—a vast, dark-but-not-dark expanse, like a great, echoless hall. All about her were hanging curtains and tapestries, massive heavy walls of patterned cloth. The bottoms of them brushed the dusty floor beneath her feet; and she couldn't see the tops of them because they seemed to reach up forever and blend into the darkness far overhead.

The tapestries made walls and rooms in the dark, dividing the great, unbounded hall up into a maze of curtains, moving gently in faint drafts of air that she couldn't feel. She gripped her staff tightly in one hand and began walking—not sure whether she was standing at the maze's edge, or trapped inside its heart.

A few minutes later, she took a wrong turning and found herself in a dead end. She looked over her shoulder, ready to reverse her steps and go back to where she started, and saw that the way had closed up again behind her. Another dark, heavy curtain hung where there had been a path only seconds before.

*Is this some kind of test?* she wondered. *Am I supposed to find the path, even when it's hidden?*

*Or is the question not about following the path at all?*

*What is a path, except for a way where somebody else thinks that you should go?*

She raised her staff, ebony bound in silver, and red fire ran down its length. She brought it forward in a sweeping overhand blow, rending the curtain from top to bottom. Light, pale yellow, showed through the gap.

With her staff she pushed the curtain aside—tendrils of smoke curled up from the edges of the fabric—and saw, through the opening, the corridor of a spaceship. She eased her way through, and was aware, with the movement, of the long black robes that whispered about her high, polished boots. The feel of a mask was cold upon her face, and the slight loss of peripheral vision brought on by the eyeholes allowed her to see the things that the worlds of men found invisible: the silver cords that traced between all times and places through the darkness under the stars.

She walked forward, her boot heels clicking on the metal deckplates, and followed the two silver cords, strong and bright, that she had to knot together. Knot them and twist them, and make a cable tough enough to pull yet another of the cords—thick and heavy, but *cut*—out of the darkness where it was drifting.

"A handhold," she murmured, and was surprised to hear her voice, deeper than she remembered it, but familiar still.

She paused and leaned back against one of the bulkheads, suddenly aware of the enormity of what she was contemplating. Betrayal of all she had fought for, all she believed, for what? For a chance, and no more than a chance, of a greater good. She pushed off from the bulkhead and started forward again.

The door to the bridge whooshed open at her approach, then closed again behind her. Two men sat in the pilot's and copilot's seats.

"Drop out of hyper," she said. "Do it now."

"With respect, my lord," said the pilot, "it's a long time before we're scheduled to drop out."

Llannat could see the silver cords drifting out of reach. She walked forward, between the two seats, and clipped her staff to her belt.

*It is not right,* she told it, *that you should see what I do next.*

# VII. The Outer Net:
## *Night's-Beautiful-Daughter*
## Nammerin: Namport

**L**ANNAT DREW the long knife out of the hidden sheath on her left forearm—*and I know someone else who wears a blade there,* she thought as she watched the events unfolding, *but who?*

She couldn't quite catch the name, or more than a vague, tickling memory of the person. She saw her hand lash out and cut the throats of the pilot and copilot strapped into their seats before her.

The men surged against the restraining webbing, then fell back as blood spurted from their severed arteries. Before the two she had just murdered were quite still, she turned back to the control panel and began the process of taking *Night's-Beautiful-Daughter* out of hyperspace.

The dropout sequence ran and the glory of the stars reappeared. She closed her eyes briefly. The two silver cords that had brought her to this moment were drifting closer, but still they did not touch. And now a third cord had appeared, one that she hadn't seen before. Good—the new cord would help her bring together the two that she needed; but the cords were not yet bound, and until they were, nothing would come of her treason.

"Not done," Llannat whispered. "Still not done."

She looked again. The third cord was far off, at the extreme range of her vision, hard to see in the distance. It brought her an impression of a person, as if it were an acquaintance whose name had slipped her mind, met in the marketplace. She tried, but no names came. Still, something had to be done.

*Do the best that you can,* she thought, *and hope to luck for the rest.*

She dipped her finger in the red blood that flowed from the neck of one of her friends and wrote upon the viewscreen in large letters, trying to describe the persons she had seen: "Adept from the forest world: Bring this message to She-who-leads. Tell her what thou didst learn."

And there, in the darkness, two of the cords knotted—one of those that she had seen earlier, and the newcomer. Odd, unexpected, but enough to pull in the cut cord. It was enough. For good or ill the future had been changed, and the long plans she herself had helped to form had been disrupted.

She sat back upon the deck, overcome by fatigue. Looking at the future always brought her near to collapse when the effort ended, and she knew that it would be the death of her someday.

Owen Rosselin-Metadi stood in the windowless room at the top of the stairs. The room smelled of disinfectant, in spite of the climate-control system wheezing and rattling through the floor-mounted vents. The dim light from a *faux*-opal glow-globe showed him a bed, a sink in one corner, and a long mirror along the far wall. In the mirror's peeling surface he could see Klea Santreny reflected behind him, locking a heavy soundproof door.

*Number Five,* he thought. *Then there are four more like this, at least.* The thought depressed him.

He forced the dark mood away. He would think about the room later, when he thought about Galcen and the Magelords and all the other things he couldn't afford to think about now. Silently, he watched in the mirror as Klea propped her staff against the door and let her day pack slide off her shoulders to fall beside it.

"Well, here you are," she said. "Whatever you're going to do, you'd better get on with it."

He didn't understand why she trusted him; he'd told her almost nothing, not even his full name, and he'd asked her for more than any apprentice should have to give.

*Like teacher, like student,* he thought. *I've learned some things too well.*

"Don't let anybody come in the door," he said aloud. "Stop them however you have to."

She gave him a quick, slightly crooked smile. "Don't worry. You could skin a swamp-devil in here and nobody would pay any attention."

He nodded, not liking the memories that stirred in the back of her mind as she spoke. *I can't deal with that now. But I* will *do something about this place before I'm finished with Nammerin.*

"You might as well make yourself comfortable," he told her. "From your point of view, it's going to be a long, dull night."

"Dull is fine," she said. "I *like* dull. I could use a little more dull in my life, if you want to know the truth."

Owen smiled in spite of himself. "Save it up while you can, then," he advised her. "Adepts don't get very much of it."

He went over to the bed—hoping that the management here at least changed the sheets between rounds, and telling himself that he couldn't afford to be fastidious—and stretched himself out on the nubbly green coverlet. Over in one corner of the room, Klea was sitting down on the floor, using her day pack for a backrest. He closed his eyes.

The climate-control system sighed and gurgled. His pulse beat softly in his ears, his breath whispered in and out. He allowed the sound of his pulse to turn to a rush and a roar, and let his inner vision expand. When he was ready, he stood up and left himself behind.

He saw himself, lying on the bed, and he saw Klea, sitting beside the door, eyes closed but holding her staff upright—she was still awake. Then he wiped all external sensory input and allowed the darkness to enter his mind.

From the darkness, he plucked a single bright spot of light, while concentrating on home: Galcen, and the small room in the Retreat where he had lived and studied for years, the place to which he felt most strongly bound. He took the dot of light, and added another to it, and then another, as he had learned the theory, until a picture emerged—a picture, then a scene, then a full world.

*Home.*

He stood on a flat surface open to the stars, with the shadowy leaves and pale waxy petals of night-blooming flowers pressing close about him, and his first thought was that he had missed his goal completely. Recognition came a moment later: this was the rooftop terrace of his family's house in Galcen's Northern Uplands.

*I underestimated,* he said to himself. *This place has more power to draw me than I thought.*

A moment later he understood that he had gone astray in time as well. A woman came up onto the terrace from the steps below, with the starlight bleaching her pale braided hair. He thought at first that it was his sister Beka come home, but then he looked more closely—this was the Domina Perada Rosselin, walking in her night garden as she had done in life.

*This is the past,* Owen realized. *I should go; I need to*

*trace the path up to the present and find Master Ransome.
I shouldn't stay here in a time where I don't belong.*

Nevertheless, he found himself unwilling to move. He
was still watching when the shadows at the far end of the
terrace seemed to darken, and a man stepped out from
what had been empty air only a moment before. Owen
tensed, knowing the peculiar frustration of one who travels
out of body and witnesses disasters in which he cannot in-
tervene.

But his mother seemed unfrightened. In fact, she came
forward to greet the stranger as if she had expected
him—a formal greeting, not the true cordiality she would
have given an old friend of the family like Master Ransome, but more kindly by far than the cool, practiced
smiles she gave to Tarveet of Pleyver and others of his
kind.

The stranger bowed. He was not a tall man, but his
body was compact and muscular. His loosely curling black
hair was going prematurely to grey.

"My lady," he said. He spoke Galcenian with a strong
accent, one that Owen didn't recognize. "It is good of you
to meet with me."

The Domina smiled. "I gave up hoping for goodness
long ago. I thought that justice would serve me well
enough instead. But since it hasn't—my lord sus-Airaalin,
let us talk."

Llannat felt a hand shaking her shoulder. "Mistress, it's
time to drop out of hyper. You left orders to tell you first.
It's time, Mistress."

Llannat shook her head and looked up. It was Vinhalyn,
the acting captain.

"Thank you," she said. "I'll be on the bridge presently.
Don't drop out until I arrive."

She was in a berthing compartment. The lights were
dim, and she was naked beneath the sheets. Her staff lay

ready to hand on the deckplates beside the bunk—the same silver-bound ebony staff that she had carried in her walking dream, and that the Professor had carried before her.

*This ship was his,* she thought, and the back of her neck felt cold. *His, and he left it here for me.*

The stranger on the terrace paused, about to speak, then looked sharply in Owen's direction. "We're being watched."

"No," the Domina said, "this place is secure."

"I think not." And the stranger began to walk toward Owen.

*That's impossible,* Owen thought. *He can't see me.*

But the man's gaze was fixed on the place where Owen stood, and he was still coming forward. Forcing down his panic, Owen shut his eyes and wiped the scene from his mind. Once again, he began the process of pulling himself to a place, dot of light by painful dot, as he had done before.

*Master Ransome,* he thought. *Not in the past. Now.*

Again the shining dots coalesced around him into a place and a time—a dark place, this one, full of the rumble of engines and the sigh of recirculating air, with close, tight walls that pressed in on him from every side. Something about the rhythm of the sound made him think of the ships on which he had traveled and worked his way between the worlds.

*But what is Master Ransome doing here? He was a pilot once; he'd never be down near the ship's engines if there was some way that he could see the stars.*

Owen frowned. This place, whatever it was, had no light, and in his noncorporeal state he couldn't touch the physical switch even if he could find it. But there were other ways to achieve clear sight, and he used them now, concentrating on his extended senses until the cell—it *was* a cell, without a doubt—became suffused with a greyish, sourceless illumination.

And Ransome was there. The Master of the Adepts' Guild lay huddled in a black cloak on the narrow bunk that was the cell's only furnishing. His features were pale and haggard; there were marks like bruises on his temples and forehead, and dried blood around his mouth.

Despair washed over Owen like a heavy, sluggish wave. Not until now had he truly believed that all the worst had happened. If Galcen Prime had fallen—if the Space Force had been defeated—even if the Retreat itself had broken under the assault—all of these together wouldn't have been enough to give the Magelords the victory. But if the Master of the Guild was a prisoner in their hands, then all was lost.

*No,* he told himself urgently. *Remember what you used to say to the apprentices—'Despair is a liar; nothing is ever certain.' You came all this way because there was something you had to do. What you see here doesn't change any of that.*

He stepped forward and went down on one knee beside the bunk, then reached out a hand and touched Ransome lightly on the shoulder. Except for the fleeting sensation of pressing against an intangible boundary, Owen felt nothing from the contact; and few beside the Master of the Adepts' Guild would have felt anything in return.

But Errec Ransome was who he was, and he came awake at the touch. The Adept Master made no sound, but his eyes widened in recognition. Owen wondered how his disembodied presence appeared to Ransome—as a cloudy phantom, perhaps, or as something even more vague and nebulous, a sigh of wind or a coldness in the air.

*Master Ransome.*

Owen strove to project his subvocal words across the immense gap between his physical body and this place where the essence of him had come. He groped for the half-forgotten words of the traditional apprentice's challenge—now so seldom used, and never before under such circumstances.

*Master Ransome, I have been apprentice to you long enough; I would claim my staff and call myself my own master.*

Improbably, Ransome's bruised mouth curved into a faint smile. *Owen*, came the answering thought. *I did not think you would come this far.*

*But now I am here. And I require . . .* The dark cell and the manacles on Errec Ransome's wrists made a mockery of the formal wording; Owen's thought stumbled, and he forced himself to go on. . . . *I require that you test me as you see fit.*

Ransome laughed silently. *If you've come all the way from Nammerin into this place, then you've passed a harder test than anything I would have set for you.*

*Then do you give me mastery?*

*I give you nothing*, Ransome said. *You have claimed it, and it is yours.* The Adept Master laughed again—no sound, only a troubling of the dark air. *And I see that the Mages have set themselves a greater task than they thought, since you are free. But if you are willing, there is something more.*

Owen bowed his head. *Command me.*

*No. You are Adept now, not apprentice. What you do must be of your own choosing.*

*Then I choose to serve*, said Owen. *Tell me what needs to be done.*

There was a terrible joy in Errec Ransome's eyes. *For this I trained you, for this I kept you from the destruction that I knew would come. Go to the Retreat. Your staff is there. Claim it, and become the Master of the Guild.*

Owen drew back, shaken. *I did not ask . . .*

*But it is given.*

*And if I fail?*

Ransome closed his eyes, as if the strength to hold them open were failing him. *Then the Adepts have no leader; our sun is set; and Lord sus-Airaalin has conquered.*

*sus-Airaalin?* Owen felt a tremor go through him at the name. *But I saw him. . . .*

The Adept Master paid no heed to his unvoiced question. *You should go,* Errec Ransome said. *It isn't safe for you to be here. But I have looked into the future and have seen how it lies. You will be the Master of the Guild when the Mages threaten us no longer.*

It was a dismissal. Obediently, Owen allowed himself to drift away, passing like a bodiless ghost through decks and conduits until he seemed to float in open space above a planet. He let himself fall downward through the upper air onto the surface of his homeworld.

After the painstaking transit through darkness from Nammerin, his progress to the Retreat was simple and almost effortless. Guided by his knowledge of the world's geography, and increasingly by the feeling of wrongness and evil coming from his goal, he floated cloudlike through the middle atmosphere until he came to the Retreat.

He knew what to expect when he came close to his destination, but what he saw sickened and angered him just the same. Within the walls of the Retreat, the courtyard was blackened and cratered. Black-robed and masked Mages stood there, and they tended fires. The fires burned the books and furnishings of the Retreat, they burned the broken staves of Adepts, and they burned bodies as well.

*I should have been here,* Owen thought, as he had protested aloud to Klea on Nammerin. *These are my people; I should have been with them.*

He knew that Klea had been right, that he couldn't have stopped an invasion single-handed. But he still felt an overpowering sadness as he passed over the courtyard, and its flagstones puddled with drying blood. Forcing himself to go onward, he entered the main building, and walked through halls he knew well toward his old room. That was the place to start the search.

And there, indeed, was his staff, leaning against the far corner, as if he had never been away. Now to put his hand upon it, and somehow bring the physical object through the vast distance to Nammerin—if such a thing was possible.

Before he could touch it, he became aware of someone else inside the room. A Mage. And like the stranger on his mother's terrace, this one seemed able to see him even in his noncorporeal state. Owen shuddered; from the dark familiarity of this one's aura, he was facing the same Magelord who had held him pinned down in Flatlands for more than two seasons.

"You've come," the Mage said. "We were certain you would. Now you can follow me to the Void, and die."

The Mage crossed the room in a stride, snatched up the staff, and gestured toward Owen. With his movement the room vanished, to be replaced by a dull grey place, skyless and groundless, and Owen knew that his worst fears had come to pass.

This was the Void, where all of an Adept's skills were useless, where reality itself was unreal, where the very nonsubstance of this nonplace leached power and strength away. And there in the Void the Magelord turned, and laid down Owen's staff at his feet.

"Come to me, Adept. Take back your staff if you can. Here you will be destroyed."


As soon as Llannat was alone again in the berthing compartment, she sat up in the bunk and looked around for her clothes. Somewhat unnervingly, she found them hung over the back of the only chair in the compartment, just as she always dealt with them when she got ready for bed.

Judging from that, and from what Vinhalyn had said to

her a minute or so earlier, she must have put herself to bed in here—after walking about the ship and speaking to people in what must have seemed to be a normal fashion.

She shivered. *If I'm going to be doing things like this a lot, I'd really like to know about them at the time.*

Her preferences, she knew, weren't likely to count for much. She got out of bed and dressed, then headed for the Deathwing's cockpit. *Night's-Beautiful-Daughter* was still cruising in hyperspace when she arrived.

"I'll be doing the dropout," she said.

The pilot looked at her curiously. "But you don't know the systems. . . ."

"I said I'll be doing the dropout."

Llannat let her fingers trace over the control panels along the patterns she had seen herself use in her trance. *This one first, and* then *the others in the sequence. . . .*

"Hey!" said the pilot. "That's not the way it says in the manuals!"

She kept working. "The manuals are incomplete," she said, speaking from the memories she had shared, trying not to think of what that other self had done in this very place. "The code for disarming the self-destruct was a matter of personal instruction only, as a final safeguard against having captured ships used by the enemy."

"I . . . see," said the pilot, as the dropout process ended and the stars reappeared around them.

Llannat straightened and stepped back from the control panels. "Where are we?" she asked.

"Gyffer system."

"Gyffer? Not Galcen?"

Again the pilot looked startled. "It's where you told us to go, Mistress. Don't you remember?"

Llannat shook her head. "It's not important. I'm going back to my quarters now; when *Naversey* arrives, let me know."

* * *

Owen felt his strength draining away wherever the grey mist of the Void drifted against him. Whatever happened next would have to happen quickly—he couldn't live here long.

*How can the Mages endure it?*

But Owen's black-robed adversary was living, standing like a statue with a glowing staff in his hand. The staff's red aura flickered off the black mask that hid his features.

"Are you the Master of your Circle?" Owen asked the Mage. He circled as he spoke, looking for position. The Mage turned to follow him throughout. "For if you are not . . ."

Between one word and the next Owen dived through the nonsubstance of the Void toward his staff. He reached for it, trying to call it into his hands. The Mage's ebony rod slammed him in the ribs as he rolled to his feet, and he felt a bone crack under the blow.

Worse, his move had taken him into the fog, and now his strength was waning further. With the last of his momentum he sprang straight up, letting the edge of his foot fly out at the Mage's head.

The Mage ducked under the kick and brought his staff around in a blazing circle against Owen's knee. All the strength fled from the limb in a hot splash of pain, and Owen went down. The grey, soul-draining mist swirled around him. He struggled again to his feet.

"Now you will die here," the Mage said. "But see, I bring friends and family to play with you in the time that remains."

The Mage gestured with his free hand, and shapes arose from the mist: Beka in her guise as Tarnekep Portree; Owen's brother, Ari; the General and the Domina; Master Ransome. All pale and expressionless, with cold and lifeless eyes, and the flesh sloughing from their bones to reveal the skeletons underneath.

"Come, embrace your kind," the Mage said.

"They're all illusion."

"Are they?"

The phantasmal Beka reached forth one rotting hand and brushed Owen's cheek. Pain followed her touch, burning and chilling him at once. Owen reacted by punching straight into the creature's face—but nothing resisted him, and his fist exploded into pain as the unreal face deformed like smoke.

"Not quite illusion," the Mage replied, laughing behind his mask. "And real enough for what I do."

But Owen noticed that his enemy was breathing hard, and that under the mask his jaw was set and tense. *So this place does take something out of the Mages as well. In that case*—Owen dropped straight down, throwing himself flat, and rolled through the grey mist. He felt a burning pain in his midsection as he passed through another of the phantom figures, and then he was away.

*Ahead of me, and to the right. My staff is there.*

Owen tried to call it to him, but nothing responded. *"An Adept's skills count for nothing in the Void."* Had he heard that lecture once, long ago, or had he given it himself? He didn't dare breathe; taking a breath would draw the grey mist into his lungs, and that would be the end of him.

He struck something solid—the Mage's leg—and grasped it, whipping around in a wrestler's throw and pulling his adversary down into the mist with him. The Mage's staff struck him low on the hips, but the blow lacked strength. Owen drove his elbow into his opponent's belly and was rewarded with the sound of an explosive gasp.

Owen slid his left hand up the Mage's arm to grab the other man's staff. His right hand was still numb from punching his sister's phantom double. The ebony rod was glowing and hot to the touch. Owen seized it, rolling as he did so to bring the Mage over on top of him.

Now the Mage's back was pressed tight against his chest. He crossed his right arm over his left to hook the other end of the Mage's staff. And then he pulled.

The short staff pressed inward against the Mage's throat. The black-robe struggled, trying to pull Owen's hands free, reaching down and striking Owen's ribs, smashing his head backward into Owen's face.

Owen felt an explosion of pain as his nose broke and the hot blood ran down over his mouth and chin. His lungs were burning. He hadn't dared to breathe since he'd gone down below the mist. He pulled back more sharply on the Magelord's staff.

The Mage convulsed. The vertebrae in his neck snapped, and he fell still. Owen rolled from beneath the suddenly inert shape and swept out with his left hand.

*There.*

He pulled his staff to him and used it as a prop to lever himself upright. If this was victory, he reflected, it wasn't likely to do him any good. The featureless fog stretched as far as his vision extended. He was tired—if not for his staff, he would have collapsed—and he had no idea how to get home.

Then a dark mound stirred where the Mage had fallen. It rose, and stood upright. The Mage.

Owen brought his staff to guard, and white witchlight flickered down its length. But the Mage neither attacked him nor spoke. Instead, the dark figure turned and ran away, and Owen ran after. His legs hurt, his lungs hurt, and his side ached where the ends of the broken rib grated together—but wherever the black-robed phantom was going now, he was Owen's last remaining link with reality.

A shape appeared before them, a pointed archway of impenetrable shadow. The Mage pulled ahead, fell into the blackness, and was gone. Owen followed him into the dark.

By the white glow of his staff he saw that he had come

into a rough stone passage, one that he recognized from the Retreat, a corridor deep underground. Doorways lined both sides of the passage. He felt himself being drawn forward and to the right, to a rough wooden door with a pull-ring in the center. He pulled, and took a step forward—

—into a windowless room lit by an opaline glow-globe, where cool air sighed and rattled through the vents in the floor. A young woman with a staff in her hand slept leaning against a wall. On the far side of the room was a wide bed with an ugly green coverlet. Owen was filled with the desire to sleep. He walked forward, staggering in his fatigue, and lay down with his staff beside him.

Much later, he opened his eyes. Klea was bending over him, cleaning the dried blood from his face with a damp cloth.

He reached for his staff. In defiance of all he had ever thought possible, it was still beside him—real, tangible, and *here*.

"We may yet win," he said. "At least, we have not yet lost."

Klea's eyes were troubled. "I had dreams," she said.

"So do we all," he replied. "So do we all."

Grand Admiral Theio syn-Ricte sus-Air-aalin paced the observation deck of his flagship, dictating to the autoscribe his report for the leaders of the Resurgency on Eraasi.

"We have now gone beyond the span of time for which our Circles undertook to suppress hyperspace communication. Within a few hours at most, messages will once again be able to pass between such links as remain physically undamaged; and I will send you this summary, together with my daily reports for the period spent out of contact, via the protected relays on Ophel.

"I cannot praise too highly the efforts of those who did this work. Many of them have died, giving themselves away completely in order to provide their Circles with renewed energy. They are heroes; let it be so written.

"We have completed the primary tasks which we set for ourselves during this period of grace. The Barrier is broken. Galcen is ours."

He paused, picturing the jubilation that his message so far would undoubtedly set off in the streets of home. Far be it from him, he reflected, to deprive the people of their long-awaited satisfaction. He let a few more seconds elapse, the better to help those who would have to cut and amend his words for their public hearing, and then continued.

"A number of our secondary objectives, however, remain to be accomplished. Those Adepts who stayed to hold their citadel are dead; and Errec Ransome himself is a prisoner in our hands—but lesser Guildhouses remain on a number of the Adept-worlds, and even here on Galcen many of the apprentices have eluded us."

He paused. "One apprentice in particular has slipped from our grasp, which brings us to the second problem.

"General Metadi and his offspring have not been located, living or dead. I have spoken to you before about the danger Metadi himself presents. As if that were not enough, his younger son, Owen, is our missing apprentice. Owen was tracked for some time by our agents on the Adept-world of Pleyver, but succeeded in vanishing—possibly returning to Galcen, since we found his staff at the Retreat. We left the staff as bait, and Lord syn-Criaamon, who had dealt with Rosselin-Metadi on Pleyver, offered to watch the trap.

"Now syn-Criaamon himself is dead, the staff is missing, and we have searched for its owner by all means at our disposal. Nevertheless, although no ship has departed from Galcen, Owen Rosselin-Metadi is not to be found.

"The possibilities," sus-Airaalin concluded, "are disturbing."

He halted his dictation as the door of the observation deck opened to admit a trooper with a message tablet.

"Report from the bridge, sir. Hyperspace communications are starting to come back up, and the captain says you might want to take a look at this—it came through on the widebands just a few minutes ago."

sus-Airaalin accepted the tablet, which was flashing the orange light that meant a stored audio or video message. "Thank you," he said to the trooper. "You may go now."

As soon as he was alone, he pressed the button which would allow the tablet to replay its message. The first thing to come up was a red and yellow design identified in the commentary screen as a commercial trademark belonging to General Delivery and Communications Technologies of Suivi Point, Limited. The red and yellow trademark faded into a white and blue logo belonging—so the commentary informed him—to Dahl&Dahl Mercantile Bankers, also of Suivi Point. The Dahl&Dahl logo dissolved into a picture.

The image in the message tablet's palm-sized screen had the fuzzy edges and dead colors of a holovid transmission picked up flat, but that didn't matter. sus-Airaalin recognized the face. In his youth he had seen a copy of the message Perada Rosselin of Entibor had sent to the Lords of Eraasi, telling them that she would see her homeworld dead rather than give up the fight; and in the fullness of years he had met and spoken with the Domina herself.

Perada was gone—*to the sorrow of the galaxy,* thought sus-Airaalin; *had she lived, things would have been different*—but the young woman in the pale green gown had the same fair, arrogant face and the same startlingly bright blue eyes. Her yellow hair was braided in the same complex pattern, and she wore on her head the black tiara of twisted metal that was the Iron Crown of Entibor.

*This one was supposed to be dead,* thought sus-Airaalin. And then the young woman began to speak.

The voice that came over the message tablet's on-board speaker didn't have much volume, but the words came through clearly and without distortion.

"People of the Republic! A Mageworlds warfleet has attacked Galcen. Singly we cannot stand against them; we must work together if we are to survive. If you have a ship that can fight, or a ship that can be made to fight, or the knowledge and skills to work such a ship, come to Suivi Point, where we will build a fleet such as can capture the galaxy. To this goal I pledge my resources; to this goal I pledge my name and sign myself:

"Beka Rosselin-Metadi, Domina of Lost Entibor, of Entibor-in-Exile, and of the Colonies Beyond."